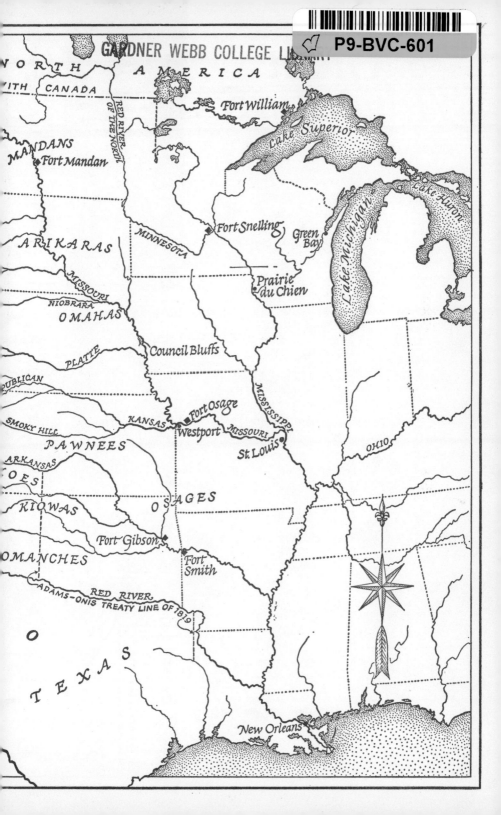

NORTH AMERICA

WITH CANADA

Fort William

Lake Superior

MANDANS

Fort Mandan

RED RIVER OF THE NORTH

MINNESOTA

Fort Snelling

Green Bay

Lake Huron

Lake Michigan

ARIKARAS

MISSOURI

Prairie du Chien

NIOBRARA

OMAHAS

Council Bluffs

PLATTE

REPUBLICAN

Fort Osage

MISSISSIPPI

SMOKY HILL

KANSAS

Westport

MISSOURI

St. Louis

OHIO

PAWNEES

ARKANSAS

OES

OSAGES

KIOWAS

Fort Gibson

OMANCHES

Fort Smith

ADAMS-ONIS TREATY LINE OF 1819

RED RIVER

O

TEXAS

New Orleans

The
Great
Adventure

By Janice Holt Giles

The Enduring Hills

Miss Willie

Tara's Healing

40 Acres and No Mule

The Kentuckians

The Plum Thicket

Hannah Fowler

The Believers

The Land Beyond the Mountains

Johnny Osage

Savanna

Voyage to Santa Fe

A Little Better than Plumb
(*with Henry Giles*)

Run Me a River

The G. I. Journal of Sergeant Giles
(*editor*)

The Great Adventure

The
Great
Adventure

a novel by
Janice Holt Giles

Houghton Mifflin Company Boston
The Riverside Press Cambridge

To
ANNE N. BARRETT
who also knows about the western wind

All of the men of the Driant trapping party and all of the Fowler men are fictional. The authentic mountain men, such as Jim Bridger and Tom Fitzpatrick and Bill Sublette, move in and out of the story in their own characters and in place and position historically true. Captain William Drummond Stewart, the Scotsman, is real, as is Captain B. L. E. Bonneville, U.S. Army.

The
Great
Adventure

one

THEY RODE FAST and jangling out of San Fernandez de Taos. It was a bright September morning and they were a wild, yowling, yipping, rambunctious crew. Their horses and the herd of pack mules raised a fog of red dust which trailed behind them.

They were trappers—beaver men—mostly young and bold, proud. All of them were reckless and tough. To the last man they were suffering a little or a lot from a final spree with Taos lightning, and sleepless from one last *fandango*. But they were either young enough or indestructible enough to ride with their heaving stomachs and splitting heads. They were saying goodby to Taos in the best possible style, riding out in a fine string, well mounted, possible sacks full, steel traps and Spanish spurs jingling.

Two men rode a little to one side. The big one, loose-coupled on a big blue roan, was named Fowler. He said, "We didn't leave nobody, did we?"

The older man beside him said, "Can't ye count? Thar they be, all twenty of 'em. I called *levé* on 'em all, personal."

Fowler said, "I would love to have seen you getting 'em up at daylight. They hadn't much more than got to bed." His mouth was so dry he couldn't even raise a spit.

"It taken some doin'," Mose Strong admitted. "Yore bed was empty."

"It was?"

"How'd you git past the little Uliballos girl's mama?"

"I didn't say that was how I was occupied."

"How else would a young coon like you occupy hisself his last night in Taos?"

"Several other ways. Was a big game of monte at Salazar's. I could have been there. Or me and Mr. Driant could have been seeing to things."

"Likely you was," Mose said dryly. He slid an oblique look at the big man. "You aimin' to marry Carmelita?"

Joe Fowler laughed. "Sheep and beaver don't mix, *amigo.*"

"Mebbe not," Mose said, "but if Carmelita Uliballos was big-eyein' me way she is you, this coon could quit beaver. Especially," he added, with emphasis, "since you'd git a fine *hacienda* and a hundred thousand acres of land and four-five thousand head of sheep with the gal. Yep, this coon could l'arn to admire sheep wool right quick and fergit all about beaver plews."

Fowler looked at the old man with affection. "You're just trying to marry me off so's you can set in the sun the rest of your days."

"I'm yore partner, ain't I?"

Fowler laughed. "There's time. She ain't but fifteen."

"Jist right fer marryin'," Mose said. "Ye'll come into Taos end of some season and find her married off to some García or Valdéz or Martinez is what yer gonna do."

Fowler shook his head. "I don't think it."

Mose eyed him slyly and grinned. Joe didn't tell all he knew. Maybe he'd spoken for the girl already. Maybe there was an arrangement. He kicked his black mule and threatened to skin him if he didn't get a move on. "Mebbe *you* don't mind eatin' dust," he told the animal querulously, "but this child does."

Fowler squinted his eyes against the harsh, brittle sunlight and winced at their tenderness. He looked over the string, his eyes observant, practiced, knowledgeable. Out in front, leading, was the owner, the Frenchman Pierre Driant, and his friend and clerk, Paul Noel. Bunched loosely behind him were the usual hands, the mixed bunch of free trappers and greenhorns to be picked up around Santa Fe and Taos any season. Half a dozen of them were camp swampers, meat hunters, horse wranglers, what have you. Their job was to take the drudgery out of the

season for the beaver men—to pack and unpack morning and
night; to stretch and cure pelts; to cook and keep camp; to do
any kind of odd job needing to be done.

The horse herder was a round-faced Spanish *chico* named
Pedro. To help him was a blue-eyed Utah halfbreed.

Besides Driant and his men there were Joe Fowler, his partner
Mose Strong, and three of their hunters, Big Starr—and nobody
knew any other name for him—young Pete Smith and Lou
Fouchette.

The brigade was riding loosestrung and now that they'd made
their grand exit from Taos, sloppy. Fowler watched them tol-
erantly. He was old enough in the trade to have worn out most
of his young foolishness, but not so old he didn't remember it.
It would be tomorrow before the outfit shook down into trail
wariness, but this near the settlements it didn't matter. Strictly
speaking, this was not his brigade. He and his men had joined
forces with it because they were heading north anyhow and
Pierre Driant needed a guide. It had suited Fowler to serve in
that capacity.

His mother had given him a fancy name that hot August night
he was born at his grandmother Hannah Fowler's home in Kentucky. She wanted to honor the neighbor woman who had
helped her through the birth, so she called him Joseph Manifee
Fowler. The family moved to Arkansas Territory when he was
still a boy and he had a chance to become plain Joe Fowler,
which he did quickly. He never liked the Manifee and was glad
to get rid of it.

He was a natural horseman, riding with a loose give in his
body. He was a tall bony man, well weathered and seasoned.
His face had been scoured by wind and sun and rain and grit
and cold until the skin fitted to the bone with little flesh pad-
ding. Spokes of weather ran out from his eyes. He was deeply
browned. The eyes were fine, deep in their sockets, clean-irised,
and they were the blue-black color of a good gun barrel.

Like all fur trappers he wore his hair long to the shoulder. In the beginning there had been practical reasons for the trappers' long hair. It kept your neck warmer in a howling blast, and it was less trouble to let it grow than to keep it cut. But it had by now become part of the fancy dress which marked a beaver man and which he cherished with pride. There was no telling what color Joe Fowler's hair had been to start with. It was now streaked and bleached and, on the surface, the color of dried weeds.

He rode a big roan horse, a true roan, bluer than gray. He was a powerful horse. You could tell something about a man by the kind of horse he liked. All trappers wanted a good animal. Some liked a fine horse and felt sentiment for them. Some just picked good horseflesh and took good care of them because a horse was a trapper's life. Get put afoot and you didn't last long. What you looked for in a horse was wind and endurance first, speed if you could get it. Some took pride in their horses and decked them with Spanish silver on their bridles and saddles and with fancy apishamores. Others, less proud and less willing to load a horse with extra weight, rode them plain.

Fowler was no less proud than the proudest, but he let his big roan's blood tell his pride. He had got himself a fine animal and he didn't deck him out.

He pulled his hat brim down. The sun was well up now and the glare was pitiless, the sky white and bright, bouncing the light back in the eyes and making them salt. Fowler roved his look over the brigade again. Most of the men were fancily dressed in beaded, long-whanged new buckskins. Strictly for show. More of the foofooraw beaver men liked when on parade. For the *fandango* last night and to ride out before the Taos *señoritas* this morning. Tonight the fancy buckskins would be packed away. Worn old wool pants or easy soft buckskins made from old smoked tepees would replace them. At work, beaver men had no vanity. Comfort came first. The fancy shirts, pants, and beaded moccasins would stay packed away till rendezvous time next summer, or if a man didn't go to rendezvous, until he came riding back into Taos and wanted to show off properly.

Fowler's eye lit on one man and he laughed. "Look at Big Starr. He's sure got himself a knot on his head."

Mose made a noise down in his throat, part growl, part grunt. "Wagh! *That* coon don't like no interference when he shines up to a squaw, Injun *or* Spanish. He made 'em *come* last night or I wouldn't say so." He slewed a look at Fowler. "You was right some yerself."

Fowler was still chuckling. "How many did we lay out?"

"*Well,* when we stacked 'em in the corner, this child counted twelve."

It was possible. Full of *aguardiente* two mountain men had been known to clean out a *fandango*. Fowler said, "What commenced it?"

"Why, one of them *palous* taken a dislike to Starr dancin' with his gal too often. Drawed a knife on him. I figgered you knowed."

"I had me Carmelita doing a reel and swing and next thing I knew Starr was owgh-owghing and swinging a table leg, laying 'em out right and left. You was in one corner taking on a handful and Pete was in another. I allowed I'd better back up Big Starr."

"You done so. 'Course, Starr had done buried his knife in the bugger clean up to the Green River, but them other *palous* was makin' him some trouble. We made 'em come, fer a fact," he ended happily. "We was half froze fer a scrape, anyways."

Fowler laughed again. "Starr must of took a whack on the cheek, way it's swole up. Puffed his eye clean shut, too."

"Pete done that, accidental," Mose said. "He ripped another table laig off and commenced swingin' it a leetle too wide and handsome. Caught Starr a lick backhanded."

Big Starr was riding slouched, huge body slack in the saddle. He was a big block of a man, toweringly big, even in a land where all men were outsize and measured by mountains. He was still young enough that his bigness could have been awkward to handle, but wasn't. It was pure joy to watch Big Starr go into action, any kind of action, from cleaning out a *fandango* to cleaning out a passel of Indians. On demand, every muscle bunched to its purpose as sleek, smooth, and controlled as a panther's, and as economical. One of those big, deer-haunch hands didn't flail around wastefully and miss its mark. Big Starr was a good man to have beside you in trouble.

He had Kentucky blood in him, too. He and Fowler had learned early in their acquaintance that their grandparents had settled up in the old days near each other, been neighbors and had forted up together many a time in Ben Logan's old fort at St. Asaph's. There was some basis to believe they might be a little kin and they had agreed it was a good thing it was not to be ashamed of.

Young Pete Smith was riding near Starr. He had his head thrown back and he was shouting out a badly off-key song. It was meant to be a slow, sad Spanish love song. But young Pete was making up new verses and the way it came out it was anything but sad. It was a saga of young Pete's prowess with numerous Spanish ladies, juicily uninhibited and profane. Don Juan would have hung his head in shame. "Listen to him," Mose growled, "makin' out he's a brayin' bull elk."

"He ain't lying too much," Fowler laughed.

Young Pete had the face of an innocent child, round, smooth, red-flushed on the cheeks, with black eyes always glittering with fun. He fooled everybody at first glance, but no man's looks were more deceiving. Though he had the face of a good little boy and the fetching grin to go with it, Pete Smith was a rip-snorting young hellion, a reckless, heedless, half-horse, half-alligator sort of man. He always gave a good account of himself.

He had been among the Moqui and Navajo Indians and along the Dolores and San Miguel rivers into the San Juan range. He had been on the Gila. He knew the Uncompaghre country and the Huajatolla country. About the only place he hadn't hunted yet was the high north country, the Wind River, Siskadee, and

Yellowstone country. He was remedying that this season. Young Pete was the kind of man who went into an Indian scrape shouting and carving and cutting and shooting. He was always "half froze fer ha'r" and he nearly always raised it.

Old Dan Sutton, a Taos trapper who signed with a different outfit every year, was riding alone far on the other side of young Pete. He rode a seedy-looking gray mare that jounced along on four long legs as stiff as sticks. As thin as Old Dan was, Fowler wondered how he could stand the mare's hard gait, but Sutton swore by her. "This child knows a thing or two," he would say when joshed about the mare. "Mules'll foller a mare to hell and back. This coon don't *never* have to go huntin' no stray pack critters. They're allus to hand whur the mare is."

"And eatin' on the mare's tail," friends hooted at him.

"She kin spare it," he would say.

The mare's tail was nearly always thin and scraggly, chewed off by Old Dan's pack mules.

Fowler watched the seedy-looking man on the seedy-looking mare. Old Dan was a man you didn't warm up to straight off. Some, and Fowler was among them, never warmed up to him at all, though giving him his due. He was a good beaver hunter, but he had notional ways and he was something of a loner. Fowler had never hunted with him, but he was one of Pierre Driant's men this season.

Mose was talking to his black mule. "You, thar, Solomon, you god-damned, tough-hided, slab-sided, cantankerous critter, git yer head up and quit snatchin' at them cactus! Ye'll git yer fool flabber-mouth full of them needles and it'll take me all night to git 'em out fer ye." He fanned the mule's head with his hat. "Git yer flea-bitten head up, do 'ee hyar, now!"

Fowler grinned. The mule was the love of Mose's life. He wouldn't have parted with him for all the beaver in the mountains. He cussed him constantly and imaginatively, daily dreaming up new obscenities to call him, but he never raised his voice at the animal. Men stood around and waited to hear Mose

Strong cuss his black mule, for it was something to hear him breathing fire and brimstone at him, threatening to cut his liver out, to feed him to the coyotes, to fill him full of lead, to hamstring him and draw and quarter him, to roast his haunches, to leave him for the wolves—and all in the softest, tenderest voice you ever heard, almost whispered in the mule's flapping ears. "Thar's the beauty of havin' a understandin' critter," he would say. "You kin blast his tough hide off and long as you don't raise yer voice he thinks yer makin' love to him."

Mose had always liked a mule to saddle. "Ain't no Injun gonna steal a mule," he would say when the men jibed. "A mule kin whiff a Injun a mile away. They can't git in thievin' range 'fore he'll hinny and warn ye. If they's ary thing a mule don't like, it's Injun smell. This coon ain't likely to lose his ha'r long as he rides a mule."

But when Mose acquired old Solomon a love affair developed. "He's a Chihuahua mule," he explained to Fowler, "and them is the best kind. I got two wipin' sticks to my rifle. I kin cuss him in English *and* Spanish, or both. Whichever comes handiest."

Having got the mule's head up, Mose sighed heavily. "He's sometimes a trial and a tribulation."

"He is *so,*" Fowler agreed. He drawled thoughtfully, "If I was to breed my blue to Old Dan Sutton's mare she would foal a better critter than you got there."

"Now, hold on thar . . ." Mose began.

A pack mule broke from the herd and capered off to the left. Fowler kneed his horse swiftly and the roan turned, but Lou Fouchette was whooping after the mule. Fowler hauled up and watched him.

He had hunted many a season with Fouchette and you could rightly say he was a Fowler man, but sometimes, looking at Fouchette with that clarity of vision which makes the most familiar person suddenly seem strange, Fowler thought that Fouchette could easily pass for an Apache. He had the same barrel chest with prominent sternum and clavicle, and the same long-stringed muscles in his thighs and legs. His wrist and hand bones, his ankles, were small and delicate. His hair was black and straight, without gloss, and he wore it banged with a red band to keep it from falling in his eyes. He rarely wore a head covering.

Fouchette was an uncommon Frenchman. He had their chattering gayness and their liking for song, but the Latin temperament which abhorred solitude and darkness and fell prey to gloom and despair when exposed to them was not as strong in him, or it had been trained out of him, for he was an old, old timer. He had broken in with the Canadian Northwest Company, one of the best-disciplined outfits ever engaged in the fur trade. You stayed a pork eater with the Northwest Company for three long years before you were trusted with a trap. By that time you were ready or you never would be.

Fouchette drifted down to Taos when the Northwest had merged with the Hudson's Bay Company, their bitterest rival for years. The old enmity was too strong in him. He wouldn't, he said, take beaver for those *cochons*. He was one of the few men in Taos before Fowler.

Coon Bastro cut out to help head the mule. He wasn't anybody Fowler knew. Big Starr had told him Bastro showed up with a wagon train a couple of years before. Claimed to have hunted buffalo for McKenzie up at Fort Union. Claimed to have lived with the Crows a spell. Claimed to be a friend of Jim Beckwith, also a Crow man, and he had hung around with the mulatto in Santa Fe some, until Jim drifted back up north.

Bastro was a short, thick-set man, with long arms and powerful hands. Didn't talk much. In the *cantinas* they said he made 'em shine at monte. He had trapped last season in the same outfit as Old Dan Sutton and Old Dan had recommended him to Driant for this season. He was an unknown quantity to Fowler and no business of his.

Among the other Driant hands was a young fellow named Jordan who either knew Coon Bastro from former days or had taken up with him. They were pretty thick. While the outfit was assembling in Taos they had drunk and prowled together. But Jordan was a rank greenhorn in the trade.

The youngest member of the Driant party was a kid named Ben Lashly. He didn't look to be more than eighteen. Could barely raise a beard. But he had a steadiness about him Fowler had noted and if he was a greenhorn he at least knew it and didn't try to pretend he knew more than he did. He kept his mouth shut, watched, listened, and learned.

Fouchette and Bastro brought the notional mule back into the cavvyard and the brigade strung out again.

The big roan shied at a tumbleweed and Fowler steadied him. They were passing the pueblo now and he looked over at the terraced adobe houses set back from the ancient wall. Dust devils swirled about the bare court and, high on the shoulder of the humped mountain behind, the aspens were showing yellow, not much yet, but a little. It had been winter when he first saw the Taos pueblo and he had been a lean and limber kid. He was pushing thirty, now.

2.

In winter, in Taos valley, the Sangre de Cristo peaks are snowy and the valley is white. The acequias are sharded with ice and the cornfields are long and flat. The heavy blind church at Ranchos is heavier and blinder under its white weight.

In winter, in San Fernandez de Taos, the plaza is windscoured and the cottonwoods rattle like old bones. In the angles of the walled streets, dried frail tumbleweeds pile, their blowing liberty lost. The *chili colorados* which have hung like red flags around the doorways of the houses have been taken in and the doors are closed and blank. In shadow the cold is like sharp knives, but the sun is shining after the snow and old men are dozing against adobe walls, waking to move a foot or two when the shadow chills them.

In winter, the Taos pueblo is still as sleep, the mountains behind it asleep and silent, too. On either side of the boiling little creek the two massed, stepped-back houses, which rear five stories and shelter every living soul of the Taos Indians, look strong and buttressed. The ladders which lead from one terraced roof to the next are like black sticks against the snow. A blanketed sentinel on the topmost roof of each house, wrapped to his eyes, is watching. Little smokes rise from the chimneys. A child may run quickly from one level to another. A hooded, booted woman may go to the creek for water. A dog may wake and scratch his fleas. These are the only signs of life.

One time a *puebleño* whom Fowler had befriended told him that the Winter People lived in one house and the Summer People lived in the other. And that the Rio Pueblo was the river of sacred water, the river of life because it flowed from a lake on the sacred mountain where the gods, the *kachinas*, lived. And that it was a good thing to live by this river because it not only furnished life through its waters but it purified all who used them or bathed in them. And this was true of all the river people even on the Rio Grande for the Rio Pueblo flowed into the Rio Grande and made it blessed. But of all the People in the land the Taons felt they were the most fortunate for they lived at the foot of the sacred mountain and the sacred river flowed through their town.

Fowler had been a young squirt to come riding into El Valle de Taos alone, not yet eighteen in fact. But he hadn't been as green a greenhorn as some. He had been trapping beaver in the streams of the Osage country in the Arkansas Territory since he was big enough and strong enough to spring a trap. Nobody had had to teach him how to look for beaver sign, or where or how to set his traps, or how to stretch and pack his skins. He had known those things as long as he'd known anything. You couldn't help it if you grew up near Fort Smith and the Three

Forks of the Verdigris and Neosho and Arkansas rivers, for they were the beginning of the west, the farthest west white settlements in a land facing west. Nothing stood between them and the great Rocky Mountains but the prairies and plains and the mountain-headed rivers. Money was beaver pelts and buffalo hides there. It was a country where the gospel came from St. Louis out of the mouths of the great fur families, the Prattes, Cabannés, and Chouteaus. One of the Chouteaus, young Auguste, had lived on the Neosho, not far from Fort Smith.

Once when he was a little boy, Joe Fowler's uncle had taken him up the Neosho with him. His uncle was called Johnny Osage because he was a trader to the Osage Indians and he was at that time courting a young teacher at the Union Mission. His courting done that day he had gone upstream to see Auguste Chouteau on business. Joe had been roundeyed at the great double-log house, its piazzas hung with skins and Indian blankets and rugs, the wealth of the establishment plainly evident in the village of buildings all about it, and the livestock and the slaves and the fields, the mill, the storerooms, presses, boatyard, and dock. He had also been roundeyed at the Osage wife and children. Riding back to Three Forks, where Johnny had his trading post, he had said, "Mama says Auguste Chouteau is living in sin. She says his real wife and family live in St. Louis."

Johnny Osage had been quiet for a moment. "Don't go around repeating what your mama says, Joe. It isn't polite. When you're a man, maybe you'll understand about Auguste Chouteau's Osage woman."

A grown man, he had.

Joe Fowler was early infected with the western fever, also. Each time he took a load of skins to Colonel John Rogers' store in Fort Smith, or over to Three Forks to Johnny's post, he heard the talk of the mountains and the rich catches of beaver in them. Beaver was playing out in this country, he heard. You got to go west. There was beaver, beaver galore out there in those western mountains, all around Taos and Santa Fe and up into the mountain country. He heard Nathaniel Pryor tell about the Lewis and Clark journey to the Pacific and back, following the Missouri River, then down the Columbia. It was 1804 when they started, the year he was born. It was 1806 when they got back to St. Louis. Nathaniel Pryor, who lived with the Osages and had an Osage wife, had been with them. He said, "Them streams that run into the upper Missouri are workin' alive with beaver. You never seen as many beaver, nowhere. And the prettiest pelts you ever handled."

It didn't take long for the big fur companies, which had been trapping the headwaters of the Mississippi and up the Missouri as far as the Mandan villages for years, to sew the upper Missouri up tight. But there were still the mountains, and Joe Fowler lived on the banks of the Arkansas, and the Arkansas led straight to the heart of the mountains. All you had to do was follow the river to where it headed and it would take you into rich beaver country. Take you into the Spanish possessions and Indian country, too, but if you didn't risk something you didn't gain anything.

Everybody talked beaver and going west, everybody wanted to go, even the soldiers garrisoned at Fort Smith talked of it, wistfully. Joe Fowler heard all the talk and as bad as anybody he wanted to go. The one memory of his boyhood that was an unchanging, undeviating constant was the waiting till he was big enough and old enough to start west.

In the summer of 1821 his chance came. A man named Hugh Glenn, who had a trading post on the Verdigris, finally found the financial backing to form an expedition to go west and hunt beaver. Joe was seventeen. He was counted a man, and a change in the family situation gave him the freedom to go. As the eldest of four children, three brothers and a sister, Joe had carried for several years a big load of work and responsibility. His mother had died, his father seemed lost, and his younger brothers and sister were but children yet. Now, however, his father had married again and his brothers were old enough and big enough to be helpful. Joe was free.

Before seeing Colonel Glenn he went to the Johnny Osage post to talk with his uncle. "I want to sign on with Glenn," he said.

Johnny Osage, only twelve years older than Joe, wasn't one to hash all around Robin Hood's barn. What he had to say, one man to another, was always straight to the point. "You gonna trap," he said, "Auguste Chouteau would give you a job upriver, likely."

Joe shook his head. "Don't wanna go with the Company, Johnny. Be stuck in one of their posts the rest of my life. I wanna get out on my own, be my own boss, do my own trapping."

Johnny accepted it. "Can you afford to go?"

Joe was puzzled. "Ain't Glenn furnishing the outfit? He's heading it up."

"Sure. He'll furnish you, if that's the way you want it. But you wouldn't be your own boss that way, either. You'd be working for him. He'll pay you a little wages, very little, and all the skins you take will belong to him. Or, if you don't do it that way, you can go in debt to him for your necessaries. Then half the skins you take will be his. Maybe you'll be able to catch enough beaver to pay him off, maybe not. If you can't pay off your debt, you'll owe him another season of work, and you'll have to go in debt again for more supplies."

"That's no good," Joe said. "That ain't the way I want to go."

"Didn't think so. Only way to do it is furnish yourself. Stay a free trapper. Then you'll owe nothing to nobody."

Well, you weren't born with all the sense in the world and you never learned as much as you needed, but if you weren't a plain fool you learned a little something from almost everybody. Joe learned about free trapping right then and he knew it was the way he wanted to work and he never varied from it. "Will Glenn sign me on that way?" he asked.

"Sure, he will. Be glad to. He wants as big an outfit as he can put together. When the season is over, you oughtta give Glenn first chance to buy your skins. You'd owe him that much for it's a protection to a man to work with a big outfit. But if you don't like his offer, if you think it ain't enough, take 'em where you want—bring 'em to St. Louis, or to me, or take 'em down to Taos or Santa Fe."

"He's heading for Taos, they say."

"Yes. He'll have to get a license to trap south of the Arkansas. That's Spanish country. Now, can you furnish yourself?"

Joe had saved some money from his trapping and for several years he had been catching wild mustangs on the prairies and breaking them to the saddle and selling them to the men of the regiment. He had a little money. "Is it enough?" he asked.

Johnny Osage rubbed his nose. "Barely. Tell you what I'll do, Joe. I'll outfit you at cost. It ain't good business and not even for kinfolks will I do it more'n once, but I'll see you have what you need. You got some ponies?"

"I got four."

"They broke?"

"Nearabout."

"Well, sell two of 'em and keep two. You'll need one to ride and one for your pack. When you've settled up your affairs come back and we'll make up your outfit."

Hugh Glenn was agreeable to signing him on as a free trapper, and when he had sold two mustangs, Joe had enough to outfit himself pretty well and a little left over for a small cash horde.

Johnny Osage gave him quality at cost. For eight dollars each, he furnished him six good steel traps which would have cost him twelve to sixteen dollars in St. Louis and more from Colonel Glenn. In a heavy skin sack he loaded the traps, along with chains, spare springs, and tools for repair. Into a possible sack he packed gunpowder, Galena lead, flints, tobacco, sewing materials, some coffee, sugar, and flour. Joe himself knew how to stow about his person a skinning knife, whetstone, awl holder and awl, tomahawk, bullet pouch, and powder horn.

Johnny also made him up a pack of trading goods—several gross of awls and knives, some needles, beads, small mirrors, shells, feathers and bells, some vermilion, and a bolt of gaudy calico. "You been around trading stores enough to know these awls and knives are the most useful things you got. All Indians need 'em and want 'em. They come cheap, but trade smart with 'em. One for one if you can get it. Sometimes you can get two plews for a good knife. Make your calico go as far as you can. A squaw can nag her man into buying a shirt length if she wants it bad enough. Get four skins if you can for a shirt length. Don't trade for less'n three. Trade your vermilion high, too. They'll give anything for paint. These bells, beads, feathers— they're for on the prairie. Give 'em a handful of them, a little tobacco, maybe an awl or knife. Something like that. Don't trade powder and lead at all. Let Glenn handle that. And I'm not giving you but five gallons of whiskey. It's for your own use, not to trade. Let Glenn handle that, too. But there'll be times when you're wet and cold, or maybe hurt some way, and you'll need some whiskey. It's not a good idea to be without. But don't mess with it with Indians. Not trading alone. They get mean sometimes."

He leaned under the counter and brought up a gun. "Your gun is too light. Here's a heavier one for you."

Joe took it and whistled. It was a Hawken, a big, heavy gun weighing around twelve pounds, with a forty-inch barrel, .50 caliber, which fired a half-ounce slug. The barrel had been bored so often it looked like a tunnel. The stock was black walnut, grained with use, and sunk into the heel was a brass plate with some fancy initial work carved on it. Joe looked the gun over reverently, hefting it, feeling it. But he put it on the counter. "I can't afford that gun, Johnny. I've killed buffalo with my gun. It'll have to do."

"I ain't selling you the gun, Joe. In a way, it's rightly yours. It was your pa's. He traded it to me some years ago, when he first come to the Territory. He needed to raise some money in a hurry and sold her to me. He would have meant you to have it some day. Them are his initials on that brass plate. She shoots plumb center and she'll drop you a grizzly or a buffler easy."

Joe picked the gun up again and looked for the initials. Now that he knew, he could make out the MF, for Matthew Fowler. "Let me pay you what you give Pa for it," he said.

"No. I'm making you a present of the gun. Never felt right about taking her. Ought to have loaned Matt the money." He laughed. "Now, take her and don't give me no argument. Matt called her the Hellraiser."

Hellraiser. So Joe Fowler had a gun with a name, like all the oldtimers, and it was a name he never changed. A boy and a gun named Hellraiser. It was the beginning of the legend.

Johnny Osage leaned on the counter and said, "I'll be out there soon. Soon as this revolution down in Mexico is over. If the Mexicans win, the way to Santa Fe will be open to traders."

"You aiming to stay in trade, Johnny? Whyn't you go for beaver?"

"Nope," Johnny shook his head, "not me. You can freeze your legs off if you want, wading them cold creeks and rivers. I'll buy and trade. Getting too old to trap. But I'll make a bee-line for Santa Fe when the time's ready."

"Well, then," Joe said, shifting the new gun, "I'll look you up when you get there."

"Do that," Johnny said. "Bring me your plews. I'll pay you as much as anybody else. I figure to be there in a year or two."

He helped the boy load his pack horse, watched him heave into the saddle of his riding pony. At the last he felt a pull of sentiment for the tall, steady boy who knew what he wanted and was headed toward it. He said gruffly, "Remember, Joe, a buffler, a grizzly, and a Injun all take a lot of killing. And don't get caught with your gun empty."

"I'll remember," the boy said, and rode away.

3.

Glenn's party left from Van Buren on the north side of the Arkansas the middle of September. Later, Joe Fowler was to say the journey west was uneventful. There was a sizable pack train and they followed straight up the Arkansas. They had the usual mishaps of the trail with thunderstorms, stampeded horse herds, flooded streams, and they ran into some bothersome Pawnees. They lost one man when a grizzly ripped him open, but those were hazards more or less expected.

They sighted the loom of the mountains at the Big Timbers and spent a month trading with the Cheyennes. Then they crossed the Arkansas into Spanish country. They were in the mountains above Taos, in deep snow, when a detail of Spanish soldiers found them. Courteously they required Glenn to accompany them to Santa Fe. He went, confident he could persuade the Spanish governor to give him a license to trap. He told the men to fort up and wait for him.

In the three months on the trail Joe Fowler had done some thinking. It was too big a party, in his opinion, and Glenn didn't have the control of it he should have had. Joe didn't much think he had the connections in Santa Fe he had led the men to believe he had, either. He decided it would not serve his interests to stick with the outfit. He was furnishing himself, he wasn't under bond, he wasn't an official of the party, and he owed nothing to it. He went to the second in command and told him he was going to cut loose on his own.

The man was gloomy. "If I didn't have some money in the

outfit," he said, "I'd go with you. We're liable all of us to end up in the calaboose."

Joe pulled out the same morning and two days later came down into Taos valley. And so it was he first saw the pueblo and San Fernandez blind and sleeping and drifted in snow.

He had no notion of where to go that first evening, or what his welcome would be. He didn't want to be picked up by the *soldados,* so he stopped at a small clump of willows beside a ditch of water and made a shelter of branches. He cached his small take of furs, made a thin flour gruel for his supper, and slept the night out.

Next day he went into the village and wandered about. From the first he liked it. It was a brown earth town, under its lid of snow, the color of earth, and it had the melted, eroded look of the ageless earth from which it had been made. Narrow lanes walled by low, flat-roofed adobe houses led into a *placita* where hitching rails fronted the road, and broad painted doors opened into the *tiendas, cantinas,* and trading places.

Blanketed Taos Indians drifted about, what you could see of them the color of his walnut gunstock. Spanish men in peaked, oilskin-covered hats, their heads sticking out of a hole in an Indian blanket or rug, tipped their hats over swarthy faces and looked at him from blazing black eyes. Chattering French-Canadians, the *bons vivants* among beaver men, trooped noisily from *cantina* to *cantina,* sampling the fiery *aguardiente.* He did not yet know them, but they were men he was later to hunt with—the Robidoux brothers, Antoine and Michel, Etienne Provost, Gaston LeClerc, Lou Fouchette. They rolled by him babbling their French-Canadian *patois.*

There weren't many Americans yet but those that were there were noticeable because they were treetop tall and they swaggered and swayed and rolled together in twos and threes, whooping and shouting. Three fourths of these early beaver men were Kentuckians, and Kentuckians just came naturally by swagger and brag. Kentuckians just naturally thought they could lick their weight in wildcats, and mostly could. Kentuckians just naturally thought they could out-shoot, out-fight, out-talk, and out-drink anything that walked on two feet, and mostly could. Put two Kentuckians together and you had a loud-mouthed majority. Put a dozen Kentuckians together and you had, by God, an army. No Kentuckian ever needed authority, Spanish, British, or American, to do what he wanted to do when he wanted to do it—nor did he ever heed any authority. Kentuckians *were* authority. Big powerful men, they strode out of Kentucky, which their fathers had settled, across Missouri, over the plains, into New Mexico and the mountains, where they roared like mountain lions and clawed and bit and scratched anything that got in their way. They were a special breed of men and Joe Fowler, by blood, was one of them.

Down the narrow lanes of Taos young boys drove little burros heaped high with wood, and sometimes a black-shawled woman went silently and alone into the church. Occasionally a girl went by, *reboso* over her head, big, black eyes splintered with light and excitement, a shuck *cigarillo* dangling from her mouth. But a shuck *cigarillo* dangled from the mouth of everybody.

Dirt town, dark people, high sky, and mountains—it was like no town Joe Fowler had ever seen before, like no town any American had ever seen before. There was nothing with which to compare, nothing with which to identify, unless you had been south into Chihuahua or Mexico City. The people were mostly government officials, petty clerks, merchants, traders, and trappers. There were a few *soldados* drifting about. And they all huddled together behind their adobe walls, inside their adobe houses, on the high plateau under the shadow of the mountains. They kept a few goats and chickens, raised a little maize and some beans and chilis, and if God willed had enough to eat and something left over.

They should have been miserable with so poor a life but they did not appear to be. For the most part they seemed to be happier, higher spirited, more laughing, readier to enjoy life, than

Americans in the frontier towns Joe Fowler had known. He had no way of knowing a deep bed of fatalism infected them. They accepted all things—as God willed them. In the meantime they smoked their everlasting *cigarillos,* worked a little, had a *baile* at the drop of a hat, gambled a lot, drank *aguardiente,* and for their sins were truly penitent in the confessional, which was not the same as going and sinning no more. The church was the center of their lives and God required much of them, but not that a man should go against the nature He had Himself given them.

In their youth, with their gusty appetites, with their inborn instinct for swagger and rule, for *fandango* or fight, the beaver men, the trappers and traders, accepted Taos as it was, enjoyed it, made of their time in it one long lusty spree.

Fowler was leaning against a corner out of the wind when he was accosted. "Howdy, *amigo,*" the man said, "this coon ain't seed you around before."

"Just got here," Fowler said.

You couldn't have told the man's age, but Joe Fowler, sizing him up, judged him to be beyond Johnny Osage's age, near forty or so. At seventeen, that made him practically an old man to Joe. He wore old buckskins, velvety with grease and dirt and smoke. He was clean-shaven although he hadn't shaved for several days. His eyes were squinched with weather wrinkles and they were a bleary blue. His face was as leathery as a saddle.

"Wagh!" he grunted, and it was the first time Fowler heard the Indian grunt which beaver men had picked up and used constantly. "As if I didn't know. This child knows ever' white man in the mountains. Name's Strong," he said, "Mose Strong. Whar from, boy?"

"Joe Fowler. From the Arkansas Territory."

"So-o-o," Strong said, drawing it out long, "you must be with that Glenn feller's outfit."

"I was," Joe said, "but I cut loose a couple of days back. You know where he is? What's happened to him?"

"*Well,* I do. He's havin' hisself a right smart of trouble down to Santy Fee. The guvmint's in kind of a turmoil jist now. But likely he'll git his permit in time. They don't do things in a hurry in these parts."

"We heard the government was favorable to Americans now."

"Sometimes they are. Sometimes they ain't. Depends the humor they're in. Glenn got any money?"

"I don't know."

Mose Strong shrugged. "If he ain't, he won't git no permit. Sumpin that jingles is usually what puts 'em in the best humor. You got any plews, boy?"

"Some."

The man studied him, then laughed and clapped him on the back. "Close-mouthed coon, ain't ye? Best way to be. You kin trust me, but you don't know that yit. This child wouldn't do no diff'runt in yore shoes. Trust me enough to go to my place and have a drink of Taos lightning?"

"Whyn't we go to the inn?"

"Ain't no use payin' out yer pesos. I make my own whiskey. It goes down like hell's own f'ar but it won't cost you nothin' and it'll warm yer guts."

Fowler went with him, seeing nothing to lose and maybe a lot to gain. Mose lived in the edge of the village, up toward the pueblo, in a miserable hovel that had only one room. There was a shed of sorts along one side and he went into it and brought back a clay jar. "Taos lightning," he said, chuckling and sloshing it around. "Take a jolt of that, boy, and it'll warm ye to yer toes."

Fowler figured the man knew. He was hungrier than he was thirsty, but he didn't want to say so. Six foot two, still angled with a boy's flatness and thinness and still growing, he was as hard to fill up as an Indian. His last meal of flour gruel had long since left him. He could have eaten half a horse, but you didn't turn down a drink.

He had some staying power with whiskey. He had learned pretty young with the men of the Seventh Infantry. When they found a whiskey runner operating among the Cherokees or Osages they confiscated his stuff and made good use of it. Most of it was as raw and fiery as this Taos lightning Mose Strong gave him. It made your eyes water and it burned your throat, but it had a good spread, as he said, and it reached to your fingers and toes. It would make you crazy wild, too, Fowler thought, if you downed enough of it. Likely kill you. He took it easy.

They talked a while and finally Mose said he was hungry and set out some food—beans and bread and meat. "Is there enough," Fowler asked, "for me to have all I want?"

"Goddlemighty, boy, you that lean? I ort to knowed. Jist come down from the mountains this time of year. Shore there's enough. Eat up, boy, eat up. Eat all you kin hold. I got a whole elk out back froze and waitin' and them beans comes cheap. Fill yer belly full."

The first mouthful brought tears to Fowler's eyes and set his gullet on fire. Blindly he reached for something to wet it down. Mose laughed till he fell out of his chair. It was worth a six-dollar plew to see a greenhorn take his first bite of *frijoles!* They all did the same things, they coughed, cried, clutched their throats. "Ain't ever eat Mex food afore, have ye?"

Fowler wiped his eyes. "Is that what it is? What'd you put in them beans? Is this your idea of a joke?"

"Hell, no, boy, 'tain't no joke. Them is freeholies with red chilis in 'em. The Spanish jist like their food hotter'n hell is all. You git a taste fer it yerself, you hang around long enough."

Fowler eyed his heaped plate with distrust. "I don't know as I will."

"Shore you will. First swaller is the worst. Hyar. I got some goat milk. Swig that along with them freeholies and the burn'll ease up some."

This was the beginning of a friendship and partnership that had lasted through the following years, through many a quarrel-springing spree and long lonesome hunt. Fowler moved into the hovel with Mose that first winter and they made Taos lightning and peddled it. The demand for it was so great it was never properly aged. They made enough money to keep in beans and when they couldn't scare up an elk or deer they stole sheep and goats and chickens. Mose would chuckle, "This coon's got more'n *one* wipin' stick to his rifle."

Joe settled into the wintering easily. Uncritical, he picked up a working knowledge of the language. Young enough to relish it, he flung *Válgame Dios* about, called Mose *amigo,* said *bueno* for everything fine, good, all right, and *carajo* for everything that wasn't. Goodby went out of his vocabulary and *adios* replaced it. He picked up *sacré* and *enfant de garce* from the Canadians, and felt traveled and wise and experienced and quite a mountain man.

He was gauche, *naïve,* and a sucker a few times, but mostly he kept his head. He enjoyed the *fandangos,* made a little love to a few *señoritas,* as much as he wanted to, got into a few scrapes with a jealous husband or lover and got himself out of them, played monte when he wanted to but wasn't seized with any gambling fever, learned, as Mose had predicted he would, to like the highly seasoned Spanish food. He thought the bread, *biscoche,* the best white bread he had ever eaten and hot chocolate the way the Spanish women made it was a drink he could never get enough of. Even when the new wore off and he saw some things beneath the surface he continued to like the place. He came to Taos with the best possible preparation for an unshocked acceptance of its easy morals. He had been reared on a frontier where white men mouthed the moral platitudes and regularly corrupted them all. He saw no new sins in Taos.

Mose found a buyer for his pelts—a Spaniard who ran a train to Chihuahua—who paid him a fair price. Between their whiskey business and Joe's furs they pooled enough cash to outfit themselves to hunt that spring, and in February they put out for the country around the Spanish Peaks—Huajatolla.

They followed the mule path up the Taos Cañon, crossed over the summit, descended, found the Canadian and trapped on its waters, moved over and trapped the headwaters of the Cimarron. They left the Raton peak to the right and moved on up the valley. This was gray-rock and cedar country, big and rugged and harsh. They circled the foothills of the Spanish Peaks. *"Las Cumbres Españolas,"* Mose told him. "Wah-to-yah. Them two peaks is good landmarks. You kin see 'em a hundred miles away. Leetle snow most allus a glitterin' on top of 'em. Ary time you're east of the mountains and git befuddled you kin git yer bearin's from 'em."

On this hunt Joe Fowler learned his first lessons in mountain navigation from Mose. A mountain was not something beautiful to stand around and admire. It was something to go around or cross over. It was usually a trouble to you. But it was also a good landmark.

He learned that it was no miracle or compass in their heads that made beaver men able to find their way around in the mountains. The Indians had been here a long, long time and the trails they had made through the mountains and over the passes were always the easiest paths to follow.

"Any place you want to go in the mountains," Mose said, "east, west, north, or south, Injuns has done been and found the best way through. They like a low, good pass. They got sense enough to know their animals has got to have grass and water, so they don't fool with no passes that's much higher'n the timberline. Ye wanna git around in the mountains, pick ye the lowest gap and ye'll likely find a Injun trail. Whur they've been, ye kin git through and yer critters'll git through."

He learned that a beaver man didn't lift up his eyes unto the snowy peaks and think what God had wrought. He breathed deep the sharp, singing air, cussed the peaks for being in his way, went around or crossed by the easiest pass he could find. Mountain men didn't name the mountains they found. But they never failed to name the new creeks or beaver streams or valley basins and holes they discovered.

Joe and Mose had come out of the gray-rock country and were trapping the headwaters of Cuchera Creek, beyond the Spanish Peaks on the edge of the plains, when Joe Fowler suddenly grew up. In ten minutes he changed from a boy to a man.

They had been out three months and had a fair catch of skins. They had broken camp that morning and were working their mules, heavily loaded, down toward the main stream of the Cuchera. Mose suddenly grunted and pulled in his horse. With his head he motioned off to the right. "*Bueno*, boy. Hyar's damp powder and no fire to dry it. Git down."

Joe looked where Mose had nodded and his heart suddenly chunked up into his throat and his mouth went bone dry. At the top of a swell, plain and silhouetted against the sky, a motionless figure sat on a motionless horse. He thought stupidly, that's an Indian.

Mose was talking to him. "Tie yer pack mules to yer hoss. Close up to thar heads. Git*down!* Cain't ye hyar? Pronto! Yer gonna l'arn whut it means to stand back to back in a few minutes or I wouldn't say so."

Joe got down. His knees felt like a melting tallow candle, his stomach was heaving, and his heart was pounding. He hoped he looked calmer than he felt. He hauled in the mules and tied them, nose to nose, to his horse. Mose then tied the whole bunch together and side-lined them. "Now they won't stampede," he said. "A Injun tries first to stampede yer critters and ketch ye afoot. They kin take ye easy then. Take yer skulp, take yer plews. Stand thar," he pointed, "behind them critters on yore side. Rest yer gun across yer saddle."

Joe sighted his rifle on the Indian. The Indian turned as Joe watched him and rode off unhurriedly. "He's gone."

"He'll be back—with the rest of 'em. He was jist scoutin' out ahead."

"What do we do?"

"Wait."

"What are they?"

"Cain't tell yit. But they'll be Comanches or Kioways or Shians. They all range through hyar. Now, you listen to me, boy. When they come, they'll charge, full run, screechin' like all the devils in hell. Jist pint yer gun and stand yer ground. Don't shoot, ye hyar? Don't shoot less'n I say so."

Joe stared at him. "We just gonna bluff 'em?"

"If we kin. A Injun don't like to git kilt no more'n we do. They know when that rifle speaks they's gonna be one dead Injun. They'll bluff and we'll bluff and we'll see who kin out-bluff the other. If we have to shoot, we'll take turns. Keep one gun loaded all the time."

When they rode over the rise it was the way Mose had said—they came with bows drawn, lances pointed, horses pounding in a dead run, and they were yelling, whooping, screeching.

Mose grunted. "Wagh! Ain't but ten of 'em."

They looked like all the Indians in the world to Joe. He looked over his shoulder and felt steadied when he saw Mose standing at his back looking like his feet were rooted in the ground, his rifle rested and sighted. Joe squirmed his own feet to a better stance, rested his cheek against the stock of the big old Hawken, took a good breath, and tightened his jaws.

The uproar was tremendous, the horses pounding, the yells and whoops deafening, the brandished guns, spears, bows, threatening. Joe thought they would be ridden down for sure. The Indians came straight at them, not pulling up or changing course, intent to all appearances on riding right over the two of them. He found his breath short again and moved. "Keep stiddy," Mose warned him, "they're bluffin'."

The Indians were less than a hundred yards away when Mose suddenly swung his long rifle up off rest. Joe did the same. The

Indians split like waves against a rock, swirled around both sides, passing Joe so close the breeze fanned his face, but shooting neither guns nor arrows.

"Wagh!" Mose snorted, "that's makin' 'em come, boy. Stiddy, now. They'll turn and come back."

Almost as soon as he had spoken the Indians had swerved, circled and, still yipping and screeching, were charging back. As if sensing that Joe was young and green they did not split this time but charged straight down his side. Mose swung around to back him up. Sliding off their mounts onto the far side so that only a heel was visible, they swept by once more. This time an arrow was released in swift, under-horse flight. It plunked harmlessly into the pack of skins atop one of the mules. The mule whinnied and stomped but couldn't run.

Joe held steady, his gun following the charging Indians. He felt quite calm, now, and though tense with excitement he felt no fear. He saw the Indians plainer, this time. They wore their hair long and banged across the front. Their horses were small and rough-haired, mustangs such as he used to catch on the prairies himself. Scalp locks blew at the end of their spears. There was the gleam of silver on their arms and the apishamores which served as saddles were bright-colored, like the blankets he had seen worn as serapes in Taos.

Once more the Indians circled to make their charge. *"Bueno,"* Mose said, "let's quit this hyar foolishness. Ain't but a few of 'em. Take the lead man 'fore he gits in too close. Reload quick, but my gun'll be ready. I don't figger they'll risk losin' but one or two."

Without question, Joe brought his sights in on a barrel-chested Indian that seemed to be the leader. He kept him beaded as the Indian brought his horse around, waited till he had him straightened out, running, then he fired. The Indian tumbled to the ground.

"Wagh!" Mose yelled, "that's makin' 'em come, boy! That's good shootin', that is! That old Hellraiser of yore'n throws 'em plumb center, damned if she don't. Come ag'in ye blasted heathen varmints!" He began shouting their own war whoop at them, "How-owgh-owgh! Git our skulps, will ye! That'll l'arn ye!"

The Indians broke off the charge in confusion, circled around and corraled about the fallen man, scooped him up and fled. "By God," Mose shouted, dancing in his glee, "boy, ye'll do! You're *some*, I tell ye! That was purty shootin', or I wouldn't say so!" He pounded the boy on the back, almost knocking him over. "Helt stiddy as a rock, never lost yer nerve, and made 'em *shine!* This coon kin pick 'em. I seen ye had the makin's in ye soon as I laid eyes on ye. Ye'll do, Joe Fowler, ye'll do. Ye'll make a mountain man that'll outshine 'em all, see if ye don't!"

Joe felt sick at his stomach and suddenly outraged. "Quit pounding me on the back, you old fool," he shouted, "you're gonna make me heave!"

"Go on. Heave. Git it over. This child knows how ye feel. Felt the same first Injun I ever kilt." He looked off in the direction the Indians had fled. "Too bad they takened him off with 'em 'fore you could git yer skulp. But this child's hyar to say he seen ye count coup. Won't nobody dispute it with me around."

Joe didn't want the scalp. He was holding hard onto his nerve to keep from being sick, taking big gulps of air, swallowing, trying desperately not to be a disgrace to Mose. When he could speak safely, he said, "Will they be back?"

"Naw. They jist happened to run up on us and made a try. Never put much heart in it. Injuns don't like a open fight 'thout the odds is a heap more in their favor."

"You ever make out who they were?"

Mose was unhobbling the mules. "Shore. Comanches."

"I thought they was Shians, way they wore their hair. Them Shians we saw at the Big Timbers wore theirs the same way."

"So does the Comanches. So does the Utes. But a Shian buck has got three cuts on his arm. Comanches make three cuts on their chest. Utes don't make none." Mose went on, "Injuns has got their own ways and places, where ye can mostly expect 'em, and they got their own friends and enemies amongst theirselves. Now, this fur east you'll likely not find no mountain Injuns. They'll be Shians or Comanches or Kioway or Pawnee. But you got to look for Rapahoes most anywhur. Them Injuns'll raid anywhur. They count north of the Platte their country, but they rove a heap. They're bad Injuns, mean as a snake. They're kin to the Blackfeet and friendly with the Shians and Pawnees and Comanche. Their worst enemies is the Utahs. The Utahs live in the mountains up north of Taos and over west, but they come onto the plains to hunt buffler sometimes.

"Now, them was Comanches, but if you couldn't of seed the three cuts on their chest and was trailin', it'd be a leetle hard to tell. Fer them and the Shians and the Rapahoes all make their moccasins the same way. Straight inside and curved around outside so their tracks is pigeon-toed. Pawnee moccasins makes a squared-off track, fer they jist gather up the hide around their foot. Best moccasin I ever wore was a Pima moccasin. Them are Mex Injuns—down in Heely country. They make the sole long in front and tie it back over the toes. In cactus country it comes in handy."

Joe listened intently at first, then he caught on Mose was running off at the mouth to give him time to get over his queasiness. It angered him that Mose should see it was necessary. He said roughly, "We gonna stand here talking all day or we gonna ride."

"We gonna ride," Mose said, grinning. "Ho-o-o-*up*, thar, mules! Let's git movin'."

But Joe Fowler felt as old as the Spanish Peaks when they rode on. Something innocent and young had died inside him. You couldn't kill a man, not even an Indian who might have killed you, know that you had sent him out of breathing, riding, eating, sleeping, loving, fighting forever, and not feel different. Not the first time, anyhow.

Mose slewed a look at him and mumbled, as if talking to himself, "Whut it biles down to is him or you. Him or you. Either he takes yore skulp or you take his'n. Gonna hunt beaver, ye're gonna rub out some Injuns. Fer killin', amongst their selves or white men, comes as natural to them as breathin'. Naturaller, fer a Injun had ruther quit breathin' than never count coup. Thar floats yer stick, ye gonna hunt beaver."

Fowler wasn't fooled nor much comforted, but he already knew there floated his stick and nothing to be done about it.

4.

For two or three years thereafter the two men found good hunting in the streams and mountains handy to Taos and Santa Fe. They worked through the dune country of the San Luis basin, around Blanca Peak, and farther north and across the Sangre de Cristo to the east. They worked the tributaries of the Arkansas and the Platte. They worked up the Pecos and down the Rio Grande. They wintered in Taos those years, coming in when the deep snows began and staying until late February or early March before going out again.

Come first, they profited most, and Joe Fowler took care of his profits. When his uncle, Johnny Osage, brought his first wagon train west in 1823, Joe banked with him and bought an interest in the trade. He had two wiping sticks to his rifle, then.

But in those years the western fever was drawing other men to Taos and Santa Fe. When the Mexicans won their revolution against Spain, the Santa Fe traders with their big wagon trains began to come, and more and more fur trappers came with them. Fowler and Mose watched them come. Ewing Young, the summer of 1823, with William Becknell's wagon train. Young planned to make gunpowder but couldn't find nitre. He quickly shifted to beaver hunting. Isaac Glover came,

William Wolfskill, Joe Walker, Old Bill Williams, Milt Sublette, and in 1826 a sixteen-year-old kid named Kit Carson turned up in Taos, a runaway from a saddle maker in Missouri to whom he had been indentured. Carson liked to tell that the old man had published a broadside offering one cent as a reward for his return. "Now, ain't I worth a heap?"

Where in the beginning there had been only a handful of trappers and mostly the long-traveling French-Canadians at that, now there were all these others. Getting crowded in Taos and Santa Fe, now.

Fowler and Mose, now able to finance and lead a party, had to go farther and farther afield as the streams were slowly trapped out. They went up into the high country, into the parks and holes of the great ramparts, and still farther north into the richest beaver country of all—the massed mountains of the Wind River range. They trapped the Siskadee, the Popo Agie, the Sweetwater, the Laramie Fork. They had frequent brushes with Blackfeet and Arapahoes, occasional brushes with the Crows, but found the Nez Perces and Shoshones almost invariably friendly.

These were long hunts and they couldn't split a season. They had to winter up and come into Taos with their catches in June or July. Johnny Osage then handled them for them and sent them on to St. Louis.

One winter in the high country they ran across another brigade of trappers on the upper Salmon. Jim Bridger was the leader. Fowler and Mose had joined their party up with Bill Huddart and nine others and they had worked across the old Spanish Trail into the Salt Lake country. They had worked up Cache Valley and the Bear, then Fowler and Mose had split their party off and headed up beyond Soda Springs into the lava country and on to the Salmon. They had run into bad luck. A band of Crows, who were notional Indians and however friendly always willing to plunder, had found their camp one day, killed the two men on guard, stolen the mules and horses and most of the beaver. The party was left with only the horses they were riding and a cache of skins hidden in another place. Fowler and Mose told the boys to fort up and they set out to find a village of Nez Perces to buy horses from them. Cutting the trail of this party they followed it and stumbled into camp in a blowing blizzard.

Jim Bridger made them welcome and sitting by the fire that night thawing out and filling their lean stomachs they learned for the first time that General William Ashley, of St. Louis, had ventured into the mountain trade and that there were several brigades such as Jim was leading now working in the north country. "Etienne Provo has went south," Jim told them. "If you come up Bear River you ort to run into him, fer he was headin' down that way."

"Cache Valley? Sevier Lake?" Fowler asked.

"Thereabouts," Bridger said. "Provo claimed he knowed the country."

"So do we all," Fowler said, "all of us from Taos. Bill Huddart's hunting down there now."

Bridger nodded. "Reckon they'll cut trails. Jed Smith has took a bunch onto the Snake. Tom Fitzpatrick is still in the Wind River country."

"Never heard of none of 'em but Provo," Mose said, spitting his contempt. "Must be greenhorns."

"Not so green," Bridger said. "We been l'arnin' right fast."

"Wagh!" Mose grunted, "this coon don't shine to them doin's. We been trappin' this country fer y'ars. Whyn't this gineral stick with the Missouri way the rest of them St. Looey companies does?"

"Ain't but one company that counts no more—American Fur Company. They got so much money back of 'em ye cain't buck 'em on the river. The general, he's cut clean loose of the river. He ain't even dependin' on the forts fer supplies. He's bringin' 'em out from St. Looey hisself—packin' 'em out. And when we git the season over, we don't have to go nowhur to trade but acrost them Three Tetons over thar. He said fer us all to meet him thar. We bring in the skins, he brings out the supplies. Calls it a rendezvous."

"Rondyvoo," Mose repeated. "Well, now, that don't shine with this coon."

But Fowler nodded. "Makes sense. Saves a heap of trailing."

"You been out long?" Mose asked.

"Just this season," Bridger said, "but, man, we got the plews or I wouldn't say so. I never seen beaver so plentiful."

"Ye've plundered our country fer it," Mose said, outraged.

"Who says it's yore'n?" Bridger said. "It's wide and open and dog eat dog. You git yore beaver, we'll git our'n. But," he added ominously, "we got ten men out fer ever' one you got, and we'll take a hundred skins fer ever' ten you git. You better throw in with us."

Fowler shook his head. "Reckon not."

Bridger laughed. "They don't come no prouder than you Taos trappers, do they? We've heared tell of ye. Well, go it alone if that's where your stick floats."

"That's where she floats," Fowler said.

They rolled up and slept. Next morning Fowler and Mose returned to their cache, unearthed their remaining pelts, traded with the Nez Perces for horses, and went their way. Mose grumbled it was about as poor paying a season as he'd ever seen.

Reunited with Bill Huddart and his boys later, they all discussed the news Fowler and Mose brought. All the boys were troubled a little, but not much. It was a big country, bigger than any one man or a dozen men could ever know, and beaver, like buffalo, had no end. There was a plenty, they reckoned, for all.

5.

Mose brought Joe Fowler out of his mulling memories. "Them two," he said, pointing with his nose toward the head of the pack train, "is gonna cut into yore and Johnny's trading business I'm thinkin'."

Fowler and Johnny Osage now had two stores, one in Santa Fe, the other in Taos. Fowler's original investment had grown so that he was now a full partner, although a silent one. He never thought of himself as a trader and never raised his voice concerning the business. That was Johnny's job. Joe was a trapper, but as a trapper he was a good field man for the stores.

He glanced along the brigade to the two Frenchmen riding at its head. Pierre Driant was riding hunched to ease his aching side, and he was looking nowhere. Fowler knew that if seen full-on the man's face would reflect the slow pain he lived with. The dark eyes would be bruised with it and though he drove himself with an iron will he had no energy left to enjoy the morning, the clean rim of the sleeping mountain behind the pueblo, the golding leaves of the aspens, or the soul-shrinking space of the vast plateau.

Beside him rode Paul Noel. Both men were short, stocky, dark, and full-bearded. "Well," Fowler said, "maybe. You can't keep a man from setting up in trade. If that's what they're aiming to do, there's nothing to stop 'em."

Driant's father was old LaClede Driant, fur merchant of St. Louis. The Missouri had been his territory, but two years before Pierre Driant and Paul Noel had come to Taos, Pierre with a hundred men to trap and Noel with wagons of goods for the Santa Fe trade. They hadn't been notably successful yet but they kept trying and they had old man Driant's money behind them. On this expedition Noel was serving as clerk, which meant keeper of stores and supplies, tally counter of skins and wages and such.

Fowler was in Santa Fe when Pierre Driant approached him about guiding his party into the high country. Back from a long sweep with Ewing Young which had taken a year and a half and led them down the old Spanish Trail into California on a horse-buying trip, Fowler had taken a wagon train of pelts, specie, and the California horses and mules on to St. Louis. He had just got back now, in August. He was trail-tired and glad to be back. St. Louis had smothered him and the long dry haul across the plains and prairies with the slow wagons had galled him. But he picked up news which he passed on to Johnny. "The whole place is simmering with what the American Fur Company is gonna do to the Rocky Mountain boys."

"What are they aiming to do?"

"They're gonna cut loose from the Missouri, too. Send out their brigades, outfit and supply 'em at rendezvous. Cut the ground right out from under 'em. They're saying that Chouteau, who's heading it up for the Company, has given orders to pay any price for beaver. Just get the furs and rub the boys out."

Johnny looked directly at Joe for a long moment, then he whistled. "Reckon what that means?"

Fowler said, "It means just what you think it means. Price war. Trade war. Somebody's gonna get hurt."

Johnny's eyes narrowed and he flipped the end of his shuck *cigarillo* onto the packed-earth floor. "You better take a *paseo* up thataway."

"I aim to."

A woman, her black skirt dust-tailed, came in. Johnny went to wait on her and Fowler drifted out. He leaned against the wall, one heel propping him.

Santa Fe was an adobe city, built around a central plaza. It was an old, old town. The Royal City of the Holy Faith of St. Francis of Assisi was founded somewhere around 1610, a full ten years before the Pilgrims landed at Plymouth Rock. It was built by order of the Viceroy of New Spain to the rigid specifications of all Spanish *casas reales.*

It was not the first capital of the province. Captain-General Don Juan de Oñate, who brought the first Spanish colonists to Nuevo Mexico in 1598—one hundred and thirty families, two hundred and seventy single men, eighty-three wagons and carts, eleven Franciscan friars, seven thousand cattle—took possession of the twin pueblos, Yuque-Yunque near the confluence of the Chama and Rio Grande farther north. He renamed it San Juan de los Caballeros and made it his capital.

But Santa Fe was old enough. It had been the capital for more than two hundred years now. It was too much to call it a city. It had a royal name but it was little more than a village. The streets were narrow and winding and red with the red-earth dust. They led whichever way the people had wanted to drive their burros and goats, whichever way they had wanted to go to the plaza to buy and sell, and up and down the little stream called Rio de Santa Fe, which bisected the town.

The Johnny Osage store in Santa Fe was on the south side of the plaza. Directly across from it, and taking up the entire north side, was the long adobe building called the Palace of the Governors. A portal ran along the front and in its shelter hot foods, live chickens and goats, wood, various things the people made, were vended. The customhouse and *calabozo* occupied the west end of the *palacio* and several huge wagons stood in front of it, with half a dozen Spanish officials clustered about them. A trader, paying up.

Fowler grinned. He had been through that yesterday. The American trader had got so good at smuggling in goods that the governor had devised a new plan. He replaced the old duty on goods with a flat $500 duty on each wagon. The result was the biggest wagons ever seen parked in front of the customhouse and a disgruntled governor. The *Yanquis* were shrewd and it was hard to outwit them.

The plaza of Santa Fe looked good to Joe Fowler, sunbaked,

dusty, slow-drifting with *mañana* people, children, burros, dogs, barefooted, bare-shouldered girls. He lounged against the wall and watched, content to soak up the hot sun and fill his nose with the smell of foods, dust, the high odor of raw skins accumulating in the traders' storehouses.

Over the roof of the *palacio* the hills rolled away northward, sparsely studded with piñon and juniper. They sprang from red earth which showed strong in the sun. The Taos road unwound like a scar over the first hills and disappeared on a far crest.

To the east of the plaza the big mountains heaved up, the red earth showing on their flanks likewise. Sangre de Cristo—blood of Christ. Like a crooked backbone they poked up beyond the San Luis basin and headed in the massive ramparts of the main Rockies.

Southward, the long high tableland, black-dotted with piñon, ocherous with red earth, stretched far and far away to the turtle mountain, the Sandia.

West was the Jemez range, saw-toothed and jagged, blade-clean against the most gorgeous sunsets in the world.

All in between the mountains, rimmed by them, fastened to the sky by them, lay the Santa Fe plateau. It was a haggard land, starved for water, and sparsely green only where water flowed, the growth stunted to sage and creosote bush, cactus and bunch grass. Along the river some willows and cottonwoods grew. Piñon freckled the hills. On the mountains spruce and fir and aspens reared up. Desert—hills—mountains. There were elk and deer and bear in the mountains, but the desert plateau supported only antelope, prairie dogs, horned toads, rats, and snakes.

Only the Indians really knew how to live in such a land. The Spanish had come looking for gold. They had conquered the land and its people, the *puebleños,* and they had remained the conquerors, but it was a land that never paid for itself. Nearly everything the people needed had to be brought to it—from Vera Cruz, Mexico City, and the last several years from St. Louis out of the United States. Which made it a paradise for merchants and traders but a poor paying proposition for the Spanish government. There had never been a year when more goods and food and metals and necessities had not been brought into the country than had been taken out. It had always been a debit country.

Johnny Osage's wife, Judith, had preached this sermon in economic history to Joe Fowler. Johnny had never needed it. He had probably preached it first to Judith. Joe Fowler liked his young aunt-in-law well enough, though he had never quite understood what Johnny had seen in the young teacher of the Union Mission to the Osage Indians. Even Johnny admitted that with her passion for learning things and judging things and even preaching about them, she talked a lot of foolishness sometimes. Joe thought she poked her nose into things that weren't any of her business. But what could you expect of a Connecticut Presbyterian? She wasn't very happy in Santa Fe. "It's a tragic land," she said, "and always will be. It has a brutal, cruel, and bloody history."

"Name me one that don't have," Johnny said. "You can't go around carrying history on your back like a turtle shell, Judith. What the Spanish did here ain't my fault. What they do *now* is what I care about."

"Yes," she said bitterly, "you and Joe are fine examples of the only kind of North Americans who can be happy here. Him," she nodded at Joe, "because anywhere he hangs his hat is home. He's a wanderer, an adventurer. He never really sees anything or thinks about anything. And you, because anywhere you can make money is a fine place to live. Those mountains," she went on, "the saintly Spanish called Sangre de Cristo. It would have been more appropriate to call them Sangre de Indios. They certainly spilled enough Indian blood here. And now you have made us Spanish by taking out citizenship papers."

"If I'm gonna live in a country and make my living off it," Johnny retorted, "I figure I owe it some loyalty."

"You don't have an ounce of loyalty to the Spanish government in you—you, nor Ceran St. Vrain, or Carlos Beaubien, or Lucien Maxwell, or any of the rest of them who have taken out citizenship. It's the easiest way to make more money is all."

She had found somewhere a little volume bound in fine cordovan leather, a volume of the history of Oñate's first year of the colonization. It was written by Captain Don Gaspar Perez de Villagra of Salamanca, the nephew of the governor. Judith held it up and read from it to them: "One of their purposes was to correct and punish the sins against nature and against humanity that exist among these bestial nations."

"I seem to recollect," Johnny said, "when one of your purposes was to convert the 'heathen Osage.' "

"Convert, yes," she said, "but not enslave."

"You're splitting hairs," Johnny said, levelly. "When you convert an Indian you enslave him."

Judith talked a lot like that and Joe sometimes thought the weight of the history was going to be too much for her. She was up-and-downy, touchy and quicky. If it wasn't that, then it was the thin air—the altitude of Santa Fe was nearly seven thousand feet—the wind and dust, the bright ever-shining sun which could make you feel brittle and cracking at the seams, longing for clouds and the sweet softness of rain, and the bare, raw dirt with so little green. Even men had trouble in the high, dry atmosphere keeping their nerves and emotions stable, grew irritable often, became shrill, easily angered. It was as if the land meant to break them, one way or another.

Joe wondered if Judith would ever learn that the only way you could live with it was to sink into it, let down, quit fighting it. He didn't much think she ever would. She would fight the dust in her house and she would fight the wind in her hair and she would fight the slow and wrinkling drying out of her body and she would fight the raw, red dirt by setting out her pathetic little fruit trees and bits of flowers, by carrying the heavy pails of water for their eternally thirsty roots, trying to make a small oasis of green about her.

A dark-skinned boy came by with a *sombrero* full of apricots. Fowler snaked one and laughed as the boy looked at him indignantly. "How much for all of 'em?"

"*Qué? Señor?*" The kid didn't understand English. The Spanish wouldn't bother to learn it.

"*Cuánto cuesta . . . ?*"

The boy's grin stretched all over his face. He offered the hat full of fruit. "*Un peso, Señor.*"

Fowler took off his own hat and poured the apricots in it, handed the boy some coins.

"*Gracias, gracias, Señor.*" The child scampered off, yipping as loud as the cur at his heels.

Fowler bit through the tawny skin into the bland, dripping flesh. He ate a dozen, then took the rest into the store and dumped them on the counter. "For Judith," he said.

Johnny, busy, looked up and nodded.

Fowler drifted around the east side of the plaza. A church bell began to ring and he looked south to the twin towers of Nuestro Señora de la Luz. The deeper bell of San Miguel joined in, then the bells of Guadalupe pealed out.

The bells of Santa Fe. If you didn't notice anything else about the town you had to notice the church bells. Joe Fowler had never thought much about them, except to know there were an awful lot of them and they seemed to ring all the time, day and night. But Judith had enlightened him there, too. "The Spanish required three taxes of the *peubleños*," she said, holding up her fingers and counting off. "First there was the tax for the government—the king's tax. Then the Church required a tithe, one tenth of everything. Lastly, there was the tribute to be paid to the local *encomiendero* set over them. When they couldn't pay, *soldados* went among them and took forty, fifty, a hundred of their strongest people and made slaves of them. Sometimes they were required to work for the government or the Church here; sometimes they were sent to the mines in Mexico. Those sent to Santa Fe were kept in slave quarters—the *barrio analco*.

San Miguel is the church that was built for the slaves. The good padres had to save their souls, of course, so they made them build a church for themselves—slave labor, slave church. Think of that when you hear its bell."

Her distress was obvious and Joe clumsily made it worse by mentioning Our Lady of Light.

"Oh, that one," she said, "it was built for the soldiers. The Spanish were very tender about their soldiers. Two buildings were erected, almost side by side—the *casa de puta* and Nuestro Señora de la Luz. Tell me," she said, "how could men in a 'cat house' hear the bell of Our Lady of Light?"

Johnny's mouth dropped open at his wife's coarseness. "You be careful how you talk," he said darkly.

"Is there a nicer way to say it?" she asked. But her eyes filled and the slow tears brimmed over. She went away.

Johnny watched her go, pity and love and concern on his face.

"What's got into her?" Joe asked.

"I don't know," Johnny said tiredly. "Once a missionary always a missionary, I guess. She don't live in the real world at all. She keeps all worked up over slavery and the Indians. This country's hard on her. She don't much like it."

Joe shook his head, glad she was tied to Johnny and not him.

By the time the bells quit ringing he was in front of the *cantina* where beaver men congregated most frequently. He bumped into Pierre Driant, who was coming out of the place with his head down, not looking where he was going. Both men backed up, begged pardon, made to pass, then Driant paused. "Mr. Fowler, a moment if you have it. May I speak with you?" He spoke English precisely and quickly, with a slight inflection of St. Louis French.

"Sure, Mr. Driant."

"Mr. Fowler, I am preparing to take a brigade up north this season—onto the Green, if possible. It will be well financed and comfortably outfitted. I have my own party made up, except . . . " he smiled wryly, "some of the old hands I would like to have with me seem loyal to you. They say they will consider hunting for me *if* Joe Fowler isn't taking an outfit out."

"Yes. Well, we're all old friends," Fowler said.

He looked directly into the dark, steady eyes and felt the man's awkwardness. If you were one of the fraternity you could ask plain out where a man was going to hunt and who he was taking with him, and he could either tell you or tell you it was none of your business and no offense on either side. If you were low on dollars you could say so plain out to an old partisan, say you had to work a season or two as a hand to get your stake back, and no shame to it. But this man was not one of the boys and not even in his need could he say, are you taking a party out this fall, and if so, where, and who will you take with you? He couldn't say, above all, what Fowler thought he most wanted to say, why don't you and your boys come with me?

And Fowler couldn't say what he most wanted to say, don't go up there into that Teton and Wind River country, mister. They are tough *hombres* up in that country. They'll chew you up and spit you out and you won't even know how they did it. They'll talk your meat hunters and trappers and voyageurs away from you; they'll find your caches and ruin them; they'll steal your pelts; they'll run the meat away from you; they'll set the Indians on you. They'll fleece you down to the raw, quivering hide and throw you to the coyotes. They know how to do it, they do it every season, for they've staked out that country and they don't want any greenhorns horning in.

"You're bound to go?" was all he permitted himself to say.

"Oh, yes," Driant said, as simply as if it were just a journey back to St. Louis.

On impulse, Fowler decided. "Well, I'm going north myself. I'll take you there. Some of the boys will go."

"That's very generous of you, Mr. Fowler. I appreciate it."

They discussed terms, the outfitting of the party, the meeting place, and the starting time. *"Bueno,"* Fowler said finally and was turning away. "I'll see you in Taos." He swung around again. "Just one more thing, Mr. Driant. You'll be the *bour-geois* of this outfit all right, but I'd like it understood we move *when* I say, and *where* I say. I couldn't undertake to guide you otherwise."

Driant surveyed him steadily. He knew Fowler's reputation. He wasn't a man who thought he knew it all. There was no arrogance in his terms now. But he was a man who knew exactly what he did know and had to have reins loose enough to operate and function. Driant said, "I would be grateful if you would take that responsibility."

Fowler liked his quick comprehension and intelligence. He seemed a sensible man. He believed he was a man with staying power, also.

Swinging into the *cantina*, he wondered a little why he had offered to do this. He had thought that he and Mose, Big Starr and young Pete, Fouchette, would make a *paseo* north, fast and rapid, the way they knew how, winter maybe on the Bear, head for the rendezvous across South Pass. He didn't feel exactly protective about Driant. He just liked the man, had liked him immediately, had learned through the years to trust his instincts, and that was about the size of it.

6.

It wasn't the size of it for Mose and he was still grumbling about it. "This coon cain't make no sense of you signin' us up fer this piece of foolishness. What we doin' leadin' a brigade fer Driant when we could be puttin' out fer ourselves? This child knows runnin' water good as anybody. So do you. Ginerally my stick floats whar yore'n does, but you've done cut my trail this time, Joe, dogged if you ain't."

"Call it a notion, Mose, just call it a notion. We're going, he's going. Might as well go together." Fowler tickled the big blue's

ribs gently. The brigade was pulling ahead and they were eating dust.

"This coon'd feel a heap better if Pierre Driant warn't ailin',
too," Mose complained on. "Man in pore health has got no business winterin' in high country. He'll be in bad shape we have to
take pore bull. Or git in a Injun scrape which we shore as hell
will up amongst the Blackfeet."

"It's him taking the chances," Fowler said.

But he glanced ahead at Driant hunched in his saddle. As
much as Mose he wished the man's health was better. He knew
Driant had had a sick spell in Santa Fe but he hadn't known it
had hung on as long as it had. If he didn't get better he was
going to be a risk for the whole party and if he got bad sick on
the way he could delay them dangerously. Fowler wanted to
get this outfit on the Green before the deep snows came, and as
slow-moving as it would be, trapping as it went, any long delays
could be disastrous. Driant himself made light of his condition.
"It is nothing," he told Fowler, "just this devilish Spanish food.
It is enough to ruin any man's stomach."

Maybe. Fowler didn't remind him he had been eating it for
a good many years longer than Driant, he and a lot of others, and
it had never ruined any man's stomach so far as he knew.

Fowler straightened up and took a long breath of the cold,
thin air. Well, he was committed now. As he had been committed so many times before. Twelve years of it. A lot of time
and a lot of country. A lot of good men he'd known gone under
and more to go under every season. Maybe on this *paseo*. But
you never thought so, and it never counted when the air grew
tingly with frost and it was time to put out again. Beaver got
into your blood, he guessed. There was always a piece of running water you wanted to try, a stream on the backside of some
mountain you'd heard a whisper about. A beaver pond in some
high grassy park, just glimpsed because the damned Rapahoes
were hot on your tail. You had to go back there. It was just over
Rabbit Ear pass, in a little *ronde* and there had been buffalo ga-

lore, too. Every season it was a pull and a passion. This year you'd be the first out, the first set, this year you'd make your richest haul. He'd made some good ones. He didn't need the money now. But the pull was as hard in him as it had ever been. Sky-tall mountains, snow-shouldered mountains, deep valleys and holes, big pine passes, white running water. These were his things, made his passion, made his life.

Big Starr skirmished his horse across the tail of the string and pulled alongside Fowler. "Whar away, *amigo?* East side the del Norte? Straight up under old Blanca?"

Fowler looked west into the blue-hazed distance. "How about if we head for Pagosa?"

Big Starr's eyes squinched with humor. "They won't be thar yet, *amigo.* They're still up at Saguache."

"Well, Saguache ain't out of our way."

Starr broke into a war whoop. "Howgh-owgh-owgh! Look out, Betsy, hyar he comes!"

He fanned his horse into a run and capered far out on the plain. The brigade broke left and angled after him, yipping and yelling and whooping. Young Pete howled a ditty:

> Sugar-eye Betsy,
> Cotton-eye Joe;
> Oughtta been married,
> Forty year ago!

All the boys knew Joe Fowler had a Utah squaw he called Betsy.

two

THEY ANGLED northwest across the high tableland, leaving behind the cleared pastures and fields, the irrigation ditches and the irregular threads of willows and cottonwoods which marked them. They rode into mesa land, sage and red earth country. Their drove of mules and horses clouded the clear air with a smothering red dust.

Their first day was hard and long, for Joe Fowler wanted the party across the Rio Grande before the night camp. Late in the afternoon they rode into a blazing sun which the red haze made a ball of crimson fire. It was throwing shadows in a long distortion behind them when they came up to the rim of the canyon the river cut through the tableland. The greenhorns stood and gaped at the canyon. You came upon it across the flats so unexpectedly, so little warned it was there. You were riding across the sandy flats and then all at once here was this big gash in the earth.

Fowler led them down the precipitous wall by a narrow, rocky trail. Twilight rose about them as they descended, deepening the lower they went, a chill from the river rising with it. At first the chill felt good on their sweaty bodies, then it set them to shivering. The deep gloom which slowly shrouded them set the French voyageurs to looking about fearfully. Apaches and Navajos had been raiding recently. They muttered about an ambush in this dark canyon.

At the bottom the party crossed on a good, gravel-bedded ford. They let the animals drink, drank themselves, washed dust from their faces, filled their water bags, and climbed out of the canyon by another narrow trail. They made their night camp well back from the rim of the gorge.

Next day between the Rio Grande and the Chama, they came into scrub growth and bunch grass and passed thousands of sheep being grazed, herded by silent, dark-gazing Mexicans. They were barefooted, ragged, mostly thin, their peaked straw hats shading their faces. They did not speak and none of the beaver men spoke to them. Paul Noel rode up beside Fowler. "Whose sheep are these?"

"Belong to Don Mateo Uliballos."

"All of them?"

"All of 'em."

"*Sacré!* How much land does the man own?"

"Dunno. Goes plumb to the Chama, though."

Noel pursed his lips and whistled. "A hundred thousand hectares, at least. The man owns a kingdom!"

"You could say so."

"Where is his *hacienda?*"

"Farther south. On the Chama."

"Is this land a crown grant?"

"No. The Uliballos got it for themselves . . . down through the years. Don Mateo got a good part of it himself."

"Oh. He is *político,* then."

"Well, he's got some influence in the palace. Yes." Fowler grinned. Don Mateo had enough political influence to get by with a considerable amount of chicanery, but he had added the last fifty thousand hectares of land to his estate by simply getting a very corrupt governor under embarrassing obligation to him. Then he had squeezed and what had squeezed out was enough land to double his holdings. An accepted practice in New Mexico and one the Anglos were finding very useful, too.

"He is not *hidalgo,* then." Noel sounded scornful.

"He is now," Fowler said. "You get enough land and enough sheep and enough peons and enough silver and you get to be *hidalgo* pretty quick."

Noel sneezed from the dust and dropped back. Fowler watched the slow-moving herds of sheep. Wool. Rough, curly, matted, smelly wool. Peons tending slow, stupid herds. Shearing. Baling and sending to market. Money and plenty of it, with never once the high flush of personal commitment. His hands remembered the silk and the richness and plush of beaver. They tightened on the reins, then flexed, he put it out of his mind and rode up ahead.

When the brigade crossed the Chama, they followed up its west bank and they slowly began to climb. The red mesa rocks gave way to pine country and the trail wound increasingly up and upward. The pack mules pulled into it doggedly and Fowler's big roan put his own head down. The men of the party quit chattering and grew silent. Again they were depressed because the yellow pines closed round them, the sun was shut off.

Mose Strong swayed tiredly as his black mule picked his way around a boulder. "This coon," he said to Fowler, "is gonna pack hisself in a hot mud bath soon as we make camp tonight. These old bones is achin'. You been pushin' this outfit, Joe."

"Rather be pushed by Apaches, maybe?"

"Hell, no. But we ain't seen no sign."

"Don't mean there ain't none."

Mose sighed. "Git on, Solomon. We gotta Injun spook settin' the pace."

They crossed the divide and began the slow descent. Now they could see far ahead a great range of gray mountains spread all across the north and west, a massive, rooted bed of mountains, with innumerable peaks, snow-capped and jagged, rising like the teeth of a saw from the range. Mose chuckled. "Feast yer eyes, *amigo*. Thar they be."

Fowler gazed at them. From this place they looked solid and unbroken, but what he saw in his mind was hundreds of beaver streams rising in springs and basins dimpled high on the mountain shoulders, flowing fast down the deep defiles and canyons which gashed the flanks of the range. Solid? No. When you got up close each peak was cut again and again across and down, with rugged, rough, gouging canyon scars.

Big Starr rode up, grinning. "Wagh! The San Juans, old coon. They don't never change, do they?"

"They don't ever change," Fowler agreed.

"Mind the first time we seen 'em?"

"I mind." Fowler met Big Starr's eyes and both men laughed.

Mose jerked at Solomon's head and growled, "Git on thar, ye black imp o' Satan. Yore feet ain't half as sore as my tail." He looked at the two men. *"Well,* way you two is behavin', this child is reminded of a couple of elk stallions. You fought over some squaw, I reckon."

"Didn't so," Starr denied. "Wasn't no need. But now *that* was the biggest kind of rendezvous, or I wouldn't say so."

"It was so," Fowler agreed. He laughed. "Old Cholly's squaw fixed a feast of fat pup that wouldn't quit, and we had a big smoke and plenty of whiskey and plenty of trade—"

"And old Cholly had plenty of beaver. Joe got reelin' drunk one night," Starr said to Mose, "and he was bound to teach the Utahs how to square dance. Thar he stood yellin' do-ce-do and swing your partners, and the Utes reelin' around and gittin' worse and worse mixed up, all of 'em laughin' their fool heads off at such a crazy dance. And Joe got mad at old Cholly's main squaw and he whopped her on her big fat rump and said, 'Whatever sense you got is down thar 'stid of in yer head.' It tickled old Cholly so he commenced calling her Big Rump. Still does, don't he, Joe?"

"I reckon. Did so last time I seen him."

Mose grunted and Fowler laughed. "Mose don't like to hear nothing about that spree because he missed out on it."

"Well, I been thar plenty since. Takes more'n one spree to make a season," Mose flared up.

Big Starr pulled around. He said, "Joe, you best speak to Driant. He's about done in. See what you think. My opinion, he cain't make it to the Springs today."

Fowler frowned and turned half around in his saddle to look behind. Pierre Driant was almost doubled in his saddle and Noel was riding close to him a hand on his arm. "Looks to be in pain," Fowler said.

"He's been gruntin' and groanin' fer some time now," Starr said. "He's got a peculiar color, too. Sort of green around the gills."

Fowler swore and rode back. Driant was hanging to the pommel of his saddle. His mouth was a thin line against the pain and his eyes were shuttered almost closed. He was worse than a little green around the gills. He was ashen, with beads of sweat on his face. Noel was talking to him in a low voice. He looked up when he heard Fowler's horse. "It's his side," he said, "he is in great pain."

"You ought to have told me," Fowler said. "Is he fevered?"

"No. He's cold. He says he is chilling."

Fowler rode around to the other side and addressed the man. "Mr. Driant, we'll make camp soon as we get to a level place. But it's a half hour ride yet. Think you can make it?"

Driant raised his eyes and looked dully at Fowler. "Where did you intend to camp tonight?"

"Well, I aimed to make it to the Springs."

"The Springs?"

"Pagosa Springs. It's a good place to camp. Plenty of water and grass. But it's too far, shape you're in. There's a level place on down a little piece and some water. We'll stop there."

Pierre Driant shook his head. "How far to the Springs?"

Fowler looked at the sun. "Couple of hours, I'd say."

Driant tried a grin, but it ended in a grimace. "Let's go ahead, Joe. I mustn't delay the party."

Fowler watched him a moment, skeptically. Then he decided. "*Bueno*. We'll take it slow. If you can't make it, holler out." To Noel he said, "Don't fall behind. If you can't keep up, sing out."

Noel's head bobbed vigorously. "I understand."

Fowler went back to the head of the string. Mose, who had got off to rest, hauled himself back in the saddle. "He gonna make it?"

"I dunno. He's pretty sick. Don't look good. Noel says his side is hurting him. He's game, though. Wants to keep moving."

"Game ain't gonna git him thar," Mose said. "Had no business comin'. But he was half froze to go."

Fowler shrugged. "It's his belly."

"Be our plews we lose we have to lay up with him sick, and mebbe our ha'r."

"Let's move," Fowler said.

They wound on down and came out into a valley, timbered with pine well out from the mountains. Another hour and they reached a clear, fast, rough-watered river. Good grass grew on either side and there was a fine stand of cottonwoods and willows. Here Fowler stopped the party. The men chose places for their bedrolls, Fowler told off the horse guards, the cavvyard was driven out to grass, and the camp swampers began to build the fires.

Driant was lying on his apishamore on a grassy plot near the river while Noel laid out his bed robes for him. Fowler went over to him. "Mr. Driant, the springs aren't far from here. Before it gets dark why don't you let me and Paul give you a mud pack. It'll rest you and ease you quicker than anything."

"Whatever you say," the man said. "I want a drink of brandy first. Paul, in my pack."

"*Oui*," Noel said and quickly searched for it.

Driant raised up to drink from the bottle, took two more swallows, capped the bottle, and handed it back. "That is good," he said. "I am ready, my friend."

Leaning on Noel on one side and Fowler on the other, he was led to the springs. He eyed their boiling, bubbling, steaming water distrustfully. "Do you intend to parboil me, Mr. Fowler?"

Fowler laughed. "No. Down here a little way, sir."

They came to a little rivulet, an overflow from the biggest

spring. Noel helped his friend out of his clothing. When he was as naked as the day he was born, Fowler told him, "Just roll in and lay back, Mr. Driant."

Driant did as he was told. Fowler squatted and began heaping the hot mud all over the man. Understanding, Noel jumped the rivulet and began doing the same on the other side. "Get it good and thick," Fowler told him. "Just keep packing it on. This is a mineral spring," he told Pierre Driant, "and the mud is full of the minerals, too. The Utes come here for these mud baths every year. They say it draws all the poisons out of their bones and bodies and makes 'em limber again."

Driant had relaxed and closed his eyes. He sighed comfortably. "I can believe it. It is good. It is restful."

"Well, you stay here and rest a while. Noel, keep the mud wet. Keep dousing water up on it and keep it hot. When the boys have got something to eat will be time enough for him to get out."

The hunters, who had fanned out all day killing meat, had unloaded it and the swampers were roasting and boiling when Fowler got back to the fires. He prowled downstream to a short bend in the river, where old Cholly's village of Utahs had erected their lodges last winter. There were still a few discarded lodge-poles and a pile of bleached bones.

Fowler picked up a pole and ran his hand down its slick, peeled surface. He looked around, as if there ought to be more sign the village had stood there, something more to show for the hive of life that had gone on. Over there had been the stages where they dried meat. The horses had grazed upstream. The lodges had been pitched parallel to the river, with the wide street between them. He guessed this was about where his lodge had stood, here where these alders clumped in the back. Where he and Betsy could plunge in the cold river waters each morning when they woke. The hot springs were big medicine, all right, and when you got used to the mud pack every day you found yourself cross-grained and out of sorts if you missed a day, but for waking, for opening the eyes, for giving a clean, fresh, fine feeling to the day, the quick, cold plunge in the river was best.

2.

Her Utah name was a cough and a grunt and he had never bothered with it. Indians did not use a personal name in direct converse. They spoke *of* a person, she who is the Mist Rising from the Valley—and a touch, a look, a murmured word, called attention when they wished to speak directly. But Americans needed a name to bawl out. So, she who was the Mist Rising from the Valley became Betsy. He didn't know why. She just looked like a Betsy sort of woman, comfortable, heavy-bosomed, ample-hipped, square work-flattened hands, an easy voice.

She wasn't Fowler's first squaw but she was the only one he had gone back to consistently, about four years now. She was old Cholly's daughter. She wasn't the prettiest Ute he'd ever seen. She was short, plump toward fatness, her nose was pretty flat, and she was older than some others. "What you want her for?" Big Starr asked when Fowler chose her. "You kin have yer pick."

"I've picked," Fowler said and went out to kill his deer for her.

He had watched her. She was a steady worker, even when chattering and laughing with other women. Her hands stayed busy and the skins she worked over were smoother, more pliant, cleaner, and better cured than most. Her own clothing showed the care she took with her sewing, and she wasn't forever talking and giggling. She wasn't glum, but she had her quiet times. A bunch of Indian women working together was like a flock of jay-birds for clatter and noise. Betsy was often on the outside of it. She had a way with herbs and seasonings in her cooking, too. The best food he ate in the village was in old Cholly's lodge, prepared by his daughter. Most of all, however, she was clean—

shining clean. The Utahs weren't a dirty people. All their women were fairly clean. But Betsy was in the river every day and she had nice-smelling root powders and some kind of sweet oil she put on herself so that she smelled sweet all the time. Her hair was always neatly parted and the part painted with vermilion.

When she dressed his deer and built their new lodge of clean, new skins and he went into it to live with her, he found it as satisfying to all his senses as he had thought it would be. She kept the lodge as clean as herself, everything in its place. His wants were attended to, almost foreseen, promptly and efficiently. When he came in wet and cold from running his traps, she got him into dry clothing, always warm, always ready, then she took care of his catch. His pelts were perfectly cured, perfectly stretched, deep-piled and silky. He was fed well, and at night she was like a little round fat stove in the robes with him. She was cheerful without being obstreperously so and she seemed instinctively to compartmentalize their life into the work of the day and the giggles and play of the night.

Before that winter was over, Big Starr and the others who hadn't seen why he had chosen her were openly envious. Big Starr's squaw, who was as pretty as a Ute squaw ever got to be, turned out to be a shrew and a scold and he had to lodgepole her often. Betsy's tongue would click against her teeth at the sounds that came from Big Starr's lodge. She didn't know why that woman talked so much and angered her man so. She and Fowler spoke together mostly in Spanish, which old Cholly's village had picked up from traders from Taos and the other settlements, although Fowler knew a little Ute and she tried a little English. They had no difficulty understanding each other.

It was a good winter, but when the spring hunt was over and the men left for Taos, Fowler was glad to go, eager to be in the settlements again. He and Betsy didn't say goodby. She helped him load his beaver. She didn't ask him if he would ever come back and he didn't say whether he would or not. She didn't stand around to watch him leave. She handed him up his Hawken when he was in the saddle and the last he saw of her she was picking over some roots she had gathered the day before.

Big Starr left his woman sticking out in front that spring. Young Pete left his in the same condition. But Betsy hadn't conceived. Fowler knew very well that Indian women knew how to control the number of children they wanted or thought appropriate. There were roots and leaves which made teas and brews which remedied an unwanted conception, as well as precautions to prevent it. Indian families did not run to great hordes of children as white families so often did. Betsy evidently didn't want kids yet and Fowler was a little glad. Children were noisy and troublesome and Indian kids were the worst spoiled brats you could find. He didn't wonder at all that there were still no children of their union. What he did occasionally wonder about was why she had never taken a Utah husband. But it was pleasant to go back, when he could or wanted to, and find her there, unchanged, a little fatter maybe, but waiting, ready to pick up where they'd left off.

3.

His mind wandered to Saguache, where old Cholly's village was, waiting for the winter before dropping south to Pagosa for the deep cold. The scouts would be returning from the Bayou Salade pretty soon now, and the young men would be preparing to go there for the buffalo hunt. Maybe they'd already gone. Fowler wanted to get on, learn what the scouts had learned, if there were buffalo, what the season was like, if there were Rapahoes or Comanches on the prod. He felt a sudden impatience with the sick man who was going to need a few days' rest in this place. With a physical effort he put it down, heaved the lodgepole away and walked back to the fire. He seized a roasting stick and tested the sizzling ribs. Half raw, they were just right. The men gathered around and grabbed portions and the swampers put more to roast.

Driant and Noel came up, Driant looking better but still needing help to walk. "It is incredible," he said, "the pain is better."

"The minerals have drawn it away," Fowler told him. "Eat, now, and get some strength."

" 'Tain't as good as fat hump or tenderloins or boudins," Mose said, "but it'll fill yer guts and do ye good."

Driant tore a chunk of meat off with his teeth, chewed and swallowed, settled back on his heels to make his meal. "I give thanks to *le bon Dieu* it has no *chili colorado*." He shuddered. "The food those *cochons* think fit to eat!"

After the meal the horses were driven in, side-lined, and pick-eted. The night guards drifted away, still gnawing on rib bones. The camp swampers took kettles and pans to the river to wash, then gathered about their own fire. The beaver men filled their mugs with more coffee. With full bellies and long grunts of sat-isfaction they pulled out their pipes, tamped them full, lit them, and settled against their saddles. Driant rolled in his robes and was soon asleep, but Noel joined the group around the fire.

It felt good, for in these high places the air at night was crisp and nipping, sharp as a winesap apple when bitten. The camp was well pitched in the grove of cottonwoods. A light wind rustled the fall-browning leaves and drifted a few down now and then, and the slim trunks speared upward and showed white in the firelight. The river flowed with a broken current, quarrel-ing and splashing around the rocks. The sky was a clear green in the east, but the dark was already fading it. The horses and mules cropped the bunch grass quietly. The firelight rose and flared with the wind, lighting, then darkening the faces of the men about it. The time for yarning had come.

Fowler drew on his short dudeen and listened. Mose was holding forth across the fire. He sat crosslegged, his rifle at hand, his old hat on the back of his head, his hair tangling over his forehead. Mose liked a long pipe and he smoked the way the Indians did—deep drafts held, then expelled from nostrils and mouth in three heavy streams. "Well, now," he was saying, "Ashley men is *some,* or I wouldn't say so. They know fat cow from pore bull. Jim Bridger's as good a budgeway as ever led a brigade and made beaver come. So's Tom Fitzpatrick and old Frapp and Jarvis. They *shine* and I ain't sayin' they don't. But this coon knows a thing or two and the rest of the boys does too. Ain't *only* Ashley men is good beaver men, and some of us has been hyar a heap longer'n them. As fer Injun scrapes . . ." his hand touched his rifle, "this old buffer stick hyar has made 'em come many a time. I mind the time Joe and me, thar, was on Laramie Fork . . ."

Garrulously he rambled on, using the stylized argot which all mountain men fell into effortlessly when together but which had become almost the only speech old Mose knew any more.

The tale went on and on. The sick man turned in his sleep and Fowler's attention wandered to him. He wondered how much trouble he had let himself in for with this Frenchman. Driant ought to turn back while there was still time, but you didn't tell the owner of an outfit what he ought to do. But he could get the whole party into trouble, no mistake about it. He lay quiet again and Fowler shifted his own position. "Tell 'em, Joe," Mose was saying, "tell 'em 'bout that big spree down on the Heely that time."

"Big Starr was along," Fowler said, "he can tell it."

Starr was itching for the chance. "Wagh, but I *can,*" he said. He drew on his pipe slowly, savoring the tale he was to tell. "Well, me and Joe, thar, and young Pete . . . wasn't you along on them doin's, Pete? Seems like you was."

"Well, but I *was.* That was the biggest kind of spree, now."

"Well, we was with a right smart party that Ewing Young was the head of. Reckon there was anyway thirty of us. We put out

from Taos and follered down the del Norte to Socorro, then we
struck out for the Mogollons—"

"Tell about them *soldados* at Socorro," young Pete put in.

"Oh, yeah. When we got to Socorro all the folks was boilin'
and weepin' and takin' on something fierce. Bunch of Apaches
had raided 'em and run off all their horses and took several
women and children with 'em. Was some *rurales* thar, but they
wasn't aimin' to risk their skins. They was standin' around as
worked up as the people, wavin' their arms, yellin' at the top of
their lungs, brandishin' their fusils but gittin' no place. Ewing
said, 'Hyar's damp powder, boys. Let's git them Apaches.'

"We taken out after 'em, run 'em down, finished off a few and
chased the rest away. Wasn't but a handful, but jist one Apache
kin make the Spanish commence screechin'. We recovered the
herd and the women and kids, taken 'em back to Socorro. Meantime, some of the governor's dragoons from Santy Fee had come
in, and they rode out to meet us. We was needin' a few more
horses and since we'd saved the herd fer the folks, thought to
take what we needed. We sent the rest across the del Norte, with
the captured women and kids and made to go on our way.

"Well, sir, the biggest kind of a screech went up from them
folks and hyar come the dragoons splashin' across the river sayin'
we was stealin' their horses. We never seen it that way, so we
stood and give 'em a volley. Them dragoons changed their
minds the quickest you ever seen. Right in midstream they
turned back and headed out in a dead run."

"Wagh!" Mose put in, "them Spaniards won't fight. They're
all wind and britches."

"They are so," Starr agreed. "That was the last we seen of
them dragoons. We allowed we was due a few head of horses for
our services. Hadn't we brung 'em back? And hadn't we saved
their women and kids? But they got the peculiarest ideas of
gratitude."

"They have *so*," young Pete said. "If I had knowed her folks
was gonna beller and bawl and raise such a fuss over one paint

horse I would of kept that little *señorita* I give a ride back on my saddle. Seemed to me their girl for a horse was a good trade. But they never thought so."

Big Starr laughed, remembering. "Pete raised his first top-knot thar. Got him an Apache scalp. Where's it at, Pete? You still got it?"

Young Pete flipped his apishamore back and showed several rings of long, dull black hair stitched to his saddle flaps. "This un is it." He lifted one. "He's kind of weathered now, but most of his hair is still thar."

Big Starr took up his story. "Well, we worked through the Mimbres, hit the Gila and worked on down through the San Franciscos. We hunted all them creeks and back then you could make the beaver *come* in that country. It's all ketched out now.

"We was down about where the Agua Fria runs into the Gila and we hadn't seen hide nor hair of nobody since leavin' Socorro. Never knowed any of the boys was huntin' the same country. One evenin' we'd coraled the cavvyard and was just eatin' when somebody, believe it was Joe, thar, said, 'Hark!' Now when Joe says hark, there's something to hearken to, so we jumped fer the guns, thinkin' it was Papagos tryin' fer the horse herd.

"We didn't need the guns, though, for there come staggerin' in three men. One was Michel Robidoux, one was Jim Pattie, him that worked the Santa Rita mines fer a spell, and the other'n I disremember. You recollect, Joe?"

"Not his name," Fowler said. "He was one of Robidoux's voyageurs."

Noel interrupted. "This Michel Robidoux, he is—"

"Antoine's brother," Big Starr said, "you've seen 'em both around Taos. They got a fort in Brown's Hole and one in the Uncompaghre country. They been huntin' beaver forever. Fouchette knows 'em good."

"*Oui,*" Fouchette said. "We hunt together wid de old Nor'-west Company."

Big Starr went on. "Robidoux was as full of arrows as a porkypine. The way he told it, a bunch of them Papagos had come into his camp and made like they wanted to smoke and trade. Robidoux had a good strong party and there warn't but a handful of the Papagos, so he let 'em come in. Then his boys got keerless and left their guns layin' around. They had a big smoke goin' when all at once the Papagos jumped up, grabbed the boys' guns, commenced drawin' their knives and shootin' their arrows, and first thing Michel knowed he had lost his huntin' party, fer thar was a big bunch of 'em hid out in a dry gulch. Michel's boys didn't have a chance. They was ambushed purty as you please.

"Jim Pattie and that voyageur wasn't hurt. Pattie said he was mistrustful of the Papagos from the start and he taken a little *paseo* up an arroyo. Other feller, he went with him. Directly they heard the owgh-owgh-owghin' and they stayed put. Michel yelled to the boys to make tracks but the Papagos was on 'em so quick mostly they couldn't. He got away hisself and run up that same arroyo Pattie was in, and they all hid out till the Injuns had gone."

"Ortent to ever trusted 'em no way," Old Dan Sutton put in.

"Well, Papagos is wayward Injuns. One time they're friendly, next time they ain't. Robidoux said he'd allus got along with 'em."

Old Dan's voice became shrill. "I tell ye, ain't no Injun to be trusted. He ort to've run 'em off when they come up."

"Well, he never," Big Starr said, "but hyar was damp powder for a fact. It taken us a good spell to pluck the arrows outen Michel. One we had to butcher out. That un give him a little trouble."

"Not so much," young Pete said, grinning, "he didn't raise ha'r when we caught up to them Papagos."

"Well, it *didn't*. He was half froze fer ha'r after seein' his boys rubbed out thataway."

"What happened?" Noel asked.

"Well, you don't *never* let Injuns git by with doin's like that," Big Starr said. "You got to l'arn 'em some respect. We put out at daylight next mornin' and found their trail. They had took all Michel's horses so they left a trail a kid could of follered. Ewing said we'd try their own tricks on 'em, so we laid back a mite so as not to come up with 'em 'fore dark.

"When they'd pitched camp, got their fires lit, we rode up, made sign to talk and smoke. And we kept Michel and Pattie and that other'n back out of sight. The Papagos hadn't seen none of us before so they didn't git up no suspicions. They made us welcome. We was a bigger party than Robidoux's, so they didn't try no tricks on us.

"We set around the fire with 'em, palavered some, Ewing brought out some goods and passed 'em on the prairie and everything was sweet as apple pie. But ever' one of us had his rifle handy and we all had marked us a Papago fer the first shot.

"Joe, he was settin' on a blanket next the chief, and we allowed he'd git *him*. When Ewing give the signal, Joe grabbed up his gun and stuck the muzzle right ag'in the chief's chest and was tryin' to pull the trigger. But that chief bounded up and grabbed the muzzle and commenced to twist and turn. Pete, you better tell it from thar. I kind of had my hands full."

"Well, you *did*," young Pete said, his eyes blazing with the remembered excitement. "Starr shot his buck all right and he went howling in to lift his topknot. Two more Injuns went plungin' towards him while he was still bent over the buck. I yelled at him and he straightened up, fired off his pistol right in the guts of one, then beat the other'n to a pulp with the pistol butt.

"I had got off my shot good and so had the others and we was layin' about with knives and pistols, raisin' ha'r right and left, when I seen Joe was havin' trouble. That chief was stronger'n a grizzly, holdin' onto Joe's gun muzzle so's he couldn't shoot. I went tearin' over to help out. Everybody was owgh-owgh-owghin' for all they was worth and the noise was *some*, now. I run over to git my knife in the chief's back, but Joe wouldn't have none of it. He yelled at me to keep back. He says, 'If this coon can't whip one Injun, he'll go under. Keep back!' That's just what he said, ain't it, Starr?"

Big Starr grinned. "It is so-o-o. Joe never did git off his shot, but he throwed the chief and keeled him good. We counted six knife holes when he got through with him. We seen sights *that* night, or I wouldn't say so. Wagh! Papagos was layin' dead all around and what was left was flyin' out of thar."

"How many was it you counted coup on?" Mose asked.

"Sixteen. Robidoux come in when the fight commenced and he got two. Joe got two. Young Pete got three."

"You got three yourself," young Pete reminded him.

"Well, I did. But it was lucky you warned me. Come close to gittin' my own ha'r raised thar."

"Did you lose any men?" Noel asked.

"Nary a one. But there was several had arrows in their meat bags." Squinching his eyes and laughing he said, "Recollect what happened a little later, Joe?"

Fowler nodded. "Give me the cold shakes for a minute or two."

Young Pete whooped. "We was settin' thar by the fire, tellin' it all over, ever'body talkin', tellin' his own fight. Joe was settin' alongside the chief he'd kilt. Somebody had built up the fire and it was blazin' good. All at once and of a sudden this damned chief raised up . . . jist plumb raised hisself up and set thar. Without no scalp, mind ye. His face skin was all sagged down and bloody and where his topknot had been was pure raw. Wagh, but our mouths dropped open at the sight. He was the awfullest lookin' critter this child ever seen. He jist rose up and then his mouth opened and be damned if he didn't give out with an owgh-owgh-owgh one more time."

"My God!" Noel said.

"We set thar thunderstruck fer a minnit. Then Joe taken his pistol and put it right ag'in the chief's head this time and pulled it off. Blowed the varmint's brains to hell and gone. But he was the hardest Injun to kill I ever seen."

"Damned if he warn't," Big Starr said. "Had more life in him than a buffler bull."

Fowler was tired of the story but the boys would never quit telling it, not only those who had been there, like Starr and young Pete, but all mountain men. Joe Fowler's chief who wouldn't stay killed had become a legend among them. You'd think that in the mountains with all their great distances and men scattered over them in little bunches nine months out of the year there would be as little talk as anywhere in the world. But let a bunch of mountain men come together around a fire and the talk clattered like women's tongues at a sewing circle. You couldn't kill a rattlesnake without every man in the mountains knowing it. Some of it was knowledge traded, but the stories that got told over and over again had an outsize quality to them, like Joe Fowler's living corpse, or John Hatcher's drunken nightmare of visiting hell, or Rube Herring's "putrefied" forest, or the California-bound party starving in the Salt desert who had eaten "man" meat foisted on them by Digger Indians as bear. There was usually one outlandish happening in any hunting season, with the quality of marvel or dream or drama to make it a legend.

Tom Jordan, one of Driant's greenhorns, was laughing. "I reckon," he said, "that tale is about half true and the other half pure lies."

The firelight glinted suddenly on flashing steel and Big Starr's knife buried itself in the earth beside the youngster. "You be keerful, son," Starr said slowly, "who you call a liar. When you got a scalp or two hangin' from your belt, like us old hands hyar, you kin call me a liar and git by with it. It'll be your privilege, for ye'll have a few of your own to tell. But till then, keep your trap shut."

There was sudden and total silence around the fire. The greenhorns were scared and the mountain men were all at once cold steel. Big Starr didn't pull his Green River without he meant it. Fowler flicked a look at Paul Noel. The Frenchman might mean to interfere. But he was puffing nervously on his pipe. Fowler pulled on his own. He reckoned Noel was too scared himself to butt in.

Young Jordan looked dazedly at the knife still quivering in the dirt. He looked around, laughed nervously, fumbled with his pipe. No one joined his laughter. It was not a joke. He mumbled, then, "I never meant nothin'. Never meant to give offense."

Big Starr heaved up off the ground, sauntered over and took up his knife. "Don't go acting the smart aleck around yer betters," he said.

Mose eased the tension by saying, "Any of ye ever hear the tale of that Mike Fink spree?"

"This child has heared that story," Old Dan said, "but never knowcd if it was a fact."

"It was Jim Bridger told it to Joe and me, and he was thar. It was up on the Musselshell. Mike Fink and his best friend, feller named Carpenter, and another feller named Talbot had come up from the Ohio to St. Louis and when General Ashley advertised fer men to go upriver and hunt beaver they signed up. They wintered on the Musselshell. Jim said Mike and Carpenter fell out over a Crow squaw."

The men around the fire laughed. "It's the commonest reason fer bad blood," Old Dan said.

"They'd passed her back and forth," Mose went on, "but Mike got to feelin' tender towards her and claimed her fer his'n. Him and Carpenter had a fight but the boys got 'em to make it up. But they fell out ag'in, later the same winter. Seems they had a stunt they'd pull, of shootin' a cup of whiskey off each other's head. They was both dead shots and they'd take turns.

"Well, one day Mike said they'd settle who got the squaw fer keeps by seein' who could shoot the closest to a leetle black spot on the rim of the cup they'd been drinkin' from. They flipped a copper to see who got first shot. Mike won. Jim said Carpenter knowed what Mike was aimin' to do but he wouldn't back down fer he'd of done the same. They had got to that point of hate.

"Jim said Carpenter never flinched. Said he stood thar and waited fer Mike's shot stiddy and calm. Mike paced off sixty steps and called out, 'Don't move, Carpenter, I'm aimin' on drinkin' that whiskey in the cup.' He raised his rifle and pulled the trigger. Bored a hole dead center between Carpenter's eyes."

Noel said angrily, "That was pure murder!"

"Well," Mose said, "it couldn't be proved. Jim said Mike stormed and tromped around and said Carpenter must of moved a little, or his gun didn't fire true. Said he'd sighted right on the black speck and he *couldn't* of missed. Said Carpenter was his friend and worse than anybody he hated to see him killed. He also mourned spilling the whiskey."

"Was nothing done about it?" Noel asked.

"What could be done about it? Ain't no law out this way."

Coon Bastro had been cleaning his rifle. He laid the gun aside. "Was something done. I knowed Mike Fink. I knowed Carpenter. I was on the Ohio same time as them. And Talbot. I knowed him, too."

"Tell it," Mose said.

"Well, it was several months after the shootin' and Mike had a big dry on. The Company had a fort downstream a little piece from where they was winterin'. Mike and some others come in and got some alcohol and Mike drowned his dry. I was thar. He got rollin' drunk and he commenced braggin'. He bragged he meant all the time to kill Carpenter and he had shot him right where he aimed to. Me and Talbot laid for him. He come rollin' along and Talbot drawed a bead on him and shot him dead. I was thar. I seen it."

"Mountain justice," Noel said.

"Wagh!" Mose said, "I'm glad to know it." He stood up. "And so that was the end of Mike Fink who allus bragged he was the Salt River roarer who loved the wimmin and was chock full of fight. He died at the end of a long black rifle. Well, it's robe time fer this coon. Day'll be breakin' and some bugger will be callin' *levé* 'fore I git my fill of shut-eye way it is."

The little knot of men broke up and were quickly rolled in their robes and blankets. Fowler thought who had camp guard and remembered Big Starr had the time just ahead of daylight and went quickly to sleep.

three

FOUR DAYS the beaver party lay at Pagosa Springs favoring
Pierre Driant's ailing side. The trappers grumbled, led by Old
Dan Sutton. "This caper don't shine to this child, it don't.
Layin' up this clost to the settlements. Beaver's done trapped
out, see if it ain't. This coon don't like layin' up, except at robe
time. This ain't gonna make no beaver come."

Fowler joshed him. "Never heard of Old Dan Sutton saying
he couldn't catch beaver before."

"You ain't hearin' of it now," Old Dan cried. "Whut ye're
hearin' is this coon sayin' he don't like the chances."

Some of the greenhorns, a season or two behind them and
thinking they knew all there was to trapping beaver, sided with
Old Dan. "Ain't but little use settin' out."

"There's beaver in the hills," Fowler said.

"Summer pelts," Old Dan snorted.

"Better'n none," Big Starr put in. "We gotta lay up hyar, we
gotta. *Bueno.* This child'll wager his fanciest pair of Pima
mocks he'll git set out 'fore anybody else and he'll lay ye his otter
sleepin' robe he'll bring in the most plews."

A wager was all they needed to send them racing to the
streams, but Big Starr lost both his bets. Old Dan got set out
first. Coon Bastro paired with him and he told that Old Dan
was in such an all-fired hurry he ran off and left him to catch up
as best he could. "Beat up that old mare," he told, "till they
was raisin' a real dust. Come to a long downhill piece all covered with brush and thickets. Old Dan was faunchin' along and
that mare lost her footin' and commenced slidin', then she put
on the brakes and Old Dan, he kept right on goin', right over

the mare's head. She threw him a good thirty foot and he landed right in the middle of a brushy thicket. I made shore he had broke his neck and it was the last of Old Dan Sutton. But dogged if he didn't rise up outta that thicket, ketch the mare and cuss her out, crawl back on and beat me to the crick. Beat me so dogged bad he was done set out and movin' upstream 'fore I could ketch him."

"That's Old Dan fer ye," Mose said. "You cain't kill the old fool."

Old Dan's eyes glinted in triumph. His voice was shrill at all times but it rose to a whinny when he was worked up. "You heared him," he said, screeching. "Ain't nobody in the mountains kin beat this coon settin' out. I'll beat ye all winter, too, don't matter the kentry or the weather. Do 'ee hyar, now?"

Fowler and Mose had worked up a small creek together and Fowler was drying the legs of his pants at the fire. His old buckskins were cut off at the knees and pieced out with blanket. Buckskin was cold and stretchy when wet and it dried tight. All old hands took their oldest pair of buskskins and whittled them off and sewed on blanket leggings. Fowler kneaded his hot pants' legs. He said, "Well, I reckon you've won yourself some foofooraw, Dan."

"Foofooraw!" Old Dan spat his contempt. He didn't care about the Pima moccasins. What mattered to him was that he had been first to get set out and his reputation was saved.

Young Pete brought in the biggest catch next morning. Big Starr handed over the Pima moccasins and the otter robe in good humor. He won them both back that night in a game of cards, along with a considerable number of other items. Sporting six knives, a carved bait horn, two extra shirts, and more ammunition than he could pack, Big Starr yelled, "You boys better l'arn to hold a hand! This coon is a rip-snortin', hell-raisin' euker player from the Rocky Mountain House in St. Louis! That's whar they separate the men from the boys. That's whar, if ye ain't good, they strip ye to the hide and walk ye nekkid down the street. Anybody for another game?"

Most of the men had had enough. They threw in their hands and went yawning to their beds. Young Pete hung on. "By jinks," he said, "I'll set to ye. I kin out-ketch ye and be damned if I can't out-euker ye, too."

Next morning young Pete ruefully confessed he couldn't out-euker Big Starr. "I got my horse, two traps, my rifle and powder left," he told Fowler. "And the clothes I'm standin' in."

Fowler laughed. "He's a hard one to beat."

Young Pete rubbed his chin. "He can run a bluff the furthest of anybody I ever set in a game with." He brightened. "Well, mebbe my luck will be better next time." You couldn't put young Pete down. His spirits rose with the sun and they usually rode as high.

Fowler and Mose went out to run their traps. Mose brought up the delay at the Springs. "Misput us some, don't it?"

"Not to worry about," Fowler said. "I'd rather to have got on to Saguache and held up there, but it don't much matter."

"Reckon old Cholly's sent his boys on up to make meat?"

"Likely."

"Well, if he has," Mose said, "it'll mean the Rapahoes ain't prowlin'. I shore hope they ain't got bad hearts this year."

Fowler spotted a float stick downstream and waded into the cold water, catching up the chain and following it to the trap, springing it and releasing the drowned beaver. He tossed it to the bank, set the trap again, bent a twig over it and doused it with castoreum. He loosed the twig and waded out, sprinkling water on the bank to kill his own scent. "What I hope is old Cholly ain't had no brush with 'em lately and we can get through the parks without no trouble."

Mose picked up the beaver and skinned it expertly and quickly, saving nothing of the flesh but the tail. He flung the carcass back into the alders and strung the pelt over his shoul-

der. "If old Cholly has stirred 'em up," he said, "them Rapahoes'll be workin' like a swarm of prodded hornets."

They worked their way up to the last trap. It was empty.
They rebaited it and turned back to camp. They found antelope and elk meat roasting. Noel, under Driant's direction, kept
the hunters ranging for meat and they found it in plenty.

Each day, also, Noel packed his friend in a mud bath. Fowler
watched the man slowly grow better. On the second day he
could walk without help. On the third day he could stand
straight, not favoring the sore side. That evening he insisted
the pain had entirely left him and that he was able to travel.

"Let's wait over one more day," Fowler told him. "Them
mud packs are helping you so much, let's give 'em a little more
time. Be certain you're able."

Fowler and his men, except for young Pete, knew the country they were heading into. None of Driant's party did. You
couldn't tell men what a mess of tumbled mountains there was
up beyond Poncha Pass, and how they were cut by hundreds of
canyons and gorges, how rough it was and steep and hard. You
had to see it for yourself and learn your own lesson of respect for
it. And if you were unlucky with the weather—and some years
the snows began as early as now, September—you couldn't tell
men how deep the snow could be in the passes, soft and full of
air so that animals sank to their bellies and floundered and the
only way you got through was to traipse back and forth ahead of
them and pack down a trail with your own feet. No use telling
Driant this and that his side had better be in as good shape as he
could get it if he was going to live through it himself, much less
take a party through. But Fowler could wait another day and
give him a little more rest, give him a day or two at Saguache, a
few days when they made meat in the Bayou, then Driant would
be at the mercy of his body, the trail, and the weather, and nothing anybody could do about it.

The night of the fourth day Driant was so impatient that
Fowler decided he'd had as much good of the rest and the mud

baths as he was going to have, so he gave the order they would leave at daybreak.

It was cold on the river and gray storm clouds boiled over the peaks as they loaded. The old hands broke out Northwest capotes or great coats or mackinaws. Big Starr and Mose liked a Navajo rug which they wore in the Spanish fashion, a hole cut for the head and the rug making a poncho about them. One of Fowler's treasures was a genuine Nor'west capote made of thick, almost waterproof blanket wool, with a hood to be pulled over the head. Driant and Noel wore great coats. Young Pete, having been reckless with his possibles, had only the shirt he wore. Big Starr offered to give him back his mackinaw but young Pete roared, "Hell's full of such give-backs! I'll win it back or do without. I'll set to ye tonight and tomorrow I'll dry ride."

Driant went among his greenhorns and warned them the clouds meant a squall and they had better prepare for it. Fowler sat the big roan patiently. Fouchette's horse was dancing. He snubbed him up and held him in. Fouchette watched Driant with a sardonic eye. "Don't they have eyes to see?"

Fowler grinned. "He'll get over wet-nursing 'em."

"By gar, he needs it himself," Fouchette said. "He goes under on us up here, Joe, who pays? How we gonna come out?"

"He ain't dead yet."

"This *paseo* don't smell good to me," Fouchette grumbled. "A sick man, a bunch of greenhorns, what kind of outfit is that?"

Fowler looked at the big Indian-colored, Indian-looking man and laughed. "When did we ever need anybody but ourselves?"

Fouchette's eyes widened, he looked startled, then he laughed. "*Sacré,* but you are right, Joe." He put up a big paw and counted off. "Big Starr, young Pete, Mose, you, me." He closed his fist. "We don't need nobody, eh?"

"Nope."

Fouchette was cheerful now, assured that Fowler had not tied them up, that they were Fowler men still.

Fowler led the brigade upstream, following the river, winding around the willow and alder clumps, through the deep shade of the cottonwoods, and sometimes riding clear for a stretch in loose sand and gravel.

A half hour after starting the squall hit with crashing thunder and a heavy, sheeted, hissing rain. The party plodded on, hunching into it, keeping their eyes wiped to see and according to their natures swearing and complaining or keeping silence, ungrumbling.

The lightning was like vicious blue spears and the thunder was crackling and explosive, doubled by the peaks and sent booming down the canyons. It made men and animals jumpy until a sudden burst, like the long roll of heavy artillery, made the pack mules jerk, bunch, squeal, and spook.

Half blinded by the rain, Pedro yelled, *"Carajo!"* He dug in his spurs and chased to head the herd.

Fouchette wheeled his horse. *"Diables!"* he shouted.

"Mah-son-ne!" the Utah halfbreed cried and kicked his horse into a run.

Big Starr yelled, "Goddammit!" and he and young Pete wheeled off to help.

Fowler hauled up, stood his weight on one leg and eased the other across the saddle, and watched the excitement. "Them mules," he said to Mose, "ain't too impressed at being cussed in four languages."

Mose talked obscenities tenderly to Solomon to ease his fear. He said, "A mule don't impress worth a damn. Mules take the measure of a man ever' time. Them mules was watchin' Pedro and they *knowed* he warn't watchin' them and they communed together and they said next big clap of thunder we'll make him some mischief. We'll show him our heels."

The greenhorns had got into the chase, too, and there was a lot of yelling, whooping, hubbub, much flapping of elbows and coattails and ponchos, much spurring and cursing and rounding and braking. "Last time I seen as much running as that was on a buffalo hunt," Fowler said. "It was a heap better paying, though."

It took about fifteen minutes to head the herd and turn them back toward the river. Fowler balanced his weight in the big Spanish stirrups again. "Let's us get outta the way, Mose, 'fore them fools run them mules clean over us."

The squall had passed, the sun was breaking through, and the mules were out of the notion of running by the time they reached the river. They trotted around, quieted, and began to munch placidly on the short brown grass. Pedro pounded up, threw himself off his horse, and swatted a few mules over the head with his hat. Outraged, he said to Fowler, "*Válgame Dios! Muchos diablos! Muchos, muchos, muchos, grandote diablos!* These *mulas*, they make the *stampedo!*"

Fowler was spreading his capote on the rump of the big roan to dry. "You're danged right, Pedro. Ain't no *mulas* ever made a bigger *stampedo*. But I tell you one thing, Pedro. They ain't ever gonna get away. If this bunch don't catch 'em for you, they'll scare 'em to death. Rope 'em, boy. We may get another squall or two before the day's over."

Pedro's head bobbed up and down. *Sí. Sí,* Señor Joe. *Sacré!*" He spat out one last oath, shifting to French for emphasis.

They moved on up the river until the stream was boxed into an alder canyon, then they left it and followed an Indian trail to the right. They made their night camp in the foothills of the big San Juan range, high pines massed upward to the peaks behind them.

Next day they began the long climb up among the pines to cross at Wolf Creek Pass. The trail was rocky and narrow and wound like a loose-flung rope up the mountainside, steep in places and in some places overhanging deep chasms. Pedro went ahead with the mules and they picked a surefooted way. The saddle horses followed. Some of the men got off and led finicky, nervous horses. "This crazy critter of mine," young Pete complained, "keeps stretchin' his neck to see what's down below."

"If he was to slip," Mose said, "he'd find it ain't no feather bed."

"That's what I keep tellin' him."

On Solomon, Mose was comfortable, even on the narrowest switchbacks. Young Pete eyed him enviously. He said, finally, "I ain't ever stole a mule yit, but I shore got a good mind to."

"Ye wouldn't lissen," Mose said. "I been tellin' ye 'bout mules. But no, you knowed best."

"Oh, well," young Pete laughed, "we ain't gonna be in mountains forever."

They were all day making the winding climb. They camped at the summit in light thin snow, began the descent the next morning, and by night were east of the divide, down from the peaks and working through the lesser hills.

The next night they made their camp beside a narrow, silvery little creek. Paul Noel came up to Fowler. "What is the name of this creek?"

"It's the south fork of the del Norte."

"Rio Grande?"

"The same. This is where she begins to head up. That's the San Luis basin out there. That's old Blanca Peak plumb across the basin."

Noel stared. The sun was still striking the sage and sand desert glittering with gold. The gray-green of the sage was like mold on an old yellow coin. The red edge of sundown was on the flanks of Blanca and they were burning in the light. The peak towered above the other mountains massed around it. The sand rose in hills toward the foot of the range, the golden dunes looking golden waves arrested at crest. "So that's Blanca," the Frenchman said. "I've heard a lot about that mountain."

"Leave it hearsay," Fowler advised. "She don't look it but she's a mean one. Full of rockslides, bad timber, deep gashes. She's wild and rugged and you can't find the end of her. Lonesome as hell. Even the Indians leave that one alone. They have some kind of legend about her."

Noel looked at him curiously. "Superstitious, eh? How?"

"Well, the Utes say Blanca is the home of some kind of jealous god. He don't want people messing around the mountain. Something bad happens to folks try to get in that wilderness."

Noel laughed. "There's probably silver in that mountain and the Indians know it and want to keep white men away."

"No," Fowler said, "it ain't that. Utahs don't fool with mining. They got no use for silver except for ornaments and they can get what they want for their trinkets from Taos. They're uneasy when they get too close to Blanca. I don't like her because when Indians leave a mountain alone there's no trails and she's so big you can get lost before you know it."

The sun was sliding down fast now and the floor of the desert was losing its gold and turning gray. A biting cold was flowing over it and Noel shivered. Fowler turned toward the stream to wash up. "How's Mr. Driant?" he asked.

Noel went with him. "He is well."

"Complaining any about his side?"

The Frenchman dipped in the water, flinched from its iciness, then doused his face. *"Non,"* he said. "He does not mention it."

You're a liar, Fowler thought. He had been watching Driant and he knew he was suffering again, though not as bad as before. He didn't look too used up yet, but riding a horse was plainly not good for him. It jolted up the sore side and brought the pain back. But he said, levelly, "That's good."

Noel nodded, squeezed the water from his beard, and swiped his hands down his shirt front. "Do not be uneasy, Mr. Fowler," he said, "Pierre Driant is indomitable."

"Think he'd be up to a long day tomorrow?"

"I think he would be up to whatever is necessary," Noel retorted.

Fowler's temper flared quickly. It was one thing to hide Driant's condition from the men if possible. It was another thing to hide it from him. He had to get this outfit where it was going and it would help if they'd tell him the truth. He flattened down his anger. "It's not strictly necessary, but we can make Saguache with a long ride tomorrow."

"How long?"

"Fifteen hours . . . maybe less."

"No rest?"

"Oh, sure. We'll noon. Ain't in that big of a rush."

Noel considered. "Pierre will do it."

"Bueno," Fowler said shortly, his temper still stretched a little. "We'll leave an hour earlier in the morning."

"I will tell the men."

When they had eaten, Fowler said, "Who's got the morning watch?"

Old Dan said, "Coon and me."

"If I ain't awake, call me at three."

"Will so," Old Dan said, nodding.

Young Pete had broken out the cards and was spreading a blanket.

"Break that up early, will you, boys?" Fowler said. "We're putting out an hour soon in the morning."

"Hell," Big Starr said without looking up from his job of straightening a corner of the blanket, "if we're puttin' out that early we just as well set to euker all night."

"I said break it up early." Fowler's voice was curt and scalding.

The big man looked up, startled, and saw Fowler's angry eyes, the red rising in his face, the tight mouth and clamped jaw. Instantly he understood that something, but not the euchre game, was hackling Fowler. He said quietly, "Why, shore, Joe. This coon's luck is runnin' downstream anyways. 'Twon't take the boys long to clean me out."

Fowler felt sorry for climbing Starr before the others. Poor thing to do, shed your temper on a good friend. He didn't like doing it, but he didn't like explaining it either, so he let it done, unrolled his robes and kicked off his moccasins.

"What's boogerin' *him?*" he heard Bastro say.

Mose answered. "Same thing that's boogerin' us all. Driant."

"*That* sonuvabitch . . . !"

"Aw, put yer money where yer mouth is at," young Pete said, "let's play cards."

"Don't deal me in," Old Dan said, "I aim to sleep."

Fowler lay a long time awake, hearing the slap of the cards, the whisper of the shuffle and deal, the trappers' laughter and bets, the jibing at losers, the crowing of winners. He gave it up when the ground felt like it was seeping right into his bones, rolled out, and built up the fire. "Want in the game?" Pete asked.

"Nope." He put a piece of meat on a stick. "I'm hungry."

Young Pete turned back to his cards. "Starr, you like that trump or don't ye?"

"I don't like it at all," Starr said. "I pass."

Each man studied his hand. Left of Starr, Mose passed then. To his left, Fouchette passed. Coon Bastro hesitated, looked at the eight of spades turned up for trumps, studied his hand a little longer, then said he'd pass.

When Bastro passed, young Pete whooped, "This child'll make it and he'll cross to diamonds! Wagh! Hyar's whur you boys l'arn what bein' eukered is like! Make your bets, boys, and make 'em big."

"Your mackinaw," Big Star said, grinning, "that ye'll not make a march."

Mose offered Starr's beaded mocassins which he'd long ago won from Old Dan.

Fouchette threw in a knife. "Wan Green River."

Coon Bastro looked at his cards, shrugged, and threw them in. "This child can't hurt ye," he said. A hand holding no face cards or trumps could be thrown in—no bets made.

Young Pete nodded. He held his five cards in a tight fan. "Well," he said, peering at them again, "this coon'll jist bet that sleepin' robe of your'n, Starr, which I taken the other night. Your lead and it don't make no difference."

Big Starr led the ace of clubs and the suit was followed until young Pete flipped out the nine of diamonds. "No clubs," he chortled.

He slapped down the jack of diamonds with a flourish. "Right bower and that's makin' 'em *come*. Come on, you Rocky Mountain beaver tails, gimme your diamonds!"

Starr laid out the ten. Mose flipped out the seven. Fouchette groaned and lost his queen.

Young Pete raked in the trick and plunked down the jack of hearts. Big Starr yelped. "Left bower, too! That gutshots the coyote." He reluctantly parted with the king.

Mose grimaced and threw off a heart. Fouchette played a low spade.

Young Pete watched the play. Neither Mose nor Fouchette had a trump left, then. With a five-card deal, all the trumps needn't be held, but they might be. Pete's face didn't show anything but Fowler had sat in too many games with him. He figured Pete didn't have the next high card—his own ace. Starr might have it. He had followed two trump leads. If Starr had it, he was going to take a trick. Pete had his hand made, had his three tricks, but the bet was on a march, all five tricks.

Pete's grin stayed stretched as he led the ace of an off suit, spades. It was followed all the way round. Pete gathered in the trick. This last lead would tell the story. Only the fire made a sound as he flung out his last card, the ten of hearts. Big Starr sighed and put on a little card. Neither Mose nor Fouchette bothered to play. Pete exploded when the ace of diamonds didn't fall.

He leaped into a war dance around the fire and rumpled Fowler's hair. "Owgh-owgh-owgh! Howgh-owgh-owgh! That'll l'arn ye, by damn! Set to euker with this coon, will ye? Oh, I'm a Rocky Mountain he-goat! A ripsnortin' bighorn he-goat! Pay me, boys, pay me! I kin out-euker ye to hell and back. Howgh-owgh-owgh! This coon'll take that mackinaw back now, Starr. Gimme them Pima mocks, Mose. I been honin' for that Green River, Lou."

The boys laughed at his capering and piled his winnings to one side. "The night ain't over yet," Mose said. "Them goods is liable to change hands several times 'fore the game is over. Come on, hyar. My deal, and I aim to deal *this* bugger a march this time."

Mose reached for the cards but he fumbled Coon Bastro's discarded hand and the cards fell onto the blanket face up. Nothing to play . . . except the ace of diamonds, one stark and lonely trump. The men stared at it, then young Pete howled, leaping up again. "Why, you yellow-bellied, low-lifed, cheatin' sonuvabitch, you! You threw in to keep from losin'! You'd have had to play that ace on my first lead! Why, I'll bury this knife plumb to the Green River in ye!" He was crouched, his knife drawn and whistling, closing in.

Bastro rolled up and his own knife flashed. "You mess with me, Pete Smith, and you'll git yer ribs tickled good. You ain't the only one knows how to keelhaul a man."

"I'll grain ye," Pete warned.

"Try it," Bastro said. "This child learned to use a knife with Mike Fink on the Ohio."

The other trappers kicked out of the way and made a silent ring. A knife fight was serious business, and bloody business, and often to the death.

Fowler stood, a deep depression settling over him, and went around where Big Starr was. Starr gave him a direct look and hooked his thumbs in his belt.

The two men circled, each crouched, knife blades glittering in the firelight, bright as they whistled, pointed, arched, flashed. They moved warily, shifting balance like dancers, flicking their knives, each watching for an opening, feinting, drawing back, feinting again. Suddenly young Pete darted in and back. The sleeve of Bastro's shirt was ripped from the shoulder to the elbow and through the opening a long red streak appeared. But Pete paid for his move with a gash in his own shoulder.

Fowler sighed. *"Bueno.* They've drawed blood, Starr."

"Which un you want me to take?"

"Bastro." Fowler grinned. "You're the biggest."

Starr grinned back. "So's he."

They waited a moment, then lunged together. Fowler made a flying tackle around Pete's knees and knocked him over. Pete's head hit the ground, bounced, he grunted, then moved dazedly. Fowler scrambled up astride of him and pinned his knife hand to the ground. Young Pete began to struggle and swear. Mose came running to help hold him down. "Give over peaceable, now, boy, or we'll have to tie ye. Ye hyar, now?"

Pete kept struggling and Mose and Fowler kept talking until finally what they were saying began to penetrate, he recognized them, quit fighting them. Mose sighed. "Damn if ye ain't harder'n a painter to keep a hold on. Git up, now."

They helped him to his feet, not yet releasing their grip on him. He was still twitching and panting. "Lemme go! Lemme go!"

Big Starr and Fouchette were holding Bastro, who was twisting and struggling. "Let go of me. I'll make mincemeat of him!"

"Both of you shut up and listen to me," Fowler said. "You've drawed blood. Now, let it go till the season's over. Then you can kill each other if you're a mind to and nobody will stop you. We're too short-handed for you to do it now. Is that understood?"

Young Pete looked like a cock in the pit that had been balked, neck feathers still raised and spurs ready. "I kin take him, Joe," he begged, "I kin take him."

"Not now," Fowler said tightly.

Bastro threw off the hands holding him. "You ain't got no

call to interfere, Fowler. I ain't beholden to you and I ain't takin' no orders from ye."

"But you are working for me, my friend, and you will take orders from me," Pierre Driant said from behind Fowler. "I will back Mr. Fowler. There will be no more fights among you during this hunting season. You will doubtless have opportunities to use those knives on Indians many times before the winter is over. Don't draw them again, except against an Indian."

"I ain't takin' no orders from you, neither," Bastro said.

"Then you had better go back to Taos, now, before it is too late," Driant said. He had not raised his voice and he had come up to the circle so quietly no one had known he was there. There was a long moment of silence, then Bastro flattened his hands, giving in. Driant stepped forward. "I'll take those knives, please."

Big Starr handed over Bastro's and Mose gave him young Pete's.

Driant tucked them into his belt. "Now, you'd better get some sleep. Your knives will be returned when your tempers have cooled."

The short, rotund man walked away without looking back, rolled in his robes and left the group astounded.

Fowler whistled low and laughed. "Danged if he ain't *some*, now. Regular banty rooster."

Young Pete looked bewildered. He glanced over at the rolled, still form, then he broke into guffawing laughter. "By damn, he jist cracked our heads together like we was school kids. Ain't he somethin', though?" He marched over to Bastro, who was sullen and glowery. "Well, Bastro," he said, "what the budgeway says goes, but jist for the hunt. We'll settle up at rendezvous. I'll cut your liver out, then."

"You won't have none yourself," Bastro promised, "nor any guts. Your friends here kin bury ye when I git through with ye."

Big Starr picked up the cards, shuffled them a time or two, boxed them and slipped them into his pack. "Well, so-o-o," he drawled, "now you got spanked, git to yer beds, boys, so pappy kin tuck ye in."

The men broke it up and turned in laughing at the spunky little French cockerel and the sudden turn of events. Fowler watched young Pete move his saddle and possibles around the fire from Coon Bastro and Old Dan, giving notice of the distance he meant to keep. He blew his breath out tiredly. There would be bad blood between the two men the rest of the season.

He lay on his back and looked up and, finding the stars he knew in their right places, let his mind run on to the quarrel. What had made Bastro pull such a fool stunt? Was he so close and stingy he couldn't stand to lose? Or was he just plain mean? Open-handed, free-hearted, give-away, rich one day, dead broke the next, was a pride with mountain men. Out-do, out-trap, out-catch, then throw it all away with gusty grace, out-drink, out-spree, out-spend. It was odd to find one who even aspired to be a mountain man who didn't know you took a cleaning-out with as much brag as you took winning. Neither condition was permanent. You wanted to hold onto everything you had, this country was no place for you.

He couldn't figure it, so he put it out of his mind. The stars already had an old and wintry look. In summer, in this country, the stars were so hot and yellow and close they looked like they could melt right down out of the sky. In winter, they were cold and silver and far away. They looked like frost, brittle and not very friendly. Well, he turned on his side, it was almost time.

Next thing he knew a hand was touching his shoulder. He came awake instantly. *"Levé, amigo,"* Old Dan said.

"Bueno," Fowler said.

He lay a moment longer, smelling the sweet chill of the cold and feeling the light weight of the darkness, the just-before-daybreak intense cold and dark and quietness, which had so little burden of the night left. His flesh crawled with the knowledge he must unroll and his blanket warmth be invaded by the cold. His old room in the Widow de Leiva's house in Taos would feel good on a morning like this. Old Lonzo would be coming in about now to build up the fire in the corner fireplace and it would wake him a little, but he wouldn't have to stir. He would nap and doze until the room was warm and in the cookroom Doña Eufemia would be making small muffled noises and soon good smells would seep under his door. And the girl, Pepita, and the boy, Luis, would begin to chatter. What possessed a man to stay unsettled and to move around like water itself in the mountains? He ought to have been married by now, had a home and family. He knew he ought, but every time he thought of it it made him restless and he put it away from him and went out again into the mountains. He knew all about cold nights and cold mornings and every kind of discomfort beaver hunting threw at you. But somehow a warm room, a warm bed, warm food, were for idle times. It didn't seem like much of a life to spend it making sure you had them.

The fire blazed up and the men began to stir, waking with sniffles and snorts and groans and mumbles. A pan clattered and a man swore. Water splashed and another man swore. The cavvyard was restless and the horse guards were moving about. Fowler flung his robes back and heaved up, went shuddering to the river to wash.

Old Dan followed him. "Coon's gone, Joe," he said.

Fowler let water dribble down his face. So the bastard had sloped off. "By himself?"

"One of the greenhorns went with him. That young Jordan feller Starr throwed his knife at."

Fowler wiped his hand down his face. "They take anything?"

"You better see."

They had taken twelve traps and two pack mules. They had raided the supplies for full loads. And Coon Bastro had taken

Pierre Driant's horse to ride. Bleakly, Fowler informed the Frenchman. Then he asked, "You want to make a search for 'em?"

Driant's eyes were dark pits in the firelight. "How much time have they had?"

"Several hours. Dan said he roused Coon at midnight. He took the far side of camp and left Coon this side. Likely Coon didn't wait long to commence moving."

Driant shivered and warmed his hands over the flames. "It would take us all day. And there are a thousand places they could hide."

"Yes."

"There is no certainty we could find them."

"No. But it's your property. You say so, we'll try."

Driant's hand went to his side and he probed it gently. "I think I shall simply charge it against them and collect it later," he said.

Fowler thought his chances of collecting were pretty poor, but he thought Driant had made the right decision. It would take time to hunt Bastro down. It would shorten the season and wouldn't be fair to the other trappers. As owner, he had all things to consider and, backed in a corner, to cut his losses. *"Bueno,"* Fowler said. "I'll tell Pedro to cut you out another horse."

Driant was still rubbing his side as Fowler went away. His side. His everlasting, tormenting side. He was so sensible about everything but himself. But iron for nerves had brought more than one man through a bad scrape, and maybe Driant's iron would serve him now.

2.

The Cochetopa hills rolled back westward to their left as the outfit followed around the great paws which splayed out into the basin. The first two hours were slow, through soft sand as they crossed the neck of the basin, then they were on hardpan. The day broke gently with the stars going down a bleaching sky, then suddenly the sun was up over Blanca, bright and reflecting and assaulting.

It wasn't a rough day's ride. The sun had heat in it, but it wasn't the frying kind of heat it brought in summer. And there were occasional small rills of water trickling down from the hills, losing themselves quickly in the sands. They didn't sweat out or go dry. But it was a long day's ride.

The sun had gone down and the basin was plum-colored with dusk when Fowler, in the lead, caught the first glint of fires, specks of red in dark timber against the hills. Mose spotted them at about the same time. He laughed. "Well, thar they be, boy."

Big Starr and young Pete saw the fires next and came galloping up. Big Starr shouted at Fowler, "Hope Betsy's stew pot is full tonight. This child's belly is plumb empty. I got a hankerin' for tender dog!"

"Can't nobody cook pup like Betsy," young Pete said.

"You'll eat at old Cholly's fire tonight," Fowler said. "What Betsy's got cooked is for me."

"Oh, I reckon my squaw'll latch onto me soon as we git in," Starr said. "By Crikey, I've tried Shian and Naypursie and Shoshone, but that Nancy is the meanest squaw I ever had. I'll have to lodgepole her 'fore mornin'. I give her pa my best hoss for her, too. That woman don't *never* quit naggin'. They won't be enough calico and beads and paint in Driant's packs to satisfy her, neither. Sometimes," he concluded woefully, "this coon thinks he'll jist go it alone."

Young Pete whooped joyfully. "Not this'n! I aim to keep my back warm this night."

Soon they could see the Ute horse herds being driven in, and then ponies cut out from the herds and came flying across the flats toward them. From the south the Utahs had so little to fear that almost any party arriving would be friendly. Fowler, Mose, Big Starr, and young Pete spurred their horses to meet the Indians, leaving the main party plodding along behind.

The trappers and the Ute young men drove head on at each other, neither slowing, until at the last possible moment the Indians swerved, split, and curved to the side, turning and coming up on the flanks of the trappers. "There's Running Water," Fowler cried, raising an arm and signaling.

"And Big Wind," Mose yelled.

"And danged if White Wolf ain't amongst 'em," Big Starr shouted.

Trappers and Utahs both began owgh-owghing, laughing, whooping together, the Indians wheeling, circling, flowing between the trappers, making a big show of their welcome. One Indian cut out and rode up beside Fowler, his face bright with delight, his tongue spitting, swallowing, exploding with Utah words. He shifted to Spanish. *"Hola!"* he cried, flinging out an arm, *"Cómo está usted?"*

"Hey!" Fowler cried, and went on to say he was fine, there was big train following, there would be *mucho* trade tonight.

Running Water whooped and veered away to shout to his companions. They dashed on ahead with the news.

Suddenly, among the trees that marked the creek, the white flash of lodges stood out against the fire glow. Fowler pulled up the big roan and the other trappers slowed to a walk also.

The camp was well pitched, as always, on a level place beside the foaming, white-water creek. The tall, roomy lodges were spaced well, in parallel lines down a broad, ample street. Fires burned down its middle, their light glancing off the war lances and shields struck before each lodge. Behind the lodges would be the drying racks for meat. The horse herd was already penned in a pole corral.

As Fowler led the way down the broad street, squaws, children, yipping dogs, Utah men, boiled out of the lodges, up from the fires, running to meet them, crying out to them, greeting them. They rode between the lodges to the central fire, Indians clinging to their stirrups, crowding around them. Here old Cholly waited for them, his blanket draped about him, one hand holding the handle of his tomahawk, its head resting in the curve of his other arm. There was dignity in his silence and in his waiting.

Fowler's eyes found a short, plump squaw who stood quietly before a lodge. He grinned at her and her face flashed joy at him. He rode on to say his piece to old Cholly and be made solemnly welcome by the old chief. It would be late before the feast and the big smoke were over, but Betsy would be waiting.

four

NEXT MORNING when she had given him coffee and meat and all the small affairs of the lodge had been set to rights, she told him more of what old Cholly had told him. He had to pick it out of a running wifely monologue accompanied by small scandalized clucks and tooth-clickings, glottal explosives and offended swallowed gutterals at the state of his clothing, his equipment, and himself.

So. And yes. The scouts had returned this many days ago. And yes. Their horses were very worn and gaunt. They had ridden far. There were many buffalo but they were farther south than usual at this time of year and they were beginning to leave the mountains. And yes. The scouts had seen the deep cold coming already in the high places. But where was the holder for his awl which was made for him . . . the one of carved and painted wood . . . ?

He had lost it.

Tongue clicking and head shaking. And so. And yes. Yes. The scouts had seen Arapahoes. The scouts had been clever. They had remained hidden in the rocks and they had watched for many days. The Arapahoes had then gone away.

"The boys didn't get into a brush with 'em?"

No. The old men had forbidden them to make war at this time. It was not wise. The need was great for meat. War could come later. They were to go quickly and watch and return rapidly so the hunt could be made. But his hair was full of sand and grit. The trail had been dusty then. And so. She would beat up the yucca root and wash it for him.

"Not now. How many Rapaho?"

A hand held up four times. This many. And this . . . many horses. Not a village. No women. A war party. Returning from a raid, probably. Did he know that the brass plate on his gun was dull? She would shine it for him.

"Yes. *Bueno*. When they left the park, which way they go?"

So. That way. Her chin indicated north and east. They went without hurry, not knowing they were watched. They were tired. The horses they had stolen were Comanche horses. An offended explosive over a long rent in his oldest shirt meant precisely what it sounded like—look what you've done now! How can you be so careless? It would have served you a while longer but it is now past repair. She tossed the shirt aside. She would make gun patches of it.

He watched her competent, work-hardened hands feel over each article, testing for strength, thickness, durability, wear. Her comfortable amplitude was spread onto her heels tucked under her. Her skin was lightened from dead brown by a copper warmth. She was *mestiza*—Spanish blood ran in her. Many Utahs had the strain from the seed of Spanish traders. Her mother, old Cholly's chief wife, now dead, had been half Spanish. But Betsy's features, the broad planes, flattened nose, full mouth, low forehead, were all pure Indian.

A shift of wind gusted down the smokehole and blew up the ashes and made the fire in the pit smoke. She scolded the wind for its bad manners, scolded the fire for waywardness, went outside and adjusted the flap at the top of the tepee's cone, came in and made the fire tidy, set the pot of simmering stew more firmly and went back to her feeling and looking and sorting. This must be repaired. And this . . . she would use this for moccasins. This shirt was still useful but he had torn off many of the whangs. She would replace them.

Fowler reached into the pot for a piece of meat and swore when he burned his fingers. She looked up at him and laughed, her strong blunted teeth white against the dark of her face.

"The greedy child burns his fingers," she told him. "You are hungry?"

"No. It just smelled good is all. Your father says the young men left to hunt nine days ago."

And so. Yes. It was decided by the old men in council that the hunt should be made earlier this year because the buffalo were leaving the mountains. It was not wise to follow them onto the plains. And so. Yes, the young men left to hunt nine days ago.

Her sorting finished, she leaned forward on hands and knees and pushed up like a cow, hind end first, making herself deliberately ludicrous for his laughter, laughing herself at her exaggerated awkwardness. She patted her broad behind. She ate too much. She was growing fat. She reached over his head for a parflêche bag and laughed when he whacked her and then pinched her. She thrust his hand away and returned to her seat. With awl, needles, sinews, she set to work on the repairs she thought were needed.

"The women made much pemmican yet?" he asked.

Her mouth bunched. He knew, didn't he, that the time for making much pemmican had not come. The hunters had not returned with the buffalo yet.

"But Ute women make pemmican whenever there's meat, and you been eating meat, and wild cherries have ripened. You made any?"

But yes. They had made some. She herself had this many bags. It was made of deer and elk and antelope meat. It was, he knew, not as rich as buffalo pemmican.

"Never mind. I just wanted to know there was any."

With her teeth and strong hands she tore the stoutest pieces of the useless shirt into strips and began to weave new whangs into the fringed sleeves of another shirt.

Fowler packed his pipe and leaned against the willow backrest and considered the things he had learned. His eyes followed the brown, peeled cottonwood lodgepoles which went up to their gathering at the top of the lodge cone in precisely spaced intervals. Pale, smoked skins were stretched over them, overlapped and fastened and without wrinkled folds. He noted that the housekeeping was in order, the bed robes rolled and placed out of the way, the floor brushed clean of extra dirt, insects, ants, and that the willow baskets, parflêche bags, brass and iron kettles were hung about neatly, where they belonged.

There was a smoky smell in the lodge, sweetened with the new grass mattresses and by Betsy's herbs and root powders. She put up a good lodge and kept it well, changed the bed mattresses, and while all lodges had a smoky, greasy smell, it was never rank and foul in Betsy's lodge. She kept the door flaps open to the air as much as possible, she aired the bed robes, she did not allow food wastes to accumulate, and all things she used were kept clean.

He felt lazy and full and good. It did not matter that they had missed the party of young men going to hunt. It would have been useful to journey with them had the Arapahoes been on the prowl, but the Arapahoes had been raiding, had gone home, and their hot blood was cooled.

The whole village was stirring with noise and life now. Horses were clattering down the street, dogs were barking crazily, children were yelling, squaws chattering and scolding and screeching. Fowler winced. If there was anything noisier than an Indian village coming to life he didn't know what it was. The waterfront in St. Louis was as peaceful as a church by the side of it. It seemed as if every living thing that opened its eyes had to open its mouth, too.

He didn't much want to move but he guessed he had better see Driant and talk. Two, three days was as much as they ought to stay here. They had to make meat themselves and with the cold coming they should keep moving. His attention came back to the woman.

Did he know that the vedettes in the hills had seen a fire and that one of them had gone to observe more closely and that there were two white men? One, a big man, was awake, keeping watch. The other was sleeping.

"Where?"

Behind the hills. Her chin pointed. Two hour's ride, perhaps. The vedettes had not alarmed them. They were men of his party, perhaps?

Fowler slid a little farther down on his long spine. "I'll be damned," he said softly. So Bastro and young Jordan were trailing north, keeping out of sight, but following up with them. "When did you hear this?" he asked. "Who brought the word?"

A messenger had been sent immediately to her father, she said. She had heard him arrive—after the feast had ended. She had listened as the messenger talked with her father. They were men he knew?

"Yes. They were with us. Run off night before last."

This was not good, then?

"Don't matter much. We'll have to keep an eye peeled is all."

It was a pretty good way to trap beaver—trail along with a bigger party, keeping just a little out of sight, just far enough to run if need be, but watching their catches and trapping in the same vicinity. The big party led you to beaver and all you had to do was mop up. The boys would have to take care. It wasn't very clever of Bastro, however. The time would inevitably come when they would catch him out and recover Mr. Driant's horse and traps.

Betsy was talking again. It was a pity, she thought, that the man called Starr did not have his own woman last night, but his woman had taken a Utah husband. But perhaps the man called Starr did not care. The woman had always had a long tongue. Perhaps the man called Starr would prefer the woman loaned to him last night.

"Don't think he wants another one regular," Fowler said.

She clucked and thought that was not good. But see these

moccasins made for him only so many months ago. His feet had walked through them. But fortunately she had made two new pairs for him. They were not much. She had used all her beads long ago—and it was good he had brought her so many—so they were very plain. And so. And yes. And see, this pair she had put the wing feathers of the little brown bird on so that his feet might run with wings.

Fowler was lighting his dudeen. He sucked it into fire and nodded over the first pair. "Good. Reckon I can use some wings on my feet."

She murmured that she was glad he was pleased. She stirred the stew. Then she handed him the second pair. They were beautiful and soft, the doeskin so bleached and cured that it was almost white, so supple and so pliant that the moccasins could be crushed in one hand. Porcupine quills, small shells and bits of metal had been sewed in an intricate design across the toes. They were made with high ankles which folded about the leg for warmth. She had spent many hours on them, he knew. He turned them, handled them, sucked on his pipe. "They're pretty, Betsy," he said, "real pretty." He laughed. "I'll not get much good of 'em, though. They're too soft for wear. My toes would walk through them in a day's time."

She lifted the moccasins and stroked the quilled design, the soft white leather. But they were not to wear outside, she told him, not looking at him, her head bent over the moccasins. They were to wear in the lodge . . . this winter . . . in the lodge, with her.

Fowler's tongue explored a rough spot on a tooth. So. She wanted to go with him this time. It was the first time she had ever asked. He moved his head, and the smell of the food cooking and the old smoke smell and the old grease smell came into his nose and mouth and he killed it by drawing on his pipe. He thrust up and walked out of the lodge into the full bright sunlight.

2.

He walked over to the rushing, diamond-clear creek and watched its purl as it boiled over the rocks, watched the hammered-bronze leaves of the cottonwood trees which had fallen sail like little boats down with the current. Across the creek and up into the hills the oak scrub was turning red, and beyond it the dark of cedar and pine climbed upward. Higher than the green the aspen groves were now pure gold, as pure as a nugget taken from the washing pan, or a woman's bracelet or wedding ring.

He had not ever followed the trapper custom of hauling a squaw around with him. For one thing his ties with Taos and Santa Fe had remained close enough that he had got back to the Spanish settlements pretty often and he had stayed a little more civilized than many beaver men who never left the mountains; who went for years without seeing a town or a white woman or a house or a street; who forgot how to sit in a chair, or at a table, or among social beings; and who had forgotten the feeling of a real bed and a floor, even a packed-earth floor, under their feet. He had not felt any need to carry a home around with him for he went home often enough to keep a sense of home in a house, in a town, among his own people.

But it had its advantages, having your own squaw with you. There were things to be said for it. You got to know each other intimately, and you settled into an easy, old-shoe, old married couple's way of living together. You learned more or less what to expect from each other and how to serve each other and how to make difficulties less difficult and hardships less hard and comforts more comfortable. Whether you were the man or the woman there was someone always there who belonged with you and who was, more or less and as much as was desired, loyal and proud and fond. It wasn't all physical, either, though there certainly was that. Sometimes, maybe oftenest, it was just sort of good to be with somebody whose voice and face were heard and seen every day, around and about, and whose ways, even of dressing or bathing in the river or starting at the back instead of the front to part their hair, were things you had together and didn't have with anybody else.

It put strings on you, though. Take a woman with you once and not only did she think she belonged with you wherever you went, you got used to having her with you and didn't much like being without her any more. You got used to the comfort, and Indian women knew how to take care of a man better than any other women in the world. They'd been taught it all their lives.

And they were a trouble wanting things. No squaw wanted any other squaw to have more than she did, in beads and shells and paint and foofooraw, and you got to where you had pride in her and in your ability to deck her out and you gave her more and more. Just like back home if your neighbor's wife had a fine pair of carriage horses you wanted your wife to drive a little finer pair, and if your neighbor's wife ordered furniture from New Orleans or St. Louis you didn't want it said you couldn't afford to let your wife order furniture from New Orleans and St. Louis.

They were a trouble, too, when the time came you wanted to cache your traps, leave the mountains, go home, settle down, marry, raise a family. Unless you'd grown a callus over every soft spot inside you, you had to make some sort of provision for them. You couldn't just abandon them. Some men, going home, passed their squaw on to a friend they knew would be decently good to her. Milt Sublette had done that with his Mountain Lamb. He'd given her to Joe Meek. Some took them back to their own village. Being a white man's squaw never hurt a woman's chances to get an Indian husband. But the arrangement was never permanent. However many years a man stayed in the mountains the time of parting always had to come unless you were willing to turn yourself into a full-time squaw man, and few men ever did.

He picked up a handful of sand, shook it, and let it sift through his fingers. You traded one thing for another was about the size of it. You bought yourself a lot more comfort. In any weather, under any conditions, you got yourself a lot more comfort. A squaw trailed along without complaining, stayed in the background doing the things you wanted a woman for, keeping the lodge, keeping food and clothing always ready, caring for your equipment and animals and understanding that when you wanted companionship it was with other men, completely different from what she gave you.

For this great comfort you traded some measure of freedom. But not much. Not much at all compared to what you traded when you took a real wife. And what was free? And what was just footlessness and loneliness?

Another handful of sand trickled through his fingers. He didn't know where Driant meant to winter. His job with him would be finished when he got him on the Green. Maybe he would winter near Driant, or with him, if he picked a place that was a good wintering place, or maybe he wouldn't. Maybe he and Mose and the rest of his boys would move out on their own. Maybe they would even come back south for the winter. Too soon to tell. Didn't much matter if Betsy went along. She could trail anywhere a man could. He could take her, easy enough. It would sure be nice to be as comfortable as she would make him. Winters were long and cold and rough in that north country. But—no need to decide right now.

A bunch of young Utes clattered up on their horses and tried to persuade him to go with them onto the flats and race his big roan. "Shoooo!" he said, grinning, "that roan would leave your critters so far behind you couldn't see his dust!"

They knew it. They just wanted to see the big roan run.

They wanted the excitement of racing with him even if it lasted only a few seconds. "Not now," he told them regretfully. "Mebbe later. I got things to do now."

They accepted it. Men of affairs, like Joe Fowler, had important things to discuss, to do. They raced off, crouched over their horses, yipping and whooping. They weren't much more than boys, too young yet to be allowed to go on the hunt, but old enough for the blood to boil high, to make them chesty and noisy. Next year they would go. And the next year, each would count his coup against an enemy, if he was lucky.

Watching them, Fowler shook his head. No wonder Utahs didn't like to follow the buffalo onto the plains and risk an encounter with plains Indians. Watch a Ute on horseback, with his short, stumpy legs, and you could tell he'd be no match for the superb horsemanship of Arapahoes, Cheyennes and Comanches. Utahs had had horses as long as any Indian—from the Spanish—but they were mountain Indians. Up and down was a Ute's trail, not away—so they never got the practice or the skills of the plains Indians with their flat sweeps for long, fast running. No, he wouldn't follow the buffalo onto the plains either, was he a Utah.

Fowler found Driant alone, resting, in the lodge which old Cholly had ordered erected for him and Noel. He knew that neither Driant nor Noel had accepted a woman last night and the lodge had a man's disorder in it. Driant's eyes were pain-darkened. He was sipping on brandy, which didn't go far toward curing that tormenting side. He spoke good morning courteously.

Fowler took in the uncomfortable lodge, the aching side, and the probable fever at one glance. "I'm gonna send my squaw over to do for you," he said. "She knows things that will ease that pain of yours and she can make you a better bed."

"I would be grateful," the Frenchman said.

Betsy brought a willow backrest, an armful of robes to make a softer bed, examined Driant's side and plastered it with a poultice of leaves and mud and beaver hair, brought him a deep bowl of her good fresh stew and some coffee, then went away.

Driant sighed. "A woman's touch, even an Indian woman's touch, is always the same. Comforting."

Fowler sat crosslegged near him. "That's their business."

He said then what he had not ever meant to say to this man and didn't like to say but felt he must. "Mr. Driant, don't you think you had better turn back to Taos? That side's not getting better and you're taking it a long way from home."

Driant moved restlessly and he said impatiently, "It is nothing, my friend. It comes and goes. This is a thing I must do. It was planned before I left St. Louis."

Fowler eyed him soberly. "About that, I don't care. That was St. Louis. You're here on Saguache Creek in a Ute village and you'll soon be in a wilderness like you never seen before. I don't know what's wrong with your innards, but it ain't Mex food. You been eating trail meat long enough if it was chili peppers and *frijoles* it would be better. I'm not one to give advice, especially when it's not asked for and maybe not wanted, but you don't know the country we're heading into and I do, and I got to warn you. If I was you I would take my men and start back to Taos soon as I felt better."

Driant's mouth twitched. "And you? You will go on, won't you?"

"It ain't my side hurting," Fowler said bluntly. "Sure. I'm going north."

"So am I, my friend," Driant said, gritting his teeth, "so am I."

Fowler rubbed his hand over his face. Well, he'd done what he could and it was more than he'd liked doing. A man had to make his own decisions. You went along all your life making decisions, never the same ones twice, some of them right, some of them wrong. You paid a big price for the wrong ones sometimes, but sometimes you squeaked through. You shaped your life with the decisions you made and each man had the right to shape it the way he had to or could. Only thing was, he didn't

have the right to shape another man's along with his and Fowler
didn't mean to let himself or his boys be shaped by Driant's
decision. If Driant got sick and couldn't ride, had to winter
up some place short of the Green, he must understand Fowler
would cut loose. That was what he had been trying to tell him.
Joe Fowler and his boys were going north. *"Bueno,"* he said,
"now let's talk."

They totaled up the things they had learned, quickly and
expertly, both men knowing they about balanced out between
good luck and bad. Good that the Arapahoes weren't on the
prowl. Bad that the cold was early. Good that the buffalo were
plentiful. Bad, but not much, that Bastro and Jordan were
trailing them. Good that they were so comfortably outfitted.
Bad, but again not much, that old Cholly had so few plews.
They left the ailing side out of it. That was settled. Driant
would ride and keep on riding until his side quit pestering him
finally or got so bad he couldn't ride any farther.

"How long will it take to finish the trading with these people?" Driant asked.

"Maybe tonight. Tomorrow, anyhow. We'll leave the day
after." He threw it in carelessly but figuring that Driant would
have sense enough to understand they couldn't go on pampering
him. It was push and ride, now, against the trapping season and
the weather.

"Oui," Driant said quickly. He touched the bandaged side
lightly. "Is there a way I may be excused from the feast and
smoking tonight?"

"Sure. You needn't of set to it last night if it bothered you."

Driant's voice was amused. "You mean, my friend, that as
long as you are present the courtesies are met, is that not it?"

"About the way of it," Fowler admitted. "I been coming to
old Cholly's village for some years."

Driant fingered his beard and laughed. "I gathered as much.
How did he come by that name . . . Cholly?"

"His Utah name sounds a little like it. Big Starr give him the name, first time we spent a season with 'em. The Spanish call him Oso Grande—Big Bear."

"He *is* a big fellow," Driant commented.

"And a smart one. Shrewd. He'll trick you trading if you don't watch him."

"Paul will manage it." He drew in his breath. "It will be a relief not to sit all those hours and listen and eat and smoke. I am not good with Indians, I fear."

Fowler flowed up to his long height. "Takes some learning. Betsy will change that poultice when it dries out. She'll probably keep you tied and bound the whole time but it will help you."

Driant's head dropped onto the backrest. "I will make the most of this brief respite."

Walking back to his own lodge, Fowler turned a mountain man's weather eye on the high blaze of blue sky, tested the wind for strength on his cheek, noted the heavier browning of the cottonwood leaves, and looked at the mountain summits. Overnight there was a powder of white on them. Change. Season's change, as slow and unsparing and inexorable as the sun coming up and going down each day. You thought winter came on swiftly in this country, but it didn't. If you watched, you could see it beginning in July with that sad lonesome purplish look over the peaks and valleys. And the sun came up later each morning and there was a longer coolness on the streams. It set earlier each evening and sometimes in late August the little shallow edges of the streams would be webbed with sharp needles of fine ice. The first thing you knew, early September, you saw a yellow leaf on a quaking asp, and there was red on oak scrub. Then one day, late in September maybe, you were standing in bright, hot sunshine in some high park and you looked up and saw a snowstorm sheeting across the peaks and then you said, winter's coming. But it had been coming for a long time.

Paul Noel and Mose were handling trade across a blanket

spread on the ground. Big Starr and young Pete were hanging around, Pete's bright-skinned youngster riding his shoulders. "She *like* to threw me out," Pete was telling, "didn't think I give her enough foofooraw. Wanted enough for her mother and her aunt and her sister and her brother's wife. God, she's got more kinfolks than ary squaw I ever seen! Was *seven* slept in that lodge last night, not speaking of me and her and this little feller."

He turned loose of the child's legs to count the seven relatives on his fingers. The youngster lurched and grabbed a handful of hair for balance. Pete yelped, pried the boy's hands loose, swung him onto the ground, whacked his fat little bottom and sent him scuttling. "Ain't he *some,* though? Look at them legs on him. They gonna last him out his life, all right."

"Gonna be bowlegged jist like all Utes," Starr said. "You made 'em *come,* all right, when you whelped him but you short-changed him on reach."

"Well, hell, he ain't *all* mine," Pete said.

"Mebbe he ain't any your'n," Big Starr jibed.

Young Pete poked him in the ribs. "He's mine, all right. Them least two ain't, but that un is mine. She didn't have no chance fer him *not* to be *that* winter."

Fowler grinned and went into his lodge. He took his bridle from its peg and hefted his saddle. Betsy scrambled up from her work, scolding. She would bring his horse. He should not do such things for himself. It was for her to do such things for him. He put her in a bad light. The other women would talk together and say she was lazy letting her man serve himself. He was always doing things which caused gossip—cutting wood, skinning meat, bringing water, saddling and caring for his own animals. When would he learn that these things were a woman's concern? When would he learn that such things were beneath a man's dignity—that they made him look small.

Fowler laughed. "My dignity can stand it," he said, "and I'm a pretty big man to be whittled down in size. I don't like anybody handling my horse but myself, you know that."

She subsided, still muttering. She didn't ask where he was going. A woman didn't. That, always, was a man's concern— where he was going, for how long, and with whom. But small courtesies were still ingrained in Fowler. He said, "I'm going out on the flats with the boys."

She watched him go, made an errand outside to watch him ride away, her eyes following him with affection. When he had dwindled in size, she turned briskly to work again. They would need these new soft robes during the long journey and winter . . . and the pemmican she had made . . . and the bags of fat . . . and this brass kettle . . . and her bag of sewing materials . . . and these new blankets . . . and her bag of roots and herbs and medicines.

And this . . . and this . . . and so.

five

ON AROUND the foothills for two days, then up the valley of the San Luis where the river pinched in, and then the high lift over Poncha Pass where the air was thin and sharp and piney with the smell of blue spruce. Down the other side, across swift brawling cascades, down from the timber into a high tableland, folded with tumbling, rumpling hills.

They forded the Arkansas well above its great gorge, near its headwaters, where it was so clear the sand of its bottom glittered in the strong sun. The high unnamed peaks tiered and massed to their left, west and north, dark green up the slope, aspens as bright as brass above the green, then gray boulder and rock, beetling and striated, crowned with the eternal snow.

They kept angling north and a little east and climbed out finally on a crest which looked down on a spread of plateau—a valley, a basin, a high park in the mountains; a hole, in the mountain man's language.

Fowler, leading the strung-out train, pulled up and let the big roan breathe. He leaned his weight on both hands on the pommel and slowly, carefully swept the basin below from one end to the other.

Pierre Driant came up beside him. "Bayou Salade?"

"Bayou Salade—South Park, Old Park. It's called several things." He continued his scrutiny until, satisfied, his shoulders eased back and slouched. He took off his hat and beat it against his knee, shaping it up.

"Anything?" Driant asked.

"Nary a thing," Fowler said, putting the hat back on, "not a blessed Indian. No Rapahoes, and no Utes neither."

"What does that mean? Weren't you expecting to find your Ute friends here?"

Fowler was still sweeping the basin. "Not specially. They could of made their meat fast and got out. Or they could of found the buffalo further south and not needed to come into the park. Or their medicine could of told 'em it wasn't very smart to follow this close on the heels of them Rapahoes. We may find their sign we get down in the hole. This far away it's a little hard to tell."

Driant nodded. "Yes. I wondered." His eyes swept the valley floor. "It is a beautiful valley."

"One of the prettiest," Fowler said. "She's about trapped out, though. Too handy."

Driant looked around at the mountain rims and he laughed grimly. "Handy? *Mon Dieu!*"

The ramparts were massed eastward beyond the park. The mountains they had come through, whose spine they stood on now, curved around to meet the ramparts northward. The corrugated hills flowed away south. Through the grassy floor of the park a stream wandered, the sun glinting off its water. "The river?" Driant asked.

"South Platte. She heads up there." Fowler pointed to the high peaks north.

It was a true basin, rimmed by the mountains, laced with a dozen mountain streams falling down their canyons to brake on the basin floor and join the Platte. They flowed in and out of lakes which were like crystal links on a chain. The lakes and streams were bordered with trees. Bank willows were tipped with saffron now. Clumps of aspen were yellow. Alders were blood-dark. And the autumn grasses were curing out russet. The whole floor of the park looked like a rusty velvet rug, patterned with the cross-hatched silver of the streams and lakes, toned over with autumn lemon and orange and gold and russet and a little green here and there, all of it sparkled over by the glitter of the sun. High country, where wind was born and blew lonely as a willow flute; where clouds were speared on the horns of peaks and split and sheeted rain on rock and talus; where snow fell more quietly than breath and piled higher than young trees.

Driant shivered. "It's too big. It's high and lonesome. It's scary and too beautiful. It's too solitary. A man is a puny thing in these mountains."

Fowler looked at him curiously. He had never heard anyone say such a thing. High, yes. Lonesome, yes—but who minded it? Beautiful, if you wanted to name it so. Solitary, sure—that's the way you wanted beaver country to be. You begrudged every other man who cut your trail. You got out of country where there were too many hunting. And that's what had ruined this park. Too handy. Too many crossing and recrossing it.

He had never in his life felt puny in the mountains. There they were, big—sure. But there was nothing in a mountain to make a man feel puny. A mountain was a dead thing. No hurt or harm in it, except what it could hide from you. You couldn't move a mountain, but you could sure go around or over them and you sure never let one stand in your way. Use your think-piece and you could outwit a mountain, any day.

Fowler shrugged. It was the French in Driant. The French, all of them, even Fouchette, were tender toward things in nature which Americans never noticed. Easily elated, easily depressed, they went up and down like a thermometer.

He scrutinized the Frenchman. The man lived with pain as his constant companion these days. He ate with it, slept with it, rode with it. It sat on him like the flesh on his bones. He accommodated it as best he could, saying little, only his eyes showing its steady ravagement. They were dark holes of endurance and the great bruises under them pouched heavier and more purple daily.

Fowler shifted his glance back to the basin. The man was game. Say that for him. Fowler had had a toothache once that rode with him three full weeks. Not a sharp lancing pain, just a throbbing dull ache that never quit. He'd nearly gone out of his wits till he got where he could have it yanked. What Driant felt must be like that. But he kept his temper and he kept his patience and he kept going on.

Fowler narrowed his eyes and pointed. "See them little black specks across there on them benches? Other side the hole?"

Driant peered. "I see them, *oui*. They are moving. They are sheep? Mountain goats?"

Fowler laughed. "This mountain air is deceiving. Them are buffalo. We'll eat fat hump tonight."

Driant grimaced. "If we had to depend upon my eyesight for our meat, my friend, I fear we should go hungry."

He eased in the saddle and swung around as Fowler twisted to look behind. The brigade had topped out and they were bunched, breathing their horses, looking down in the valley. Mose, Big Starr, young Pete, Fouchette were pointing, gesticulating. Fowler chuckled. "They're telling, no doubt, about the time they chased some horse-thieving Shians into this hole and raided 'em before daylight and got their cavvyard back."

"They did that? Truly?"

"Oh, sure. You don't let an Indian get away with your cavvy, can you help it."

Betsy was off the horse Fowler had bought from old Cholly for her, tightening the cinch after the long climb. Fowler watched her soberly, then grinned. She rode like a lump of dough—all give and easy. But she rode, and that was what counted. He wondered if a wild bronc could pitch her off.

Driant smiled, watching her. "Your squaw, she is a capable woman."

"She's pretty good," Fowler admitted.

She was looking to his pack mules now and from the set of her face he knew she was muttering—scolding the mules, scolding the packs for slipping, scolding the scrub that had scraped the packs awry, scolding the mountain for the long climb. But she was also placating. Since everything had life and spirit—

trees, rocks, water, sand, wind, fire, the utensils of daily use, the hides and clay and reeds and grasses that made them, the clothing one wore—everything must constantly be placated, must not be offended, must be pled with—to be kind, to be friendly, not to be an enemy and troublesome. All the right things must be said, the right things done, if one would live with the great power dwelling in all things and in every individual thing.

Learning that Betsy was going with Fowler, young Pete's squaw had squalled to go also. But young Pete had been adamant. "With three kids? My God, no! I ain't got time or room to pack a whole Utah village around with me."

She cajoled, then threatened, then when she could not have her way pitched his gear out of the lodge. He collected it and moved in with Big Starr and laughed at her. "Sister, you ain't misputtin' me none atall. Easy come, easy go. There's plenty more Injun squaws. This coon'll git him a little Shoshone or Naypursie that'll make you look like the tail end of nothin'."

Fouchette, who had decided to take his own squaw, joshed him. "Why you not take her, my fran'? The papooses, they help keep the back warm."

"Not three of 'em," Pete grumbled. "They don't keep you nothin' but awake. And they wet on you."

"But what is a little wet?"

"It ain't a little. It's a river! Take yer own squaw, Lou. I'll git me another'n and make a fresh start."

One of the greenhorns, the youngster named Lashly, also took a squaw. The boys jibed at him. "Ye'll wish ye hadn't," Big Starr said. "When ye see them Shoshone gals or one of them Sweetwater Shians, ye'll wish ye'd left that Ute woman behind."

"Until I see 'em," young Lashly said levelly, "I'll make out with her."

He was a colt-legged kid, long in the flanks, with a shock of sandy hair and steady gray eyes. Eighteen, nineteen years old, Fowler judged, the boy knew how to keep his mouth shut and his hands busy. He was learning fast. Watching him, studying him, Fowler thought if he kept on the whole season the way he was beginning, he was going to prove up fine—make a real beaver man. Next to Old Dan he was the best of the crop of Driant's hands. He'd picked a good steady squaw, too, which showed more judgment than you'd expect at his age.

Fowler raised his hand and signaled for the train to move. They wound down into the valley and made their camp in a copse of alders and willows which hid them from prying eyes.

Fowler sent the men out in pairs to comb the valley for sign and he and Big Starr rode south toward the hills. They sighted a larger herd of buffalo which were grazing slowly, moving almost imperceptibly southward, and which obviously had not been hunted and alarmed. They did not find any sign of old Cholly's young men—not an old encampment, nor any tracks, nor any evidence of a hunt. Fowler studied, watching the buffalo.

Big Starr rode a circle and came back. "They must not have come clean up into the park," he said. "Biggest herd must be down in them hills further."

Fowler shifted in the saddle and his spurs clinked. "Probably," he said. It was the likeliest answer. The Utah scouts had reported Arapaho in the basin. They had reported the Arapaho gone. Cholly's boys wouldn't have been afraid to come into the basin—unless further sign had been found. He would know more about that when Mose and Old Dan Sutton came in, and the other boys. But, on the face of it, it looked as if the south-moving buffalo had been encountered below the park.

"*Bueno,*" he said abruptly. "Let's go. This herd will make all the meat we can pack."

"Shore," Starr agreed. "Two days' kill, if them greenhorns kin shoot."

They loped easily back toward camp, the eyes of both, by habit, wary and constantly scanning. "Joe," Big Starr said suddenly, "is Driant aimin' to winter on the Siskadee?"

"He's not said."

"We aimin' to pull out we git thar?"

"If he's aimin' to winter there, yes. Wouldn't nobody but an elk winter in that wind tunnel. He said for us to get him there. We get him there, we're done."

"*If* we git him thar," Starr said.

"Yes."

Fowler's spurs touched the big roan's ribs and in his thighs he felt the big muscles slide and stretch. He pulled away from Starr. He didn't like to talk about Driant's chances. The man was doing all he could. He, Joe Fowler, was doing all he could. Driant would either go under or he wouldn't, but it surprised Fowler how much he hoped he wouldn't. He hadn't expected to feel much about this man. Some, yes. But not so that his sickness would drag on him. His circle of friends and trusted associates had been closed a long time and he hadn't expected to open it, even this small slit, again. But the fellow was so damned game you couldn't help wishing he'd make it, and if he didn't you knew you were going to be sorry about it.

It was one thing to put out every season hale and sound and take your chances. Never was a man put out didn't know it could be his last, but you never gave it much thought. You learned a little something each time about how to keep your hair safe. What you mostly learned was that about all you'd ever learn about Indians was that you weren't ever going to learn much. Because they didn't have your white man's mind and you didn't have their Indian mind.

But it was another thing to put out for as rough a season as you could ask for, with your innards wrong in some way and your guts hurting and not knowing if you could make it or not. Foolish, sure, but damned game.

Back at camp, they found a few men already in. Others rode in in pairs. Nothing but old sign, they said. The Arapahoes had camped there, and there, and there. Old fires and some meat bones told the story. No sign of any trouble with Cholly's boys. No fight. It looked good and a wave of easiness ran over the camp.

"No sign of Bastro and the Jordan feller, either," young Pete reported.

Fowler shook his head. "Wouldn't have expected any. He's likely a couple of days behind."

Mose and Old Dan Sutton didn't get back to camp until after dark. They talked as they ate. Old Dan said, "We cut their sign, all right. They trailed out up a canyon over thar," he waved eastward, "up a easy slope. Headed east by north. Sign about three weeks old. I tell 'ee them Rapahoes has got a big cavvyard. Made a big steal on somebody. Is some Injuns some place is missin' a heap of animals."

Fowler nodded and looked at Mose. Mose threw a rib bone away and reached for another. "We follered up to whur they topped out the canyon onto the main trail up the mountain. Warn't no use goin' no further, 'thout we aimed to foller 'em clean home. Either they kept goin' or they're still up thar. Last camp, up by a spring at the head of the canyon, was old."

Fowler nodded again. The Arapahoes could be in their own country on the North Platte by now, or they could still be messing around some place. Whichever, it had to do, and it was good enough. Just the same, he told Pedro to put three men on horse guard every night they were in the basin, and he and Big Starr, young Pete and Mose took turn about on the daylight shift of camp guard. No use risking a surprise.

2.

They made their surround the next morning and killed meat, shooting until their guns were hot. The swampers and squaws took three days, then, to cut out the meat, strip it, and jerk it

over slow fires, while the hands worked the streams of the basin
rapidly for beaver.

They worked in pairs, as usual. Mose and Big Starr teamed
up; Fouchette and young Pete went out together. Old Dan
linked himself with Ben Lashly. That had been happening
more and more often since Coon Bastro had left. Old Dan was
a picker. He had noticed, too, that young Lashly had the mak-
ings of a beaver man.

Fowler didn't hunt. He turned blacksmith. They had some
climbing to do when they left the basin and some rough country.
He and Pedro and the Ute halfbreed, Shell, went over the
whole cavvyard, hoof by hoof, to make ready for it. Driant
watched them, helped a little, walked around some, and sat in
the sun a lot and seemed to feel better. Noel went out with a
couple of the Driant hands each day.

The catch was pretty good and the nights were full of the
stories of each day's work. Mose fell in a beaver pond. "This
coon cain't swim a lick," he complained. "He warn't sired by
no beaver. I like to drowned. That fool Starr jist stood thar
on the bank and helt me a pole. Wouldn't even git his feet wet.
Jist helt me that saplin' and fist over fist I clumb up it, him
standin' thar bustin' his sides laughin' at me."

Starr said mildly, "If he warn't the outlandishest lookin'
critter you ever seen. Flouncin' and flappin' and yellin' he was
drowndin'. Like to flounced that pond plumb dry. Skeered
the beaver over to the other side the mountains, likely."

Mose glared at him. "Next time, I'm aimin' to crown ye with
that pole. Ye could of fotched me in a heap quicker'n you did.
You was enjoyin' yerself too much."

Starr was plaintive. "I got ye out, didn't I?"

"Barely. I shuck fer a hour 'fore I got warmed up from that
dousin'."

Old Dan told of a black bear that chased Lashly up a tree,
and he brought in the forepaws to prove he'd killed it.

"Your gun misfired, did it?" Fowler asked the youngster.

Lashly turned red. "I shot too hasty, I reckon. First time me and a bear ever come face to face and I got excited. He just kept coming. Dan told me after where to shoot."

"It takes some learning," Fowler said.

Fouchette and young Pete were very mysterious about where they were working. For two days they brought in the biggest loads and they were queried by the others as to the stream they'd found. "We found it," Pete bragged, "and we'll keep it. Ye'll have to track us to find it."

"If Pete don't break his dam' neck," Fouchette said. "He always go too fast. Leave me behind. Lay his rifle on de bank. He gonna lose his hair wan of dese days."

Fowler looked at Pete sharply. "Pete, I told you. Stay with your partner."

"Aw, he ain't never fur behind. Mostly in sight. Fouchette's allus bumblin' around."

"Some day," Fouchette warned, pointing his pipe at Pete, "some Shian or Rapaho is gonna shoot you. They be hidin' in de bush. You be in de creek. Your gun be onna bank. Boom! Bang! Young Pete gonna be dead."

"Pete," Fowler said seriously, "Lou's right. Now, you hear me. You're asking for trouble rustling around by yourself. Them beaver ain't gonna run away. You stay with your partner."

"*Bueno, bueno,*" Pete said, his hands flapping impatiently. "I'll stick with old Granny hyar, makes ye feel any easier."

"It ain't just my feelings," Fowler said. "You bring trouble on yourself, you'll likely bring it on the whole outfit."

"I said all right. You needn't to keep on harpin' on it."

Young Pete had more liking for Joe Fowler than any other man he'd ever known. Joe was a man didn't claim to know everything, which was the mark of a good man who knew more than most but didn't put on airs about it. Wise as an old coon, Joe was still listening and learning. He had never known Joe Fowler to let hurry goad him into imprudence. That was why

Joe was leading brigades and he was still following him. He wished he was more like him, but he knew he never would be. He was just cut from a different bolt of cloth. He had been with Joe a length of time now, and he thought he probably always would be. He was a Fowler man and he didn't know anything better or actually want anything better. He was ashamed Joe had had to call him down.

Driant's hands were doing well enough with their trapping, also, although Old Dan's nose was a little out of joint at being beaten by Fouchette and young Pete. He was even more glum and silent than usual. "This child never did like this hole," he quarreled, sniffing the air as if it smelled. "Been too much comin' and goin' hereabouts. When we movin' on?"

"Take one more day," Fowler said. "We'll put out day after tomorrow."

3.

But the next day young Pete and Fouchette came in early, empty-handed. Fouchette's face was dark and young Pete was in a faunching rage. He stormed over where Fowler was salving a dry patch on the big roan's leg, thundering mad, his eyes blazing. "Traps stole," he snapped, "every blasted goddamned trap me and Lou put out has been stole. Bastro and Jordan run the whole line and takened all twelve of 'em. I'm not askin' ye now, Joe, I'm tellin' ye—I'm goin' after that bastard. You oughtta let me cut his gizzard out before. Fouchette and me are gonna git him good this time."

Fowler handed the pot of salve to Betsy. Her breath hissed in and she slewed her eyes at him. Fowler wiped his hands. "Sure it was him?"

"Sure I'm sure! Who else could it be? You think we ain't watched for sign? Ain't no Injuns anywhere near this hole.

Ain't been that first sign of 'em. That sonuvabitch has just snuck in and cold-camped so's we wouldn't know he was around. Waited for his chance and tuck it. Well, it'll be his last one. I'm gonna keelhaul that Salt River roarer for good. You ain't tellin' me nay, neither, Joe."

Fowler took the last of the grease off his hands and Betsy took the soft old piece of deerskin from him. He looked up and around the rim of mountains and he felt heavy. This was something Pete had to do now. It would be something any man had to do. Every man was his own man, most of the time. But there were ways of doing and acting and feeling common to all, and this was one of them. When you were a little boy, sometimes another kid would draw a line in the dirt and dare you to cross it. You almost always did because if you didn't your size got so small you could feel it in your waistband and it wasn't a feeling to like.

Maybe it *had* been a mistake not to let Bastro and Young Pete fight it out. Maybe it had been a worse mistake not to take the time to recover what he'd stolen from Pierre Driant. A man got to feeling mighty big when he got by with something. But Bastro had drawn a line in the dirt now and he had drawn it on Lou and young Pete. They had to cross it.

"Pedro," Fowler called, "cut out two fresh horses, will you? And a mule."

He rubbed a scar on one thumb and looked around the mountain rims again. "Mose and Starr oughtta be in 'fore long."

"This ain't nothin' to do with them," Pete said. "Me and Fouchette kin take them two."

"Well."

Fowler walked with him where Fouchette was already helping Pedro cut out the horses. "We'll haul out in the morning," he said. "Make for the North Fork. You don't catch up to us time we get there, we'll be moving along up thataway. Towards the hot springs in the Middle Park."

Fouchette nodded. "Me an' Pete, we finish dis *cochon* quick. We ketch you pronto."

Pierre Driant came up and in a few words Fowler told him about the theft. Driant nodded and walked away quickly. Fouchette's squaw brought his bedroll and a pack of food. He lashed them behind his saddle. Pete brought up his own bedroll. When Driant returned, he handed young Pete a knife. "Return this to our friend," he said.

Young Pete thrust it in his belt and grinned. "Right between the ribs."

Driant flashed a smile briefly. "It was what I had in mind. If he has not ruined my horse, Pete, I would be grateful to have him back. The beast I am riding has a hard gait."

"We'll bring him," Pete promised.

Betsy had laid a parflêche pouch on the ground and was doing various things with colored powders and small sticks and feathers and roots, mumbling to herself as she passed things from one hand to the other, made prayers and incantations. She approached Pete and Fouchette and made signs over them, smeared stuff under their eyes, on their cheeks, around their mouths, and blew yellow powder about. Pete fanned it away. "Quit it! That's enough medicine. Don't blow no more of that stuff in my eyes."

Fouchette, more superstitious, was more patient. "Make *good* medicine," he told Betsy, "make heap good medicine."

His squaw tied a prayer stick to his blanket roll, a small stick with various little articles, a shell, some beads, a few feathers tied to it. Unceasing and placating prayer would thus accompany him constantly, be with him where he went, interceding, protecting. Betsy had made a prayer stick for young Pete which she tied to his bedroll.

Fowler watched them ride away then and he wished Old Dan Sutton had never taken up with Coon Bastro and brought him into Driant's party. But he put his feeling of exasperation down.

There was more than one scoundrel in the mountains. It was a good place for men running from the law to hide, for men who for one reason or the other couldn't live with their fellows, for men whose sense of honesty and decency and justice were on a lower level than those of their fellow men. You were bound to run afoul of one of these men now and then. Bastro was obviously one of them.

There was a lot of talk among the trappers as they came in and learned what had happened. Old Dan's snarl rose into a high whine as he told what he thought of Coon Bastro. "This child hunted with him a season is all. He made the beaver *come* now, or I wouldn't say so. He warn't no slack-off in work, neither. Done his part. Good eye fer sign and honest, fur as ye could tell. But do 'ee hyar now, thievin' horses and traps from a man's own kind don't shine with this coon. Bastro has turned renegade and ruint hisself in the mountains."

"He won't never git a day's work with *no* outfit if this child has his way," Big Starr said.

He was feeling aggrieved that Pete hadn't waited for him to come into camp so he could go with him. He was missing out on a big scrape and didn't like it.

4.

The sun was down and long shadows were casting across the basin when the squaws went out to gather wood for the night. There was suddenly a wailing which brought every man to his feet, reaching for his gun. "What the hell . . . ?" Big Starr began.

"Sh-sh-sh-," Fowler hissed and he motioned flat-handed for quiet. The men silently rolled into shadows and behind tree trunks. Young Lashly stepped up beside Fowler. They listened intently.

The high keening of the first squaw was joined by the squalls and wails of the other two. "What is it?" Lashly asked. "They been ambushed?"

"Mebbe," Fowler said. "Listen, now . . . "

But there was no sound of an ambush. No sound of horse's feet, no voices, no shots, no mixed confusion that would indicate the women were being taken. There was just the women crying and wailing.

Fowler grunted all at once. "That's their grieving cry. They ain't hurt. They ain't scared. Something's making 'em grieve." He walked out toward the women and Ben Lashly followed him. Some others, Mose, Driant, Big Starr, Old Dan, trailed along.

They came upon the women huddled on the ground beside the trail, their wood dropped, all of them with their hair loosened and veiled around their faces. Fouchette's boy, on his mother's back, frightened by her weeping, had joined his wails to hers.

As he came up, Fowler spoke to Betsy and she ceased her wailing long enough to reply to him. The prayer stick which Fouchette's squaw had made for him had fallen loose. It had been found here . . . in this place. He would have no protection where he was going. Something bad would happen to him.

The tightness in Fowler's chest loosened. He looked at Mose and Big Starr and on past them to Old Dan. He pointed to the prayer stick Fouchette's squaw was hugging to her breast. Not a man smiled or made light of the woman's fears. They had been too long in the mountains to mock Indian ways and, to some extent, with this fetish or that, they themselves believed in medicine. You went too long in a bad luck streak of not finding beaver, a little medicine was sometimes a help. Your gun took to throwing crooked on you, medicine might straighten it out to throw plumb center again. If every Injun you met seemed bent on raising your hair, make a little medicine and it might overcome some of their cantankerousness. The men weren't awed by the happening, but they understood how the women felt and were sobered themselves. Even Driant understood. "I would be uncomfortable if I lost my beads," he said.

Young Lashly tried to comfort his squaw.

"Leave her alone," Fowler told him. "Don't try to stop her. They got to screech long enough to scare off the spirits still hovering about. Some spirits made that stick fall. They got to frighten 'em away. They'll quit when they think they've done it."

The men went back to the camp, and word of the incident spread among the swampers and meat hunters. Most of them were French and an easy prey to fear and gloom. Fowler made no attempt to lighten it. You had to work through these things your own way. What was in a man's heart and mind was his own mystery. He had to deal with it himself. Every man had to walk his lonesome places.

Driant puffed on his pipe beside Fowler. "How will the women placate the spirits now?"

"Dunno," Fowler said. "All that howling does something. And they'll think of something else. Whatever it is we got to go along with 'em or there won't be no peace amongst 'em."

"*Mais, oui,*" Driant agreed. "That is understood, my friend."

After supper, Betsy told Fowler what the women wanted. There should be a big smoke and dance, twelve men participating. And there would be the twelve poles of power . . . and there would be the dancing before the poles . . . and there would be the drum which Shell, the Utah, would beat . . . and there would be the eagle feathers to send the prayers to Fouchette . . . and there would be the drifts of colored powders crossed into the earth and danced upon and trod into the earth, so that the earth, too, would be full of power and prayer.

Fowler considered. The twelve-pole dance was just about the most powerful dance the Utahs had. It was used mostly before going to war. It would take all night and most of the men. "That's too big a dance," he said, "six poles and six men. We'll take turns."

Betsy shook her head. He did not understand. It would take a powerful dance to make a big enough prayer to overcome the power of the spirit which had caused the prayer stick to fall. She told him softly but insistently, her eyes full of apprehension, that the power of this spirit could fall on the whole party if it were not vanquished. It must be appeased and it must be shown that its medicine was not as strong as theirs.

"Betsy," Fowler said reasonably, "a twelve-pole dance wouldn't give nobody any rest all night. The boys'd be too beat to put out tomorrow. You'll just have to make do with a six-pole dance and me and Starr and Mose and the others'll dance extra time."

She wasn't happy about it but she accepted it and went to go with the other women to cut the poles.

Fowler sighed heavily and reported to Driant, who chuckled. "A six-pole dance, eh? I have never seen such a dance. I shall be interested."

"I expect," Fowler told him, "you'll have to dance a little. The men with the most power must do the dancing. There's nobody in the outfit has got as much power as you."

"He is not well enough to dance this heathen dance," Noel said sharply. "This is foolishness, Pierre."

"Even so, Paul, I shall dance a while. These things must be honored. When I falter, you can take my place."

Noel scowled, stood abruptly and walked away. Driant watched him go. "Paul is a good man," he said thoughtfully, "but he does not have much patience with new ways and new ideas. He must do all things his own way." He brushed ashes from his shirt. "Tell me about this dance. I have no idea what I must do."

"Just watch me and Mose and Big Starr. We've seen it. We halfway know what to do. Likely we'll mess it up and the women will squall, but maybe it'll satisfy 'em." He laughed. "A little brandy would give us more staying power."

"It will be furnished," Driant promised.

The fire lit the court the women made with the poles and, stripped to their waists, painted, feathers stuck in their hair, eagle feathers in each hand to waft the prayers on their way, the men danced solemnly. Fowler, Mose, Old Dan, Young Lashly, Big Starr and Pierre Driant led off. They would be relieved as they tired, but Fowler knew he and his boys were in for a long night. Betsy counted on them for the most power and she would be distressed if they weakened.

Shell's drum was a hollow piece of sycamore log with a deerskin for a head. His palms stroked it steadily, pacing the dance. Shell looked the way a Utah ought to look doing something as important as stroking out the pattern for a pole dance. He looked like a piece of brown rock, his mind turned inward to the variations of the dance, feeding them down to the palms of his hands, so that he was there, in the same way a rock would be there, and with no more knowledge of being there.

The dance went on and on until Fowler felt like a sleepwalker. His legs were heavy and ached in the knees but they obeyed the drum beat automatically. A man dropped out now and then, his place taken by another, and refreshed himself at the brandy keg.

Pierre Driant held out considerably longer than Fowler thought he would, longer perhaps than he should, for when he dropped out he was purple-faced and wet with sweat. From the corner of his eyes Fowler saw him bend over, gasping, and stumble to the group of seated men. He also noticed the confusion for a moment as nobody took his place. It should have been Noel, to keep the big power going, but the man who came forward finally was one of the camp swampers. He was supposed to keep silence but Fowler broke it. "Where's Noel?"

"He is not here," the man whispered. "He went away."

Fowler swore softly and glanced at Betsy. She was scowling and unhappy and he judged the power had been broken a little. Suddenly he felt ridiculous and angry at himself for allowing this piece of craziness. Anybody saw them dancing around these poles would think they were lunatics and be more than half right. He must have been deranged to consider it. He wanted to drop out and call the whole thing off. Instead his feet moved on, shuffling, advancing, retreating, circling, and his hands kept on waving the eagle feathers. He shuttered his eyes and made his mind a blank and heard the drum in the beat of his pulse and the hinge of his legs and suddenly felt tireless and limber and easy-jointed and knew now he could keep on till it was over.

It was over as the first pale light of daybreak rose above the mountains. Watching intently, Betsy suddenly signaled to the halfbreed and the drum stopped abruptly, even its reverberation silenced by the firm flat palms. The dancers took a few more steps before their consciousness was pierced by the silence of the drum. Betsy's hands signaled to Fowler and he spoke. *"Bueno,* boys. That's enough. It's done."

They dragged over to the fire, put on their shirts and dropped to the ground. Quickly the women put pots of food on to heat and the swampers surged around with coffee. Mose laced his cup with brandy and swigged at it. "If *that* don't make them spirits come, ain't nothin' will. This coon is shore flattened out."

Only Fowler and Big Starr and young Lashly had danced without relief through the entire dance, and Betsy served Fowler with deep pride in his strength and power. Much power, she told him, he had much power. The spirits would know with such a man dancing their strength was too feeble.

"If he's got so much power," Mose drawled, "how come the rest of us had to dance, too? Whyn' jist Joe do the hull thing? Don't look to me was any use the rest of us warpin' ourselves to a frazzle if he was so powerful."

Betsy gave him a disdainful look, told him obscenely that while his power was so small it was not needed, he was so repulsive an object he was perhaps useful in frightening the spirits. Then she marched huffily away.

Mose wrinkled his nose. "I got a feelin' I don't stand very high with Betsy."

"You sprung that trap on yourself," Fowler said, laughing.

"I reckon I did. God, this coon's too old fer such doin's. I've done hamstrung myself." He nudged Fowler. "Lookit Starr, willya? Lettin' Lou's woman wait on him hand and foot. Ain't he the big chief now?"

Fouchette's squaw was serving Big Starr with pride and honor and the big man was lolled back allowing all the attention he could get. Mose grunted in disgust. "He'll be lettin' her spoon-feed him next."

"Wish it was you, don't you?" Fowler jibed.

"When I want a squaw to tend me," Mose retorted, "I can git one. No, I ain't wishin' it was me."

Ben Lashly's young squaw was almost overcome by the prowess of her man. Doe-eyes limpid with love she hovered near him, touching him a little, handing things, trying to foresee his wants. Fowler watched the boy keep his dignity, refusing this, allowing that, asserting his manhood and his mastery. He had a swift soft-ness for the youth of the boy, his illusions and innocence. They would go, all of them—youth, illusions, innocence—hardly with his knowing, eroded away slowly so that he could not say when or how they had gone. But they were things Fowler remem-bered in himself, with some wistfulness for their passing. It was good to be that young. It would be better if you knew how good it was.

The youngster caught Fowler's eye and he turned red, but he grinned manfully. It's foolish, the grin said, but it's fun. Fowler nodded, agreeing.

Noel came out of his lodge, scowled when he saw the cluster of men and walked briskly over. "I suppose," he said to Fowler, "we won't move today, after that all-night *fandango* of yours."

Fowler stuck the tip of his knife delicately into a piece of meat and lifted it to his mouth. He chewed it slowly and with relish. When he had swallowed he said, "Why, yes. We'll put out soon as we get done eating. Was you thinking a one-night *fandango* would weary us so bad? Now, if it had been three, four days hand-running, we might need some rest. But I recollect one time we danced four days and nights and rode fifty miles when we got done. When was that, Starr?"

Starr rose to the occasion. "Couple of seasons ago, I reckon. We was on the San Juan and old Cholly was makin' medicine fer the warpath. We danced with 'em, then rid into Taos."

"Of course," Fowler said gently and apologetically, "we was a little likkered up and wasn't to say feeling much. Don't know as we could do it cold sober."

Noel snorted and poured a mug of coffee.

Fowler searched for another tidbit in the bowl, carefully moving the less choice pieces aside. "Mr. Driant asleep yet?"

"He's asleep," Noel snapped.

"I would wake him if I was you," Fowler said, "so as not to delay the leaving."

Noel flushed and swung about.

Big Starr eyed his retreating back reflectively. "That little *mangeur-de-lard* is about ready to be cut down to size," he said, "and this coon is half froze to do the job."

"Don't trouble yourself," Fowler said, standing and stretching. "He'll get whittled down without anybody's help."

six

THEY HAD blue silk skies these October mornings, but autumn had come to the high country. It was shaking cold under the peaks until the sun got up, and ice had come in thin glass across the ponds and streams. Some mornings there was hoar frost on the dried grasses and spruces and the whole unbelievable country glittered like spun sugar frosting. The golden light of their first days in the high country was going and all the golden tones and hues were darkening. The light was later coming up over the mountain rims and it had none of the glory and the flame and the sunburst splendor it had had in September. It was a darker light now, blued and slated by the gray rock peaks, shadowed sooner and deeper, and sooner gone. Down in the canyon bottoms a new black showed and rock and moss and dark spruces were somber with it. Pierre Driant's French people were almost always melancholy these days.

But the pelts they took as they moved slowly northward were early-prime, thick, glossy, rich, and heavy. While Pierre Driant's French swampers gloomed in the grayness, the trappers gloated over their catches. "Look at that," Mose would say, tangling his fingers in the thick fur, "jist look at it! October prime!"

Mose's eyes glittered at the richness and his mouth worked as if he could taste the quality on his tongue. "Only full prime is purtier," he told young Lashly. "And sometimes not so purty. Come a season of thick ice and a long cold, they git ga'nted down. The pelts ain't so thick then." He stroked the thick pelt. "This was real beaver country once. When me and Joe first hunted it. We taken fifty packs to Taos more'n one time. Jist the two of us." His bile and spleen rose up and spilled over. "Them days you could work a season and never cut trail of nobody. Stay out nine months and never see another living soul but Injuns. Nowadays the mountains is workin' alive with hunters. Like a big ant hill, with a army of ants swarmin' around. Ye can't go *nowheres* 'thout runnin' into another party of trappers. Ye can't hunt thirty days 'thout cuttin' trail somewheres."

"We ain't seen nobody yet," young Lashly said.

"Because the brigades figger this country is trapped out down hyar is why. They're north of hyar. Doin' the same thing up thar they done down hyar." He spat in disgust. "Gittin' as populous as St. Louis 'round hyar."

They stayed east of the divide a few days until they hit the North Fork of the South Platte, then they began to angle roughwest. Fowler's intention was to take them straight up the park system, from South Park up through the Middle Park and on up through the North Park. There they would hit the North Platte and follow it along a piece, then cross the alkali flats over to the Green.

An easier way, but longer, would have been to stay east of the divide all the way up, follow down the Sweetwater west. But his two-pronged purpose, to trap as he moved and to get there before deep winter, made Fowler choose the rougher, shorter, furricher route. Though they trapped as they moved, they moved steadily. With a party their size it didn't take long to trap out the streams—a day or two here, a day or two there, as they moved.

After the first week the men began to speak of Pete and Fouchette, wondering about them, where they were, why they didn't catch up. "Looks like they ought to be back by now. Unless they've run into trouble."

"Reckon they've had their topknots lifted? Gone under?"

"It wouldn't be surprising. *Or* they mought of been put afoot."

"Or," another added plainly, "Coon could of laid for 'em and got *them* first."

"What do you think, Dan?" young Lashly asked.

"This child don't hold with none of them idees," the old man said. "It's takin' time is all. That Coon Bastro is good on the trail. He makes 'em shine a trailin', or I wouldn't say so. Likely he stole them traps early in the night and was fur away time Pete and Lou found they was gone. This hyar is hard trackin' country, too. Heap of rock. A clever feller could travel all day and leave no sign. No use lookin' fer 'em yit. It's jist takin' time, I tell 'ee." He shook his head. "Coon is jist leadin' 'em a real good goosechase."

Mose agreed. "He says true. Ain't no use expectin' 'em yit. Keep yer eye on Lou's squaw. When she commences watchin' the back trail, ye'll know it's time."

Fowler let it alone, even in his mind. It was a hard case, but Pete and Fouchette were on their own now. They weren't greenhorns. They knew how to move around in the country. Unless they let it be known they were in trouble and needed help, the outfit would keep moving. They knew where to catch it up, how to reach it. They might catch up tomorrow, they might never catch up. They might go back to Taos, they might get caught by weather and have to winter some other place. They might even straggle in after the outfit reached the Green. As long as you didn't know, it was a waste of breath and body to fret. Pete and Lou would do what they had to do, what was best for them to do, and no matter how long it took, it would be foolish to change any plans.

They slowly climbed up out of the basin and crossed a high pass with a foot of snow blanketing the trail. It wasn't as deep as Fowler knew it could be and halfway expected it to be at this time of year and he felt lucky.

They slithered down and wound up canyons, bucking and twisting their way, crossed rock slides, skirted the peaks, followed up bouldered trickles, snaked around jutted angles which balanced over depths God knew how far down. And always above them towered the true peaks, breaking back, benched, the spires rising slim and beautiful against the sky. It was the rugged, rough country Fowler had told them about.

Driant gaunted down, but he crawled on his horse every morning and hung on. And although he used Noel, he never turned over the reins to him. Watching him, Fowler saw how well he kept his job in his hands, stayed watchful, kept command.

They were all tired to their bones by the time they reached the hot springs in the Middle Park late one afternoon. The whole day had harried them off and on with fine, driving, biting snowstorms. They rode into and out of them, one moment in sunshine, the next in a gray swirling maelstrom which almost blew them off their mounts. Typical mountain snowstorms, and the mountain men shrugged up the collars of their coats and capotes and sloped into them. But wind and cold sapped a man's blood-warmth fast and drained his strength. You felt as if you were ten pounds leaner after a day of wind and put cold with wind and it made an old man of you fast.

When they came down to the springs, they came into calm, only a skift of patchy loose snow on the ground. They crawled off their horses stiffly and made for the vaporing springs to thaw out their hands and faces. The swampers limped about making camp and the squaws got up their lodges quickly. Fouchette's squaw was still attending Big Starr and except for moving into his lodge with him could have been his own. She took care of his animals, his skins, cooked for him, cared for his clothing.

Fowler and Mose, after drinking copiously of the hot bubbling water, watched her put up Starr's lodge. In his cradleboard, Fouchette's baby was crying. He had been crying a long time and his husky first wails had subsided into a thin, hopeless rise and fall of discomfort. He was cold and wet and hungry but he had to wait a while longer and he seemed to know it. Mose pointed his chin at the lodge almost completed. "Starr'll take her in one of these nights. Then there'll be the devil to pay when Lou gits back."

Fowler's legs ached and his feet were so cold they had no feeling in them. It felt as if his legs ended in rocks. Inside his moccasins he wiggled his toes. Well, at least they would still move. He shook his head. "No . . . he won't. He'll give Lou time. If Lou don't get back this winter, though . . ." He left it hanging and they both laughed. A man wasn't going to sleep cold and wait on himself all winter with a woman ready and waiting. And Lou wouldn't expect it, either.

Fowler looked around. The gray had closed in and snow was feathering down. "We'll take a breather here," he said, "couple of days."

"Yep," Mose said, "we're due. Them pork eaters of Driant's is nervy. I never seen a Frenchie, savin' Fouchette, didn't git lower'n a cellar in the mountains. Seems they're skeered they'll fall down on 'em. They ain't got no spirit at all."

Fowler nodded and moved absently toward his own lodge. Driant's French hands didn't bother him. They would live, low-spirited or not. Driant did bother him. For a couple of days he had thought the man's belly looked swollen.

Mose ambled on to help Pedro and Shell with the horse herd, and Fowler went into his lodge. Betsy had it neatly arranged already, had the fire going and the stew pot on. There was also a smaller pot of water heating and she was digging into the parflêche bag which held her roots and herbs and powders. Fowler folded down on the bedroll and she came to take his moccasins and leggings off. She exclaimed over his white, cold feet and rubbed them briskly, then slipped dry moccasins on them and placed them toward the fire. Fowler sighed comfortably. "You think," he asked her, "Mr. Driant is sicker? Looks to me his belly is swollen. You noticed it?"

Yes. And so. He was not well. She was making a root tea for him now.

Fowler considered. The hunters had not found much game in

the wilderness of canyons through which they had come and there had been little fresh meat. Betsy had been making pemmican stews for them. Pemmican was rich—dried meat pounded to a meal, wild cherries or berries added, the whole sealed in melted fat in a pouch. It was food heavy with grease, a good winter food which the man with a good digestive system relished and took no harm of. But Driant—he didn't know. Maybe it was too rich for him, set too heavy on his stomach. Something was bloating him, that was certain. "Don't fix no more pemmican for him," he said, arriving at an uncertain conclusion. "Make him a jerky stew tonight."

Betsy spoke quickly, rapidly, arguing and scolding. Fowler cut it off. "Just do what I say, will you? No matter if you do think different. May be that pemmican is what's hurting him." He rubbed his feet together and shifted them nearer the fire. "He better soak in the springs here, too."

That would be good, Betsy thought, but it would be better for him to sweat. She would build such a lodge for him. But tomorrow. Not tonight. There was not time for such sweating tonight.

She turned her back on him then, to show her displeasure, and squatted, her well-padded backside spread on her heels. Fowler grinned and shot his foot out against it suddenly, bowling her over. She crawled all over him, pulled his hair, whacked his chest, pummeled him angrily until he caught her hands and held her helpless. She heaved chestily a moment longer, then went limp with giggles and was soft and heavy against him. He tumbled her over in the robes, wanting her intensely suddenly, and then, feeling easy and limber again, warm all over, feeling the blood-warmth in hands and feet again, in his skin and even in his bones, he shoved her away and stood, arranging his clothing.

Affectionately she watched him, her eyes soft on him. He was so tall he could stand fully erect only in the middle of the lodge. A Utah man would have come no higher than his chin. He was hard and he was lean and he was a good man . . . and he was hers. Pride in him swelled inside her and she touched his ankle, yearning out to him. He looked down and winked at her and made a coarse comment in her own language which set her laughing. She agreed they made good medicine in the robes.

When he left she did not do the things she knew to do for herself. Instead she drew a pattern on the sandy floor and drifted a design with colored powders and small shells and bits of beads and she said things, the right things, to herself and to the great powers, that this seed she was keeping would be fruitful. And when she had finished she rubbed it out and made the brew for the sick man and dropped the hard, dried strips of jerky into the stew for him. She felt soft and heavy and warm, as if the medicine they had made were already nourishing, darkly and moistly, within her, already forming, already growing.

Fowler found Driant resting. He looked tired but refreshed. "I had a good wash-up, my friend," he said. "These hot springs in this country are remarkably beneficent."

"They are *so*," Fowler agreed. "Good to drink, good to bathe in. And hot water gets you cleaner than river water."

"Yes. Unfortunately, we don't often take the time to heat water and bathe regularly."

"Regularly?" Fowler's eyebrows shot up. "Most of us don't get a bath the whole season. Water's too cold and time too short and all of it too much trouble. Most of the boys think the dirt and grease help keep you warm, too."

He jackknifed down beside the Frenchman feeling oddly, again, that there was a whole world of difference between them. You didn't often remember how this man had been reared. It took a word or two now and then, like the regular bathing, to bring to mind he had been brought up with grace, in a big fine home with servants to attend him. That until he came west he had never, probably, in all his life worn the same linen two days running. That he had never gone dirty. That he had slept in good beds on fine sheets . . . had eaten only the best foods, served with beautiful silver and on fine china. That he had been given every advantage and luxury . . . and then been sent west to sloven it in the mountains.

He had never heard Pierre Driant utter one word of complaint at the conditions of his life now. He ate what there was to eat, got dirty and smelled as high as any of them, picked lice off his bedclothes and kept, mostly, a good heart. On top of all that, he was sick and pain-ridden. He didn't complain about that, either. He was ignorant about the mountains and didn't pretend he wasn't. He didn't put on airs about his learning in other matters, though he had let slip once that he had been sent to France for his schooling. He listened, in these present circumstances, to a man who was his better, but he learned so quickly he never made the same mistake twice. There were plenty of men in the mountains with the old grit in them and the hair of the grizzly on their chests. But they hadn't had much unlearning to do. Mostly they'd roughed it all their lives and they took to the mountains without strain. For plain, raw guts, Fowler had to hand it to this St. Louis Frenchman. He didn't know if he could have done as well.

"I been thinking," he said, "we better hole up here a day or two. We got a pretty heavy load of pelts. We oughtta cache 'em. No use packing 'em any further."

"This is a good place for a cache?" Driant asked.

"Good as any. You make a *good* cache and any place'll do. Not even an Indian can find a cache made the right way." He pulled a long frayed thong loose from his sleeve and drew it back and forth between his long, bony fingers. "Ought to be some right fair trapping close by, too."

He carefully did not say maybe the hunters would find elk and deer in this more sheltered basin, that a change of diet might benefit the Frenchman, that drinking the hot water and resting a few days certainly would.

Driant watched the thong passing and repassing through

Fowler's fingers. The man was so low-keyed and had such iron control of his nerves that any restlessness in him gave away some inner tensions. "Are you worried about your friends?" he asked quietly.

"Pete? Fouchette? Lord, no." Fowler fiddled the strip of leather, then he dropped it and locked his hands about one knee and rocked back. "The whole outfit is trail-tired, Mr. Driant. They ain't used to such rough going. They need to make camp a few days."

"You mean *my* men are trail-tired. My men aren't used to such roughness. You and your men would have been on the Green by now, wouldn't they?"

Fowler said casually, "Maybe. Maybe not. Your boys are doing pretty good. But we ain't out of this rough country yet and it's no use pushing 'em too hard. And like I said—we gotta cache these skins soon anyways. Might as well do it here where we got a comfortable camp."

"I see." Driant reached into his sack of belongings and drew out a bottle of brandy. He set out two cups. "How much farther to the Green, *mon ami?*"

"We're maybe half way."

Driant handed Fowler a cup of the brandy. "We have been a month and a half on the trail. Would you say it would take that much longer?"

Fowler took the brandy and looked directly into the stubborn, unadmitting, undespairing, unrelenting eyes with their dark pouches of pain shadowed beneath. The eyes bruised him where he was softest inside. You may not make it, my friend. You may not make it.

He dropped his eyes and looked at the brandy, swirled it, and sipped, savoring its rich body. "Thereabouts," he said. He gulped the rest of the drink, handed back the cup and pushed onto his feet. "Betsy wants to sweat you out a little tomorrow— the Injun way."

Driant laughed. "What the good Betsy wants, she shall have. I would not be much help digging a cache, so it would be as well for me to sweat. I shall be interested in that process."

"It ain't too pleasant while it's going on," Fowler said, "but when it's over you feel fine."

Driant touched his sore side. "If you can guarantee that, my friend," he said softly, "it will be worth it."

2.

The next day while Driant sweated in the stone-heated, steam-vapored lodge the squaws built for him, the cache for the pelts was made. Only a few men knew the location, Fowler, Mose, and Big Starr for the Fowler interests; Old Dan, Lashly, and Noel for the Driant firm. It was so cleverly hidden in the middle of a willow thicket, the scrub so carefully taken up and replaced, that no sign at all was left and no one, not knowing the secret marks, could have found it. The copse of short willow shrubs had no look of having been disturbed.

Driant was still as pink as a parboiled lobster when Fowler went to give him the location of the cache and the marks by which it could be found. Fowler laughed at him. Above his red face Driant's luxuriant curly black hair had been twisted by the heat into small upstanding horns. His bushy eyebrows were swept upward and his beard had kinked and flared. Altogether he looked hot, disheveled, disgruntled, and rotundly satanic. He was also petulant. "All right," he said. "Get on with it."

"The cache is a mile upstream from this place, north side the creek," Fowler told him. "There's a half blaze above the first crotch of a cottonwood tree a hundred feet east. A full blaze on another cottonwood south by fifty feet from the first one. A half blaze on the far side of an aspen two hundred feet west."

"Write it down," Driant snapped, "I can never remember all that."

It was the first time he had ever been short spoken, but Fowler kept his patience.

Driant burst out suddenly. "I have sweated until I am weak and your Betsy has allowed me nothing to eat all day. She has required me to drink copious draughts of some bitter brew of her making. It was a nauseating mess. It made me retch and vomit."

"That was the idea," Fowler said calmingly. "I forgot to tell you. The Injuns don't only sweat out all the poisons in their systems, they drink this tea that makes 'em vomit and clean their bellies out, too."

"You also forgot to tell me," Driant said acidly, "that after being sweated profusely I would be immersed in ice cold water. I am still having chills from the shock of it."

"That's to seal up the pores," Fowler told him. "You'll feel better tomorrow."

"I would like to feel better now. Have you ever undergone this torture, my friend?"

"Many a time," Fowler lied cheerfully. "It's good medicine or I wouldn't say so." He had successfully avoided ever entering the sweat lodge, but he knew the Utahs swore by it and its theory made sense to him.

"I am hungry," Driant said shortly. "I want something to eat."

"Soon," Fowler soothed, "soon, now. Betsy's fixing it."

Noel came in and looked sourly at Fowler. He had not approved of the sweat lodge experiment, but he did not approve of very much that was done these days. Fowler guessed that Noel was afraid of his influence with Pierre Driant, afraid that if it became necessary for Driant to give up the command of the outfit, he would choose Fowler to take his place. He needn't have worried, but, his own streak of contrariness rising up in him, Fowler didn't say so. He let the man stew.

Noel looked closely at Driant and said, "You look sick. I do not understand you, Pierre. Why do you submit to these heathen treatments? How do you know one of these concoctions that Indian woman prepares isn't poison?"

Driant's good humor returned. "Why would the good Betsy want to poison me, Paul? Be sensible. These brews of hers may do me no good but they can't do harm. The Indians have dosed themselves for centuries with natural herbs and they are no worse for them."

"We have medicines in the bag," Noel said, "if you need dosing. You know the treatment for a stomach disorder is a purge."

Driant laughed. "One of your blue mass pills, I presume."

"Precisely. They are recommended and you could be certain of good benefits."

"He could be certain of no sleep tonight," Fowler said dryly. "He'd be trotting all night." He handed Driant the bit of paper on which he had written the signs marking the cache. "Remember, it's a mile upstream from the springs."

"I made a note of it," Noel said testily.

"Fine," Driant said, "it is good for each of us to have the directions. Should we become separated, either of us can find the cache." He folded the paper and put it in the pouch slung about his neck.

"You want Betsy to bring your supper here, or you gonna eat with the rest of us?" Fowler asked.

Driant hesitated. "Perhaps she should bring it here, Joe." He smiled apologetically. "My legs are a little tottery yet."

"*Bueno.*"

They had eaten, but the men were still lingering, talking around the fires that night when Fowler heard something and motioned for quiet, his head tilted and listening. In the quick silence the only sound was the soft slide of guns being drawn across the sand into their owners' hands.

Mose raised his hand, listened intently, then spoke. "Horses. Trottin'."

Big Starr nodded. "Them, I reckon."

There was a visible relaxation among the men but no one moved, no one stood to be silhouetted against the fire, until the vedette posted beyond the cavvyard sang out of the dark, "It's them! Pete and Lou!"

The men clambered to their feet and some, young Lashly, Big Starr, and others went running to meet them. Fowler stayed by the fire and waited.

The men were noisy with their welcome, yelling and shouting. "Hey, *amigo,* you git 'em? You find 'em?"

"Hey, you fix 'em? How'd it go?"

"God's name, where you been? We been lookin' for ye better'n a week."

The shouts, cries, questions, whoops, laughter, suddenly faded off, drained away, and a strange stillness took their place. Fowler's right hand opened wide, the fingers stiff, then closed again into a fist.

Out of the gloom, into the firelight, rode one horseman, young Pete. He looked like a pouch of meal, shapeless and collapsed, bent almost double over the pommel. Behind him, led by the rope still clutched in one hand, followed the pack mule, loaded with furs and jangling with traps. Big Starr was leading Pete's horse and he stopped him at the fire.

Fowler went slowly to meet him, heaviness settled in him. When the horse stopped, young Pete raised his head and stared, first at the fire, then around at the group of men. He lifted one hand in gesture meant to be a salute, but the hand dropped limply. Fowler looked up into the face. It was black and rocky with weariness and some other thing, so tamped down and flattened and controlled it made the face a mask. The new beard was scruffy and Pete's eyes were dark burned-out holes sunk deep in the sockets, glazed with dullness. He was so cold the dry shakes twisted him in spasms.

Fowler said, "Fouchette?"

Young Pete said, "Rubbed out."

That was all.

Big Starr came around beside Fowler and the two men lifted Pete from the saddle as if he were a baby and carried him to the fire. Dan and young Lashly led the horse and mule away.

The squaws came running, then, and Fouchette's woman knew the truth instantly and set up her wailing. She tore at her hair until it fell loose, she tore her face with her fingernails till it streamed blood, she tore her dress. She scooped up ashes and spread them on her head and face. Betsy and young Lashly's squaw joined her and the valley was filled with their high, horrible animal howls. It was a tremulous, concerted sound, thin as paper but as piercing as a high whistle. The squaws squatted and swayed, howling, their eyes rolled back showing the whites, ripping at their flesh, their clothing, their hair. The sound spread out from the fire and filled the whole night—the dark, hopeless, wild sound of wild things, reasonless and mourning, the cry for the thing done but not understood, especially lonely and bereft because it was reasonless and not understood, the anguish of the doomed assaulted once more by their doom.

Driant came from his lodge, a buffalo robe thrown about him, with astonishment curving his eyebrows. Beside him, Noel was cursing at the noise.

A long shudder racked young Pete, and Fowler flew into a rage at the women. He cuffed Betsy and sent her sprawling. "Shut up! Shut up that crazy yowling! This ain't no Ute village and we don't follow no Ute ways! Shut it up now, you hear!"

Betsy rolled over and sat up, scuttled crabwise out of his reach, with no pause in her ululating howl. Fowler caught her and clapped a hand over her mouth, the other pinching her nostrils shut. She clawed and fought, but as her breath ebbed she had to subside. "You get in the lodge," he ordered her, "and take the others with you. All of you get quiet."

Big Starr came to help and his big ham-hands whacked and shoved and propelled Fouchette's woman and young Lashly's behind Betsy. The women covered their mouths with their hands to muffle their cries, but they did not hush. The ritual of mourning with all its desolation had begun and was already hypnotic in them. They stumbled before the driving men into Fowler's tepee. "I'll lodgepole you," he warned Betsy, "if you make enough noise I can hear you up at the fire."

She broke off her wailing and glared at him. "You would not allow the twelve-pole dance. The power of the six-pole dance was not enough."

A chill, beginning at the base of his neck and progressing down his back in slow, widening waves, was as cold as a trickle of ice water. Fowler gave her another shove. "Just get quiet, will you?"

He walked back toward the fire.

The dance had nothing to do with Fouchette. No power, no spirit, no prayer, nothing. Indian superstition, was all. Six men, twelve men, or a hundred men dancing around poles, waving fans, scattering powders while a drum beat couldn't have saved Fouchette a hundred miles away from them. It was a ceremony, a ritual, that was all. Some contrary corner of his mind argued back at him—that was what all religions were, the faith as the cornerstone, then ceremonies and rituals. It had always made as much sense to him to offer smoke in six directions, to set out a prayer stick, to dance a prayer into the earth, as it did to tell your beads, to recite the litany, to genuflect, or even to roll and howl and talk in unknown tongues the way the revivalists did. Just depended what you believed was all.

A shame and a blame rolled up inside him at the memory of the six-pole dance. He'd felt that way once when a boy, when his sister Savanna, seeing him eating a piece of pie, had begged a portion. He had broken it and, too greedy, had given her the least piece. It had ruined the rest of the day for him. It wouldn't have hurt to have had the twelve-pole dance. One day of delay? In the long winter of cold day after cold day, what could it have mattered? He caught himself thinking he had been niggardly with Fouchette, then he came up to the fire and shook his dank thoughts aside.

Driant had been quietly watching, taking in the whole scene. "It is Fouchette?" he asked, when Fowler returned to the fire.

Fowler nodded.

"How did it happen?"

"We don't have the particulars yet. Pete was too tuckered and them women set up their howling straight off. Soon as Pete can talk, we'll know."

The women's wails, softer and less invasive, could still be heard. "Can't you make them stop that?" Noel asked.

"We tried. They'll squall all night. Can't nothing stop 'em. But they won't be right underfoot now."

Mose had set a kettle of pemmican before young Pete and he was bolting it down ravenously, the grease dripping from his chin and streaking down on to his chest. He ignored the coffee set before him and dipped up bowl after bowl of the stew, gulping it down. "Hyar," Mose said, gently stopping the bowl finally, "git yer breath, boy. They's time enough and the kittle ain't gonna run dry. Ye'll glut yerself. This ain't hump meat or fat rib. This hyar's pemmican. Slow down a mite."

Pete looked at him dully but he comprehended and obediently he made the next bowl last longer.

Big Starr squatted in front of him and slipped off what was left of his moccasins. He examined the feet for frostbite. They were white and shriveled. "Water soaked," Starr said. He pressed and prodded, then nodded. "Ain't froze." He rubbed them a little, then covered them with a warm robe.

Fowler watched young Pete's face. Some color was returning to it as the heat of the fire penetrated, and slowly his eyes began to have some life in them. He ate more slowly and, seeing the coffee, swilled some of it. Long shudders still ran over his body, and Fowler threw a blanket around his shoulders. A dry sob caught in Pete's throat and his chin nuzzled the warm wool like a child at a woman's breast. Fowler wined as if a tender wound had been touched. It had been bad, real bad, then. Pete wouldn't have come in like this and carried it inside him the way he had, if it hadn't. He filled his short dudeen and lit it and puffed slowly.

Pete smelled the tobacco and sniffed, traced it around to Fowler. He held out his hand and Fowler put the pipe in it.

Young Lashly came up with Pete's saddle and fixed it behind his back so he could lean on it. Mose put the kettle of stew out of the way. Old Dan silently appeared and dropped down beside Fowler. "He brung in the traps that was stole," he muttered, "and a pack of thirty skins, and two extry guns. One of 'em's Lou's. He was plumb outta meat and nigh outta powder. He's made 'em *come,* but whut this coon'd like to know is did he raise ha'r on Bastro and Jordan."

"He'll say," Fowler said.

The men had gathered around. The fire was built up and they talked together in low voices. Young Pete lay for a time, smoking, his eyes closed. Fowler would have thought he slept except for the moving arm which lifted the pipe now and then. He began talking all at once. The men gave him dead silence.

"We trailed 'em clean down onto the San Luis. He's a hard one to foller, that Bastro. Hard as a Injun. But we stuck with 'em. We'd lose the track, nose around a while, then we'd find it again. They was movin' fast but we was movin' faster. We knowed we had 'em boxed in when we found their cache, close by their last camp. And we wasn't more'n two hours behind 'em. The coals was still red in the fire. He kin brush his trail, Bastro can, but he can't make a cache worth a damn. A kid could of found it.

"We follered on feelin' good. He had headed up one of them arroyos that pinches in tight and we figgered he'd made a bad mistake. We allowed we could trap him easy. We follered up. It was a rocky place with a lot of scrub cedar—big boulders, rough, thickety and tight. Well . . ." the voice slowed, "they ambushed us."

He sat up so suddenly the blanket was thrown off his shoulders. He looked directly at Fowler, his eyes anguished. "They was up above us on a bench and first I knowed we was closin' in on 'em, they shot. I'd been leadin', but I'd had to stop and git a rock outta my horse's hoof, so Fouchette had taken the lead. I heared the shot and then I seen Lou commence to fall, real slow like. There was another shot straight off and they got his horse. I flung off and taken cover in a thicket and tried to find 'em. Kept crawlin' towards Lou but it wasn't no use. They had a lot of fun with him. If he wasn't dead the first shot they made damn sure. They pumped him full. It was like they was tauntin' me, wastin' their lead, showin' what they could do, they was so sure of theirselves.

"I holed up. I knowed Lou was gone. Wasn't nothin' I could do for him. I jist holed up behind some rocks and cedars and kept watchin'. Mebbe a hour later, mebbe two, I couldn't say, I seen a piece of arm showin' behind a rock high up. I wanted more'n a arm so I helt my fire. My gun was rested so I figgered I could hold on till dark. I jist centered my sights and hung on. I hadn't fired a shot yit. They didn't have no idee where I had got to. They could see Lou and his horse, dead, out in the open at the bottom of the arroyo, but for all they knowed I had got clean away."

Fowler filled him another pipe. The men were tense, listening, but nobody said anything. Nobody asked a question or made a comment.

"Finally, I seen a hat inchin' up over the rock—real slow. Seemed to me it taken an hour for his forehead and eyes to show."

One of the greenhorns could not contain himself any longer. "Bastro!" he breathed.

Young Pete shook his head. "It was Jordan. But I squeezed

off and got him. He rolled down the ledge and bounced like a big rock all the way. He come to a stop not more'n six foot from Lou. His gun come clatterin' down with him. I left 'em thar for the time. I was wantin' to git Bastro."

He drew on the pipe then handed it to Fowler. "It don't taste right," he said, "git mine, somebody."

Fowler said, "It's right there, in your possible sack, Pete."

Pete fumbled and found it, filled it. "I didn't git him," he said. "He got away durin' the night. He didn't shoot no more and I never seen the first glimpse of him. Where he had his horses, I don't know. We was trailin' horses plumb up the arroyo, but they jist quit at a rock slide and they didn't pick up nowheres. It was like they'd had wings and flown out."

Mose nodded. "He either brushed his trail or kept to the rocks."

"I reckon. Well . . . I buried Lou and brung his gun and possibles back. I come by the cache and taken all he had in it —traps and skins. And then I come on in."

Pierre Driant, across the fire from him, waited for him to go on, and then he realized he wasn't going to go on. That was all of it. That was the end. He felt shocked at the quiet breaking off, at no telling of freezing nights and starving times and rough trailing back to the outfit. He looked curiously at Fowler and Big Starr and Mose and saw that for them, too, that was the end. With a sense of awe he understood, then, that men like them did not think it worth telling about freezing nights and starving times and rough trailing. Those things were too commonplace. They took them for granted. They weren't unordinary in any way. They were part of every season, part of every man's experience and so casually accepted they were only discomforts and nothing more. The story ended with the fight. After that, a man came on in—that was all.

There was a long silence as the men thought over and digested Pete's story. The softened crying of the women was in the background, not intrusive, just part of the night, the fire, the rimmed valley, an appropriate and fitting curtain call to the drama just heard.

Young Pete spoke again. "I'm sorry, Mr. Driant, I didn't get your horse for ye."

Driant stared at him, then cleared his throat noisily. He could think of nothing to say except, "It isn't important, Pete. Bastro has probably ruined him."

"Yes. I'd think it."

"*Well,*" Mose said, "Lou Fouchette was a good man fer a bastard like Coon Bastro to put under. This coon vows to git even fer him."

"No, you don't," Big Starr said, rolling up onto his feet, "this coon aim's to git him."

"I'll slit the one touches him," young Pete said tensely. "You've done forgot he's mine."

Fowler made a pushing downward motion with his hand. "Not no more, Pete. He's *ours.* Lou was one of my boys. The first one of us who crosses Bastro's trail, maybe you, maybe me, maybe Starr or Mose . . . the first *one,* Bastro is *his.* Hear?"

The named men nodded, each as his name was mentioned, and Pierre Driant, seeing their faces solemn and stony as they nodded, thought it was as if they were being charged, were taking an oath. A death sentence had been pronounced and Coon Bastro would be running from it the rest of his life. Driant shivered. Bastro was as good as dead this moment.

seven

A WEEK LATER they had climbed over Rabbit Ear's Pass. The snow was forearm deep on the horses in some places, though mostly it was only knee deep and they could flounder through. Fine, blowing gusts of snow needled the faces of the men and collected around their collars. It melted down their necks. The French swampers were miserable, unhappy, spooked, and full of nerves. They did not like this penetration of the high country, they did not like these mountains, they did not like this cold and snow, and they did not like the ghosts of sickness and death which rode with them. The beaver men swore at them, drove them, shoved, pushed, and hauled them over the pass.

They slithered down into the North Park, hit the headwaters of Grizzly Creek right on the nose and trapped down it to where it flowed into the North Platte. Here, under the Medicine Bows to the east and the loom of the Sierra Madre on the west, they made a base camp from which the beaver hunters could fan out onto the creeks hidden in the slopes. There was snow even on the floor of the basin, now, but it wasn't deep and there was no hard ice yet on the creeks. Beaver could still be trapped and the pelts were the best of the early prime.

The trappers paired off and went out like the spokes of a wheel in all directions. Joe Fowler paired with young Pete. Pete had recovered from the death of Fouchette. The way it was among beaver men, maybe you were as used to a man as if he were your own brother, liked him fine, hunted with him on good terms, but if he got rubbed out you couldn't sit around and brood about it. It wasn't you, and you had traps to set and moving on to do. You buried him as deep as you could, piled

stones—if there were any—over his grave to keep the wolves or
Indians from digging him up, said a prayer if you could remember one, and left him. You remembered him, sure, and you'd
tell things you'd done together around the fires at night, but he
was gone and nothing to be done about it. You were living, to
tell of it.

Fowler and Pete rode out southeast toward a tall peak and
found a brawling stream they liked. They leapfrogged their sets
upstream, but Pete was too reckless. It had been a long time
since Fowler had hunted with young Pete and he had forgotten
his way of prowling ahead too far, leaving too big a gap between
him and his partner. "Quit this foolishness, Pete," he told him,
when he caught up with him next time. "Can't either of us
help the other if you're out of sight and hearing."

"Aw," Pete ridiculed, "you're a worse granny than Lou. I
aim to take more skins than anybody. I don't aim for Old Dan
Sutton to beat me."

"You keep this up," Fowler snapped, "and maybe you won't
have no skin yourself. When you work with me, you don't get
out of sight, you hear?"

Pete laughed but he hung back the rest of the day.

When they came in, Paul Noel met them. He was standing
up to the trail pretty well but he looked like he had a deep hole
inside him now. "Pierre is very sick," he told Fowler. "He
didn't sleep much last night and he is still in great pain."

Fowler was cold and his wet britches and leggings were stiffening with ice but he went immediately to Driant's lodge. The
Frenchman was in such pain that his long control of himself was
gone. He could not lie still. He was rolling restlessly from one
side to the other and he was moaning in the low, subhuman way
of animals in pain. Joe put his hand on Driant's forehead and
found it dry and hot with fever. As he squatted by the bed,
Driant rolled again and a stench of foulness filled Fowler's nostrils. "You give him a purge, didn't you?" he asked of Noel.

"Yes," Noel said. "I persuaded him to take one. All doctors," he continued loftily, "recommend it."

Fowler swore. "And he's been trotting ever since and cramping, and now he's too weak and fevered to trot any more and he's fouled his bed. Whyn't you call me last night?"

Noel was sullen. "You haven't been able to help him—with your Indian squaw's potions. I did what I thought was best for him."

Driant's eyes flickered open but he did not muster his usual smile nor did he speak. Fowler didn't think he recognized him. He probed the swollen side gently. "God," he said, "it's as hard as iron."

Noel nodded. "I've had your woman keep water hot all day and I've kept hot compresses on it. That should have reduced the swelling and the mass, but it hasn't. He's been out of his head the last few hours."

Fowler stood up. No use berating Noel for giving Driant the purge. He didn't know, actually, but maybe it was needed. He wouldn't have given it, if it had been left up to him, out of plain compassion for the man, but he didn't know enough about medicine to know whether it was the right thing or not. Generally speaking, and from his experience in the mountains where you let nature heal herself not only from theory but from lack of anything else to do, he held with the notion that the less you had to do with medicines the better. But it was the plain truth nothing they had tried had done much except help the man temporarily, not even the sweat lodge on which Fowler had pinned a lot of faith. There was something bad wrong with this man which was having its way with him.

"You got any opium pills in your medicine bag?" he asked Noel.

"We had some," Noel said, "but Pierre has been taking them. For a long time he has been taking them, at night, so he could sleep. There are no more now."

Fowler gazed down at the sick man. Sensible about everything but himself. How long ago might he have had to give up if he hadn't secretly bolstered himself with a false ease? What was driving him to make him cling so hard to his purpose? "We oughtta get him quiet," he said. "Whatever's wrong with him it ain't doing him any good to thresh around that way. I reckon you've tried whiskey."

"Brandy. As much as he would swallow."

They poured more down him, and with two of them, one could pry his jaws open while the other poured, and they managed to get a considerable amount down him. They waited for it to take effect.

Noel pinched his under lip nervously. "He is very sick," he said.

"Yes," Fowler said flatly, "he's very sick. Well, he's quieter now. Betsy'll come clean up his bed. I'll come back in an hour or so." He pulled the tent flap aside and went out.

No use fooling about it now. You put a good face on something as long as you could and sometimes it turned out all right. But if it got worse there came a time when you had to look straight at the worst and face up to it. If Mr. Driant wasn't a gone gosling he looked mighty like it. He had death written all over him or Fowler had never seen it on any man, and he had seen too many go to be much mistaken. Fowler's frozen leggings rattled as he walked and he hit one fist against the other. It was a pity, a waste and a pity, for the man to go now.

Next morning Driant was still quiet. Fowler had spelled Noel during the night because the man was fagged from nursing Driant that day and the night before. They kept him quiet with whiskey and they kept the hot rags on his side all night, too. Betsy and Fouchette's squaw, who had mourned for Fouchette three days, then moved into Big Starr's lodge, had kept the fires going and hot water waiting. Big Starr had come several times, Mose, Old Dan, young Lashly, had all offered to take a turn sitting with Driant. "Later," Fowler told them. "If he don't get better it will take us all to nurse him."

The swampers were gloomy and they eyed Driant's lodge surreptitiously, their fears easily aroused again. The whispers ran quickly around the camp. "If de boss dies, who pays?" What would happen to the outfit? Would they go on? Would they turn back? Who would say? Some of Driant's trappers were also uneasy. They stood to lose a season's profits. Noel sent them out to run their lines.

Fowler found Big Starr saddling up. "I won't go out today," he told him. "You and Mose stick with Pete. He can help you run your lines, then go with him and run ours. Don't let him go over on that creek by himself."

"I'll hogtie him if I have to," Starr promised.

Fowler clapped him on the back, then he grinned. "Fouchette's squaw gonna make you a good woman?"

Big Starr laughed. "She's got the makin's. I mightn't have picked her to commence with, but I ain't finicky right now." He tightened the cinch and the horse danced a little. Starr slapped his flanks. "Be still, you. You know that kid of Lou's is a cute little booger, Joe. He's real bright, too."

"Sometimes they are," Fowler said. "Stick with Pete, now."

Starr nodded and heaved up in the saddle. "Hope Mr. Driant feels better today."

The squaw came up and handed Starr his rifle. Fowler looked at the little boy in his cradleboard. He couldn't see much brightness in the round baby face. And all Indian kids had those glittery shining black eyes.

He swung around as Starr rode off. He never had thought much about the halfbreed youngsters the trappers and traders fathered. There were a lot of them. As long as the trapper and the squaw stayed together the kids were traipsed around with them. Then usually they were raised in the village, among the mother's people. If Lou had lived he likely wouldn't have stayed with this woman the rest of his life, though the French did that sometimes. The kid would have been raised by his mother, never known who his father was except a Frenchman named Fouchette who had passed through a few seasons and moved on. Mostly, a trapper's kid was all Indian. A few men, thinking the white in a halfbreed could be cultivated, had tried civilizing them. Like General Clark, who had taken Sacajawea's boy to St. Louis, given him an education, even let him go to Europe to study. And what had come of it? He was right back with his mother's people, right here in the mountains, working for trappers, guiding and hunting for them. Didn't amount to much either, Baptiste Charbonneau. Fowler shrugged, wondering if Big Starr was going to get sentimental about Fouchette's kid.

The day moved on slowly. Fowler let Noel sleep until nearly noon, then roused him to take over the nursing while he slept an hour or two. Driant was about the same and they couldn't tell whether he was sleeping or whether he had lapsed into a coma. His face was swollen and its skin was deeply flushed. His breathing was stertorous. The right side of his abdomen wasn't so swollen, however. Nor was it so hard and tight. Probing it, Fowler found it softer to the touch and he thought that was a good sign. Whatever had blocked the gut had passed on or softened up. He didn't like the man's dark, earthy look, but it was bound to be a good thing that the side wasn't so hard and swollen.

2.

Betsy waked him, as he had told her to, when the lodge was dim with twilight. She whispered that food was ready. She would bring it. She went outside for something. Fowler moved his legs. Sleep had not rested him much. He was still tired, bone-tired and aching, but he knew some of it was the tiredness of helplessness. He could not help this man who was so sick. He did not know how to help him. He could sit beside him and put hot cloths on his sore side, he could straighten his bedding, he could even hold the hand that occasionally seemed to be searching for something, that strayed about, picking at the robes, hunting—but he could not see inside his body and see what it was that was wrong with him and pluck it out. It was one thing to lose a man quickly, the way Fouchette had gone. It was another, and more grievous, to watch a man go down and down one little step at a time, one losing moment after another, right before your eyes and be unable to stay those slow steps. It was a wearying thing because it was such a load on the heart.

Betsy came hurrying back into the lodge. There was trouble, she told him, her hands flying rapidly to tell the trouble—the three men, the ones called Big Starr and Mose and young Pete, they were here. The man called young Pete was hurt. He had been shot. The men called Big Starr and Mose had brought him into camp. He was by the big fire now. The man called Mose was also hurt, but not badly. His hand was bloody. He did not have to be assisted from his horse.

Fowler was on his feet with one lunge. "Rapahoes!"

He charged out of the lodge so fast he took a couple of poles with him and brought the whole tepee down. He fought his way clear of the clutter and left Betsy squalling with rage and fright. It was a bad thing for a tepee to fall.

As he neared the big fire in the middle of the camp, Fowler slowed. Young Pete wasn't killed, that was a sure thing. He had been put on a blanket and he was propped up, holding one leg with both hands. He was cursing—loudly, obstreperously, beautifully, lucidly. Young Pete was an artist at swearing. He was putting all his artistry to work right now. The profanity was inspired. It was curdling, blazing, withering, but it was imaginative and unrepetitious.

He caught sight of Fowler coming up. "It was that bastard

Bastro," he shouted, "he's the one done it. There was jist this one shot—jist one. He plunked her in right where he got Fouchette. Only this coon fooled him. I got to the bank and the thicket, 'fore he could reload. And they wasn't no Tom Jordan to back him up. He didn't have nobody but hisself this time!"

Big Starr hadn't seen Fowler. His back was turned. He said, "Well, it was Rapahoes this coon seen down by them alders where me and Mose was at. And it was a Rapaho arrow nicked Mose."

Fowler put his hand on Starr's shoulder. "Tell it," he commanded.

Starr turned. "Five of 'em. Ambushed us on your and Pete's lines. Pete was ahead, like he allus is—out of sight. Them that laid for us didn't have no guns. They was usin' arrows. One that got Pete had a gun."

"Warn't no Rapaho got me," Pete insisted with vehemence, "I tell ye, it was Coon Bastro!"

"You see him?" Fowler asked.

"No, but I didn't need to. Them Rapahoes didn't have no guns. Starr says so. But Bastro had a Hawken, same as all of us. And he plunked me jist below the knee same as he done Lou. If I'd have fell where I was, he could have taken his time reloading and he could have filled me as full of lead as he did Lou. That was what he was aimin' on doin'."

Fowler nodded, but he said, "Injuns have been known to get hold of Hawkens. Don't nobody trade 'em, but all it takes is one ambush and a dead trapper and the Injun has got himself a Hawken."

Pete was stubborn. "I know that, but it was Bastro. He plugged me jist exactly the way he done Lou. Cripple ye first is his way, then pump ye full. It would of taken a awful lucky shot for a Rapaho to shoot that good. You know's well as I do, they jist don't shoot that good."

The men gathered around were nodding, agreeing. Fowler

looked at Mose. "It was Rapahoes laid fer us," Mose said. "And hyar's the arrow that nicked me."

Fowler took the arrow and examined it minutely. It was an Arapaho arrow and no doubts about it. The wrappings, the feathering, the paint marked it unmistakably. "Have to butcher it out?" he asked Mose, looking at the dried blood on his left hand.

Mose was pouring coffee. He swiveled to show the hole in his shirt. "Naw. It jist glanced. Jist sliced a hunk of meat off. 'Twon't even stiffen up on me."

Pete groaned and lay back on the raw beaver pelts that had been piled up behind him.

Fowler dropped the arrow. *"Bueno.* Lashly, tell Pedro to set a picket a hundred yards out from the herd tonight, on all three sides. The camp guard will cover the creek side. Tell him to put Shell in the middle and relieve him himself at midnight." He swung around. "Let's have some wood on this fire. I got to see what I'm doing."

Two camp swampers brought the wood and built the fire up to a high blaze. In its light Fowler knelt beside young Pete. "Lemme see that leg, now, boy."

With his knife he slit the leg of Pete's old wool pants. He worked fast but the wool was tough and wet and the knife jerked along. Pete swore when the leg was jostled. The wound lay bare finally. Noel had come up and he and the other men crowded around to look. Nobody said anything. The men juggled about until each had looked. Each then backed off. They looked at each other, shook their heads, dropped their eyes. The circle of men slowly fell away leaving only Fowler, Big Starr, Mose, Old Dan, and Paul Noel. Noel's face was screwed in nausea.

Young Pete's lower leg was shattered between the ankle and knee so badly that pieces of bone were sticking out through the flesh. It was a mess of torn flesh and splintered bones. The men had seen too many mangled beaver legs not to know that Pete's right leg would never be any good to him again—if he lived, and more than likely gangrene would set up and he'd be a gone gosling.

The silence grew, only Pete's breath sucking in and out and a deep groan from him now and then breaking it. "She's got to come off, ain't she?" he said, finally.

Out of his knowledge, and sickness of the knowledge, Fowler said steadily, "Yes, it's got to come off."

"I knowed it would. I seen it 'fore the boys come for me. Well, git busy. Go ahead and cut her off."

Noel choked a little and gagged and Fowler looked at him. "You stay with Mr. Driant. You won't be needed here."

The man stumbled away.

Fowler said, "We got to get some things ready, Pete. Stay with him, Mose."

"He's done had a leetle jag of Taos lightning," Mose said. "We dosed him to git him in."

"He'll need a lot more," Fowler said. He looked at Big Starr, who nodded and went for a jug.

Fowler went to his lodge. Betsy had her poles up again and was quarreling at them for falling. Fowler spoke to her and from her parflêche pouch she brought him fine, drawn sinews of deer skin, so finely drawn they were almost like thread. He got his skinning knife and tested it, sharpened it more.

Betsy watched him, understanding what had to be done. She murmured a word or two and Fowler shook his head. "No, this is a man's job. Keep the other women out of the way."

When he got back to the fire Old Dan had shooed the other men away. Left to assist were only himself, Big Starr, Mose, and young Lashly. He had a good bright fire going and was squatting by it watching a piece of iron that was heating in it. Big Starr and Mose were pouring whiskey down young Pete.

Young Lashly was standing helplessly to one side. His face was white and he looked sick. "Go on away," Fowler told him, after a quick glance.

The boy shook his head. "No. I'll stay."

"Well, don't get in the way," Fowler warned him. "Help Dan with the fire."

It took a while to get Pete drunk enough to work on, but they waited. When Mose said, "He's about as fur gone as he's gonna be, I reckon," they laid him flat on the blanket.

"Who's gonna do it?" Old Dan asked.

"You ever cut off a man's leg?" Fowler asked.

"Nope. This child ain't ever been called on to do sich. Ortent to be much different from butcherin' off any kind of leg, though. Now, you take buffler . . ."

"This ain't no buffler," Mose growled, "this hyar is a human bein'. This is young Pete. He ain't got much chance to pull through but if he does he's got to have somethin' left to walk on. It's got to be a good, clean job of cuttin'."

Pete opened his eyes and bleared at them. "This child'll pull through," he mumbled drunkenly, "jist don't fergit that. I ain't goin' under yit. If ye're all too chicken-hearted to saw that laig off, gimme the knife. I kin do it."

Fowler laughed. "We're gonna commence right now, Pete. Hang onto Mose and Starr."

Fowler's knife made a clean slice through the mangled flesh. Pete howled, cursed, and gripped Starr and Mose so tight it was like their arms were in a vise. Seeing Mose wince at the hold on his arm, young Lashly elbowed him aside and took his place. It was about then that young Pete went limp. "Good," Big Starr said, "he's done swooned. Git through now, Joe, quick, 'fore he comes to."

There wasn't much to it, after all. The bone was so shattered there was no solid piece to saw through. Fowler made as good a job of it as he could. He whittled the flesh off as evenly as possible and left a flap on the under side of the leg. He pulled out the splintered pieces of bone and tied off the arteries with the deer sinews.

"This arn's red-hot when yer ready," Old Dan said.

"I reckon we're ready," Fowler said.

Old Dan brought it with a pair of tongs. Young Pete groaned and moved and opened his eyes. He saw the white-hot iron and yelped, sat bolt upright. "No, ye don't," he squalled, "ye ain't searin' off that stump with no hot arn! Cuttin' off my laig is one thing, but searin' that stump is somethin' this coon ain't havin'. Jist take that arn away!"

"Ye'll bleed to death without it," Old Dan said, "or git the gangrene in it."

"Them is chances I'll take," Pete said. "Git that arn away from me. And don't you boys try to hold me down and use it."

They wavered, then Fowler waved the hot iron away. "He's the one to say, Dan. Take it away. Give him some more whiskey, Starr. I got to sew this flap up, Pete."

"Ye won't put no arn to me? Yer word, Joe."

"My word, Pete. No iron."

Pete gulped down the whiskey, but he wouldn't let them wait. "Go ahead. Stitch her up."

He fainted again before Fowler finished stitching the flap up around the stump.

The job finished, Betsy nudged Fowler's elbow. She held out a bowl full of some kind of dark mess. "What the hell is that?" he asked.

She told him. While he was working she had had every man in the camp chewing tobacco as hard and as fast as he could. The softened cuds, stirred into a mass, were ready to put on the wound.

"By crackey," Mose said in admiration, "if she ain't the beatin'est! I was jist fixin' to git a mess of beaver ha'r to poultice on it, but terbacker's the best. Plaster it on, Joe. It's the best thar is to draw the pizen out and make it heal even."

Betsy pushed Fowler aside and laid the tobacco on thick. Then she bandaged the stump. Fowler saw that she had sacrificed one of his linen shirts. He had almost left those shirts in his room in Taos. He was glad, now, he hadn't. Pete needed a soft bandage worse than he would ever need the shirts.

They didn't move him. They covered him warmly and let him lie where he was by the fire. They sat about it themselves, ate and drank coffee and talked. Fowler cleaned his knife, digging the blade into the sandy soil until no blood remained on it.

"Well, pore old Pete," Starr said, shaking his head. "Reckon he'll go under for shore, now. This child has not knowed of many pulled through losin' a limb."

Mose agreed somberly. "Ginerally the gangrene sets in and putrefies 'em."

"He ort to let me seared off that stump," Old Dan put in.

"That kills about as many as it helps," Fowler said, "and it's an awful agony to put a man through." He looked around. "Where's the foot? And all that mess?"

Young Lashly spoke up. "I've done buried it."

"*Bueno.* I don't know as I could have," Fowler said.

The boy dropped his eyes at the praise. "I didn't help much elsewise." He looked up again, wonder and awe still showing on his face. "He sure took it good, didn't he?"

"He's got the old grit in him, Pete has," Mose said.

"I sure hope he makes it."

"If thar's a man in these mountains *kin,* losin' a laig, it'll be Pete."

"You think it was Bastro got him?" young Lashly asked Fowler.

Fowler spitted a piece of meat on his knife and bit into it. "I don't know," he said slowly. "I would think so, except for them Rapahoes. It don't seem reasonable, them and him at the same time, in the same place."

"Mebbe he's with 'em," Big Starr said. "He was a Crow man once. Said he was, anyhow."

Mose was rubbing his arm to ease its ache. He paused and

reflected. "Mebbe it wasn't Crows he lived with. Mebbe it was Rapahoes."

"They don't much cotton to a white man," Big Starr went on, "but once in a while they do. Milt Sublette had him that Rapaho squaw, remember? And he had a whole village of 'em doin' whatever he said fer a couple of years."

Old Dan wrapped in his robes by the fire and slept. Young Lashly went to his lodge. The three friends continued to sit. Mose and Big Starr talked softly and Joe Fowler brooded into the fire. He went once to Pierre Driant's lodge and peered in. Both Driant and Noel were sleeping.

Beside the fire again he felt a great weariness seeping all through him mixed with a great compassion for both these men crippled and helpless now—for Pierre Driant, who had fought his trouble for so long but was losing the fight and was sliding slowly down into darkness. And for young Pete, who might, and probably would, follow him down that long lonesome way. And who, if he didn't go under, would always lurch around on one leg; he who had always rolled so wildly and recklessly and brawlingly on two. Fowler's mind did not say to him in so many words that one of the most terrifying things about nature was its complete disinterest in human fate, but he felt it in his sorrow and in his anger at what was happening to these two men. Nor could he reason clearly enough to see they had brought it on themselves. He just felt sad and bad about it.

"He was up ahead of you, was he?" he asked, coming back to the event.

"Well, he was. You know how he was," Big Starr said. "Didn't *nobody* move fast enough to suit Pete. Yeah. He was up ahead, by hisself. He stayed with us and worked our sets with us. Then we went over to work his'n. He knowed where the sets was at. He moved on, fast. Next thing we knowed, arrows was flyin'. We flang down and taken 'em on. I heared the shot but wasn't nothin' we could do. We was too busy ourselves. We made them Rapahoes scamper, then we went to see 'bout Pete."

"He was layin' in a thicket holdin' onto his laig and cussin' like the Old Nick hisself," Mose said. "Told us he had jist taken a beaver from the trap when the shot come."

"And *his* gun was on the bank where he couldn't get to it," Fowler said.

"It was *so,*" Mose said, laughing. "Warn't no more use to him than if he didn't have none. But he made a good try fer it. He didn't go down in the water. He floundered towards the bank and crawled out and got his gun and got hisself into them alders. But he never seen who shot him, and there warn't no more firin'. Jist that one shot, then nothin'.""

Fowler picked up a twig and drew marks in the sand, absently, studying. "It *could* have been Bastro," he said then. "It could have been. He could have been layin' up. It could be just a happenstance them Rapahoes come along when they did. *Or,* he could have been with 'em. What puzzles me is why, if Bastro wasn't with 'em, they picked the creek Pete and me had set. If *that* was an accident, it's a mighty queer one."

"More and more," Mose said, "it don't appear so to me."

Fowler flung the twig down. "Well, we got to hole up here a few days anyhow, account of Mr. Driant and Pete, so you and me and Starr will make a quick *paseo* and see what we can find out."

Mose nodded. "Figgered that's whut we'd do."

Young Pete moaned and Fowler got up to go to him. He was twisting his head restlessly. His eyes slowly opened, stared, and then focused. "Joe?"

"It's me, Pete."

"I got a big dry."

"That ain't surprising. You want water or whiskey?"

"Water."

When he had drunk he caught Fowler's wrist. "Joe, you won't pull a Jim Bridger on me, will ye?"

"What you talking about?"

"You know. Jim went off and left old Hugh Glass 'fore he was gone. Time the grizzly clawed him."

"Jim wasn't nothing but a kid then. He didn't know no better."

"But you and the boys won't leave me, will ye? I got to hear ye say it, Joe. I know you got to move on, but I kin travel. Take me with ye when ye go. Jist don't leave me behind."

"We ain't gonna leave you behind," Fowler promised roughly. "Either we stay with you, or you go with us. You got my word if you need it, but I don't know how come you to think we would."

"Ye might think I would be too much trouble," Pete said, turning loose of Fowler's wrist. "I jist don't wanna be left."

"You won't be. How's it go? Hurt pretty bad?"

"Not as much as ye'd think. I reckon I kin sleep all right."

Fowler and Mose and Big Starr stayed beside him the rest of the night, whichever of them hearing him getting up to wait on him. He slept by fits and starts and so did they.

It seemed to Fowler that he didn't sleep at all. He heard all the night sounds of a camp—the ruffle of the creek, the stamping and whiffling of the herd, the soft movements of the camp guard, the cry of Fouchette's boy once and its quick breaking off as the mother gave him her breast, the hiss of the fire and its crackle when a log burned through and dropped, the rub of limbs against each other in the wind. The sounds had a magnified sharpness and loudness and he knew he was hearing them through a thin layer of sleep, for when he came full awake they were normal and not loud at all.

3.

Next morning Paul Noel made a fuss about Fowler leaving the camp. "With two men sick here," he said, "you mean to go off and leave the camp unprotected? And with Arapahoes known to be in the vicinity?"

"Best protection is to find out where they are," Fowler said, "and that's what I aim to do. They pester you while we're gone, you got plenty of men and guns."

Noel stomped around a little and blustered some more. "What about him?" He jerked his head toward Pete. "My hands are full with Pierre. I can't take care of him for you."

"We take care of our own," Fowler said shortly. "Betsy'll see to him."

"What if he dies?"

"I'll be sorry."

"You have a duty to Mr. Driant," Noel tried to remind him.

"I'm trying to do it," Fowler said.

"If it was one of Pierre's men who had been shot," Noel said peevishly, "you wouldn't be so eager to hunt down these redskins."

Fowler looked at him studiedly. Noel was wearing down and his nerves were getting edgy on him. Fowler admitted there was plenty to wear him down, with Driant so sick and the outfit's season and profits endangered. Noel must be pretty distraught, not knowing what to do. But it was no use getting edgy. You let your temper and nerves fray out on you, you just worsened yourself. All you could do was the best you could do, one thing at a time. He said mildly, "Wouldn't no mountain man let Indians count coup on him, Mr. Noel, without trying to strike back. Wouldn't make no difference who in this outfit it was. And the worst thing we could do is set here and do nothing. If we don't do nothing but learn some things, we got to." Betsy brought up the big roan and Fowler took the reins from her. "Won't take us long—two, three days." He climbed into the saddle.

"What if you don't come back?"

Fowler looked down at him and grinned. "Three of us? You

think they can rub out all three of us?" He swung the big blue around. "We'll be back, Mr. Noel."

They were back at the end of the third day. All they had found was the trail of fast-moving Arapahoes which they had followed over the Medicine Bows onto the headwaters of the Laramie. There they quit and turned back. There was no mistaking the trail. The Arapahoes were heading for home and in a hurry. Several of their stolen horses were shod so it was impossible to tell if Coon Bastro was traveling with them or not. It was about what Fowler had expected, but you had to do what you could to know. The outfit could rest easy about one thing now. There wouldn't be another brush with the Arapahoes.

Young Pete hadn't died and neither had Pierre Driant. Young Pete was in the better condition of the two, however. He was making an astonishing recovery. "Aw, ye can't kill a old coon like me," he growled at them when they remarked on his ability to sit up, eat with good appetite, and cuss with undiminished vigor. "If you was thinkin' ye was rid of me, ye made a big mistake. This child'll finish the season with ye."

"I believe it," Fowler said.

He went on to see Pierre Driant and found him rational and free of pain but very weak. "You better, Mr. Driant?"

"I am not suffering," the man said. "Sit down, Joe. Tell me about your journey."

"It was cold and never come to much," Fowler told him. "They was a little bunch broke off the main bunch of them Indians we cut trail on in the South Park. They was in a powerful hurry and we never caught up to 'em."

"Do you believe our friend was with them?"

"Hard to tell. But it don't make much sense if he wasn't. No good reason five or six of 'em would cut over here unless they was helping Bastro get revenge." Fowler grinned. "He ain't using his head, though, if he's with 'em. It'll be all over the mountains, what he done to Pete. He oughtta head for

Sonora, clean outta the country. Instead, he's heading straight into country where every beaver man's hand will be against him."

"His kind do not use their heads, my friend," Driant said. "They use bluff and bluster, a knife and a gun, and think themselves invincible. A little reflection would teach them better, but they are incapable of reflection. You will find this man some day."

"Yes, sir. We'll find him."

Driant hunted around in his robes and pulled out an oilskin pouch. He fingered it a moment. "In this pouch, Joe, is a letter and some directions which must be delivered to a man on the Green. I would feel better about it if you would keep it in your charge now. If anything happens to me . . . you will see that it reaches him? It is very important."

Fowler took the pouch. It was perhaps ten inches long by six wide. It didn't weigh very much nor was it very bulky, but he knew immediately he was holding in his hand what had been driving Pierre Driant. He did not say to Pierre Driant, why don't you give this pouch to your friend, Paul Noel, to deliver. He knew why Driant had chosen him. Only Joe Fowler would see, or could see, one way or another, without fail, that the pouch reached its destination. "On the Green," he repeated.

"There, or thereabouts," Driant said. "You will understand he could not be more specific."

"Yes, sir. Who is the man?"

"He is a Captain Bonneville. He is leading a fur expedition, a very large one. His plans were to winter in the vicinity of the Green."

Fowler didn't ask what was in the pouch. It was none of his affair. "When did he come out? This spring?"

"No. Last year. He left the Missouri settlements in May. I was back in St. Louis last summer. This pouch was given to me there. Captain Bonneville is my good friend. He is well-known, well-liked in St. Louis. I agreed to find him and deliver this pouch to him. Its delivery has taken priority over my own plans."

Yes, Fowler knew that now. He tucked the sealed, water-proofed package in the overlapping fold of his shirt. "I'll see to it," he said.

Driant sighed. "I had plans for a great adventure, my friend. For a great adventure." His dark eyes fixed on Fowler. There was some sadness in them, and more in his smile, but there was no fear nor begging nor despair. There was just the intimation of sadness and, perhaps, acceptance finally. *"Le bon Dieu* sometimes has other plans."

Fowler was uncomfortable and he tried to think of something to say but couldn't. You couldn't fool this man. If he had given up, he knew it was time. He hadn't ever given up as long as he had had anything at all to hang onto.

"I do not know," Driant continued then, "what your own plans may be. I do not ask you to set them aside. But if Captain Bonneville should have need of your services, I hope it may not be inconsonant with your own plans to do so." He smiled slightly. "You would serve him much better than I, but I should have counted it a privilege to go with him."

Go with him? Fowler waited, but Driant said no more. "It will depend, sir," Fowler said finally.

"Of course. On your men, on what you find, on many things. But if you can help him, it would be as if you were helping me."

Bonneville. Bonneville. "This Cap'n Bonneville," Fowler said slowly, "I knew of a fellow by that name once. Was a lieutenant name of Bonneville in the Seventh Infantry, back at Fort Smith, where I come from . . . Arkansas." As he spoke his memories cleared more. He looked at Driant shrewdly. "He was French, come to think of it."

"He is the same man," Driant said, smiling. "He is a captain now. He is on leave from his regiment, which is presently stationed at Fort Gibson. I believe that is not far from Fort Smith."

"It ain't but sixty miles." Fowler mused over the coincidence. "Ain't that something? I used to know him . . . didn't know him good, you understand, but my father knew all the officers of the Seventh. Most of 'em used to come out to our place on the river. There was a good place for 'em to race their horses. They all had good horses and a considerable amount of money used to change hands amongst 'em." He laughed. "Lieutenant Bonneville had a fine horse. Used to win pretty regular. Bonneville was a short little feller, dark-skinned, sort of jolly, good-natured man."

Driant nodded several times quickly. "*Oui. Oui.* That is Benjamin. And yes, he is French. He emigrated from France when he was quite young. Through the friendship of an American patron he was given an appointment to West Point. He had spent most of his military life in frontier posts."

Fowler nodded. "Yes. Fort Smith, Fort Gibson." He laughed. "He'd get the fur fever all right in them posts. It's mostly where I got it." His astonishment wouldn't die away. "I would like to talk to him. He might have news, later news than I have, of my family."

"You have never mentioned a family, Joe. You are married?"

"No. I didn't mean that. But I have a father, two brothers, a sister, back there. At least I *did* have." He stirred. "You get out in the mountains you almost forget you got anybody but yourself. You don't get back often. You hole up in these mountains season after season and a time comes you even forget to think about other folks. When you do, you think next season you'll make the trip back, go see 'em, see how things are with 'em. But next season you don't do it. Or if you do, like I done this summer, you're in a big hurry. You got to get your business finished and get back. Takes so danged long to *get* there and back. You ain't got the time to do nothing while you're there."

Driant nodded and Fowler saw he was tiring. He shoved up

onto his feet. "You rest now, Mr. Driant. I'll take care of this for you if there's need."

"I know you will, my friend. You will go to the Siskadee."

4.

Some time during the night he died. Paul Noel was in the tent with him, but he was asleep. "He was resting comfortably," he told Fowler next morning. "He said he felt more comfortable than he had for days. He required nothing. He was sleeping, so I slept also. When I awakened just now he was dead. He died in his sleep, I am sure. If he had called out, I am certain I would have heard him."

Noel had wept a little for his friend and employer. His eyes were reddened and there was real grief on his face. Fowler didn't much like him, he wasn't too much of a man, but within his limits he had done all he could for Pierre Driant—give him that much. "That must have been the way of it," Fowler agreed. "I am sorry, Mr. Noel, real sorry. He was as good a man as I've ever known. I hate for him to go under."

It was the best he could do. He felt flat and as if he had suffered the loss of some part of himself. He thought he had thought so much about this man there would be a strange emptiness now it was no longer necessary.

He went to look at him. The body was cold and stiffening. Several hours, then, he'd been gone. The unrelenting, undespairing eyes were closed and his face wore that unclouded, innocent look of the dead. Rubbed out was the right way to say it. Troubles, pain, fret, ambition, hopes, joys—all were rubbed out and rubbed off the faces of those who died. What was left was a personless mask, as if no person had ever been. This was not Pierre Driant, and Fowler felt nothing in its presence. He touched his shirt, then remembered he had put the oilskin pouch in his possible sack. He had one more duty to perform for the man who had inhabited this body.

He went outside where Noel was waiting. Noel drew a long breath. "He was a very good man." He turned away from the tepee and braced back his shoulders. "We will bury him here, of course. And then we must make some decisions—I and my men."

Fowler looked at him obliquely. Command was already sitting on his shoulders. "So?" he said.

"Yes. We must consider whether or not to continue this expedition, and if we do not, where we shall spend the balance of the season, how we shall hunt, whether or not we should return to Taos—now or later. Many things must be considered. I have been doubtful of the wisdom of . . . of several things for some time."

"I expect you have," Fowler said evenly, "I expect you have." He rubbed his chin which still had a three-day growth of beard on it. "We will help you bury Mr. Driant, Mr. Noel, then me and my men will be putting out. Early in the morning."

"But that's . . . you're under contract . . ."

Fowler guessed that Driant had said nothing to Noel about the pouch. He did not mention it or the charge given him. He shook his head. "No, I ain't under contract to you, now. I was under contract to Mr. Driant."

"It is the same thing. It is the same party. You are under contract . . ."

"I was under contract to Mr. Pierre Driant. We'll be putting out early, Mr. Noel."

"But . . . but we might decide to go on to the Green."

"Why, then, you can tag along. There'll be room."

Noel's temper rose and he turned red. "I consider your contract still valid, Mr. Fowler."

"Do you? Well, that's interesting. I don't want to appear disagreeable, Mr. Noel, but I don't. You can tell the camp guard if you want to be roused."

"I will inform Mr. LaClede Driant that you did not fulfill your contract and that payment for your services should not be made."

Fowler did not reply. He just looked at Noel for a long moment, then walked away. It was foolish of Noel to make that threat. You didn't threaten an old hand and Mr. LaClede Driant, an old hand himself, would know that. Mr. LaClede Driant would pay Joe Fowler every penny due him. The Company haggled over expenses and squeezed every penny three times before letting go, but they didn't haggle over a man who knew his business or what he charged for doing it.

5.

There wasn't much ceremony to burying Pierre Driant. There was a hole in the ground, the body laid in it wrapped in a blanket, Noel mumbling a prayer, the hole filled up. The men were mostly worried about themselves, what would happen to them now. Pierre Driant had lived, Pierre Driant had died, and that was it. It happened all the time. Shoveling dirt on top of him Fowler thought bitterly that there wasn't a man in his outfit qualified to recognize Driant's grace and valor. Possessing neither, they had not known their presence in their midst. They shuffled about awkwardly, doing their last duty toward him, but eager to get at the most important business of deciding what they would do next.

The meeting between Paul Noel and the Driant hands lasted the rest of the day. It went on and on, hour after hour, with loud words, much arguing, and heated differences of opinions.

Fowler and his men stayed away and tended to their preparations for leaving the next day, as far from the palaver as they could keep. Young Lashly finally left the conference and hunted up Joe Fowler, where he and Big Starr were rigging up a litter for young Pete to travel in. "Can I join up with your party, Mr. Fowler?" the boy asked. "They ain't going no further. Gonna stay here in this park for the winter."

"They've decided, have they?"

"Just about. Mr. Noel, he don't want to go no further. He's guaranteed the contracts for the boys if they'll stay here and hunt. Says he can't do it if they go on. Too much risk, he says."

"Some of 'em want to go on?"

"Several . . . yes. Old Dan wants to. One or two more. Most, though, would be better satisfied not to. He's done told 'em you are putting out. He claims you are violating your contract. Says you ought to stay with the party."

"Yes. He told me." Fowler finished off the lashing on his side of the litter and stood back to watch Big Starr finish his. "You certain you don't want to stick with 'em?"

The boy rubbed his foot back and forth in the sand. "Yes, sir, I'm certain. They promised when we signed on we was going to the Green. That's where my stick floats, sir."

Fowler grinned. *"Bueno.* You signed on to go to the Green. They ain't going. I reckon your contract is null and void, too. What about your possibles?"

"I furnished my critters and traps. I'm on a free line. I ain't got supplies, though."

"Powder? Lead?"

"Oh, I got them, all right."

"You got as much as we have, then. Won't be no luxuries rest of this trip."

The boy laughed, then hesitated. "If they had gone on, I would of stuck, Mr. Fowler."

"Ain't nobody doubts that," Big Starr said. He lifted the litter, pulled and tugged it this way and that. "She's stout. I reckon she'll hold Old Pete if he don't git to faunchin' around too much."

None of them noticed that young Pete had become Old Pete, nor knew that he would never again be thought of or called young Pete. With one leg gone, he had entered the patriarchy of mountain men—Old Gabe Bridger, Old Dan Sutton, Old Milt Sublette—men who through age or crippling had had some of their wildness and recklessness tamed down. It would be Old Pete Smith from now on.

"Well," Fowler said to young Lashly, "we can use another hand. Cut your critters out and put 'em with ours."

"Yes, sir." The boy's face lit up. "Yes, *sir!*"

He started to walk away but turned to say, "I'd like to say, sir, I appreciate getting to be a Fowler man."

Fowler laughed. "Better wait till the season's over 'fore you commence appreciating."

Young Lashly shook his head. "Being a Fowler man is good enough for me. I ain't ever heard of a Fowler man wasn't thought well of."

It was after dark before Noel reported to Fowler what the men had decided. He was curt about it and did not go into detail. He said only that the Driant outfit would not continue, and that young Lashly had been released. He asked Fowler to make up a bill for his services to this point.

"I'll send my bill to Mr. LaClede Driant," Fowler said.

Noel's mouth tightened. He said, "Very well." Then he left.

Old Dan Sutton sat with them for the last time around the fire that night. "This coon ain't likin' the idee of settin' hyar in the North Park all winter and scrapin' these hills fer the leavin's, but I got a leetle different contract, bein' sort of the head beaver man, and I don't figger I kin run out on it. Don't know what's got into the feller to winter hyar."

"Worst thing he could do," Mose said. "Either he ort to take the boys back to Taos and cut his losses quick, or he ort to take 'em on to good beaver country. Way it is, he's lettin' hisself in fer a full season of wages and expenses and little hopes of enough beaver to make it profitable. Wagh! Makes me think of a feller won't take the trump in euker because he ain't got both bowers. He ain't the gambler Mr. Driant was."

"He ain't the *man* Mr. Driant was," Fowler said quietly. "I hope you well, Dan. You're doing the right thing, sticking by him. He'll sure need an old hand like you."

"I dunno as I kin pull him through, but I reckon I got to try," Old Dan said.

Next morning they wrapped Pete in warm red flannel, tucked him deep into buffalo robes, lashed the litter between two horses, and swathed his head in red flannel to his eyes. He blistered them with oaths when they jostled his stump and squalled over the wrappings. "What ye aimin' to do? Smother me out? How ye think I kin breathe, all this swaddlin' over my face?"

"We got to put up with ye," Mose told him, "we don't aim fer ye to freeze to death on us. Now, shut up before I take a tomahawk to ye."

They trailed out and left the camp watching them, except for Noel, who did not come out of his tepee. Fowler led, a pack mule on a rope behind him. Betsy followed leading another. Then Big Starr rode next leading the two horses that carried Pete's litter. His squaw followed, two pack mules roped on her lead. Young Lashly and his squaw came next, and Mose and two more mules made the tail of the string.

It was snowing. The little party headed into the snow and was swallowed up in it. A hundred yards from the camp they could no longer be seen and had anyone looked back the camp had vanished. It was as if a curtain had been drawn over it and it had vanished, gone away somehow in the thick screen of snow. But nobody looked back.

eight

Even with a man in a litter, Fowler's party moved fast now. With five men, three squaws, one papoose, and sixteen animals he had a good party, a manageable outfit. To be sure, he had a man in a litter, but that man was Pete Smith and Pete was only slightly incapacitated by being hauled cradlewise. All of his instincts and most of his skills continued to work for him.

The three squaws could do more camp work and do it better, handle more skins and do it better, than four times their number of camp swampers. The papoose was no more trouble than a light pack on its mother's back, and sixteen horses and mules for eight people was nothing but a routine.

The first thing Fowler did was to abandon his plan to move cumbersomely out of the North Park by way of the North Platte River. Instead he cut directly over the mountains to the Little Snake. It was shorter, the boys had a right to the beaver they would find, and it was feasible now.

Rid of the drag and delay of a big party with its big herd of horses and mules, its big packs of trade goods and supplies, its greenhorn hunters and camp swampers, all the spooking uneasiness and fear that had kept Driant's outfit stewing and bothering, Fowler's party was a lean professional group scaled down to a fine maneuverability which he could use like an extension of his own hands and fingers. He felt like a man cut loose from bonds.

They could put all their skills to their own use now and, with the exception of young Lashly, who was fast learning, they were four of the most highly skilled men in a trade and a place which required a man's life to be almost total skill. With Mose leading the outfit one day, Fowler mused that all men have it in them to become, through experience and necessity, skillful at one thing or another, but in the settlements his skills could be relaxed between the necessities of using them. Watching Mose's head constantly turning, constantly looking, watching, he thought how a beaver man's life was all skill. He lived his skills twenty-four hours a day or he didn't live to try them again. And his total skill was a combination of a thousand acquired and instinctive skills.

Fowler didn't often think about such things. Years of experience had made his skills as habitual as eating and sleeping, but because even with Mose leading his own wariness was not fully relaxed he thought what a mountain man had to be, not once in a while when he felt like it but all the time, every second of his life. He was a weather man, a map maker, a trapper, a hunter, a scout, an observer of minute and almost invisible signs, and an interpreter of them. His memory must be prodigious and unrelenting and unfailing, holding in it ten thousand minutiae of detail, configuration, movement, of terrain, wild life, Indian customs and habits, weather, distances. His immediate judgment was complexly formed of remembered minutiae and his forecasts were based upon them.

What was the best way to get over this range of mountains, not only in terms of the immediate, but in terms of distant destination and projected time of arrival there? Do you go up this canyon and around? Or up this one and over? Which pass? Had the snowstorm that morning left an accretion of six inches or two feet in the pass? How gaunted down were the animals? Could they make it? Where was the next best feeding place for them? How old was that sign by the trail? Who made it? Men or animals? How many men? What kind of men? Coming or going? And what had been their mood?

That movement behind the shrub, just for a fraction of a second . . . was it movement or some trick of vision? What moved? Bear? Elk? Deer? Indian? What was making that gaggle of geese on the creek so noisy? What was an elk doing on that particular rock? What did that broken limb floating downstream mean? Every minute of every day every detail had to be skillfully registered, skillfully weighed, skillfully judged, and a skillful conclusion reached. Or you went under. Got rubbed out. If the Indians didn't ambush you, the weather caught you, or you got starved out. This didn't mean you rode around the mountains all tied up in knots of fear. It did mean that, in time, you learned to see a dozen things at once, instantly, and it did mean that, in time, you learned to judge and conclude immediately also. Out of that prodigious memory, out of ten thousand experiences, recall was made, identification was made, and judgment was made. A beaver had scared the geese. A beaver had also cut the limb which floated downstream. A bear had scared the elk. And that snowstorm on the summit had endured an hour, thick but brief. The accretion would be nearer six inches than one foot. The horses' feet were sore, but skin moccasins put on before they began the ascent would take them over and there was a good stand of cotton woods on a little creek the other side whose bark would make rich feed for them.

Time . . . and remembering. All the things you'd seen and done, been a part of, were there ready to be recalled and used again.

Pete rode in his litter the first week, though he squalled about it incessantly. One morning Big Starr got enough of the fuss Pete made and threw the lead ropes down. "This coon ain't listenin' to no more. My ears has done wore out. Somebody else kin lead this old b'ar for a spell till I git rested up!"

Pete bawled back at him. "Come back hyar! Ye ain't gonna leave me thisaway!"

"If I was to tell you whichaway I'd *like* to leave ye," Big Starr said, "it would be an abomination even to the squaws. Ye don't like the damned litter, whyn't ye git off and walk?"

"By God, I jist mought," Pete squawked. "Soon as I git me a pegleg whittled, I'll show ye. Bring me up a critter, Joe. I kin straddle a hoss with this stump. I'm everlastin' tired of swingin' in this hyar cradle. This child warn't never cradle-rocked nohow!"

"Just be glad it ain't a cradleboard," Joe told him, trying to pacify him. "That stump ain't healed good enough yet for you to ride, Pete. You'd bust it open."

Pete howled but he remained in the litter. Young Lashly said he'd lead for a few days.

Next morning they were angling down the comb of a ridge that ledged off steeply to the Little Snake. There was an old slushy snow on the ground, patched here and there with ice slicks. A gully opened and young Lashly swung his horse wide to jump it. The horse jumped but landed in a slick and had to scramble for its footing. The horses bearing Pete's litter spooked and began sidling, jerking, whiffling, stamping, and dancing nervously around. Young Lashly threw himself off his horse and fought them, but the near horse stumbled, kicked up, bucked, skidded, and slid, and Pete was thrown out of the litter over the rim of the ledge. "Oh, my God!" Lashly yelled, "Starr! Starr! Come here quick. Pete's done fell out. He's gonna be killed!" He stood helplessly holding onto the horses and, bug-eyed, watched Pete slide and roll and plummet down the long, steep, ledgey slope.

Fowler and Big Starr raced up and flung off their horses, ran to the rim of the ledge and halted, appalled. Pete's red flannel wrappings had come loose and were flapping like sails in a full wind as he banged and bumped from ledge to ledge and slithered and tobogganed downward. Howls, oaths, yelps were added to the crashing noise of his chute-the-chute ride, until almost at the end he was banged into a big boulder and catapulted over it, red flannel billowing, flung at least ten feet into the air and over into two feet of shallow water in the river bed. A dreadful silence followed as the red flannel settled over him like a bloody shroud. "He's killed," Fowler said, awed. "That's done for him, sure."

Big Starr's eyes were as big as coffee cups as he peered at the wet red smudge in the river. "I be danged! Goddlemighty, whut a way to go! Whut a avalanche! Pore Old Pete. Pore old feller. To be rubbed out thataway. Ever' bone in his body is likely broke."

They had begun to scramble downward when suddenly the red flannel stirred, billowed, heaved, and Old Pete sat up, flinging and fighting at the wrappings. Fowler and Big Starr stopped in their tracks and watched, gape-mouthed, as Pete's head came clear. Muffled noises became curses. Pete had lost his red cap, too, and his hair was streaming over his face. He got his arms free finally and began to beat violently at the water. He spied Fowler and Big Starr. "Well, don't jist stand thar gapin'! Come on down hyar and fish me out. This dang-blasted river is colder'n frozen hell. Git me outta hyar, quick, 'fore I turn to a goddamned blue-drippin' icicle!"

Fowler recovered first. "We're coming, Pete. Just hold your horses."

A howl of outrage went up. "Whaddya expect me to do? Swim this dang river? Shore I'll hold my horses, settin' right hyar on my butt. Git a move on, you two!"

Big Starr slithered along behind Fowler. "My, Gawd, Joe," he muttered, "he's harder to kill than your old Papago Injun. Why, ye can't kill that danged bastard. He's got more lives'n a cat. Anybody else would of stove his head plumb down to his belly when he hit that big rock!"

They rolled Pete out of the river and poked and prodded at him until he fought them off. "I ain't broke nothin'," he yelled at them, "quit yer pokin'. I ain't got ary bone broke. I'm jist skun up hyar and thar."

"Let me see that stump," Fowler said.

Unbelievably the wound had not been broken open. Fowler rewrapped it, feeling dazed. It seemed impossible that a man could have made that long landslide with no more damage than a few cuts and bruises, but that was exactly what Pete had done.

"You must of rolled in a ball like a groundhog," Fowler told him.

"I never had time to do nothin'," Pete growled. "One minute I was flat on my back in that damned litter, next thing I knowed I was flang into the air, next I was bein' heaved and hoed about, next I was settin' on my butt in that cold water!"

"Well," Fowler told him, "you've come to no real harm."

"I've done told ye, ye can't kill this child."

"I believe it." Fowler shouted up to Lashly, "Bring them horses with the litter down here."

"No, ye don't," Pete squalled, "don't ye bring that confounded contraption down hyar, Ben. You bring me a horse with a saddle on it. I ain't havin' no more of that blasted litter. I'll gutshoot the feller tries to make me. See if I don't. That danged thing like to been the death of me."

Young Lashly hesitated until Fowler called, "Do what he says, Ben. Saddle his horse and bring it down."

They threw the litter poles away, set him on his horse, and he rode like a man from then on. That night he began whittling a peg to wear on the end of his stump. "I aim to be walkin' on two legs even if one of 'em is wood," he said, "time we git to the Green."

When the Little Snake made its southward bend toward the Yampa, they left it and Fowler led them rapidly across the wasteland of the alkali flats—across Alkali Creek and the Bitter and the South Bitter, all stinking and tasting poison and bitter.

It was cold going across that high treeless tableland. It was land that didn't have any stopping place, beginning, or end. Once you got out into it, it was like being nowhere, no sky, no horizon, just the middle of nothing. There wasn't any sky because there was nothing to fasten it to, and there weren't any directions because without the sun they were all the same, round like a cup. The only thing you could be sure of was that under a foot of snow there was the ground, and you knew this mostly because when your horse broke through the crust it jolted you a little. After five or six hours of the everlasting sameness you almost began to believe none of it was real, and after two or three days you began to believe maybe you, yourself, weren't real. You had to have an awfully strong grip on yourself not to feel as wraithlike as everything about you looked.

The snow was deep enough to be troublesome, but worse, it was encrusted with a frost rime which made it brittle and which cut the horses' legs as they broke through. The wind never let up, either. And there was no shelter. There was only this vast plain, windscoured, snow-bedded, with sage bushes sticking up here and there through the snow.

The water was bad. The squaws melted snow for the men, but the animals had to drink the alkali water and it gave them all the scours. They gaunted down considerably and they all had sore feet. "Be nice," Fowler told Mose about the fifth day, "if we'd meet a band of Crows so we could buy some horses. We lose more'n one or two of ours and it ain't gonna be very comfortable."

They didn't meet any Crows, but they lost only one pack mule. Then they reached the wide, wide valley of the Green where Black's Fork poured in and there were willows and cottonwoods again, with bunch grass for the animals, with good water, with relief from the everlasting wind. They splashed through the shallow water and made their camp.

2.

Middle of November. The Green—Colorado of the West—Seeds-kee-dee-agie—Siskadee, take your pick. Green, to the British and to the Yankee traveler, because of its color. Rio Colorado to the Spanish because in its lower stretches it became red-silted. Seeds-kee-dee-agie to the Crows, in whose Absaroka heartland it rose and began its long journey to the Gulf of Cali-

fornia, because the prairie hen abounded along its banks. Siskadee to the mountain men, because that was the best they could
do with the Crow language. By any name, it was a grand, wonderful, powerful river, at this place wide, clear, rapid, the color
of all God's green apples piled together.

"It sure is one hell of a country," young Lashly said, reflectively, that night. "If a body hadn't seen Texas and New Mexico
he wouldn't believe it, would he? He'd think he was having a
nightmare."

"Whut did ye expect?" Mose growled at him, rubbing his
cold hands and trying to thaw them out.

"I dunno. More like the park mountains, I reckon."

"Whut do ye think them is over thar?" Mose's head tilted
northeast.

"Well—mountains, but they don't seem so high . . ."

"Them is the Wind Rivers, boy, and thar ain't no rougher
mountains nowhar. Ye're gittin' into some *real* mountains, now
. . . the Big Horns and the Salmons and the Tetons, the Yellow-
stones and the Bitterroots. You take them Wind Rivers, now.
Thar ain't but one way through them anybody has ever found.
Even the Injuns mostly go round. Ain't but one kind of human
critter knows them mountains at all and them's the Poordevil
Injuns."

Lashly looked over at Pete, who was whittling on his pegleg.
"He's joshin', ain't he?"

"Nope," Pete said laconically, "he's tellin' true."

"Well, I ain't ever heard of 'em."

"And ye ain't likely ever to see one of 'em," Mose said, "but
that don't mean they ain't thar. They're *wild* Injuns. Broke off
from their bands. Some of 'em is renegades. Been run off. Some
jist take off fer whatever reason they got in their flighty heads.
They live to theirselves up in the cliffs and canyons. Miserable
critters. No horses. No guns. Ain't much better'n animals. All
ye ever see of 'em is a track or a smoke. But one time one come
into our camp. He was half starvin'. He talked Shoshone. Said

they was some Crows and Blackfoot with his bunch, though. When an Injun can't live with his own band no more, he hunts out a bunch of Poordevils and they kind of make up a band of their own."

Lashly shrugged. "Don't sound much account to me."

"They ain't. Except they kin steal a critter good as ary other Injun. And they know them Wind Rivers." Mose waved his hand generally north. "Up thar is the head of some of the mightiest rivers you ever seen, too. The Missouri, she heads up thar—in three branches. The Yallerstone heads up thar, and Lewis's Fork of the Columbia, the old Snake. Hyar is the dividin' place, boy, 'twixt the east and the west in waters. The Missouri and the Yallerstone and the Big Horn, they head up hyar and they turn towards the east and the big Mississippi and the Gulf of Mexico. The Snake, she turns west and flows into the Columbia and the Pacific. The old Siskadee heads up hyar and she flows south and west and empties into the Gulf of Californy. Or they *say* she does. Don't nobody rightly know. Whar ye are settin', boy, is nigh onto the head of the biggest waters ye'll ever see. And mountains? Ye think ye've seed 'em down amongst the parks. Ye ain't seed nothin' yit. Wait till ye git to trappin' the Wind Rivers and the Absarokas and the Salmons and the Bitterroots. Them are mountains to make a man of ye."

"They as rich in beaver as they say?" the boy asked.

"Richest beaver country in the world," Mose said. "Why else ye reckon the Company and the Rocky Mountain boys and the Britishers are workin' in it? But the meanest Injuns is hyar, too. That's Blackfoot country up thar, boy, and they don't git no meaner than a Blackfoot. Don't make no difference what band they are, Gros Ventres, Piegan, Blood—they're all the same, and pure mean as a snake. Hate whites. All whites."

"How come? Can't nobody git along with 'em?"

Fowler had come up and he was listening. He felt good tonight, better than he had for two weeks. He had got the outfit through to the Green ahead of the blizzards and they had pemmican to eat, wood to burn again, food for the animals, and they were back in buffalo country. All his muscles had stretched out long and easy again, felt limber and thawed out. Mose looked up at him. "You tell him, Joe. You got more learnin'."

Fowler folded his legs and sat. He grinned at the boy. "Well, one reason everybody tells," he said, "is that when Lewis and Clark were going back from the Pacific, back in 1806, Lewis was exploring up on the Marias River and had a brush with a little bunch of Piegans. Had to kill some of 'em. Some say the Blackfeet have hated whites ever since. But some say the British, the Hudson Bay Company, keep 'em stirred up. The British seem to get along with 'em better'n anybody else, for a fact. But, again, it could be they're just smart enough to know the whites are plundering their country—running off the buffalo, taking their beaver."

"Which do *you* believe?"

"Little of all of it."

"They as mean as Mose says?"

Fowler spooned up some stew, and nodded. "About. Don't do to put your dependence in any of 'em. They generally got bad hearts."

"The Company get along with 'em?"

"Some. The Company works with the fort system up there, along the river. If a band of Blackfoot want to take their skins to Fort Union or Fort Cass, they do. But the Company ain't been able to keep no fort in Blackfoot country no more'n anybody else. Tried it on the Marias and got burned out and run out. They're notional Indians. Best way to trade with 'em is in a stockade with a cannon or two for protection."

Young Lashly finished up his own stew thoughtfully. "This ain't Blackfoot country in through here, is it?"

Fowler laughed. "That's what's eating you? No, it ain't, though they roam around in through here when they please. They're kin to the Rapahoes. They come through here going visiting. Sometimes they come down here for buffalo. But this is Crow country. Absaroka."

"Crows friendly?"

"Mostly." Fowler leaned forward in the firelight for a coal for his pipe. "You can't take *no* Indian for granted, Ben. Not none of 'em."

"Yeah," the boy nodded, "I'm a-learning that."

"And don't fergit it," Mose put in. He chuckled, then. "Joe, tell him that speech old Rotten Belly used to make . . . 'bout this country."

"Your idea," Fowler said, "you tell it."

"Aw, I can't keep it all in mind."

Fowler made no move, so Mose yanked a blanket up and draped it around his shoulders, ran his hand down his face to wipe off all expression.

"Who was Rotten Belly?" young Lashly asked Pete.

"Crow chief. Listen, now."

Mose's voice rumbled out, flat, long-voweled, atonal. "Crow country is a good country," he began. "The Great Spirit has put it exactly in the right place; while you are in it you fare well; whenever you go out of it, whichever way you travel, you fare worse.

"If you go south, you have to wander over great barren plains; the water is warm and bad, and you meet the fever and ague.

"To the north, it is cold; the winters are long and bitter, with no grass; you cannot keep horses there, but must travel with dogs. What is a country without horses?

"On the Columbia they are poor and dirty, paddle about in canoes, and eat fish. Their teeth are worn out; they are always taking fishbones out of their mouth. Fish is poor food.

"To the east, they dwell in villages; they live well; but they drink the muddy water of the Missouri—that is bad. A Crow's dog would not drink such water.

"About the forks of the Missouri is a fine country; good water;

good grass; plenty of buffalo. In summer, it is almost as good as the Crow country; but in winter it is cold; the grass is gone; and there is no salt weed for the horses.

"The Crow country is exactly in the right place. It has snowy mountains and sunny plains; all kinds of climates and good things for every season. When the summer heats scorch the prairies, you can draw up under the mountains, where the air is sweet and cool, the grass fresh, and the bright streams come tumbling down out of the snowbanks. There you can hunt the elk, the deer, and the antelope, when their skins are fit for dressing; there you will find plenty of white bears and mountain sheep.

"In the autumn, when your horses are fat and strong from the mountain pastures, you can go down into the plains and hunt the buffalo, or trap beaver on the streams. And when winter comes on, you can take shelter in the woody bottoms along the rivers; there you will find buffalo meat for yourselves, and cottonwood bark for your horses; or you may winter in the Wind River valley, where there is salt weed in abundance.

"The Crow country is exactly in the right place. Everything good is to be found there. There is no country like the Crow country."

Finished, Mose dropped his head. He pulled up his shirt and rubbed his belly. Pete left off his whittling and watched, his eyes glinting. Even Fowler looked attentive. From the depths of Mose's belly there came a rumbling, a long grumbling rumble which erupted into a loud crackling belch, an air-popping, satisfying, explosive belch. Pete yipped and whooped and carved the air with his knife. "By grannies, Mose, I didn't know if ye still could, but that was as good as ary'n you ever brung up! Ye ain't lost the tetch. Ye kin still go jist *like* old Ara-poo-ash!"

"I didn't know if I could or not, neither," Mose said, laughing. "Been a time since I done that. Wuz it as good as I used to do it?" he asked anxiously.

"Ever *bit* as good," Pete assured him, "ever *bit*. I don't know as I ever *knowed* ye to belch no louder or more satisfyin'."

Mose threw the blanket off. "I got to keep in practice more."

Young Lashly looked puzzled. Fowler laughed. "That's a set piece Mose has learned. All the boys like to hear him do it."

"That chief . . . Rotten Belly," Lashly said, "he never really said all that, did he?"

"Well, not in exactly those words, maybe. But Mose has got the best part of it, all right. *Including,*" Fowler chuckled, "the belch. Reason we called him Rotten Belly was because he had gas on his belly so bad he couldn't talk without belching."

Mose guffawed. "What he had was *wind*. And he could belch or break it louder'n anybody I ever seen."

When the laughter subsided, young Lashly said, "Is that all true? About the Crow country? Is it that good?"

"Nearabouts," Fowler said. "It's a bountiful country. Except for the wind. But you wouldn't expect him to name any fault in his country. The wind blows like no place else you ever been."

Mose raised a finger and waggled it. "Another thing he never named. Crow squaws has got the least morals of any squaws ye'll ever find, boy. Don't *never* take a Crow squaw. Anything built like a man kin crawl into the robes with 'em and they jist as soon bed with a dozen as one. They ain't got the least idee of bein' married. And ye'll git the French disease from 'em quicker'n any other bunch, too."

Young Lashly's eyebrows shot up. "I like Annie just fine," he said.

"The Shoshone squaws is purty clean," Mose went on, "and the Nay-pursies have got almost the same idee of stickin' to one man as Utahs have. The Bannocks is purty good, too. But leave them Crow squaws alone."

Young Lashly said stubbornly, "I like Annie just fine. I ain't looking for another squaw."

"Well, ye mought some day. I'm jist a-tellin' ye."

Pete looked up from his whittling and pointed his pegleg at Mose. "Lissen to who's gabbin'. Old Mose ain't had him a squaw in ten year, boy. Pay him heed and ye'll sleep alone."

Mose huffed up. "In my time I've tried 'em all and ye know it, Pete Smith. I've had me a Bannock and a Shoshone. I've had me Utes. I've had me Shians. I even had me a Ricaree one time. I kin have 'em ag'in, do I want 'em. But red blood jist don't shine with this coon no more. They're all sluts and out fer nothin' but foofooraw. Ain't enough traps to buy 'em what they want in scarlet cloth and beads. A red woman's breast is the hardest kind of a rock to lay yer head on, this child's thinkin'."

Pete jeered at him. "Your own blood's jist got thin, old man. Ye can't make 'em happy no more."

Mose flung a cottonwood pole at him and stalked off to his robes. Young Lashly watched him go. "You oughtn't to said that, Pete. He ain't all that old."

"He's older'n God," Pete said cheerfully. "Aw, he knows I was jist joshin' him. What he says is true. He's had 'em all. Could still have. He jist got tired, like he said, of the trouble."

Big Starr and his squaw came up with their arms full of wood which they dumped by the fire. "Joe," Starr said, "is a lot of light towards the west, like a big party is camped thar."

Fowler looked up. Bonneville, he thought immediately. Driant had said he had a big party. He would be in the vicinity of the Green. Fowler had not told the boys yet that he was looking for the man. "About Ham's Fork, would you say?"

"Well, I *would*. Mebbe twenty fires. Ye can't see from down hyar in the draw but me and Mamselle was up on that little rise gittin' the wood. They make a purty good shine from thar."

It had been a bawdy joke among the trappers that Fouchette called all his squaws Mademoiselle. Fouchette never explained it so no one ever knew whether it was a delicate insult to the Indian women or whether some innate courtesy lingered in the man. Nobody knew much about Fouchette's past beyond his trapping days. He never talked about it. But for whatever reason, Fouchette's squaws were all Mamselle and, having inherited the latest one, Big Starr continued the name.

Fowler reflected whether or not this was the time to tell the men he was looking for Bonneville and decided to wait until he learned who was camped so near them. "We better take a little *paseo* over there in the morning," he said.

Starr dropped down by the fire. "Figgered so."

3.

But it wasn't Bonneville. It was Tom Fitzpatrick, a brigade of the Rocky Mountain boys, and a village of Shoshones. There was a great reunion; Fitzpatrick was delighted to see them. "What! Joe Fowler, old man! Ye ain't gone under yit? This coon heared ye'd been rubbed out. Warn't nobody had seed ye in a coupla seasons."

"Didn't hunt for two seasons," Fowler told him. "Went mule-buying to California with Ewing Young, then made a *paseo* to St. Louis to sell the critters. Just got back in August. And here I be."

It was a big encampment, thirty fires, forty lodges, thirty men in the brigade, a big cavvyard, and there were over a hundred Shoshones in the lodges pitched nearby. And it was an old encampment. They had been here, Fitzpatrick said, nearly a month. The Indians and his boys had found buffalo up the valley and they had been making meat. The fires were built up, the feasting began, and the men settled to their exchange of news.

Fitzpatrick led Fowler to his own fire. "Well, now, *amigo,* this coon is pure glad to see ye and to know ye've not lost yer topknot. It wouldn't be the same country if Joe Fowler was to go under. Set to the fire and sink yer teeth in some fat hump Cap'n Stewart brung in this mornin'."

"Stewart? He's a new one on me," Fowler said.

"Yeah. He's a Britisher. Friend of Bill Sublette's. Come out this summer for the rondyvoo and been travelin' with me since."

"Where's he at?"

"Oh, he'd ruther to hunt than eat. He's out tryin' to git him another cow or two."

"What's he doing? Trapping? Trading?"

Fitzpatrick shook his head. "Don't nobody know. Jist a rich Britisher. Ain't no beaver man. Ain't no trader. But he's got dollars to fling about and got him some good horseflesh. Best gun and powder this child ever seen, too. And there's grit in him. He shines, he does. He'll stand back to back with ye right enough. Done so with me on the Big Horn jist lately. But what he's doin' out hyar, don't nobody know. Jist a sport, I reckon. Says he likes the life. Was in the British army and fit ag'in Napoleon and can't seem to git settled down since. He's gittin' the lay of the land all right. Been up amongst the Assiniboins and Chippewas, round Fort Union and Cass. He gits around considerably. Ever'body likes him. Does his part. Ain't no trouble. And he don't skeer easy. Stood right up to that bunch of Crows up on the Big Horn."

Fowler looked up at Fitzpatrick quizzically. "Crows, Tom? Ain't you getting your Injuns mixed up some?"

"No, I ain't. I mean it's Crows givin' us trouble right now. Makin' all sight of trouble. Jim Beckwith is back with 'em and he's workin' fer the Company. He's the one has led 'em astray. Led 'em right into Company pay, and I kin prove it. Lemme tell ye, Joe . . . ye wouldn't believe it . . ." He settled back and began. "We cleaned the Company good at rondyvoo this summer. They had Fontenelle comin' out from Fort Pierre with their goods. Vanderburgh and Drips was headin' up their brigades and they follers us to the beaver, not bein' used to the mountains. They stuck on our tails tighter'n ticks. We couldn't shake 'em in no way. Well, we had the rondyvoo hyar on the river this summer. Campbell got our goods through on time, but Fontenelle was late. So we cleaned 'em. We bought ever' pelt takened this year and done a good business outfittin' the boys. We got 'em all. We made 'em *come,* boy."

Fowler pulled a knee up and propped his chin on it. "I heard in St. Louis this summer the Company was putting brigades in the mountains. It's true, then."

"They done *put* 'em," Fitzpatrick said, "they done put 'em, boy. They was hyar all last summer. Like I said, Vanderburgh and Drips headed 'em up. Pore old Vanderburgh, though. Jim Bridger and me, we led him a goosechase up on the Gallatin into Blackfoot country, and he got rubbed out." There was the long, detailed story of the Blackfoot ambush, how they killed Vanderburgh, stripped the meat off his bones and threw the bones in the river, and because he was a brave foe ate his heart.

Fitzpatrick then spent a ribald hour telling about the rendezvous. "And then we put out. It was this coon's intention to make trouble fer the Company up on the Big Horn, 'round Fort Cass, amongst the Crows. Jim Bridger and me, we worked up thataway, then he split his boys off and taken 'em over onto the Marias. Me and my boys, we run into a big village of Crows. Beckwith was with 'em. We was flush with fresh goods and horses and traps—ready for the season. They wanted us to camp with 'em, but this child was kind of nervy about such a bunch of 'em. We camped a few miles off. But, natural, I taken some of the boys and some trade goods and went over to trade. Well, whilst I was at the Crow village, Beckwith and a bunch of the young men went to *my* camp. Warn't nobody thar but Cap'n Stewart and some camp swampers. And durned if they didn't hold him up and take ever' trap and gun, all the skins, all the goods, and our horses. Held him at gun point and takened 'em."

Fowler kicked a snapping coal back into the fire. "Don't *sound* like this Cap'n Stewart has got as much grit in him as you said."

"Whut could he do? They had guns on him. But he was

madder'n hell when I got back and ready to light into 'em with me. We rode over and raised a storm. We got back some of the horses and most of the traps. We got our guns back. And the biggest part of our goods. But our skins was gone. We seen 'em down at Cass, with our RMF mark on 'em, but old Tulloch said he'd bought 'em off the Crows and warn't none of his business whar the Crows had got 'em. Too bad for us if they stole 'em, but warn't nothin' he could do."

"The Company got Beckwith to steal 'em?"

"I think it. Why not? Hell, they knowed I was gonna git the Crows on our side if I could." Fitzpatrick laughed ruefully. "It's dog eat dog nowadays. They jist beat me to it, is all."

He told how that wasn't the end of the bedevilment. Short of goods, traps, and horses, he had abandoned the idea of working through the Big Horn country and had marched back down on-to the Green. "I got to git me some more horses. From the Nay-pursies," he said. "Them Crow varmints tracked us ever' mile and stole back most of our herd. Them animals you see in the cavvyard is mostly the Shoshones' critters. They ain't got none to spare. I been stickin' hyar to make meat and so's I kin travel with the Shoshones. Them Crows has got bad hearts this season."

Fowler puffed on his short dudeen and let Fitzpatrick ramble on. What Fitzpatrick was telling was what he had come to learn, and no man would know more than Tom Fitzpatrick. He had been an Ashley man. He had been leading brigades in the high country for eight years, and he was a partner in the Rocky Mountain outfit now. "Ye wouldn't believe it," he said. "They's more trappers in the mountains now than they is beaver! Ye never seed the like of it. The Company has got out their bri-gades. Us Rocky Mountain boys has got four or five out. And they's a coupla dozen free trappers from down your way workin' around hyar. And the lid's off for prices! The Company is payin' as high as nine dollars for plews. And the Hudson Bay boys is edgin' into the mountains closer and closer all the time.

They got their forts on the Columbia, but ye'll run into Erma-
tinger and Payette way east of the Bitterroots nowadays. Jist
edgin' in. And last summer, hyar come two more outfits."

"Did?"

"Did so. One's a New Englander name of Wyeth. He ain't
gonna do much. Other'n is a army feller name of Bonneville.
Captain Bonneville. Now, he's got all the money in the world
behind *him*, though can't nobody figger where he got it, and he's
got a big outfit. He flings his dollars around right smart, or I
wouldn't say so. Pays as high as four hundred dollars a year
wages. But he's a real greenhorn and he's a fool. Built a stockade
hyar on the Green . . . up at Horse Creek. Real log stockade,
mind ye. Called it Fort Bonneville." Fitzpatrick laughed.
"Boys call it Fort Nonsense."

You could never have told Joe Fowler had ever heard of Captain Bonneville. He appeared to be curious, as any mountain
man would be at the appearance of another outfit, but not overly
so. "Take much beaver?"

"Nope. Not enough to pay his expenses. Lost one whole
brigade up in Blackfoot country. Jist sort of wanders around.
Covers a lot of ground but don't git no skins to amount to
nothin'. Jist another fool got fur fever and thinks he kin git
rich hyar in the mountains. He ain't gonna. Not the way *he's*
goin' about it. He brung his trade goods in wagons plumb to
the Green—twenty of 'em."

"Sounds like he brung plenty of goods," Fowler commented.

"Oh, he's got the trade goods, all right. But he jist wastes 'em
palaverin'. Don't git hardly no skins in trade."

"Where's he at now?" Fowler asked.

"On the Bear, I reckon. After rondyvoo him and some of his
boys was up near Fort Union, on the Yellowstone, and he
shipped what skins he'd took home by boat—down the river.
Sent most of his outfit back with 'em. Then he come on back
down into the Wind Rivers. Reckon he's got a cache at his stockade. Anyway, him and a handful of his boys come by hyar last

week. Said he had a outfit on the Bear and he was aimin' to join 'em. Said they'd pick where they was goin' to winter, then."

"Where'd he winter last year?"

"On the Salmon. Up close to the Lemhi Pass. Amongst the Nay-pursies." Fitzpatrick chuckled. "We plucked him good last year. Milt Sublette heard he was aimin' to hunt on the Malade. Milt taken his boys thar and beat him to it. Me and Jim was up above him in the Bitterroots, and Payette and his Hudson Bay boys was over on the Boise, so he didn't have no-where to go. Jist rapped around hyar and thar. Aw, he's a real damnfool greenhorn, Joe. Easiest pickin's you ever seed."

"How much longer you think he'll last?"

"Depends. Now, you know he ain't flingin' his own dollars around. Don't no army captain make that much money. And he's regular army—ain't no doubts about that. He's jist on leave. They's somebody with good money backin' him, but they'll git tired makin' no profits one of these days. I figger he'll have to give up, one more season. Have to git back to soldierin' if nothin' else. Funniest thing, Joe. He's one of the gamest sports ye ever seen. Ever'body likes him. Ye can't help it. He laughs at hisself fer his green ways and he gits along good with the Injuns. They all like him fine, too. He's a good-natured feller and this child will say this for him. He don't wear down. He lasts. He covers more ground than any other leetle, short-legged feller you ever seen. He's been out hyar a year now, and he's been all over this country. Ain't a hole or a mountain he ain't poked into. He even clumb that big peak in the Wind Rivers. Recollect that high one ain't nobody ever tried to climb? Well, he went plumb up it. And he's got all sorts of compasses and surveyin' things and thermometers and he's got a measurin' thing he calls a sextant. Looks like he'd ruther to measure things than trap beaver, way he's allus marchin' around and climbin' and crossin' and recrossin'. But he's a educated cuss and you couldn't expect no different. West Point, they say. Reckon he jist wants to find out."

Fowler tapped out his pipe. "Sounds like it, don't it."

Fitzpatrick laughed. "Them Crows was a trouble to Bonneville, too. Up there in the Wind Rivers he had his boys in two parties workin'. One of 'em was out by hisself. Crows run onto him and had the biggest *kind* of fun with him. Stripped him mother naked, teased him and plucked him, skeered the hell outen him, then turned him loose 'thout a stitch of clothes on to make his way back to camp. Bonneville said that feller never would git over the shame of it. Come in 'thout a hair left on him, bald as a hen egg, froze stiff, but not hurt in no way."

Fowler laughed. "A wonder they let him go."

"Oh, they warn't countin' coup. Got plenty. They was jist havin' some fun with him. Well, dang, this coon's been doin' all the talkin'. You tell, now. Ye been to Californy, ye say. I ain't never been. What's it like?"

"Like what old Jed Smith told you, I reckon, Fitz. Warm, easy country. Spanish. Rich land some places. Cattle, tame Indians, pretty *señoritas*. Horses and mules is endless. That's what we was doing. Buying up critters to sell in Missouri."

"Beaver?"

"Not none. Oh, maybe up north. But the British has got a hold up there."

"It ain't for me, then," Fitzpatrick said. "This coon is purely a beaver man." He added reflectively, "Joe Walker's workin' fer Bonneville. Bonneville sent him to Californy end of August—after rondyvoo."

"Walker? With Bonneville?"

"Yep. Right-hand man. Come out with him."

"Like to see him. I've not seen Walker in years."

"Been the lawman back in one of them Missouri settlements, he said. Said he was down around Fort Gibson one time, run into Bonneville, and hired to him."

"And he sent Walker to California, did he?"

"Yep. Joe taken about twenty of the boys with him. Bonneville brought Mex passports for 'em with him from St. Louis."

"Well," Fowler said, "if he's looking for beaver over there he'll be disappointed. If he's buying critters, they got a-plenty."

A lot had been made of Pete Smith's accident when Fowler's party first arrived, and the talk drifted back to it now, and it was told again how he had lost his leg and how Coon Bastro had ambushed him and Fouchette. Several of Fitzpatrick's men knew Bastro. "He's a mean bastard," one of them said, "real, low-down mean, the way Jim Beckwith is. Cut his own mother's throat if it would serve him. When I knowed him he was workin' fer the Company at Union. Huntin' buffler for 'em. And thick as thieves with Beckwith. He killed a man for layin' with his Crow woman. Feller was a Company trader. Reckon that was why Coon drifted away. I ain't heared where he was last few years."

"We'll find him," Fowler said.

"We'll watch out for him," Fitzpatrick promised.

"Don't nobody take him," Mose said. "That bastard's our'n."

"Shore. Shore," Fitzpatrick laughed, "we'll jist watch sign and let ye know."

About half drunk when he went to his lodge, Fowler found Betsy asleep and taking up all the robe room. He shoved her over and she roused a little, murmured sleepily, then came completely awake to scold and fuss at him for forgetting to take off his moccasins. When she had slipped them off he turned, luxuriating in the bed she had warmed, and slid her into the cup of his legs and body. "You're better'n a fire to get warm by," he told her, nuzzling, putting his cold hands under her shirt against her bare flesh.

She fussed at their coldness but held them close against her to warm them. He was half asleep when she began to talk. The man called Bastro, she told him, was with the Crows now. He had joined them two weeks ago.

Fowler was jolted full awake. "The devil you say! How'd you find that out?"

She had been talking with Shoshone women. While he was visiting at the fire. And so. And yes. And thus. The man called Bastro had appeared from the south, riding alone, and he had visited with the Crow village five days before going north.

"He ain't with the band that's been pestering Fitzpatrick?"

No. He had not stayed with the village. The Crow chiefs had palavered with him and he had gone north. It was said he would join his friend Beckwith.

Fowler grunted. "Two of a kind. Well." He turned on his back and stared into the gloom in the cone of the tepee. Well, so. They had Bastro pocketed now. They could find him. But first he had to find Bonneville. Then there would be time for Bastro. Things were working out. Bonneville was on the Bear and Bastro was up on the Yellowstone with Beckwith. He'd better tell the boys tomorrow which way his stick floated, so they could set to it.

His eyes closed slowly. Fitzpatrick's whiskey, Betsy, the warm robes, the news he had learned . . . he could sleep well tonight.

nine

"**I** SAY WE SPLIT," Pete Smith said stubbornly. "Me and Starr will go for Bastro. You and Mose and Ben kin find Bonneville."

"That the way the rest of you feel?" Fowler asked.

"Well, now," Mose said reasonably, "I dunno. We know whur Bastro's at. He ain't gonna git away. You and Starr go hightailin' it up thar after him right now, he'll be lookin' out fer ye. Be expectin' ye. Beckwith could hide him out and lie and ye'd never find him. But if we wait a little, let him git his guard down, let him commence to think we done lost his track, we could ketch him by surprise. Whyn't we all go with Joe. Find Bonneville, winter up, do our regular trappin', then when Bastro's least expectin' us, make a *paseo* up that way and take him."

Pete snorted. "You're jist tryin' to git us to wait so's you kin be in on it."

"Well, s'pose I am! Makes sense to wait a leetle. Git him off his guard."

Big Starr, surprisingly, agreed with Mose. "That shines with this child, Mose. It *do* make sense to ketch him off guard."

"It don't to me," Pete said with heat. "Supposin' he gives us the slip? Supposin' he puts out somewhere else?"

"Where could he go?" Fowler asked. "He can't get a job anywhere now. And he's bound to know every outfit in the mountains has got their hand against him. The reason he went back to Beckwith and the Crows is because he knows that. He ain't got nowhere to go, Pete."

"He mought go back to the settlements."

Fowler grunted. "He's running from the law back in the settlements. You think he'll head back there and land in jail some place? No, we got him in a pocket, now. He ain't going no place. He can't get away. We got him. We can take care of him when it suits us. Now, I ain't reminding you boys you're Fowler hands. I ain't gonna do that. You can make your own choice. Decide amongst yourselves and let me know."

"You go for Bonneville, is that it?" young Lashly asked.

"I go for Bonneville right *now*. I'll go for Bastro, too, when the time comes. But it was me promised Mr. Driant to find Bonneville. It's got nothing to do with you boys."

Suddenly Pete gave in. "We stick, dammit. I ain't goin' ag'in Joe. But if that damned bastard gits away from us . . ."

"He won't," Fowler promised.

They stayed on with Fitzpatrick long enough to hunt and make meat, and they bought new supplies from him, coffee, sugar, flour, tobacco. They traded a few gaunted horses for new ones with the Shoshones, and Pete finished whittling his pegleg and strapped it on. The stump was still too tender for him to wear the leg very long but time would take care of that. He was a man with two legs again. And being a two-legged man again he took himself a Shoshone squaw who was angular, squint-eyed, and so slow-moving the boys promptly dubbed her Pokey.

Young Lashly didn't pass up the chance to jeer. "Yah! Them Shoshone squaws is the purtiest in the mountains. Just wait till you see a Shoshone woman. You'll be sorry you taken a Ute. Jeeeeesus, Pete, I ain't ever seen a Utah as ugly as Pokey. How you know whichaway she's going with them crossed-eyes? She looks one way and goes another."

"Wagh!" Pete rumbled. "Her feet tracks, don't they? I jist foller where her feet goes. They ginerally go where I want 'em to go."

There was some coarse bantering about where Pete mostly wanted her to go, but like most mountain men Pete had picked a steady workhorse of a woman. She could stay right alongside Betsy, who was the best working squaw any of them had *ever* seen, and that was more than Big Starr's Mamselle or young Lashly's Annie could yet do. "And she gits outta hand," Pete said, slipping off his pegleg and brandishing it, "I got me somethin' to lodgepole her with that'll shore make her shine, or I wouldn't say so."

They met the Englishman, Captain William Drummond Stewart. They hunted buffalo with him and they admitted he was as good a shot as they had ever seen and he had the finest English rifle they had ever seen. It was a Manton doublebarrel. "It cost a heap of dollars," Mose said, handling it reverently, then handing it back, "more'n this coon could pay out."

They all hefted it, even shot it with Captain Stewart's gracious urging. But not one of them would have traded his own big Hawken for it. "She's fancy," Big Starr said later, "and mebbe he kin make her throw center, but Joe's old Hellraiser thar is the best rifle ever this child come down on a buffler with. She don't *never* throw off-center."

They liked the Englishman, but he was an odd fellow to them and they couldn't make him out. Nobody could figure his game, and they didn't try hard. He was sociable, free with his whiskey, and he appeared to have the hair of the grizzly on him. For the time being he had him a Shoshone squaw. "Jist fer now," Fitzpatrick told them. "He don't keep one regular. But he shore tries 'em all." He was twitting the captain, who was present.

"I like variety," Stewart said, laughing. "Variety does not stale."

He was a man of middle height, in his late thirties, sturdily built, with dark skin, hair, and eyes. He had a hawkbill nose and went clean-shaven except for a mustache which drooped handsomely about his mouth. In spite of his buckskins, he stood and walked like a soldier, and camp routine and discipline sat easily on him. He was used to it. He amused them with some stories of army life and told them in some detail about the battle of Waterloo. Then Fitzpatrick intervened. "The captain hyar is the one shot that mad wolf I was tellin' ye about."

"Now, that taken guts," Big Starr said. "Thar's two things this child'll run from: a grizzly that's been hurt and a mad critter. I'd a been up a tree till now, had it been me."

Captain Stewart chuckled. "Well, my rifle was loaded and I was nearest the animal." He went on. "I was frightfully upset about the whole episode. If I hadn't been expecting a female guest that night George Holmes would not have been bitten. We shared a tent. I asked him to sleep outside that night. When the wolf appeared and ran amuck through the camp, George had his ear torn off. The least I could do was kill the beast to prevent further injury."

The men had already heard how Holmes had fallen ill ten days or two weeks later, had drifted into melancholy, then become dangerously sick, and how finally he went out of his mind and ran away to his death. "Beauty" Holmes, he had been called, because he was such a handsome lad. One of Tom Fitzpatrick's young hunters.

Captain Stewart liked Fowler's big roan and tried to buy him. "I covet every handsome piece of horseflesh I see," he said. "I'll give you five hundred dollars for him." His black eyes glinted and his hawk nose twitched with eagerness.

Fowler just laughed.

"Well, put your own price on him," the captain insisted. "Name it and I'll pay it."

"There ain't enough money to buy that horse," Fowler said. "He ain't for sale."

The captain looked at him directly, then nodded. "I wouldn't sell him, either, if he belonged to me. I respect your feelings." He ran his hand down the big blue's flanks. "But, God, what a horse! Ever run him?"

"Sometimes."

Behind him, the boys snickered. They had all won plenty of dollars on Joe's big roan.

"You coming to rendezvous this summer?" the captain asked.

"Likely."

"If you do, we'll have a race. My bay against your roan. But it will be a real race, I warn you. My Jezebel can run."

"I wouldn't be interested if she couldn't," Fowler said, "it would be stealing your money."

Fitzpatrick grinned. The news of the race would travel all through the mountains, and next July men would ride a thousand miles to see it and bet on it. They would bring furs with them, and the Rocky Mountain boys ought to do real well again.

Next morning Fowler led his outfit out, heading north of west a little, bearing on the Beer Springs to hit the Bear River. If Bonneville was still on the river, he'd be somewhere near the springs.

2.

Some called them the soda springs. Beer or soda, the place was eerie. Created by volcanic action, it gave you the feeling it wasn't over yet, what with cracks in the earth steaming and vaporing, springs oozing and gushing, the hot insides of the earth grumbling and rumbling. You had the feeling the Lord hadn't finished here yet, and what shape he had in mind was still his own secret. You wanted to walk easy and breathe soft so as not to disturb the delicate equilibrium and start a belch of fire and lava again, that might maybe swallow you up.

What you saw first from the summit of the last ridge before you started down into the small cupped basin was the dazzle of white earth. The whole floor, from river to mountain, was white. If the sun was shining, the white was glittering and blindingly brilliant. If it wasn't, the clay had the gray look of dirty marble. The ridges which rimmed the basin were black with basalt and studded with black-green cedar and pine. The river was piled with lava rock. An occasional grove of cedar and pine grew around a spring and were stark against the white floor.

Joe Fowler knew the region well. He had traversed it often and he had wintered sometimes farther south in the Cache Valley. But he never came near the springs without feeling a little out of joint. He didn't believe, as most mountain men and all the Indians did, that it was devils or bad spirits which made the gassy springs froth the river bed and crack the white earth with steam vapors, rumble threateningly and smell up the place with that queer, sulphurous odor. Mountain men said, "It's a hell of a place and the devil hisself lives in it. Why, the damned place even *smells* like fire and brimstone."

Fowler knew better than that. He knew vaguely what had created the place, but knowing even a little about it didn't do much for the uncomfortable feeling it gave you. Letting the big roan pick his way down through fallen pines and big black boulders he had again the disquieting feeling that this place ought to be let alone. It wasn't any place a man had any business being, except passing through. There were grotesqueries of nature, which, natural in themselves, were still unnatural for man. This place was one of them. So was Colter's Hell up on the Yellowstone. So was the great salt lake below. So were the sandy deserts. Not everything natural was friendly to man.

Young Lashly was riding beside Fowler as they came out onto the clayed floor. His eyes bugged when he saw the numerous springs, and he winced when the ground rumbled under his horse's feet. "You aiming to camp us here?" he asked.

Fowler shook his head. "We'll go on past the springs. You couldn't get one of the squaws to pitch a tepee anywhere near these springs."

"I wouldn't blame 'em," young Lashly said positively. "It ain't no fit place. Why, even the river's a boiling and bubbling."

"There are springs in its bed." Fowler pointed to tracks. "Looks like Bonneville's been here. Pretty good-sized party, too."

They halted and Mose and Starr came up. They studied the

tracks and found they went downstream. "Well, he ain't left the river yet," Mose said. "Let's git on down to the steamboat spring."

"Reckon he'd be camped thar?" Starr wondered.

"Not if he's got any old hands with him," Mose said.

They followed the river down, picking their way through the big lava rocks, for three quarters of a mile. Immediately on the riverbank there, where the basin narrowed with the spur of the ridge pressing in, lay the biggest of the springs. They could see its jet thrown into the air before they reached it. "Thar she is," Mose said to young Lashly, pointing. "She's throwed up out of them rocks. She's allus three foot high but ever' hour as regular as yer watch ticks they's a kind of rumblin' down inside them rocks and she's throwed up a heap higher. Not as high," he said, "as that 'un in Colter's Hell, which I ain't never seed and don't hanker to see, but she's throwed up several foot."

The spring erupted from a mouth of rock which over the years had formed from its minerals. It was now urn-shaped and colored the rusty red of iron oxide.

The men were dismounting, milling about the spring, and the squaws were finding cups and utensils for them. "Git down," Mose said, "you got to drink some of these waters. They taste jist like beer."

Young Lashly got down but he was skeptical. He caught a cup of the water and tasted it and dashed it to the ground. "It's hot," he said, "and it don't taste like beer, it tastes like iron. We had a well one time, back home, was iron water. Couldn't use it. Turned Ma's clothes red and was putrid." The boy ran his tongue over his lips. "And this water stings, too, like it had pepper in it."

"It's good water, though," Starr said. "Shore it tastes like iron, but that don't hurt it none. It's good fer ye."

"Not for me," Lashly said, "I'll stick to the river water."

About that time there was a low rumble and panting bubbling, sounding much like the bass throb of a steamboat engine lying up. Mose shouted, "She's goin'. Hyar she comes, boys. Stand back and let her rip!"

The rumble slowly increased into a broken-throated roar and suddenly the spring was jetted eight or ten feet into the air. The men whooped and waved their hats and ran well back out of the way of the steaming spray. "That's why she's called the steamboat," Big Starr told Lashly. "She comes on to spurt with that put-puttin' sound jist like a steamboat engine. Jist like one tied up at the wharf in St. Louis gittin' ready to depart. *Don't she now?*"

Young Lashly shook his head. "I ain't ever seen a steamboat. But I don't like this here spring."

Pete called him suddenly. "Come over hyar, boy, and see *this.*"

The men looked at each other and winked and nudged elbows. Young Lashly went where Pete was standing and looked. "See that thar teeny little hole," Pete pointed, "now watch."

In a moment a blast of hot air with a light wreath of smoke escaped the hole and there was a slight grumbling in the ground. "Smell it," Pete said.

Young Lashly put his nose down and took a big whiff of the gas, then he staggered back, fanning at his nose and mouth. He reeled off, choking and gagging. The men guffawed. As greenhorns they had all had the same trick pulled on them. They knew the gas was making young Lashly dizzy and might, if he'd got a big enough whiff, make him vomit. Lashly's squaw ran up to guide him to a rock where he could sit. She glared at the men, whose laughter slowly died away. "Aw, he'll git over it, Annie," Mose said. He chuckled. "Recollect that time we come up on old Rube Herring hyar? That time he was makin' medicine?"

"Well, I *do,*" Big Starr said. "We got hyar long about sundown and old Rube was settin' right thar, on that rock, a gazin' at the spring. He didn't much more'n look up when we pulled in. Said kind of mournful like that they was the worst kind of devils in them waters."

"Recollect we asked him if he was campin' hyar," Mose said, "and he said he was. Said he'd been downed on too often to be skeered by what could come out of them waters and not even that devil hisself could shine with him. He'd had the worst spell of luck he'd *ever* had. The Injuns had stole two of his animals and all his skins and three of his traps. He just had his ridin' horse left. He made medicine when he thought we'd all gone, but me and Starr was hidin' in them canes over thar. We watched him."

Still a little groggy, young Lashly looked up. "What did he do?"

"Well, first he filled his old redstone pipe and then he walked around the spring three times. Then he set hisself down and lit the pipe. He got her to smokin' then he p'inted the pipe stem down towards the spring three times. Then he puffed a mighty cloud and he blew it in the four directions and towards the sky and the ground. He said several things in Injun we couldn't hear, then he rolled hisself in his robes and went to sleep."

"Did it work?"

Mose drank down another cup of the water. "Dunno. We left him thar. Ain't seed him since, but he's still around some place. Leastways, *this* child ain't heard of him goin' under. So I reckon it worked."

Fowler's head turned slowly, studying the spurt of the spring. Medicine. Man had always propitiated his gods, made medicine before them, begged them, pled with them, placated them in one way or another. He was so small and lonely, in such a big and hostile world. Even small favors were so acceptable, and any gesture which might be the right gesture must be made. Betsy didn't want him to drink this water. She had begged him last night not to touch it. Evil spirits, she said, lived under the ground, talked through the ground, made the water full of bubbles and smells and bad taste. Please do not drink the water, she had said, it is not good. Some harm will befall you.

He didn't believe it, but he did not drink the water. He had drunk it before, without harm of any kind to himself—it was just water. But he didn't like its taste and he told himself, not dipping his cup now, that he was not drinking because he didn't like the hot, metallic taste. Why drink it if he didn't want it? But studying the gas-filled water he had the feeling he was making medicine in his own way. He was not going through incantations and motions, the way old Rube Herring had done, but he was not tempting the gods.

He moved away, studied the tracks that milled about the spring, let the men drink their fill and tease the squaws who would not touch it, then he said, *"Bueno,* let's move out."

Perhaps three miles farther downstream they saw the smoke of fires, smelled the smoke, and a few minutes later heard the talk and laughter of men. They halted, listened, and heard a wild yippee and heard somebody yell, "By God!" Fowler eased in his saddle. "Bonneville's men, I reckon."

They single-filed and moved on. A good mile from the camp they were halted by a vedette who lowered his rifle when they came around a big boulder into the clear and he saw they were white men. Fowler did not know the man. He called to him, "Joe Fowler here. This is my outfit. I'm looking for Captain Bonneville."

The man slid his rifle to the ground. "Shore, Mr. Fowler. I've heared of you. Camp's jist on down a piece. Captain's thar."

They rode up to him. "Injun trouble?" Fowler asked. "Or just taking care."

"Jist takin' keer," the man said. "We done had enough Injun trouble to do us a spell."

The sun had slid down the mountains and the camp was in shadow when they arrived. It was a small well-made camp of four fires directly on the river, tepees pitched properly, luggage and packs well disposed, animals corraled and penned for the night already. Fowler noticed and thought the Seventh Infantry wouldn't have been ashamed of Captain Bonneville. Indians pitched a good camp. Old mountain men pitched a good camp. And nearly all military men pitched a good camp. A small village of Bannocks were camped below, and the Indians were milling about noisily.

Two or three of Bonneville's men were old hands and recognized them as they rode up. They surrounded them and gave them a gleeful welcome. The men dismounted and the squaws, under Betsy's direction, led the animals off and fanned out to erect lodges upstream a little, in a copse of cedars clear of old snow.

Fowler's men scattered among the fires, picking out old friends, shouting, whooping, clapping backs enthusiastically. From a large, comfortable lodge a short-legged rotund figure emerged to see what all the shouting was about. He had a Scotch plaid capote thrown around his shoulders and a battered, beat-up old cap on his head. His hair was long, dark, and tangled. Seeing strangers he strode toward Fowler, who went to meet him.

There was no mistaking him, Fowler thought. He walked with the same military bearing and air of authority he always had, that any good officer of the Seventh always had. He had a little more girth on him now, but he still looked strong and fit. His color was high and good and his eyes had the same dark, twinkling gaze Fowler remembered. He still looked like a man with a great zest for life.

Even in first youth, Fowler remembered, Bonneville had been short, stocky, solidly built, with a tendency toward plumpness. But he had always been, also, surging with energy, restless and reckless. He had liked the good things of life, had them when he could, but could do without them. Life in frontier posts did not often provide them. Fowler knew that under that beat-up old cap the crown of the man's head would be bald. It had been when Bonneville was in his twenties.

"My name is Fowler," he said, grasping Bonneville's hand. He stood a full head taller than the captain.

"The great Joe Fowler?" Bonneville said, his eyes flashing pleasure and his mouth stretching in a wide smile. He pumped Fowler's hand heartily. "The old mountain man? But you aren't old at all! I expected to see an ancient if I ever had the pleasure of meeting you."

"Age is measured by your time in the mountains out here," Fowler said. "Me and Jim Bridger are about the same age . . . and Fitzpatrick and the Sublettes. All old hands now."

"To be sure. To be sure."

They exchanged a few more pleasantries. Fowler pointed out his men, said their squaws would make camp a little upstream, they wouldn't intrude. "But you will be my guest tonight," the captain protested. "The boys will want to exchange news. We have meat, my friend, plenty of meat. The Bannocks found buffalo a few days ago. We are in the midst of plenty. But come into my lodge and have a drink with me while we talk."

3.

Inside the captain found two mugs and filled them. Fowler tasted and laughed. "I see you've learned to cut your trade alcohol with wild honey."

Bonneville's eyes were merry. "It must be cut with *something*, my friend, to go down."

Fowler stretched his legs and swirled the drink around in the mug. "It goes down as good as that Cherokee rotgut your boys used to bring into Fort Smith."

Bonneville's eyes widened, his brows lifted, and his mug

stopped halfway to his mouth. He set it down slowly. "No man would know about that goddamned Cherokee whiskey who hadn't drunk it. You have been in that country, Mr. Fowler?"

Fowler laughed. "Grew up in it, sir. I knew you when you were first posted to Fort Smith. You used to race your pretty bay mare in the Arkansas bottoms on my father's place."

Bonneville gazed at him, thunderstruck. "That was Matt Fowler's place . . . Fowler? *Fowler!* By God, you're Matt Fowler's boy, aren't you? Joe Fowler! Joe *Fowler,* of course!" He struck his forehead with his hand at his stupidity. "Joe Fowler, the kid who used to go out on the prairie and catch wild mustangs and sell 'em to the boys of the regiment! Used to go on scouts with my corporal, Abe Lathrop. Never was anything with four legs that young Joe Fowler couldn't ride. Why, you used to trap beaver, too, and sell the skins to Colonel Rogers in the village!"

"Well, I *did*," Fowler admitted, pleasure at being remembered so well running through him.

"Why, you were just a long-legged colt yourself, those days. You can't be a grown man yet . . . not Joe Fowler, the mountain man!"

"Well, but I am. I'm twenty-nine years old, Captain. Been in the mountains twelve years."

The captain gazed at him and shook his head in disbelief. "How fast times goes by. It's not possible. Not *possible.* But why didn't I guess? I've been hearing about Joe Fowler ever since I reached the mountains, didn't even think . . ."

"It's not an uncommon name, sir. Must be many a Joe Fowler."

"But . . . Well, I was posted to Jefferson Barracks for a while and when I returned to Arkansas the garrison had been moved to Fort Gibson . . . but the name should have meant something to me."

"I reckon that colt-legged boy stayed on the Arkansas and never growed up, in your mind," Fowler said.

The captain's round face was wreathed in smiles of pleasure. "Think of it! Joe Fowler—Matt Fowler's boy, here in my tent on Bear River. It's a world of space and change, and who could have guessed we would meet and cross trails in these vast mountains. But here we are. I am delighted, Joe. I am delighted."

He suddenly reached out and took the mug of metheglin from Fowler's hand. "That is not fit for this occasion, Joe. This requires something special." He rummaged in his pack and found a flask. "This is brandy. Real brandy from St. Louis. I've been saving it for a special time, and I should say the meeting of two old Arkansawyers is a very special time indeed." He poured a generous libation and lifted his mug. "To Fort Smith, Joe, and the old days."

Fowler raised his own mug, and for a moment there passed through his mind, like a panorama, the look of the Arkansas bottoms, the bend in the river, the way the old log house sat in its grove of pecan trees, the wide dogtrot cluttered with saddles and trappings and dogs and plows and harnesses, and the people of the house were in the vision, young as when he had left it, his sister and his brothers, bursting with youth and life and sound and laughter. He saw the long and prairie look of the country toward the old fort, the bluffs ledged above the river, and the sand and willow islands which they had loved as children. Where they had so often beached their old dugout and built sand forts and shot imaginary Indians with sweet gum balls.

It passed and he came back inside the tent on Bear River, faced the pudgy, stocky captain whose dark face was lit with happiness. "To Fort Smith," he said, "and the old days."

They drank and sat, then, and talked about the old days— Major Bradford and the old garrison at Fort Smith; the removal of the Indians to the Indian Territory; Indian agents, Indian traders, soldiers, whiskey runners; the Osage-Cherokee wars. They spoke of the people they had known there, Colonel Rogers, who began the village of Fort Smith near the fort;

Nathaniel Pryor, the Osage agent, who had been to the Pacific with Lewis and Clark; Auguste Chouteau, still the biggest name in the fur trade in that region. Fowler thought how when he was a boy the name Chouteau always meant Auguste Chouteau, up on the Neosho. He didn't know there were any more. He didn't know about St. Louis and the vast fur empire. Now, the name Chouteau meant the Company, the enemy of the Rocky Mountain boys and all free trappers.

Captain Bonneville told him about the removal of the garrison to Fort Gibson, sixty miles west, when the Osage line was shifted; about Colonel Arbuckle, the commandant, who was never, he thought, going to retire. "Gibson is a hard duty," he said. "They built it . . . you remember that low land lying near the Three Forks? Right there, just above the canebrakes. On the east bank of the Neosho." He took a piece of lava rock and drew the three rivers coming together—the Verdigris, the Neosho, and the Arkansas, and he located the stockade. "A sickly place, for many. I seem to be immune from malaria, but many have died of it there."

"Yes," Fowler said. "My sister's husband, Captain Brooks, died of it there."

Bonneville half shut his eyes, remembering. "By Jove, he did. Savanna's first husband. Well, it was a rough duty for gentlemen, and many of us drew it as our first duty when we left the Point. But I like it. I always did. I thrived on it. Its roughness never bothered me. I liked the Indians and I liked the traders and I liked the the life. It gave me my first taste of the West and it infected me with a fever to know more about it." His black eyes twinkled. "It must have bitten you there, too."

Fowler laughed. "Well, it *did*. You'd have had to be deaf and blind not to see and hear the West there."

"When did you leave?"

"September of '21," Fowler said. "I come out with Hugh Glenn's party."

"Ah, yes. I remember that one. Been back?"

"No. Never been back. Just to St. Louis a few times. Always mean to go back, but somehow never get down there. Always in a hurry to get through my business in St. Louis and get back here. But Savanna writes to me occasionally."

The captain's foot started swinging and he chuckled. "Do you know, Joe, I was more than half in love with Savanna myself. While she was free. After Captain Brooks died and before she married Abe Lathrop. We all were in love with her. Every unattached man at Gibson was. Even Colonel Arbuckle was smitten with her. She could have had her pick of the officers." He continued, musing, "She's one of the most beautiful, bewitching, infuriating women I ever knew."

"She's also one of the most fiery-tempered and bull-headed women the Lord ever made," Fowler said. "She gets into, and out of, more hot water than any dozen women have any right to."

"Oh, that," the captain shrugged. "I never minded her temper or her stubbornness. They only made her more intriguing. But she wouldn't even *look* at me. Wouldn't consider my hand at all! That was what infuriated me. And then, with every officer in the post pursuing her, she married a sergeant. My old corporal, Abe Lathrop! And promptly has twins by him. You knew that, I suppose." He darted a quick look at Fowler.

"Yes, I knew that. But you are behind times, Captain. Savanna is married to David Holt, now."

"The post surgeon! David Holt . . . but Abe? What happened to Abe?"

"He was killed last fall."

"On that Dragoon expedition! I heard of the expedition. I knew he was with them. They were going out to treat with the Comanches . . ."

"Well, it was Pawnees who killed Abe." Fowler gave him more details and there was a long silence as each man remembered, soberly and regretfully, a man they had both liked and respected.

"He was a good man," Bonneville said finally. "One of the best scouts I ever had." He cocked his head and squinted through his pipe smoke at Fowler. "But I always said he wasn't the man for Savanna. Savanna was cleverer than Abe, and she could not long have loved and respected any man who was not as clever as she. Nor was Savanna cut out to be an enlisted man's wife. She was made for the officer class."

Fowler smiled. "She was complaining about it before Abe was killed. How she missed being on the inside of things. David, now, well, David has loved her since she was a child, of course. She married Captain Brooks to get away from home and our stepmother. She married Abe, I suppose, out of infatuation. But David is right for her. And David can control her."

"Well," Bonneville said staunchly, pouring more brandy, "I would have given him a run for his money had I been there. He wouldn't have won her easily." He lifted his glass again. "To Savanna, the bravest and most beautiful of them all."

"To Savanna."

Enough time had been spent on the past. Fowler reached inside his shirt and pulled out the oilskin pouch. "My mission in finding you, Captain, is to deliver this." Bonneville reached for it, but his eyes were questioning. Fowler said, "Mr. Pierre Driant asked me to deliver it to you."

"Pierre! Yes. Where is he? He was to meet me. To bring me word . . ."

Fowler had then to tell him of Driant's death. Bonneville sat unmoving, not twiddling the pouch, holding it, appearing for the moment incurious about it, listening to Fowler's story. At its conclusion he shook his head. "Poor Pierre. He would much rather have gone under at the hand of an Arapaho. A long, painful, lingering illness . . . it must have galled him badly."

"Until the last he didn't show it," Fowler said.

"No, he wouldn't." Bonneville looked at him quickly. "Did he tell you what was in this pouch?" He slapped the oilskin against his palm.

"No. Just said find you and give it to you." Fowler stood. "And now I've given it to you, sir. I can get on with my own affairs."

Bonneville said, "I must read this immediately . . . you understand. But accept my hospitality. Join my fire. I will be with you shortly."

Fowler nodded and went outside.

4.

It was a rip-snorting evening. The metheglin which Bonneville ordered to be circulated freely was a potent brew of straight alcohol, river water, and wild honey. One drink and you felt fine and happy and mellow. Two drinks and you felt like all your strength had come to you. You were a bull elk or a grizzly bear. Three drinks and you were raring to go, able to take on all the grizzlies that ever stood on their hind legs, a whole tribe of Injuns, or, by God, all of Bonneville's men!

There was wholesale drinking, bragging, and boasting, there was yarning, there was euchre and the hand game, and there were three fist fights. A normal evening for two outfits of mountain men with the hair of the grizzly on their chests and the old grit inside them.

The Bannocks got into the act, too. They crammed their stomachs full of buffalo meat, drank watered-down alcohol, and felt their hearts grow strong and brave. Their crests rose, their feathers ruffled, and they felt called on to blow their own horns before their white brothers. They organized a war dance and stepped and strutted up to the fire and back, around it and beyond, swelling their chests and beating them, vaunting their courage and great deeds, their valor and their victories.

They boasted gloriously of their victories over the bandits of the north, the Blackfeet. They told one at a time, severally, and then all together how they had beaten the Blackfeet, how they had reduced their towns to ashes and ruins, how many warriors they had killed, how many scalps they had taken, and they dared the Blackfeet to come, now, this very moment, and try to take revenge. They would show them what great warriors the Bannocks were! When they received no reply, they sneered at the Blackfeet, insulted them, called them cowards and squaws and mutilated men. It was all very safe. The Blackfeet were several hundred miles away, up north.

Bonneville laughed. "When they roll up in their robes tonight they won't even put a guard over their horses. The Blackfeet have stolen almost every animal they possess. We had to furnish them horses to make this buffalo hunt."

Fowler nodded. "Mostly wind and britches, the Bannocks. Nearly always friendly, though."

The carousing was noisy and they were silent for a time, watching the Bannocks, laughing at their antics, lifting and lowering their cups. Bonneville said, then, "You run into an Englishman yet? Fellow named Stewart? *Captain* Stewart?"

"He's with Fitzpatrick," Fowler said.

"Still with 'em, eh? What did you think of him?"

Fowler gave him a quick, surprised look. "Never thought nothing. Appears to be enjoying himself. Appears to have plenty of dollars. Appears to get around considerably—cover the territory. If he come out here to see the country, he appears to be seeing it."

Bonneville, listening, seemed bemused. He stared in the fire, studying it. Then he roused. "Yes," he said, "yes. The Britisher certainly seems to be doing all those things."

They talked on and on, Bonneville eagerly questioning, Fowler answering out of the rich lore of his knowledge and experience. About Indians, Bonneville was especially curious. What tribe lived here? And there and there? How numerous was it? What were its special habits and characteristics? What was its attitude toward the whites? With a pointed lava rock

Fowler drew him a map, tracing in rivers and mountain ranges. "Put the Pawnees here, on the lower Platte," he said. "One branch of the Cheyennes on the Arkansas. South of them and across the plains are the Comanches. North, and along the upper Platte are the Arapahoes. The Wind Rivers and the Yellowstone are Crow country. Sioux and Ricarees further down on the Missouri. Shoshones west of the Blackfeet, along the Snake and down into this country. Utahs in Spanish country, amongst the parks. Bannocks all through here, mostly on the Snake. Flatheads and Nez Perces on the upper Columbia. They all drift around to hunt. Move about, fight each other, and except for Flatheads and Nez Perces you can't trust none of 'em. They're friendly when they're in the notion. They'll jump you when they ain't. But I never heard of the Flatheads or Nez Perces making war on the whites."

Bonneville nodded. "So I've heard. Why? Why don't they?"

Fowler hesitated. "Several reasons, I reckon. Goes back to Lewis and Clark for one thing. They treated 'em right and Clark doctored 'em. But I reckon the biggest thing is the Hudson Bay boys. They're mostly Canadians and Catholics. They have taught these Indians some religion. They're Britishers and they're edging into our trade, but they have good relations with their Indians. Better'n we do, generally."

Bonneville nodded. Fowler talked on. So many Pawnees, horse people, at war with Crows. So many Arapahoes, horse people, also at war with Crows. So many Blackfeet, horse people, kin to Arapahoes, also at war with Crows. Bonneville laughed. "Any of them friendly to the Crows at all?"

Fowler laughed also. "Not many. You know why they're all at war with the Crows, don't you? The Crows have got the best country in the west. It's the richest in beaver, got the most buffalo. The others are always raiding and invading, and you can't rightly blame 'em. But it's Crow country and they aim to hang onto it. Crows have got the most horses. They are the best horse stealers amongst the Indians. They make the best robes. All them Sioux war bonnets you see, Crows made most of 'em. Them fine Blackfoot moccasins, Crows make 'em. They trade with 'em all—and fight 'em. Shoshones," he added, "are kind of cousins to the Crows. They're pretty friendly with 'em."

The talk turned then to the state of the beaver trade, the fierce rivalry between the big St. Louis empire, the Company, and the Rocky Mountain boys. The steady encroachment of the Britishers of the Hudson's Bay Company from the Columbia. "How many posts do they have on the Columbia?" Bonneville asked.

"I ain't ever been, but the boys say they got four. They got one at the mouth of the Columbia, another one—and it's the main one—at Vancouver about seventy mile upstream. Then they got one at Walla Walla and another one at a place they call Colville. But them posts are just factories, like. The way they take beaver is the same as the Company or any of us. They send out their brigades. And used to, they hunted mostly in their own territory, but of late you run into them brigades everywhere. On the Siskadee, on the headwaters of the Arkansas, on the Platte, the Missouri, down in the Spanish possessions. Getting so you can't cross a pass any more without running into a Hudson Bay brigade."

Bonneville made a humming sound deep in his throat, coughed, lifted his cup, swallowed, wiped his mouth, and said, "Precisely."

He reached to pour another drink but Fowler stayed him. "Them Bannocks," he said, "and the boys can keep this up all night, but it's robe time for this child, Cap'n. I've had enough. I got to shut my eyes."

Bonneville agreed it had been a long evening and they said goodnight.

Ten minutes later Fowler, remembering that he had meant to tell Bonneville where Pierre Driant's furs were cached and hadn't, went to his lodge. But he let it go. Bonneville was busy scribbling in a small black notebook, so busy he didn't even hear Fowler come up. Fowler concluded it could wait till the next day.

ten

THE TWO OUTFITS lingered on near the Beer Springs together for a few days. Bonneville said he had left half his party on the Snake, or Lewis's River as some called it, and he thought he would take this Bear River party there and winter near the Bannock villages. "The Bannocks are friendly," he said, "and about as honest as Indians get to be. They can help keep us in meat for the wintering. There's some good forage there for the animals, and there's good water. About as good a place to winter as the country affords, to my mind."

Fowler liked Cache Valley. More sheltered. Though he didn't say so. Every leader decided for himself.

The weather had turned mild and it was a lazy time for the men. Except for a little hunting they loafed and gambled and yarned. Bonneville stayed busy climbing mountains, roving up and down the valley, using various instruments, making notes, taking measurements. Fowler went with him sometimes. He pointed out landmarks, told what he knew of the usefulness of the valley, who had been there so far as he knew, when, and what they had found. He asked no questions. A fool could tell that Bonneville was surveying, but Fowler figured it was purely Bonneville's business and none of his.

But one day Bonneville said, "Pierre told you, didn't he, that I am on leave from my regiment?"

"Well, he did."

"Yes. Well, no man is ever totally on leave from the army, my friend. I am charged with doing some tasks for the army out here." He laughed. "I doubt my leave would have been approved had I not accepted these tasks. I am making charts, keeping notes, taking altitudes, surveying. I brought with me all the necessary instruments for surveying and charting— theodolites, a sextant, an Arnold chronometer, quadrants, compasses, hydrometer, scales, thermometers, chains . . . everything that would be needed. A cartographer can take my charts, Joe, and make a most acceptable map of the country. Which," he squinted through his sights, "is badly needed. There is no good map of this western country." He straightened up and laughed. "On paper, that is. You mountain men have the map in your heads. The army wants it in the files of the War Department."

Fowler looked at him directly. "Yes. That's why you been sashaying around all over the country." He laughed. "Boys been wondering why you don't stay put one place or another and trap a little fur."

"Oh," Bonneville said quickly, "we trap. I sent fur down the river in August."

"Yep," Fowler said, "all of thirty pack. Didn't pay your men's wages, I'd think."

Bonneville brought his eyes round and stared straight at Fowler. "How much else did Pierre Driant tell you, my friend?"

Fowler met his look. "Not a damned thing else." He held Bonneville's eyes quietly. "You pay four hundred dollars a year wages and that's almost double what the Company or the RMF boys are paying. You built a stockade on the Siskadee. You brought wagons plumb to the Siskadee, the furthest west wagons had ever come. You sent your parties in every direction last year. You, yourself, have covered more territory than most fur brigades. You sent Joe Walker and a party, with Mexican passports issued in St. Louis before you left, to California. You ask me ten million questions about Indians, where they are, how they feel toward the whites. You are interested in an Englishman who is also covering a lot of territory. You are a fur trapper who only took thirty pack of beaver and you are a captain in the U.S. army, sir."

Bonneville dropped his eyes and studied the ground. Then he chuckled. "You are very shrewd, Joe. The other boys talking along those same lines?"

"Nope, they think you're a greenhorn fool. Call your stockade Fort Nonsense. Bonneville's Folly. They ain't interested. They just mean to see you don't take no beaver . . . they just mean to skin you."

Bonneville's eyes lit up merrily. "Good. Good. That's precisely what I mean them to think." He sobered quickly, then, and said seriously, "I am going to take you into my confidence. I know your family. I know your reputation here in the mountains. I know Pierre trusted you. Besides you have guessed too much. How much do you know about the Oregon question?"

Fowler looked at him quizzically. "What we all know. Hudson Bay Company has got a stranglehold on it. Don't reckon none of us rightly know where it commences and where it ends."

"Precisely. Well, Oregon has been an open territory for a good many years. Our country and the British have a joint trade agreement. We are both free to hunt and trap in it. But Oregon has certain loosely fixed boundaries. We know where the Mexican territory ends and begins in the south. We know that the northern boundary is somewhere between the forty-ninth and fifty-fourth parallel. On the east, the continental divide draws the line of longitude and of course the Pacific Ocean marks the line on the west."

"It's a big land," Fowler admitted.

"Much more extensive than is realized back east. Much more, although the government is beginning to eye it with considerable interest. Now. The Hudson's Bay Company is supposed to be a private firm. We know where their posts are. But you, yourself, have told me how they operate, and how they are encroaching. You know how all this began, don't you?"

"I know how the story goes out here. Mr. Astor had a post at the mouth of the Columbia and the British took it over from him during the War of 1812."

"They did, and without even a fight. Mr. Astor had mistakenly trusted the loyalty of some British-Canadians who had worked for him on the lakes—in the old Michilimackinac Company. They were pleased to lower the flag of the United States and raise the British flag over the Columbia. Our government, Joe, is beginning to think it is about time our flag was raised over the Columbia again."

Fowler looked straight into Bonneville's eyes and held them. They met his gaze unflinchingly. "Our government, Captain," Fowler said, "or Mr. Astor?" He leaned forward. "Are you working for the Company, Captain Bonneville?"

"I am not," Bonneville said immediately and unequivocally. "I have nothing to do with the American Fur Company." He waited a moment then he, too, leaned forward. "What I am about to tell you must be divulged to no one, Joe, not even your partners."

Fowler nodded.

"I am working for the government of the United States. My immediate superior is, naturally, my commanding officer, Major General Alexander Macomb. But this mission is under the orders of the War Department and the Secretary, Mr. Eaton."

Fowler drew slowly on his pipe, puffing, studying. "Beaver hunting just a blind, then?"

"Well, you could call it that, yes. Though we take what skins we can, of course. But I can tell you that beaver skins are of very secondary importance."

"Whyn't the government just send out a straight military expedition—like the Lewis and Clark expedition?"

"It would have tipped our hand to the British. And it would have been very expensive and tedious in gifts and agreements with the Indians. This way, I can move freely about the country, pick up information . . . this expedition is even privately financed, Joe. Mr. Astor has put up all the money for it," he held up his hand, "and before you jump down my throat and say you *knew* the Company had a stake in it, let me tell you that Mr. Astor is severing his connections with the Company. He's getting old. He's selling out his fur interests. But Mr. Astor has for many years been well known in Washington and he has loaned money many times to the government. It was natural the government should turn to him for the backing of this particular expedition."

Fowler grinned. *"Bueno.* I'll accept that. But if the government takes over Oregon, Mr. Astor can reopen Astoria, isn't that it?"

Bonneville looked a little exasperated. "I have no idea. I asked no questions."

"All right, Cap'n. I got my own connections in St. Louis. I already knew Astor was selling out and I already know it don't mean a damned thing. The old man may sell out, but Astor interest will still be served. What is it the government has sent you here to do?"

"To cover the country, as much of it as I can. To survey and map it. To learn all I can about the Indians living in the country, where they live, how many are in each tribe, their customs and habits, what their attitude toward us is. To learn all I can about the British intentions in Oregon. To discover if a wagon road to Oregon is feasible. To look at the land and discover if it would support settlers. I forgot to mention that there is a clause in the agreement concerning Oregon with England. Either nation can terminate the agreement at any time, by giving notice one year ahead of time."

"And that time has come?" Fowler asked.

"It may have. It may have. My job is to see if it has. Our government must protect its own interests, Joe."

Fowler nodded. "You think this Captain Stewart is doing the same thing for the British?"

"What would you think? A British army officer running around all over the country, in good standing with our own fur men." Bonneville suddenly sounded bitter. "Britain has been shrewder than we. They have placed their spy right in our midst, with a free pass to every bit of information he can collect around the campfires. He got himself accredited with the right men, Bill Sublette as it turned out. He moves right into the heart of the Rocky Mountain boys. He travels with them, sticks with them tight as a burr. A better way to learn all the British want to know couldn't be found. Fitzpatrick's boys spill their guts every time they open their mouths. And the brigade moves around enough Stewart can see all the country he pleases."

"And nothing to do about it," Fowler said slowly.

"Not one thing. He passes as a wealthy sportsman. He pays his way and who's to say he isn't what he says he is and nothing more. But he makes it all the more imperative for me to do what our government requires." He leaned forward and touched Fowler's shoulder and levelly, tapping each word out with a pudgy finger, continued, "There are men in the government, Joe, and there are an increasing number of them, who believe with Senator Benton that it is the manifest destiny of this nation to reach from one ocean to another. That this continent, from the Atlantic to the Pacific, must be ours. Do you know what that means?"

"It likely means war," Fowler said, "for it means California as well as Oregon." He put his tongue in his cheek. "Well, you've done sent Joe Walker to California . . ."

"Precisely. It is a bold, bright vision, Joe, and it must come to pass. One nation, from sea to sea. We cannot have sore spots like Texas and the New Mexican territory sticking up in our middle. We cannot have the British in Oregon. The geography of the land demands it. When the first adventurers landed on the Atlantic coast, it was inevitable they should eventually reach the Pacific and that it should belong to them."

Fowler pondered for a moment and he saw and touched briefly something of the greatness of the historical process. In his mind's eye there unrolled all the land he knew, from the Mississippi to the Pacific coast, the long middle prairies, the peaks and canyons and parks of the mountains, the sandy hot wastes of the deserts, the valleys and the sweet warming winds of California and the sea . . . and he saw the people moving like a great surging tide across them. And he knew instantly and unquestioningly that it *was* manifest destiny and that it was inevitable. He himself was a drop in the first wave of that relentless tide. He wondered only, and in some surprise, that he hadn't seen it for himself sooner.

But you didn't think much about your own part in making history. It was a personal thing. You did what you wanted to do, followed your own particular star and destiny, and along with a million others doing exactly the same thing, doing what they wanted to do, following their own particular stars and destinies, you created an age, an era, a historical process. It was not the men of action who gave it a name, nor was it they who directed it. Back at home, not doing or daring, were the men with time to think, standing up big enough and tall enough to scc over the heads and shoulders of the men on the move, to call it a movement, an age, an era, to call it manifest destiny.

Bonneville interrupted his thinking. "That pouch you delivered to me contained more instructions, Joe. When I get my outfit settled for the winter, I am going to the Columbia."

Fowler whistled. "Middle of the winter?"

"It can be done, can't it?"

"Anything can be done, if it's got to be. I ain't been, but . . ." he pondered. "Indians get across them Blue Mountains dead of winter. I should say a little party of the right white men could. It ought to be a *small* party, though, traveling light and fast. Fast as they can."

Bonneville laughed. "Fine. Fine. That means you, me, maybe a couple more."

It was calling his hand. By a little stridency in Bonneville's laugh, Fowler knew Bonneville knew it, too. Bonneville was setting up to him and betting all he had he could call a march and make it. But Fowler wasn't thinking of Bonneville just then. He was traveling back to a murky, pain-filled lodge in the North Park. Its sour smell of illness filled his nostrils and Pierre Driant, dying, was before his eyes. "I had plans for a great adventure, my friend, for a great adventure." Fowler could see his dark eyes with the sadness in them. He could hear the voice again, which had held neither fear nor petition. *"Le bon Dieu* has other plans." He could hear the acceptance, the necessary acceptance.

He said, "He was going with you, wasn't he?"

"He was going with me," Bonneville said. "If the instructions so provided—and they did. He was going with me."

There was a long stillness between them then, a long stillness. Then Bonneville turned, his own sadness gone, his eyes squinted merrily and he looked up at Fowler, who stood such a height above him. "Come with me yourself, Joe. What better have you to do with the winter? Come with me. Are you going to hibernate like some great bear? Sit and grow fat with your squaw? Come with me . . . let's chart the canyons of the Snake! Let's climb the Blue Mountains! Let's see what's on the other side!"

He knew instantly he would go—knew he had to go. For men like him the other side of the Blue Mountains was never more than a few steps away. You kept taking them day by day. He had walked right up to them, now, and he had to walk right on over them. *"Bueno,"* he said. He grinned. "I'll set to ye. We'll climb them Blue Mountains."

2.

Fowler's men and their squaws liked being with the larger party. It was like moving into town after a long and solitary sojourn in the wilderness. More men and squaws made things livelier and more pleasant. There was a different set of companions to gamble with, hunt with, yarn with, and squabble with.

The joint outfits left Bear River on the fourth of December and made their way up the Portneuf to its confluence with the Snake. Here they settled in, some three miles from the Bannock village, near enough to visit and enjoy each other, far enough away they didn't have Bannocks for breakfast, noon, and night.

Preparations went forward for the journey. Bonneville had agreed on a small party, a very small party. "You are right," he said to Fowler, "the fewer we take the easier the journey will be. Three or four of us at the most. Enough to support each other but not so many as to be cumbersome."

Fowler nodded, but since only a few were going he had some ideas of his own as to who they should be. "You got in mind who you want to take?" he asked.

Bonneville eyed him shrewdly and chuckled. "You have some of your own boys in mind, don't you?"

"Well, I *do*," Fowler admitted. "I been working with most of my boys a long time. I know 'em. Know what they can do. Know what to expect of 'em. You know your men that good?"

"My best men are scattered around," Bonneville said promptly. "Joe Walker is in California. Michel Carré is back east. Adams is out with a brigade. This is a fair bunch I have with me, but I wouldn't say I know the full stretch of any of them yet. Who did you have in mind?"

"Big Starr," Fowler said. "Be the biggest help to us of anybody. Tough as a buffalo bull and don't make mistakes. He's clever and he's got good judgment."

"If you say so," Bonneville said, accepting Fowler's judgment at once. He pondered a moment longer. "Tell you what, Joe. Your party's small anyhow. Why don't I put 'em all on wages for the rest of the winter and you pick another of them to go with us. Four men is about right for the party."

"If it suits," Fowler said.

He thought about it the rest of the day. Only one man was physically fit to make the fourth on the Columbia journey. Mose was too old and rheumatic for a winter journey and Pete's stump was still too tender. It had to be young Lashly.

At their own fire that night he talked with the boys about it. "Me and Starr and Lashly," he said, "will go with him. It'll be fast. He aims to be back here for the spring season. Everybody will be on wages."

"Suits me," Mose said cheerfully. "We got to winter somewhur. Might as well be here. And I ain't ever been paid wages for winterin' up before."

Pete had his wooden leg off. He thumped it idly on the ground. "You know I could make it, don't you?" he said.

"Sure, I know you could make it, Pete," Fowler said. "But it'd be better not to abuse that stump. Give it a chance to harden over 'fore the hunting season comes around. You boys earn your keep a little helping Bonneville's boys stay in meat."

"Suppose you ain't back in time?"

"Go ahead and make your hunt. Pick up that cache in the North Park. Head for Taos or the rendezvous, whichever you'd rather. I'll find you."

Mose nodded.

Pete fitted his pegleg on and laced the thongs up around his stump. "What about Bastro?" he said, without looking up.

"I ain't forgot him," Fowler said.

Pete heaved himself up and prodded his peg a time or two against the ground, settling the stump into the cup more comfortably. "I ain't aimin' to let you," he said.

Fowler laughed. "I got as much reason as you to go hunting Bastro come spring."

Pete thrust his wooden peg out straight. "No," he said, "you ain't. You ain't walkin' around on one of these."

Fowler's eyes went hard. "Pete," he said, "you want to go hunting for Bastro now, right now, say so. We'll put out. You gonna keep growling, we'll get it over."

Pete flung himself down again. "Aw, hell," he said, "don't pay me any heed. I just got to growl, I reckon. Can't go with you on this journey. Lay around with a bunch of Bannocks all winter. Make a little meat. All on account of this damned stump."

"You're entitled to growl some," Fowler said, "but don't keep throwing Bastro in my teeth. I've done said we'd get him."

Young Lashly wanted to go, was proud he'd been picked, but when he learned the squaws would be left behind he wasn't too happy about it. "I don't much like leaving Annie amongst all them Bonneville fellers," he told Fowler. "They ain't gonna have no regards for a feller's rights. With me gone, they ain't."

"Mose and Pete'll see to your rights," Fowler said.

"I ain't sure they can," young Lashly said.

"Ben," Fowler said, laughing, "if Annie wants to take up with one of the boys while you're gone she will, and ain't nobody can stop her. Mose and Pete'll do what they can. But Captain Bonneville says no squaws and you've got to make up your mind you want to go, the way he says, or don't you. That's all there is to it."

The boy went around the rest of the day pretty mournful but he finally decided to go. Mostly, Fowler thought, because he knew he would never hear the last of it if he let a squaw keep him from going. But for whatever reason, he would make a good hand on the journey and Fowler was glad he was going.

Young Lashly wasn't the only unhappy person about Bonneville's edict. Betsy didn't like it either and her tongue clacked considerably. Did he not know, she told Fowler, that she could travel wherever he could? Had he not had proof of it? There was no place a man could go she could not go. Who, she wanted to know, would care for his things? Who would have dry clothing waiting for him? Who would see that his food was properly prepared? Who would clean his skins and order his lodge?

"Me," Fowler said. "Sure, I know you can travel good as me. If it was up to me you could go. So could the others. I'd like it better. Be a heap more comfortable. But Captain Bonneville, he says no. No squaws."

And so. And who was this man who could tell her own man, Joe Fowler, what he should do? Was he more of a man than her own man?

"On this journey, yes. He's the boss. What he says goes. And we ain't gonna hunt. Be no skins to clean and pack. We're just gonna make a quick *paseo*. Be back here by spring . . . by the time of grass coming to life."

And yes. But, with a quick suspicious look at him, did he think a Flathead or Nez Perce woman could do all the things he required for him as well as she?

"I ain't gonna take me another squaw, Betsy. You needn't to worry about that. Now, I've done told you a dozen times. You stay. There's plenty for you to do while I'm away. When I get back everything I've got will be wore out. See to it you make me plenty of moccasins and clothes. Help Mose much as you can. He don't get around as spry as he used to. If I ain't back when it's time to hunt and Mose and Pete leave, go with 'em. Ain't nothing gonna bother you."

And suppose he did not come back. Many things might happen. She did not like this big and desolate country. She would not remain in it. She was far from her village and her own people. Who would see that she returned to her own country and her own people?

Fowler laughed. "You could get back there by yourself if you had to and you know it. And take Annie and Mamselle with you. You know your way through the Bear River country and across the Uncompaghre. Old Cholly's took your village through there many a time. But I'll be back, never fear. Just do what I tell you and hush up."

There was no good reason the women shouldn't have gone. They could have made the journey as well as any of the men and would have made them all more comfortable, but Bonneville still had some of a more civilized man's notions of women. "They would delay us," he said, "and be a distraction."

"A right enjoyable distraction," Big Starr said grumpily when told. After grumbling, however, he, like young Lashly, accepted it.

In the privacy of his lodge, as Fowler prepared to leave, Betsy was brusque with him, refusing to touch him or to allow him to touch her. *"Bueno,"* he said, "if that's the way you want it. Maybe I *will* find me a Flathead squaw after all."

She gave him a daggered look and spewed a string of Spanish at him which set him to laughing. If she heard he had done such a thing, she promised, she would follow him and she would kill that woman. She would cut her in little pieces and feed her heart to the coyotes. She would learn, that woman, what happened to a woman who took a Utah woman's man!

Fowler gave her a spank, pinched her fat bottom one last time, and left. Her anger with him had not kept her from packing well for him. What he would need, as far as she could foresee, he would find when he needed it.

They left on Christmas Day, each man riding his own horse. Young Lashly led a pack mule and Big Starr led an extra horse. Five animals were all Bonneville would take. It was a lean, stripped party, for speed. There was eighteen inches of snow on the ground, which didn't much matter. It would have been better if it had been frozen harder so the animals didn't break through, but they sloshed along pretty well. They made nine miles for the day.

Anywhere along the Snake was cold this time of year, but in the middle of this plateau, with no timber to break it, the wind was like an ice river flowing over you. Sage wood, called wormwood by some, was all there was to burn, and you could warm a little pemmican, heat a little water, before it burned out, but unless you hauled up about a ton of it you didn't have a fire that would last any time.

Bonneville was full of good cheer, however. For a Christmas surprise he broke out a meal he had had cooked and packed. "We may eat leaner later on," he said, "but we'll have a good Christmas dinner."

He was a stout, solid figure in his old Scotch plaid capote and his warm old cap covering his bald pate. He was a man who didn't down easily. Listening to him joke Big Starr and young Lashly about their cold and lonesome bedrolls that night, hearing him tell how the worst of the journey would be this side the Blue Mountains, how much distance he believed they could and ought to cover each day, what they could expect to find on the Columbia, Fowler got a strong notion that as much as the winter and the mountains, it would be a good thing to be a little wary of Bonneville's everlasting cheerfulness and hopefulness. You wanted a man who was game with you, but you also wanted a man who didn't always look for the best in everything. You got in a fix, what you needed was a man who saw it for a fix and helped do something about it. Bonneville, he figured, would let down on all this rosy glow when he got to know them better. They didn't need it. You didn't have to keep him and Starr or even young Lashly buoyed up with cheerfulness and rosy hope. They had some rough going ahead of them, but there wouldn't a one of them undertaken it without knowing it could be done. Bonneville would learn that, would quieten down and settle into it. Being French, he was excited right now, had to talk a lot.

He could hold a man's attention, though, with his stories. Like them, what he knew had come to him second-hand, but he knew details unknown to them of the disastrous overland journey of the men of the old Astor venture. They had been the trailbreakers, the first over this route. Bonneville regaled them for an hour telling how most of their disaster had come about right along this river. "They thought it was navigable," he said. "They were mostly pirogue people anyway—not used to traveling horseback and overland. They were delighted when they reached this river. They abandoned their animals and took to canoes."

"God," Starr said, "didn't they know about the falls and the rapids? And the canyons?"

"You must remember they were the first. Nobody knew about this river in those days," Bonneville said.

"Why, the Injuns did. Must of. Injuns allus know about sich things. Whyn't they ask? Find out?"

Bonneville mulled it over. "You know, I hadn't thought of that. I don't know why they didn't listen to the Indians. Lewis and Clark always did." He picked up his narrative and told them how big and cumbersome the party was. How they were baffled by the country. How they grew discouraged and how one error led to another and then another until they split in disharmony into numerous parties. Men were lost. Goods were lost. "They mostly made it to Astoria, one way or another," he said, "but it took something out of them that they never recovered. It's a country that can easily defeat you," he said reflectively. "It's so big . . . so big, and so unnatural. And it's so far away."

Big Starr belched comfortably. "This coon ain't worried none about the *country*. We ain't never seen none that could lick us. What this child wonders is if them Hudson Bay boys won't run us off. They done got it staked. Mebbe they won't take kindly to bein' visited."

"Oh, I understand they treat guests hospitably," Bonneville said.

Big Starr flopped his robes out flat on the space cleared for sleeping. "I hope," he said, "you've done understood right."

eleven

I T HAD BEEN a long time since Joe Fowler had followed another man. Not since he was a kid greenhorn with Mose teaching him all he knew had he put his life on the line under another man's judgment. To the extent that it wasn't in him to risk his life or that of his men in the test of another man's wisdom, he wasn't following Bonneville now. He was going where Bonneville went, in the way Bonneville wanted to go, was all. Back deep in his insides was the knowledge that if things went wrong he wouldn't hesitate not only to refuse to follow Bonneville, but to step in and take over. Not that he expected to have to do it. It was something simply elemental in him and every other old hand in the mountains. You got in a real rough scrape you *knew* what you could do. You never knew till he proved up what a new man could do. The inner man appreciated having Big Starr along, too. He was glad Bonneville had not been contrary about it.

But Bonneville on the trail was proving a good leader. Back in camp he had been one of the boys, jolly, hearty, easy-going, full of good spirits, maybe a little too buoyant and cheerful. He didn't ride herd on his boys much and he turned his head the other way on many of their high jinks. On the trail he kept cheerful and hearty, but he suddenly firmed up. He became a man who seemed to know what he was about and how to go about achieving it. He didn't fool around. He had a job to do, it wasn't going to be easy, but you got the feeling he didn't doubt he could do it. Taking note of it, Fowler was amused. It wasn't a fur trapper leading this outfit. It was a tough old Seventh Infantry officer, and Fowler felt a lift of pride in the kind of training the old regiment gave its men, and more than a little sentiment to be associated with it again.

Within two days Bonneville had taught Big Starr and young Lashly how to use the surveying instruments. He had turned over to young Lashly the thermometer. It was Ben's job to set it in a good place and to read it the last thing at night and the first thing in the morning. He taught Fowler to use the sextant and it became his business to take the noon observations. Big Starr had charge of the animals and packs. Bonneville himself was everywhere, observing, taking notes, sketching, collecting rock and soil specimens, making charts. He organized the camp work, the horse guard, the day's march, as if they had been on a military patrol.

Fowler settled into it smoothly. For a day or two he watched to see how Starr and young Lashly would take it. They might have been troublesome with so much discipline. But the stuff Bonneville was made of, the steel and guts and nerve, and his tirelessness were too obvious and they earned respect. He didn't ask anything of one of them he couldn't do himself and usually do it better. Inside that short-legged, chunky, solid little body was as much staying power as they had ever seen. For every job he gave them to do, he took ten on himself. He wasted a little energy with his bustling, but a Frenchman had to bustle a little. He didn't move into his work slow and smooth the way a mountain man would have done. Bonneville *attacked*. But he lasted, just the same. He led off in the morning, full of energy, fiercely ready for the day. He was still out in front when they halted at night, showing little wear. Whatever came of it, Fowler thought, it was likely to be a journey none of them would ever regret.

They moved down the left bank of the Snake. The river was frozen hard enough so that they could have crossed back and forth on it with their horses, but they didn't. Bonneville stayed back from the banks and crossed the tributary streams well back from the width and fullness of their mouths. Which was smart and gave them little trouble. It was also the way any wagon road would have to follow. There was always snow to mush through, deeper in some places than in others, but the first several weeks they never saw the bare ground. It was expected and it didn't bother them much.

They passed the American Falls and camped and surveyed their height. In the Cassia valley Bonneville scratched under the snow to sift the soil. "Good," he said to Fowler, "it's good dirt. But too cold and dry for farming."

The long dry wind watered Big Starr's eyes and he looked as if he were weeping. "Farmin'?" he said. "Hell, Cap'n, you just as well try to farm the moon as this country."

Bonneville poured a small amount of the soil into a little pouch and labeled it, "Cassia valley dirt." He said, "From now on, Starr, one of your jobs, and *never* forget it, is to take a soil sample. Noon or night, it doesn't matter. Just be sure you get at least a cup full. And be sure you label it."

Starr shook his head, but it was interesting to all of them how much that one little chore gave them a sense of *where* they were all the time. It tied them to the earth, a particular piece of earth in a particular place. When Starr, excruciating over his labels, announced with pride, "Raft River dirt," "Salmon Falls dirt," "Bruneau dirt," "Owyhee dirt," it distinguished the place, gave them at least a temporary home in it.

In the Cassia valley they spent half a day exploring a small mountain of mica slate nearby. They found its slopes strewn with rusty red stones. "Garnets," Bonneville told them, after examining a handful. "They polish up and make beautiful jewels." He had a big pack bag into which he flung samples of rocks and interesting stones. Fowler and Big Starr and young Lashly all had the same thought of taking the pretty stones back to their squaws. "They'd like 'em better if they was turquoise," Big Starr said, "but I reckon they'll be pleased enough with these red ones."

Fowler turned a large one over and over in his fingers. The

dark stone, broken from its chrysalis and polished, would be a blood red, a Sangre de Cristo red. Betsy would like it. Unlike most squaws Betsy did not wear a lot of geegaws. She said they were troublesome when she worked, dangled in her way. But around her neck she wore one silver chain which she never took off. When she worked she tucked it inside her shirt. Even Fowler knew that it was very beautiful. She had made it of coin silver got from the Spanish in Taos. She had taken pains to make each link perfect. And then she hung from it whatever beautiful stone or jewel or bead or piece of metal she thought worthy of it, which she could fashion somehow into another bit of beauty. There were many turquoises worked into the necklace, but there was also a pearl he had brought her from California, a small gold coin from St. Louis, and a blazing green stone he had found in Chihuahua which had cost him ten prime beaver plus.

She would work patiently with this large rough garnet. She would cut it skillfully out of its rock shell and then she would chip and carve until the red was pure jewel. She would polish and shine it. Then she would make a tiny silver hasp and attach it to the silver chain. He dropped it in his tobacco pouch for safekeeping. He didn't know whether he would find anything on the journey she would like more than this bit of garnet rock. And to go back without a present for her, for any Indian squaw, was asking for trouble.

When they left the Cassia valley they came into a country that was strange and wild and eerie. It was black with lava rock and cratered with volcanic formations. They picked their way around the boulders and up and down and through the craters with care. The rock was as sharp as knives and could cut the horses' feet.

It was country as hollow as a bone and nothing lived on it. There was no vegetation of any kind, no grass, no timber, nothing but sage brush, and it was scant and stunted. Under the snow there was only black sand, and crisscrossing in all directions were deep cracks in the surface. It was a wrinkled, writhen earth not yet recovered from its hot convulsions. "Wagons, Captain," Fowler said wryly at the end of the first day, "will have a rough time of it through here."

Bonneville's face was always ruddy but the wind had whipped it into fire. He wiped his wind-teared eyes and blew his wind-dripped nose. "But wheels will roll over it one day, just as sure as we are riding over it on horses."

"Is he talking out of his head?" young Lashly asked Fowler later.

"No," Fowler said. "He brought wagons to the Green. Somebody, some day, will bring them to the Snake . . . to the Columbia, maybe."

Young Lashly was not convinced. "Besides," he said, "what would they want to come for? You don't need wagons to hunt beaver."

"They wouldn't be hunting beaver," Fowler said, and let it go.

The wind blew straight down from the snow peaks of the Salmon Mountains, which they could see to the north. It shrieked through the hollow bones of the country like a tormented, anguished soul. It tore at them and pushed and shoved and wrangled and wrestled them about, as if it were a personal enemy. It sucked their warmth and their strength. Snow blew with it some days, fine and keen and cutting, rasping their faces like sandpaper. It was a thoroughly uncomfortable country.

Wrapped in his old plaid capote, living off his fat, Bonneville humped into it unaffected. Neither country nor weather ever seemed to bother him. He was too interested, there was too much work to be done. He fretted now only because the surveying and charting had to suffer and the noon observations often could not be taken.

To Big Starr it was weather and country and that was all. Wherever you went you had weather and country. Good some places, bad some others, hellish, like this, in a few. He wasted no energy fighting it. He looked after the animals and saw to his own comfort. He swore some and took to putting his saddle under his robes at night. "Crawlin' into a saddle froze as hard as a piece of iron on a mornin' colder'n frozen hell ain't this child's notion of makin' 'em shine," he said.

Young Lashly was the most affected by the wind and desolation. But he hit on a dogged way of following right behind Joe Fowler. Where Joe Fowler went he figured Ben Lashly could go, and if it didn't scare the fits out of Joe Fowler, it oughtn't to worry Ben Lashly. If he didn't lift his head, didn't look too far ahead into the long nothingness, if he just concentrated on the rump of the big roan and the broad back of Joe Fowler, he'd be all right.

To Fowler, except for the lava rock about which they had to take care, it was much like the plains below the Wind River Range, and the wind was like the river of wind that poured down from those peaks. It wasn't pleasant, but it wasn't new to him. He kept his mind focused on the stories he had heard from the men who had made the journey before. When you got to where the Snake made its turn north, they said, you got out of the wind. You got into country not nearly as cold as in the mountains. Even in the winter you'd find a little grass, and the streams would be free of ice. Nobody knew why. It had something to do, they said, with the Pacific coast. It was just naturally a warmer country over there.

Some days were clear, less windy, with a high big sky that added another dimension to the endlessness of the plain. The sky was so high and so wide you couldn't believe that by putting one foot in front of the other you would ever, in any foreseeable time, come again to where any piece of it was tied to the earth.

Occasionally they approached the Snake, and whenever they did they always found it flowing through chasms with steep perpendicular sides of black rock. "Basaltic rock," Bonneville told them. Far below, a hundred, two hundred feet, would be the river, sometimes a glassy deep slide, other times, when boulders had filled the stream bed, it would be a white boiling gush. Dark, gloomy, wild, dreadful. It was not a river to love.

Their first landfall was the Fishing Falls, and they reached them on their tenth day out. Here the black walls of the canyon reached a height of two hundred and fifty feet and as far as they could see downriver the walls marched and guarded it. The river was filled with huge blocks and fragments broken off and the water was a rough boiling torrent. At the beginning of the canyon the falls fell in a pitching cascade, their spume and spray hanging in silver mist over them. The sound of their tumult was a thundering roar.

They set up their instruments and determined that the falls were forty feet in height. Then they moved back away from them to make their camp. "Right here," Big Starr said, shaking his head, "is about where them Astor men give up on this river. This coon would have, long time back. She ain't nothin' to fool with, this old river."

It was a cold camp, the wormwood so sparse they had found only enough for a quick fire which didn't even thaw their pemmican. They were taking what comfort they could from their pipes. Bonneville, his old plaid about his shoulders, his old cap pulled over his ears, looked up from his notes. "She is formidable, the Snake. Dangerous."

"Power," Fowler said, drawing on his dudeen. "First thing you see about the Snake is power. I don't know as I ever saw a river that give you more of an idea of power." He spoke of other rivers he knew. "The rivers east of the divide get spread out and silted up and lose their power. The Missouri and the Platte and the Arkansas. Muddy rivers. Red dirt rivers. The mountain rivers have got the power. The Green—now, down through the Flaming Gorge. She's mighty there. And after the Grand flows into her farther down, they cut a gorge that Pete Smith says is a mile deep. Biggest canyon anybody ever saw. But this one, the Snake, has got power from the start. And the boys that have been say this first canyon ain't nothing to compare with the one just before she turns into the Columbia. Lord, the water she pushes into the Columbia. It will be a sight to see."

They spoke of what it might be like. Then Bonneville said, "We will explore this canyon, though."

"Explore it!" Starr exploded. "What fur? It's jist a big long crack!"

Bonneville's eyes twinkled. "The business of explorers is to explore, Starr. Whatever they find."

"*Well,*" Starr said emphatically, "I don't know as this child likes bein' a explorer. We git down in that canyon we ain't likely ever to git back out."

"Oh, yes, we will. Digger Indians live down there. They get in and out. We'll find a way."

"How you know Diggers live down thar?"

"Nathaniel Wyeth told me. He was down in this canyon last year."

"If he's done explored it," Starr said, "let's us just leave it alone."

"But he *didn't* explore it. He had no instruments. He simply visited the Diggers." Bonneville took off his old cap and rubbed his bald head. He had a habit of doing so every few minutes, either from nervous compulsion or because the old wool cap made it itch. "We must survey it. Besides, Wyeth said the Diggers caught the salmon that can't get above the falls and dried them. We can use some extra provisions."

"Who," young Lashly wanted to know, "is Nathaniel Wyeth?"

"He's a fellow from Boston," Bonneville said. "Used to run an ice house there. Got the fur fever and came out several years ago. Joe's heard of him, I expect."

Fowler nodded.

"He didn't do very well," Bonneville went on, "his first year, but he got the lay of the land with one journey to Oregon and came to the conclusion a man could make his fortune by trapping out there and by salmon fishing in the Columbia. He bought a ship and loaded it with trade goods and sent it around the horn. Aimed to ship his furs and dried fish home himself instead of carrying them back by land. Then he took a party to the Columbia overland. He came to grief with that plan. His ship was lost at sea and the Hudson Bay people wouldn't let him get one inch into any kind of trade on the Columbia."

"He quit?" Big Starr asked.

"Not a bit of it," Bonneville said. "He was at rendezvous this year making more big plans. Going to supply the Rocky Mountain boys next summer. Made a contract with Milt Sublette."

Fowler knocked out his pipe. "He made it with the wrong Sublette. Milt is a partner in the trapping end of the business, but Bill is the boss in the carrying trade. It's Bill that says who'll carry."

Bonneville gave him a quick look. "Well, perhaps. But things are changing, Joe. There's talk Big Bill may be getting out. An enterprising man might get his foot in the door."

Fowler gave him a direct look. "Don't get any ideas in your head, Captain. When Bill Sublette gets out, one of the Rocky Mountain boys will take his place. It's a closed empire. There's no door going to open to no outsider, not that first little chink. It'll be Jim Bridger or Tom Fitzpatrick or one of the boys that steps in. That's the way they've done since the day General Ashley started the outfit, and that's the way it'll be till the day there ain't no beaver."

"Oh, I have no ideas personally," Bonneville hastened to say. "No ideas at all. My career is in the army. I will return to my regiment." He dismissed the subject. "You know the Digger Indians, don't you?"

Fowler nodded. "They're in the southwest—in the desert. You see 'em on the way to California."

"You have any trouble with them?"

"No. We didn't have any. Some do, though. They'll steal you blind is about all. Poorest critters on the face of the earth.

Got nothing. Worse off than the Poordevils. But they want what they've not got, same as everybody else—guns and horses and traps. Have to keep a close watch on 'em."

"That's what Wyeth said too," Bonneville said.

Next morning they found a way down to the river through a rough, narrow canyon cut by a gushing little stream. They came out on the banks of the river where white water, wild and noisy, boiled all down the current. The snow was only patchy at the bottom of the canyon and they were surprised at the room on the banks. The shelf of the river bank was much wider than it had appeared from the top. But what they mostly noticed was a feeling of warmth they had not felt for days. "No wind," Fowler said gratefully. "Man and boy," he went on, "I'd rather be out with it below zero and have it still than to have it barely freezing and blowing. Wind pulls you down quicker than anything."

Shortly they found a footprinted trail and they followed it down the river. Toward evening they negotiated a long bend and came out in sight of a small Indian town built on a wide shelf. Bonneville called a halt and said to Fowler, "Can you speak with them?"

"I reckon," said Fowler. "Don't guess I've forgot what I knew."

There were six huts built like small haystacks of willow reeds thatched with grass. Fowler reckoned there would be thirty, maybe forty people in the hamlet. Twelve of them, he supposed, maybe fifteen, would be adults.

Bonneville's horse got a smell and began to dance nervously, then it whickered. Suddenly the haystacks erupted and boiled over with people. Women and children fled to caves in the cliffs and the men, a handful of little, stunted, wild-looking brown creatures, bravely faced them with their arrows drawn to the bow. Fowler held up his hand in the peace sign and then he got off the big roan and walked toward the Indians. The Diggers jabbered together and dropped their bows. They came to meet him. Bonneville and the others walked their horses forward slowly.

The Diggers were naked except for a loin cloth and a blanket of sorts knotted about their shoulders. When they came closer it could be seen the blankets were brief robes, not more than three feet square, made of rabbit skins pieced together. They were unbelievably dirty and smelly. Their hair was coarse, long, matted with grease, and it was so full of vermin the lice crawled in plain sight. They were of such short stature they looked more like misshapen dwarfs than men. Bonneville watched them with interest and curiosity, but Big Starr and young Lashly had a hard time hiding their disgust. "I've saw dirty Injuns in my time," Starr muttered, "but I ain't ever saw none to beat these."

Young Lashly said, "If one of 'em gets within touching distance of me I'm aiming to cleave him with my axe. They got lice running out their ears."

"Be still," Bonneville commanded them.

Fowler talked with the Indians and suddenly they broke into an excited jabbering and high, giggly laughter. They brushed past Fowler and ran toward the horses. Bonneville stood firm but Big Starr looked frantically for some way of escape. There was nothing but the river. It was fast here but shallow. He kicked his horse and plunged him into it. Young Lashly spurred his own horse after him.

"You fools," Bonneville shouted at them. "Come back here. Bring those packs. We have to trade with these people!"

Big Starr didn't pay any attention to Bonneville. He yelled at Fowler, "Tell 'em to keep back. Tell 'em no trade if they don't keep their distance. Tell 'em we'll lay it out on the ground for 'em."

Fowler was laughing, but he spoke to the Indians, who were plunging into the river trying to follow Starr and young Lashly and the pack animals. Slowly and reluctantly the Diggers returned, still jabbering and pointing. Fowler made them understand they must stay away from the horses and the packs. He was stern with them and they drew back. At a further word from him, they fled to the haystacks for the things they had to trade. They brought out packs of dried fish, dried roes, and baskets of a gray-looking mealy flour made from dried and pounded roots. This was their wealth, their riches, all they had.

They spread it out and jabbered. "They want meat," Fowler said to Bonneville. "Buffalo meat . . . antelope, deer, elk, anything just so it's meat."

"But . . . meat?" Bonneville was puzzled.

"Sure. Meat. They got no horses. No guns. They got no way of hunting except on foot. You don't kill much meat that way. They're fish people, but they're tired of fish. They want something they can chew on . . . something that'll fill up their mouths and they can get their teeth in. Meat, Cap'n."

They had not made meat themselves since leaving the Portneuf, but they had some jerky they could spare. Bonneville let the Diggers have what he could. In return they got basket after basket of the best dried fish they had ever seen. "They may be miserable creatures," Bonneville said, examining the fish, "and they live meanly, but they have learned this one thing to perfection."

Chewing on their jerky the Diggers let it be known then they wanted mirrors. "What in God's name for?" Bonneville wanted to know. "One look in a mirror ought to scare the wits out of them. Do they have any idea what they look like?"

"Well, they can see one another," Fowler said, "I reckon they do."

Small mirrors were a staple in the Indian trade. Bonneville had more of them than anything else except beads. He got them out. The Diggers were feverishly excited by them. The women had overcome their first fears and had come down from the cliffs. They swarmed around now, snatching and screeching and giggling. As each Indian got hold of a little round mirror he withdrew to preen, touch his eyes and nose and mouth, watch the movements reflected and go off into high gales of laughter.

They babbled to each other and made a big show, gestured, mocked, held the small mirrors off, brought them near, to watch the changing reflection. With a mirror in their hands, their interest in trading subsided. They could do nothing but experiment with them.

One woman did not go away. Fowler saw her standing to the side looking on. She was small, old, foolish looking. She wore nothing, no garment of any kind, not even a rabbit skin robe. She was as starkly naked as the moment she was born. But around her neck was hung one single, solitary blue bead strung on a length of fiber. Fowler gazed at her and didn't know whether to be sorry or to laugh. He nudged Bonneville. "Trade that one another bead, Captain," he said, "so's she'll be better dressed."

Bonneville gawked, then he gulped, then he swallowed the gulp. Then the fine dark eyes glowed and the full mobile mouth softened. "Poor old soul," he said. He sorted out a handful of beads and a mirror, then he went to his pack and hauled out a shirt. He advanced toward the woman holding them out to her. The woman eyed them greedily. When he was near enough she suddenly stretched out a long claw and snatched the beads and mirror. Clutching them she scuttled crabwise away, her toothless mouth stretched in a wide grin. The captain was left with the shirt still draped over his arm. His mouth dropped and he blinked. "Well, I'll be damned," he said softly and unbelievingly.

Fowler and Big Starr whooped and young Lashly was goggle-eyed. "Now, ain't that the craziest thing you ever seen? Not a stitch to her name, and it freezing cold, and she taken the beads and mirror. These Injuns ain't got a *bit* of sense."

Fussed a little at having his good impulse backfire on him, Bonneville hastily stuffed the shirt back in the pack. Fowler straightened his face and he gave Starr a look to shut him up. He became loquacious, for Joe Fowler. "They don't feel the cold way we do, Captain. They're used to it. She's probably got a robe some place. Don't feel the need of it today. I recollect," he went on, "when I first come to the mountains I felt the cold real bad. Was used to a house in the winter. But after a few seasons I got so it took an awful deep cold to make me miserable. You winter up every season and your hide just gets tough, I reckon. You get so that heat in a house sort of smothers you out."

Big Starr had been gathering up some sage wood and he set it to blazing. Fowler put a dozen fish in it. Big Starr took up the thread of talk. "Mountain men ain't sick much, neither. You don't hardly ever see one with a head cold or the catarrh, or a bad stomach. About the only unhealthiness there is in our trade is Injuns. And you get old you sometimes get the rheumatism. But folks in the settlements get rheumatism along about the same age, so that don't signify."

Bonneville was over being outfaced and flustered. He scratched idly under one armpit and nodded. "It is a remarkably healthy life. I've noticed that. And I never felt so well in my life, either."

They ate and Bonneville set about writing up his journal. But he was restless, moving his shoulders, his arms, his legs, scratching and clawing now and then. Suddenly he clapped a hand to his ribs. "Something is crawling on me!" He heaved himself up, upsetting all his paraphernalia, and started pulling off his shirt.

Big Starr grinned. "You got 'em, Cap'n. That's what me and Ben was tryin' to keep away from. You got lice, Cap'n. And you'll keep 'em the rest of the winter. Ain't no gettin' rid of 'em till summer."

Bonneville turned his shirt inside out and eyed with loathing the repulsive small gray things infesting the seams. He was horrified. Frantically he picked at them, throwing them in the fire. Starr and young Lashly snickered and Fowler watched him, grinning. "First time you've had lice, Captain?"

"Of course it is! I detest the things!"

It told a lot about the captain. He had not taken a squaw, for one thing. You couldn't live with an Indian woman, even the cleanest of them, and not get lice. All Indians had them. The best of them rid themselves of them regularly, but there was never any real end to them. Within a week or two the lice were back. Fowler built up the fire and taking one end of the shirt, cautioning Bonneville to hold the other, he passed it back and forth across the high blaze. "Take off your pants," he advised.

Between them they rid the captain's clothes of the worst of the visitors. But he still passed a restless night. Whether there were lice crawling on him or not, he thought there were. He was eager to leave the Digger village behind next morning.

They traveled on in the canyon several more days and then they came into a region where the cliff walls were more broken. "We'd better climb out of here," Bonneville decided.

On the plains again, they cut directly across avoiding some of the worst bends of the river. They came back to it again at the mouth of the Bruneau. Here was also the biggest village of Diggers they had yet seen, at least a hundred of them. Bonneville hurried past, not stopping to trade.

It was open country here. The high walls of the river were gone and the banks were of ordinary height. There was almost no snow and there was no ice at all in the river. The deep penetrating cold was softened, too. There was a silky feeling of moisture in the air which they breathed in gratefully. Lungs used to the knife of the dry cold of the plain expanded and filled full again. They went on several miles and found a place with a little forage for the animals and large thickets of scrubby wormwood. With a lot of work gathering the sage, they could keep a fire going. "Only thing measlier'n a sagebrush fire," Big Starr grumbled, "is one of buffler chips."

"But they're lastier," young Lashly said.

In spite of having passed the Digger village they weren't rid of the Indians. They followed and crowded around, jabbering, fingering, trying to steal. Any tool or utensil the men put down for a moment disappeared unless they looked sharp. It took all of them to watch their small things, such as knives, hatchets, cooking pots, ropes, even the pack thongs and lacings. Bonneville passed out some tobacco and awls and shooed them off, but they pestered off and on all night. Fearful for the horses, he set two men to stand guard each stint. It was a broken and unpleasant night. Bonneville used part of the time to scribble in his journal and sketch a map of the Snake across the plains. "What day is it?" Fowler asked, in an hour when he wasn't on guard duty.

"Twelfth of January," Bonneville said, without looking up. "We have been out eighteen days."

Fowler didn't need to ask how far they had come. He knew. About two hundred miles. Bonneville planned to make for the British post at Walla Walla first. From there, if there was time, he hoped to go down the Columbia to Vancouver. Fowler laid the distance they had come against the distance they had yet to go. They were not more than one third of the way yet and still had the Blue Mountains ahead of them. He didn't much expect they would do all Bonneville hoped they would. He was spending a lot of time surveying and charting, but maybe it was as important as anything else he had in mind. One thing was sure. They weren't going to get to Walla Walla and back to the Portneuf by the end of March. It didn't bother Fowler. His affairs were in pretty good order. He could go as far and stay as long as necessary. But he wondered if Bonneville didn't realize they were behind in schedule already and were likely to get further behind.

Here, at the mouth of the Bruneau, the Snake began its long bend northward. Moving on the left bank they followed it, going north, but going downstream. For the next several days they made good time. The valley of the Snake was pleasant here. It was broad and wind-free, there was no snow, and there was even a little green forage for the animals. The Snake was tranquil and there were no large tributary streams to be crossed. They were able to cover many miles each day.

The Owyhee was the first large stream they reached, coming in from the west, and a day's march beyond was the Malheur. They crossed this river and made camp a few miles beyond it, opposite the mouth of the Payette, which flowed in from the east. The camp chores were done and the horses hobbled to graze when a small party of mounted Indians rode up on the opposite bank. They called across. Bonneville studied them. "What are they, Joe? Flatheads?"

"They got horses and guns like the Nez Perces," Fowler said, "and they're dressed like 'em."

"Well, whatever," Bonneville said, "tell 'em we'll trade. My nag is giving out and I need a new horse."

The Indians crossed the Snake. They turned out to be more Diggers, but they lived in the Boise Valley and were neighbors of the lower Nez Perces. From them they had got horses and guns and they lived much better than their brethren below. They were friendly, mild, and inoffensive. They had none of the thieving traits of their southern relatives. They willingly agreed to take Bonneville's tired horse and give him a fresh one. They had a large quantity of dried fish with them and a little antelope meat. They wanted tobacco and ammunition for their guns.

Trading finished, Bonneville offered them the hospitality of the camp for the night, which they accepted. They did an amazing thing before they ate. They went to the river and washed their hands and faces. Then at the meal, before they ate, they folded their hands, closed their eyes, and recited together some kind of prayer. Fowler could not understand it. It was not any Indian dialect he knew. It was not French, and it certainly was not English. "Who taught you that?" he asked, when they had finished.

Their leader said Payette had taught them. He said the factor of the Hudson Bay post on the Boise had taught them to clean their hands before eating and to say certain words. They were medicine words, the Indian said. Big medicine words. They were the same medicine words Payette said. Payette always said these words before he ate.

Fowler nodded. He said to Bonneville, "Hudson Bay men are nearly all Catholics. I reckon that was a table grace Payette has taught 'em."

Bonneville shook his head ruefully. "I should have recognized it. But Latin with a Digger accent isn't entirely easy to recognize. A more astonishing thing has never occurred in this world, Joe. Fancy meeting in this wilderness a bunch of Digger Indians who say a Catholic table grace in Latin! Nobody would believe it! Nobody!" Absent-mindedly, amazed into perplexity, he reached up and pulled off his old cap to scratch his head. The Indians broke into a babbling, jabbering, pointing excitement. Their eyes grew round and wide and their hands flew to their mouths as they scooted back away from him. *"Now,* what the hell?" Bonneville said.

Fowler listened, then began to laugh. "They never saw a baldheaded man before. They think you've been scalped."

Bonneville clapped his cap back on his head. His hands flew in the sign language, but he gave it up quickly. "Tell them," he said.

Fowler told them Captain Bonneville, this man here, had not been scalped. He was a great chief among white men. But among white men sometimes a man's hair grew thin . . . it fell out . . . it did not grow back. The man became bald. The Indians listened attentively, then rounded their mouths. They patted their own thick coarse black pelts and laughed. Then they crowded around Bonneville. "What do they want?" he said, fending them off.

"They want you to take your cap off again."

"Nonsense!"

Big Starr and young Lashly had given up trying to keep a straight face. Suddenly Bonneville saw the humor of it and took the cap off again. With a big grin he allowed the Indians to feel his scalp. They circled around him, touched and talked together. "What are they saying?" he wanted to know.

"They say an Indian's hair does not grow thin and fall out. Better if you would become an Indian. Perhaps your hair would grow in again," Fowler translated.

"Too late," Bonneville chuckled. "You can't grow hair on a bowling ball."

The Indians sat down again but they continued to giggle over the bald head and point at it and discuss it. Fowler suddenly laughed. "They have given you a new name. You couldn't pronounce it, but it means 'Baldhead.' "

"Well," Bonneville said philosophically, putting his cap back on, "I am at least in good company. The only other man I know to have been honored with such an epithet was Charles the Bald."

"You better remember not to take your cap off no more," Fowler said.

But that, too, was too late. The news of the baldheaded man spread from the Diggers like prairie fire ahead of them. From then on every village of Indians they met asked for the cap to be removed so they could see the bald head. "It is a doubtful distinction," Bonneville grumbled, but he never failed to comply. The surest way he could win the good will of the Indians they met henceforth was to bare his head.

The Diggers also agreed that one of their number should journey with the party as a guide through the mountains. The one who volunteered had no gun. As pay he asked to be allowed to carry one of their guns and to hunt for them. And yes. He knew the way through the mountains. He had been to the Columbia. He would lead them there. Bonneville agreed he should hunt for them and he promised him a gun of his own when they reached the Columbia.

For several more days they continued to have good traveling down the broad and pleasant valley. The weather was mild, there was little snow, there was good pasturage for the animals, and men and horses profited by it all. They made long miles each day and Bonneville found it impossible not to be buoyantly happy. His spirits soared. He went about his work singing.

"Wyeth told me about a river a little farther on," he told Fowler one day as they rode along, "that flows in from the west. Powder River. He hadn't explored it but it was his opinion it might provide the best way through the mountains."

Joe Fowler was looking at the mountains that now loomed ahead on both sides of the river. To him they had a look of the Wind Rivers about them, the same rooted, bedded look which meant they had a big, wide spread. They were following a rough map Wyeth had drawn for Bonneville which would bring them out on the head of the Imnaha River beyond the mountains. But Wyeth had admitted it was a rough trail even in the summertime. "A river would be lucky," Fowler said. "Make it a heap easier for us."

"If it's promising, we will follow up it," Bonneville said.

Fowler nodded and then broke into laughter. Their Digger guide was not quite foolish but he was near enough to make them wonder. Bonneville had kept his word and furnished him with a gun. All day every day he dashed about looking for something to kill. Each morning he promised them fine deer and antelope. Just over the next hill. They would see. He was a fine hunter. They would not lack for meat now that he had a gun. A shadow was enough to send him chasing off and he fired endlessly at nothing. He was never discouraged by the fact that at the end of the day he did not bring in any game. Tomorrow would be different. Tomorrow they would feast.

Fowler pointed now. The Digger was on the chase again. He was racing wildly ahead of them. He was shouting, waving his gun. "If he's seen something this time," Fowler said, "he'll scare it off with all that noise."

Bonneville groaned. "He was a bad bargain. He is no more a guide than I am. And as a hunter he is equally useless."

The Digger hauled his horse to a sudden halt, flung himself off and threw himself down full length on the ground. "What in God's name is he doing now?" Bonneville said.

"Looks like he's wrestling something," Fowler said.

The Digger gave a shout suddenly and heaved himself up and held his game up in triumph for all to see. "A rabbit, by God!" Bonneville said, clapping his hand to his forehead. *"Sacré,* what a hunter we have!"

The Digger rode back bearing the rabbit across his saddle as proudly as if it had been a deer. His eyes glistened with excitement and pride as he told how he had flushed it and chased it. It had run into a hole, he said, but he had not let it escape. He had reached down in that hole and caught it and in spite of its struggles, which were many and strong, he had brought it out. "Why didn't you shoot it?" Big Starr asked. "That's what yer gun is for."

It was plain the Digger had forgotten he had a gun. Instinctively he had done what his people had done for generations. He had chased the rabbit into a hole and dragged it out. He looked at the gun in puzzlement, now. Then he handed it to Bonneville. It did not shoot straight, he said. That gun was not a good gun. He had not killed any game at all with that gun. But he had killed a rabbit with his own hands. Better for a man to hunt his own way, he said. He would not require that gun any more.

Late in the afternoon half a dozen mounted Indians appeared on the other side of the river. They did not cross, nor did they appear to want to trade. The Digger spoke with them. He said they were hunting and would not stop. Some time in the night he crossed the river and next morning there was no sign of him or of any of the other Indians. He had taken nothing. He had joined them with nothing but himself and his horse and he left with nothing but himself and his horse. "At least," Bonneville said with relief, "he was an honest fool. We are better without him. He was useless and one more mouth to feed."

The mountains were closing in now, although they were still only hills with meadowy places between. They came into snow again and there was ice once more in the river. It was slushy hummock ice but it was a warning of what was to come. They plodded on, and three days after the Digger left them they came in the late evening to a small village of Indians in a pretty meadowy basin with a clear little creek rushing through it. There were only five families of the Indians, but their huts were fairly substantial and they had horses.

They were not frightened by the white men. They were friendly and hospitable, but they spoke a language no one in the party could understand. It was totally strange to all of them, with no dialectical clues. Fowler tried several tongues with them and got no response. When he hit on Nez Perce one man, taller than the others and dressed a little differently, nodded and replied. He was Nez Perce, he said. He was visiting these. They were Skyuses, he said.

Fowler relayed the information to Bonneville. Bonneville shook his head. "Never heard of 'em. They aren't in the literature and Wyeth didn't mention them. You sure you understood him?"

Fowler had the Nez Perce repeat it, slowly, so Bonneville could hear each syllable. "That's what it sounds like," he admitted. He grinned. "You think we have discovered some new Indians, Joe?"

"I misdoubt it," Fowler said. "But I think we have probably found the first of the Columbia River Indians. They are likely kin to the Cayuses."

The Indians had nothing to trade and they had only dried camass roots for food. Bonneville's party made out to eat and Fowler talked a long time with the Nez Perce. No, he told them, they should not go up the Powder River to get through the mountains. The snow would be very deep and bad. The trail would be impassable. They should keep to the Snake, he said. Until they came to the big gorge, he said, they should follow down the river. When they reached the big gorge, he said, they would have to cross the mountains.

Had he been there this winter? Did he know the conditions? No. He had not been that far north this winter. But it would be bad. The snow would be deep. It was always bad in the winter.

"Ask him if he will guide us," Bonneville said.

The Nez Perce shook his head immediately. No. It would be very foolish.

Did the Skyuses know the way? Yes. They had relatives on the Columbia. They crossed the mountains. But later. When the snow had melted. Would one of them serve as their guide? The Nez Perce spoke to them. They looked solemn and thoughtful, then they, too, shook their heads. The Nez Perce said they would not go either. It was not wise to go on such a journey at this time of year. It was too dangerous. Bonneville could follow the gist of the talk. "Won't any of them go, will they?"

"No."

"Ask if we can get through to Walla Walla."

They did not know. Perhaps. It would be very difficult.

"That one," Bonneville said, "he's from the upper Nez Perce, isn't he? Ask him when he is going home. Ask him if he will guide us to his home. Tell him when we get there I will give him a horse."

The Indian laughed. He had fifty horses at his home. He did not need more horses.

When would he be going home? He shrugged. He did not know. When the snow melted. Perhaps. It was pleasant here and he might visit the rest of the winter. No. He could not lead them to his home. He was not going home just now.

So. Fowler left it with no comment. He let the facts, as bald as Bonneville's head, sink in. They had not learned what the actual conditions in the mountains were this year. They had only learned what the conditions usually were and that Indians would not, without great reason, risk a crossing in the winter. If these Indians had been starving, had been without horses and guns, one of them might have been persuaded to lead the party. But they were in comfortable circumstances and Bonneville didn't have anything big enough to offer for the risk.

If Bonneville had any moment of hesitation or indecision it didn't show. He didn't discuss the situation further with Fowler or the others. He turned in and as far as Fowler knew he slept sound. Next morning the camp work was quickly done, young Lashly read the thermometer and packed it away, Big Starr and Ben measured the basin, Bonneville took the altitude, then he gave the signal to saddle up.

Fowler looked at the mountain which loomed up behind the basin. The sun struck the snowy slopes and dazzled back in the eyes. The block turret was massive and behind it were more turret tops and more and more. Later, men would call these the Wallowas. Now they were nameless—just part of the range known as the Blue Mountains. The sky was clean of clouds, high, pure, light, dry, the fresh blue of the cornflowers his mother used to grow in her garden patch. It was cold and a fresh snow had fallen in the night. Fowler threw the saddle across the big roan's back.

The big horse stretched his neck back and nuzzled Fowler's neck, working his lips over it but not nipping. Fowler ran his hand along the long beautiful neck, felt the smooth rippling muscles beneath. "Boy," he said, "your guts are gonna be stretched the next week or two, and your wind and your legs. The name you've made for yourself, you better live up to, and it's a heap more important than any race you ever won."

The big blue whickered and nuzzled again, then fell to cropping the dried grass. They rode off, the Indians in the doorways watching them silently. Inside, Fowler felt satisfied. There was nothing to say white men couldn't go where Indians wouldn't go. More than once he had, and he wouldn't be here today if he hadn't. Give a beaver man a few years in the mountains and he was as good as any Indian finding his way, and better than an Indian staying with it, for he thought more clearly. He was tight inside, though, with a kind of good tightness. Without examining it or even putting it into thoughts, he knew elementally that from now on it would probably be Joe Fowler's skills and Joe Fowler's judgment and Joe Fowler's endurance that would count. It was, now, what he was used to, and he was satisfied to have it that way.

2.

Twenty-three days later they came out of the mountains into the green soft valley of the Imnaha. The last mile down the last slope of the last ridge of the last mountain had been a fever-ish delirium of slide and slip and slither, thin gaunt men and emaciated horses barely able to walk, losing their footing and falling easily. From the top of the ridge, seeing the valley below, they weren't certain it was not a mirage. They had never lost hope, but they had lost count of time in the eternity of snow and mountains. They had no idea how far they had come, nor did they know how much farther they had to go. The valley was almost unbelievable in their state of mind. Fowler was leading, as he had been for several days. He had pulled up the big roan to stare. He gazed at the greenness, at the crystal stream, rubbed his eyes and gazed again. It didn't go away. It was real. He called to Bonneville. "We've made it. Here it is."

Bonneville, his skin sagging on his fatless bones, made the effort to ride up beside him. He was snowblind and he had to prop his eyes open with his fingers. He stared a long time, his eyes filled with tears of pain and relief. He tried to speak and couldn't. He cleared his throat. "Let us go down," he croaked.

Fowler went first, leading a bony pack horse. Bonneville fol-lowed. His eyes were bandaged, with slits cut so that he might see a little when it was necessary. Behind him came Big Starr leading young Lashly's horse. Young Lashly was in a stupor. There was no pack mule. He had long ago been killed and eaten. The packs had been reduced to a minimum. The sack of rock specimens had been abandoned, and the pack of trading goods. Bonneville had clung to his instruments and his chest of medical supplies, and each man still had his personal pack. But when the mule had been killed for food they had had to lighten the load. The last thin gruel made from the last pinch of root flour had been eaten three days before. There had been nothing to eat since.

They slithered down the slope, crossed to the river, and made their camp. Slow work for Fowler and Big Starr, for they were weak. Bonneville could help himself a little, but he could help with nothing else. Fowler laid out his bedroll for him and he fell onto it and was immediately asleep. Big Starr eased young Lashly out of the saddle and onto his bedroll. Then he and Fowler hobbled the horses and turned them onto the good grass to graze. They sat down, then, out of breath. They were winded by the efforts they had made, and their legs were shaky and rubbery.

They looked at each other. Fowler saw a big man so gaunted that the bones of his face were like sharp rocks. The eyes were like black holes in his head. The nose had been frozen and was sore and scabby and there was frozen pus on the tip. The lips were full of sores that had scabbed over and the beard was dripping water from the ice that had begun to melt.

Looking at Big Starr, Fowler knew how he looked. He couldn't talk without his lips cracking and bleeding. When his nose dripped he rubbed skin away with the drip. His eyes felt as if hot wires were pulling them back in his head. He was so thin that riding had been a torture on his bony behind. He pulled in a long breath and looked back where they had come. "You believe it, Starr?"

Starr rubbed his hands together, and pulled a nail loose from a frozen finger. "Not yet, I don't. Don't seem real yet."

"No."

"But I knowed when you took over we'd make it. I *knowed* that."

"Did you?"

"Didn't you?"

The grass was soft under Fowler's hand. He pulled a handful and smelled it. He nibbled a blade. "I reckon. We have been through some bad times together, you and me, and we have had some close scrapes. But I don't think we'll live long enough to go through anything rougher or closer than this one."

Big Starr looked back at the long slope. "We wouldn't have made it if you hadn't took over."

Fowler looked at Bonneville. He was so exhausted that he was sleeping like a man in a coma, dead asleep. "No. He'd of made it. There ain't no give-up in him. But he was wearing us all out to no use. Wearing us all down. It was best to let me go ahead and find the way."

Big Starr picked at a scab on his lower lip and cursed when it came away and the blood flowed. He stanched it with a handful of grass. "It's all the same. You *found* the way. I don't know how you done it. When you come back to git us you looked more dead than alive."

"He gave me the last of the mule," Fowler said. "It sufficed. Barely." He grinned but the grin cracked his lips and hurt and made them bleed. He cursed. "And I had one of the compasses."

"And we come out dead on the Imnaha." Starr shook his head. "Don't tell this child, Joe. I got a length of bones in this carcass. Next summer would of found 'em bleachin' in the sun, hadn't been for you."

They had rested a little now. Fowler pushed up on his hands and groaned. "We better get up some wood and make a fire."

"Wagh," Big Starr grunted. "Only good thing about these mountains is wood. Plenty of pine."

They moved around like old men, stopping to rest often, but

they kept at it until they had accumulated a big stack of wood. They started the fire and fed it until it was a good blaze. Then they hunted for camass and kouse roots. Fowler felt a sudden sense of aggrievement to be doing this. Betsy ought to be here. Hadn't been for Bonneville she would have been. He was too sore and stiff to be gouging around in the dirt this way. He hadn't thought of Betsy for weeks and he put it from him now. A man worn out and hungry and lucky to be alive could hold the strangest grudges.

Big Starr found the Indian tracks. "Joe, here's sign. Heap of sign."

They examined them and then stood like two silly geese grinning at each other. They were Nez Perce tracks. "It's not far to their town," Fowler said. "Can't be. Tomorrow we'll find 'em. Tomorrow we'll eat meat."

Big Starr licked his lips. "Meat. I've done forgot what it's like."

They found plenty of roots and rolled them in the ashes to bake. "Reckon we ought to wake the captain and tell him about them tracks?" Big Starr said.

Fowler glanced at the captain, who hadn't moved. "Take an earthquake to wake him," he said. "Let's let him sleep it out. We can't move till tomorrow anyway."

They lay on the grass and waited for the roots to bake and they talked. Their minds, as yet, could not comprehend much except what they had been through. It was all still with them, as if they hadn't got free of it yet. They went over it again, in detail. They talked of the first days after they had left the village of the Skyuses and followed down the river. It had been pretty rough then, they thought. Big boulders and the trail narrow and slush ice in the river. Too slushy to hold their weight so they couldn't cross to the other side when the bank was better over there. And winding around up ridges when the trail got so narrow they had to leave the river, then winding back around them to get back to the river. Finally the edges of the river froze so they could make their way on the ice some-times.

And then at last the walls pinched in and there was no trail at all. The walls pinched in and came right down to the water. Nothing to do then but leave the river and climb the steep slopes and begin the plunging into the heart of the mountains.

At first Bonneville had stayed high-spirited, though he fretted because they had passed Powder River and, too late, he wished they had followed it. "There *must* be an easier way through these mountains," he said.

"Wasn't long after that," Big Starr said, "till we got into the worst mess of mountains this coon ever seen. And the deepest snow."

"They put me in mind of the Wind Rivers from the start," Fowler admitted.

The snow had been belly deep on the animals. The horses had to plunge and buck through it. And sometimes it was too deep and they had to tramp a trail out for the animals. Tramp and then haul the horses along. Then stop and tramp again and haul the animals another quarter of a mile. Up one ridge and shelf only to find another and higher one waiting for them. Endless toothing of sierra and shelf and slope and turret and rampart. Endless maze of canyons. Wind tearing into their hearts. Horses growing gaunt and wearing down. Men hungry. Food almost gone. Mule killed at the end of the second week. Bonneville now beginning to be snowblind. Young Lashly fell down a precipice and hurt his head. He remained dazed, his speech impaired, not making much sense when he talked. He was almost helpless and a burden to them.

Bonneville never lost his nerve. He never did give up. But it was then, when they were camped for the night on a windy summit it had taken them all day to reach, a blizzard howling around them, that he said, quietly, "Joe, perhaps we should turn back to the river. If we can reach the river we can kill the horses and eat them. Nourish our strength. Then we can make boats of their hides and we can take our chances on the river."

It was the only sign Bonneville gave that he was losing his judgment. They could never have made it back to the river. They had come too far and they were too weak, their horses were too weak. There wasn't anything to do but go on. Fowler had said, just as quietly, giving no sign that he knew he must now take over, "Before we try that, Captain, I'd like to go ahead by myself and look out the way. We may be nearer the end of this mess than we think. There's no sense everybody being worn out this way. We'll make a good camp tomorrow and Ben can get some rest and the horses can rest up." He was tactful and didn't say the captain, too, could rest. "I'll go as far as it's safe and mark out the best way."

There was nothing Bonneville could do but agree. It was a sensible idea. He may have known Joe Fowler would go anyway, even if he had forbidden it, but he didn't say so. He thought about it, then said, "It's worth trying, I suppose. We surely *must* be near the end of this maze."

Next morning they slid a little way down from the summit to a more sheltered place and they dug down into the snow to hole up. They built a fire and Bonneville made Fowler take the last of the mule meat. For those left behind he had the hoofs, part of the tail, and the ears. "We will manage," he said grimly. "We won't need as much. We won't be working."

Fowler knew it ate into the little short-legged man's pride to let him ride off this way, but neither admitted it, by word or by action. Fowler wrapped the hunk of mule meat in his bedroll and got on the big roan. "If I'm not back," he said, "by the end of four days I won't be coming back."

Bonneville nodded. Big Starr, who had to stay behind to tend the ailing, hit his fist hard in the snowbank. Fowler had a sudden intense wish to touch him, shake his hand, throw his arm around his shoulder, make a fist and hit in play the hard belly. What you got to feeling for a man like Starr you had worked with a long time and ridden with and fought with, and got drunk and wenched with, was that you made a kind of world together, which you understood together and liked together and nobody else belonged in it much. It was as if you had sewed some kind of skin between you that the same blood and muscle and guts worked in. If it happened that in your life a man like this came into it, or one like Mose or Pete, however much a loner you might be, or think yourself to be, or take pride in being, you didn't want to be without them. You weren't all yourself, even your lonely self, without them.

But he only said to Starr, "This'll be a tale to tell at rendezvous, won't it?"

Starr looked up and swiped his big ham-hand across his mouth. "You damned right it will," he growled.

"Well."

Fowler started to raise his hand but he didn't. He pulled the roan around and rode off.

He didn't now, he admitted to Starr, remember all about those three days he was gone except he kept moving. The big blue never faltered and he thought it was as much the horse as himself that found the way out. About the middle of the second day he and the blue reached a narrow canyon with a small stream gushing down it. A game trail went up the canyon and without thinking about it enough to remember the thinking, the old skills worked elementally. Where game had worn a path, men could usually follow. He followed and the trail led him over a pass till he could see this valley. He went back, then, and led the others out, much slower and in another blizzard. They nearly didn't make it.

The roots had baked. They warmed some water and mashed one big mealy one in a cup of the water. Then they roused young Lashly and fed him. Like a fledgling bird he opened his mouth when they told him, took the food, and swallowed.

When the mug was empty he lay down again and went back to sleep. "Reckon he'll ever be in his right mind again?" Big Starr asked.

Fowler looked down at the boy and pity for him stirred in him. He hadn't been old enough for what he'd been called on to face and do. He'd had too sudden a toughening. He'd been asked to be a grown man too soon. "Sure," he said, "he'll be all right in a few days. He'll be warm now, and when he comes to himself and sees he's out of the snow and the worst of the mountains he'll be all right. It wasn't only that knock on his head. He had got kind of crazy, thinking there wasn't any end to the snow and the mountains."

Then they, too, rolled in their robes and slept.

3.

From then on it was all downhill, nothing to worry about. Next day Bonneville waked refreshed and full of energy. His eyes were better, although he decided to wear his bandage still. Young Lashly was better. He said he felt like a piece of wet rag, but he made a little better sense when he talked.

By noon they found the Nez Perce village and the Indians were all kindness and hospitality. They made pets of them, in fact. They fed them, and the women swarmed around to admire Bonneville's old plaid, and he had to take his cap off dozens of times. They had heard of his bald head, of course. The young men took their horses out to graze with their own great herds and the old men sat with them and talked and plied them with kinnikinick for their pipes. They began to feel they were back down on the same planet with other human beings again.

The food given them was all fish and bread and baked roots, however. It filled their stomachs but didn't last. They were constantly hungry. "They've got meat," Fowler said. "Bound to have. They're horse people. They just don't want to bring it out."

"We have so little to trade," Bonneville said. "If we had only been able to save more of the pack goods." He brushed impatiently at an old squaw who was tugging and fingering at his capote. "What in God's name do these old women see in this plaid of mine! I wish they would go away and leave me alone."

Fowler watched the old woman creep away a few feet then slowly inch back, her hands reaching again to feel the thick wool of the cloak. His eyes squinted in his pipe smoke. "You *could* trade that plaid for some meat, Captain," he said.

"Trade it . . . ?"

"Sure. Whack it in pieces and trade each piece for a hunk of meat. They got such an admiration for that capote I'll bet any of 'em that's got a piece of meat hid away will bring it out."

Bonneville hesitated only a moment, one hand running down the good heavy warm folds. Then he whipped it off and drew out his knife. "Tell her," he commanded Fowler, "tell her to tell all her friends. One piece of plaid for a piece of meat. Elk . . . antelope . . . deer. No fish. No roots. Meat. One piece of the wool for one big hunk of meat."

It worked like magic. The squaws clustered around with their hoards of meat, elbowing and nudging each other, afraid the plaid wouldn't last till their turn. Bonneville wasn't as niggardly with the pieces as he might have been. He hit on the idea of giving each one enough to make a turban and then he turned milliner and showed them how to wrap and fold the length about their heads. The meat piled up, and for several days they feasted like kings.

The Nez Perces had hundreds of horses, and they traded fresh ones for the party's jaded animals willingly. Fowler even left the big roan in the care of a young man who, for the price of one hatchet, agreed to care for him like a baby until Fowler's return.

They moved down the Imnaha to the Snake again, and through the tablelands down the Snake. They were passed on from one village of Indians to the next with guides and runners, and they were consistently treated with kindness and hospitality. Once they reached the Snake again they came among more prosperous Nez Perces and fish as a food became a thing of the past. There was meat, plenty of meat, even buffalo jerky which had been hunted on the plains last season. With little to trade, Bonneville broke out the medicine chest and paid for their food by treating sore eyes, running sores, wounds of various kinds.

As they moved steadily down the river they gradually left the tablelands behind them until near the end of February they came into beautiful rolling meadowlands. The Nez Perce guiding them told them they were only six sleeps now from where the river emptied into the Columbia. But Fort Walla Walla was not on the Snake. It was on the Walla Walla River where it flowed into the Columbia, below the confluence of the Snake. Bonneville said they would leave the Snake here and cut across the rolling land to the fort.

All across the gently swelling land they rode through good grass already greening. They found small clear streams and wooded groves. There were fogs in the morning and good hot sun on their backs at noon. The nights were cold, but the days made them feel like new men. Bonneville tried the soil and said it was as rich and fertile as any he had ever seen.

Fowler dug down and sifted the rich loam through his fingers. "You could turn it as deep as you wanted with a plow," he said, "and it would be as rich as the top six inches."

"It's better dirt than you ever turned with a plow, Joe," Bonneville said, laughing, "back on the Arkansas."

Fowler nodded. In his young years he had worked his father's farm on the Arkansas. It was red dirt there, cotton-growing dirt. This was black, heavy, deep, loamy dirt. He took up a handful and smelled it, and suddenly he could feel plow handles in his hands, he could feel the buck as the plow bit deep, and he could feel the strength in his arms holding the heavy plow down, or hoisting it to make his turn. He could see this rich dirt curling back from the deep shovel. He could smell it as it curled back and broke, and his feet could feel it breaking under them. He looked off across the rolling grassland to where a grove of young trees marked another stream. A hill swelled up behind the grove and framed it. It made him think of some place he had been . . . some place he had seen . . . a pretty place like this, a peaceful place . . . a place that had pleasant associations. But he couldn't think of it.

Bonneville called to say they might as well noon here, and Fowler went to get the sextant. He took his sights and gave Bonneville the reading. But his mind was still trying to sort out places he had been. They finished eating and went on. Not Arkansas. It was too flat there on the river. Too scrubby in the hills. Not the Osage country. That was prairie and black-jack oaks. Red rivers, red earth. Missouri? That long stretch before you got to St. Louis? A little, maybe. But something was still wrong. It wasn't quite the look.

He turned in the saddle to look back, and as he did some-thing, the changed angle, the difference in distance, a change in light, altered the picture and the frame, and as plain as he ever saw anything in his life he saw his grandmother Hannah's home on the shelf above the Hanging Fork in Kentucky. He pulled his borrowed Nez Perce horse up, laughing at himself. Sure. Sure, that was it. The house in the grove had been missing.

He was ten years old when his father left Kentucky and moved to the Arkansas. His grandmother Hannah's house on the Hanging Fork was now an old and faded picture in his memory. But he had been born there. And when he was a little fellow, just a kid, they had gone to spend the day on Sundays many a time. They would load up the wagon and drive from their place on the river over there. It was that look of the trees and the hill back of them. That was the way, when

the wagon rounded a bend in a gap of the hills, his grandmother's place had looked. A rambling old log house set in a
grove of trees on a shelf above a creek, the hill—and now he
remembered the spring where they went for water—rising behind it. His first sight of the place, when the wagon came
through the gap, was what he had seen just now. The long
rolling meadowland lush in front of the house and the creek
—endless and swelling and rolling, the grass greener than anything he had ever seen since, until today. And the dirt black
and good. It put his mind to rest, remembering. He was glad
to have the memory placed and pocketed. It would have worried him for days. But it had been a time and a time.

He laughed again to remember that *that* had been a saying
of his grandmother's. She would welcome them when they
went. "It's been a time and a time since you've been." A time
and a time. Twenty years and two thousand miles later, it
came to him as naturally as if the tall dark woman were saying
it now. What a boy soaks up, he thought, a man doesn't forget.

He looked about him again. Fruit would do well here.
Apples. Fine apples ought to grow here. And grain would
do well—wheat and barley. And the things a woman liked in
her garden patch ought to do fine, beans and squash and pumpkins and potatoes and such. He said it out loud. "It's good
farming land."

Big Starr, riding beside him, agreed casually. "Yep, if that's
where your stick floats, this part of Oregon is real good country."

Fowler tickled his horse's ribs and laughed. "Oregon? You
could as well call it Kentucky."

4.

The first week of March they reached the fort at the mouth
of the Walla Walla. Fur trading posts were nearly always lo-

cated at the junction of rivers, for the convenience of Indians and brigade leaders and for the convenience of shipping. No thought was ever given to the appearance of the surrounding country or to the weather and climate. Fort Walla Walla was as isolated, as lonely, as dreary, as ugly a trading post as was ever built. It stood on the north bank of the Walla Walla River and on the east side of the Columbia in a sandy, gravelly, treeless waste which the wind kept whipped into a fine dust. The stockade was made of driftwood which was untrimmed and had been set up any which way so that it had a crazy dilapidated look. It was built in a square with blockhouses at two opposite corners. A small cannon was mounted in each blockhouse. Quarters for the factor and employees were also built of driftwood around the inside of the stockade fence.

Pierre Pambrun was the Hudson Bay factor at the post. He had four employees, a clerk who kept the records and daily journal, and three others who took care of the furs and did other odd jobs about the fort. The principal Hudson Bay post was down the Columbia near the mouth of the Willamette. Dr. John McLoughlin, who was at the head of all Hudson Bay operations in the Columbia country, was the factor at Fort Vancouver. Walla Walla was merely an outpost, a place to receive furs from the Indians and the brigades, and a place for them to resupply.

Pambrun was expecting them. Word of them had started down the Snake to him almost as soon as they reached the first Nez Perce village on the Imnaha. He was a gracious host. He made them welcome and was handsomely generous with his hospitality. The Nez Perces and Skyuses made gardens for him in season and he had dried beans and pumpkins to set before them, as well as fresh milk from his cow and new eggs from his flock of chickens. He quartered them on the ground floor of one of the blockhouses in which some fairly good carpenter had constructed real beds in the four corners. Real beds, milk and eggs, potatoes and pumpkin pies. "Lordy," young

Lashly said, dumfounded, "this is like back home, ain't it?"

For two days, while Pambrun and Bonneville talked, the other men loafed, wandered around aimlessly looking over the place and its surroundings. The Nez Perces had the run of the place, coming and going constantly. There was a difference in their dress from the mountain Nez Perces. Their robes and shirts were buffalo or elk or ibex skin, but their ornaments indicated their nearness to the sea. They were most often sea shells and mother of pearl. Often, too, they wore mantles of fine rich otter skin. Fowler used his own letter of credit, drawn on the Johnny Osage stores, with Pambrun to trade for a few of these things—shells and mother of pearl for Betsy and enough otter skins for a sleeping bag for himself. The squaw of one of the employees set to work to make it for him.

He and Starr roved down the banks of the big river—the Columbia. It was fast and deep and about three hundred and fifty yards wide at this point. "Reckon he'll go on down to Vancouver?" Starr said.

"I've got my doubts," Fowler said. "We lost too much time in the mountains." He felt little curiosity about the downriver country himself. Felt no wish to embark on the Columbia and go on down. He wasn't pushed by any great exploring yearning to see any more of it. After the Snake, he didn't think too much of it anyhow. He wondered a little if the Snake wasn't the real Columbia—and he had seen, and would see going back, as much of it as he wanted to see.

The talks went on, with Bonneville writing up his notes each night. Then one night, when they had been there several days, he came into their quarters bristling with anger. He had gained back most of his fat and his cheeks shook with his anger. "We leave tomorrow," he said brusquely.

Big Starr was lying on his bunk. He raised up on an elbow and looked over at Fowler. His bushy eyebrows went up. Fowler was working over some new moccasins, softening them with grease. He met Starr's glance then looked at Bonneville. "Downriver?" he said.

"No!" Bonneville exploded. "I want no more of these British! We will return to the Portneuf!"

"Well," Fowler said, getting up slowly, "Starr and me had better pack the supplies, I reckon . . ."

"There aren't any supplies," Bonneville said. "He wouldn't sell me one thing, not one thing! No trade goods, no food, no ammunition! Not a thing would he sell!" Bonneville's eyes were black fire and his face was flaming. He stood at his straightest, most military five feet seven. "Would you believe it?"

"Well, this child would," Big Starr drawled. "I ain't a bit surprised. Wonder is he taken us in at all."

Bonneville brushed it aside. "With letters of credit drawn on Mr. Astor he refused to sell me any supplies at all. He said we were welcome to stay as long as we wished. The hospitality of the post would be extended. But in the interests of the Hudson Bay Company he could not sell me supplies. He said, frankly mind you, they could not afford to outfit a competitor."

Fowler wasn't surprised, either. In fact, he would have been surprised if Pambrun had consented to outfit them. It was policy all over the mountains to keep competition down. Men would go to any length to help each other survive, but they wouldn't sell that first bead to help them trade. Fowler sat back down and went to work on the moccasins again. "You tell him we just needed the supplies to get back?"

"Of course I did! Of course! He had the insolence to tell me that no one coming into this country came with any good will or intentions to the Company and that they came at their own risk and had to return the same way. He said this was Company policy. I shall put this in my report, Joe. I shall certainly include this in my report. These Hudson Bay people are too arrogant. By our agreement with the British Oregon is open country—open to Americans and open to British. But they have it sewed up tight through the Hudson Bay Company. The Company has the Indians coerced. Wyeth told me you couldn't buy a skin on the Columbia. Food, horses, yes—but you try to trade for furs and they won't do it. Their furs go to the Company. They are too sure of themselves." He looked about him at the rickety walls. He said with contempt, "Why, one squad of my men of the Seventh could take this fort. Did you look at those cannon, Joe? They are so old and rusty if he tried to fire them the barrels would split! Why, the four of us could take this fort! It wouldn't *take* a squad."

Big Starr swung his feet off the bunk. "You want this fort took, Cap'n?"

Bonneville stopped his pacing midway across the room and stared at Starr. "I am tempted," he said, "I am strongly tempted."

Fowler chuckled. "I don't know as the U.S. government would appreciate you commencing a war, Captain."

Bonneville began laughing. "No, of course not. But this is an incredible insult to the United States government. An incredible indignity. It is an outrage!"

Starr reached for his gun and his wiping stick, and the big ham-hands went to work cleaning the barrel methodically. Starr cleaned his gun for various reasons, only one of them being to get it clean. He cleaned it to pass time, when he was weathered in or bored for any other reason. He cleaned it sometimes when telling a long tale, the wiping stick being used for emphasis. He cleaned it to calm his nerves when he was upset. He cleaned it, even if it was already immaculate, when something threatened. Fowler wondered now if Starr thought they were, after all, going to attack Pambrun before the night was over. He said, "Pambrun don't know—I don't reckon you told him—that you represent the United States government, Captain."

Bonneville halted in front of him. "No. No, that's true.

He does not know my official capacity. But I don't doubt, sir, that if he knew his behavior would be precisely the same. These British are too sure of themselves out here. They have had it their own way too long. It is high time our government called off that agreement." He began pacing again. "I have learned much. They have such faith in their hold on the country he was frank. There is a small fort at the mouth of the Columbia—Mr. Astor's old fort. They rarely have more than three or four men there, sometimes only two man the fort. Vancouver is of course the heart of the trade. It is the only strong post they have. It would garrison a hundred men if there was need. Wyeth told me about it. Pambrun confirmed what Wyeth said. But they don't *have* a hundred men in the country. There is then this post, and you have seen it. You know how indefensible it is. Colville is on the north fork and Pambrun says ordinarily they have three men stationed there. It is an even poorer post than this." He quit talking but he kept on pacing.

Fowler gave him five minutes more. "Don't you reckon the government would rather negotiate with the British over this than fight 'em?" he said then.

Bonneville flung himself down in a chair and pulled a big sigh up from way down inside. "That is the slow way. But I suppose . . . we have the treaty, yes. The problem can be settled by negotiation. Our government can give notice the agreement is at an end and some boundary must be drawn." He brought his fist down on the rickety table near his chair. "But I would swear one company of cavalry could rid Oregon of the Hudson Bay Company! Of the British! And it may come to that. It may well come to that. I shall certainly present the facts in my report and I shall certainly recommend that our government must move, *now*. They must either take these posts by force, or they must break off that agreement and settle the boundary question once and for all. If they wait," he jumped up and began pacing again, "if they wait, these people will bring in more and more men, they will build more and more posts, and they will infiltrate the country until it will take a war to be rid of them."

Young Lashly was playing euchre with the clerk and the other employees and he wasn't present to hear, but the captain was talking plain in front of Starr. Fowler thought about saying something but he didn't think much about it. He went back to working over the moccasins. When a man had a craw full he had to get rid of it or bust a gut. And the captain had a craw full. Anyway, Starr was as safe with the secret as he was. But Starr, uncomfortable with all the talk, got up and said he believed he would join the boys at euchre.

When he had left, Bonneville talked on and on, discussing what must go in his report—the richness of the whole West, all its rivers, all its land, all the information he had gathered about it, its weather, its mountains, its Indians, and their ways and locations. He would tell the story of the whole fur trade and all the men who had engaged in it. Oregon was but one part of the whole, a part they should not let slip, should not give up, but it was the whole West, all of it, the government should know about, how valuable it was, how important it was. It had been written off too soon as wasteland. It was not. It was a rich, rich land and it held the future of the country in its heart.

As he talked on and on the fire in him burned out and his anger left him. His good mind organized the details of the report, and he had them all at his fingertips, from the price of prime plews to the number and habits of the Piegan Blackfeet. What he had seen and what he had heard was squirreled away in his mind, and what he didn't have at immediate recall, he had in his notebooks. Listening, Fowler thought the government could not have used a better man to get facts and figures. He tossed the moccasins onto his pack. "When do you aim to write this report?"

"When we get back to the Portneuf. When Joe Walker gets back from California. Then all the facts will be in. I will send it down the Missouri after the rendezvous next summer," Bonneville said.

Fowler latched his long fingers around one knee. "Send it? You're not going back yourself?"

"Not yet. I've been thinking, Joe. I want to come back out here. Next fall I'll bring a larger company. Leave earlier and have more time here. And I'll be *well* outfitted."

"You must have an indefinite leave," Fowler said.

Bonneville grunted. "My leave was up last year," he said. "I applied for an indefinite extension. I *suppose* I have it, but I don't know. But this is an important job and I mean to do it right. I don't want to leave one stone unturned."

"You didn't hear about your leave in that pouch I brought you from Mr. Driant?" Fowler asked.

Bonneville laughed. "Oh, that. That was from Mr. Astor's man, Alfred Seton. It was simply to tell me they would finance me indefinitely. I needed to know how much money there was before I undertook any further explorations."

Fowler laughed. "And you took off pronto soon as you knew you had the backing. Well, I hope the army and the War Department agree with you."

"I may as well be hung for a sheep as a lamb. I wouldn't consider I had done my duty unless I learned all the facts," Bonneville said. He rubbed his hand across his eyes. "Well, we'll leave early." He said ruefully, "We could have used those supplies going back. We'll be short of trade goods."

Fowler grinned. "You can get us back to the Imnaha with your bald head and your medicine kit. Time we get there it'll be warmed up and we'll find game. We'll make out. We won't hurt none."

Bonneville began to undress. "I suppose not." He stopped with his shirt half off. "But you know, Joe, I would dearly love to set a slow match to these old driftwood walls. What a bonfire they would make!"

"It might light up Washington and London, too," Fowler said. "Just pinch out that candle, Captain."

twelve

Early in May they got back to the winter camp near the mouth of the Portneuf. They didn't actually expect to find anybody there. Bonneville's orders had been for the men to get out for the spring hunt as early in April as they could whether he was back or not. He expected to be back, he told them, but if he wasn't they were not to wait. When he got back, he had said, he would move on over to the Bear. They would all rendezvous on the Bear early in June and they would wait to see if Joe Walker got back from California in time to go with them to the big rendezvous on Ham's Fork of the Green in late June.

In spite of knowing there probably wouldn't be anyone at the winter camp, they were anxious to get there and know for sure. They were all eager for news. They wanted to know how the winterers had fared and what they had been doing and what else had been happening in the country. And they were eager to see their own people again. Young Lashly made no bones of the fact he wanted to see Annie again in the worst way and just as quick as he could. "I dunno as I ever missed anybody more," he confessed.

"A woman shore gits to be habit, don't she?" Big Starr said, laughing at him.

"It ain't just that," the boy said, turning as red as a piece of calico, "a body just gets used to having 'em around. Doing for you. Company to you. They're a kind of comfort to you. I ain't going off and leaving Annie no more," he said emphatically, "and I hope we hunt beaver for a while and quit this here exploring."

"Got your craw full of exploring?" Fowler asked.

"Well, I *have,*" Lashly said. "We been a right smart piece and seen a sight of country. And not that I don't appreciate the wages and of course if you was to sign us on again I'd go. Sure, I'd go. But I kind of hope you don't. I'm tired of wandering."

"The wages don't make up for the miss of Annie, neither, do they?" Big Starr teased.

"They *shore* don't," the boy said fervently, "they shore don't, and not for no kind of wages am I gonna leave her behind no more."

Bonneville had cached some extra supplies before leaving for the Columbia, flour, coffee, sugar, tobacco, ammunition, some other odds and ends of things. Fowler, Big Starr, and young Lashly had stowed their traps in the cache. When they dug into the big hole they found everything in good condition, which mostly meant to them nobody else had been into the hole, or if they had it was somebody as careful as they had been. If you made a good cache, located it well, wrapped all perishables in waterproof packs, there was no reason goods stored away shouldn't keep several seasons.

Fowler, Big Starr, and young Lashly retrieved their traps and Bonneville completely emptied the cache. He was moving his base and didn't know whether he would ever be back in this place again. Then Fowler found that somebody had been in the cache, for gripped in the teeth of one of his traps was a note. When he saw it was from Mose he grinned. Mose could burrow in a cache so cleverly that even if you set a trap for him you couldn't tell it. The note was addressed to Fowler. It was dated the second day of April and it said: "We air leaving out for the Blackfoot river and we will hunt through the mountains down thataway. Will go by beer springs to the bear. Bannocks is going with us to hunt buffler. Yore wimmin are with us."

Fowler read it aloud. Bonneville was pleased. "That's a

good plan . . . a good plan. And it gives us our route. We will follow them up the river."

Young Lashly couldn't hide his disappointment. "I was hoping the women would be at the Bannock village," he said.

"Aw, it won't take us long to ketch 'em up," Big Starr said. "It ain't no piece down into the Blackfoot range."

For days they had been looking forward to having bread and coffee again, and they were starved for sugar. Pambrun had had bread and real coffee at Walla Walla, but he had been short on sweetening. They baked up a pile of hoecakes and made their biggest kettle full of coffee. Then Big Starr poured sugar into it until it was almost syrupy. Hot and black and extra sweet it tasted better than metheglin to them. With real tobacco again for their pipes they felt lapped in luxury. Indians rarely smoked straight tobacco. It was too strong for their palates. Even when they had it in plenty they mixed the red willow bark with it to make the mild kinnikinick. "Kinnikinick is better than nothin'," Big Starr said, drawing in a satisfying deep draught, "but not much. I'd jist about as soon smoke cornshucks like I done when I was a kid."

The buffalo were coming south, so next day they killed and butchered meat. They feasted on liver and boudins and fat hump. They didn't bother to strip any meat out and make jerky. It was buffalo time now and there would be plenty of meat all summer. They didn't have to think about smoking jerky until fall.

For two days they stayed at the winter camp and ate and slept and loafed. Bonneville caught up his journals. He also sorted through and repacked his instruments. He had measured and surveyed and charted this entire region long before, and his instruments could be laid aside for a while. The weather was perfect. Without wind, it was like smooth silk. There was a high cloudless sky and the sun, up in the day, was hot. They kept meat roasting all the time. They ate and slept and waked to eat and put more meat to roasting, then they slept again.

Lying on his back once, between waking and drowsing, Fowler stretched his legs out long and thought how you could feel the winter-bound muscles loosening and limbering and you could feel the blood feeding and surging with new life, and the nerve ends got fattened over and didn't rasp and scrape and keep eating away at you. A man was built to be a good animal, but if he didn't treat his body with as much care as any animal took, it got seedy and run down. You had to have a quiet time once in a while, to let it lick itself and preen itself and let it mend up what you'd taken out of it.

The morning of the third day when they got up they all felt it was time to move on. They had eaten and slept themselves out, and Bonneville had finished his chores.

The Blackfoot River rose in the mountains south of the Snake and it flowed into the Snake several miles above the mouth of the Portneuf. The Bannock village was on their way. When they came in sight of the shelf up from the river flat where the old village had been, they saw smoke and a few lodges. Fowler counted ten, and five separate smokes. "They are old people," he said. "Too old for the hunt. They been left behind."

Bonneville, always curious, nosing out facts, said, "Do all the tribes leave their old people behind when they go to hunt?"

"Mostly. Of course if they're moving on to make a new village everybody goes. But if it's just a hunt the old ones are useless. They're just a trouble and bother and it's easier on them and everybody for them to stay home. They kind of keep things done up for the others to come back to."

As they came closer they could see people sitting in the sun in front of the lodges and some were moving about. Several women were working near one of the fires. "I'm glad there's somebody here," young Lashly said, "they might have some news that's later'n Mose's letter." The boy touched up his horse to a trot which set the traps hung to his pack rattling and jangling.

The others quickened their pace also. Fowler grinned and said to Big Starr, "The kid's really hurting to see his squaw, ain't he?"

The village dogs had seen them and had set up a fierce and frantic yipping and yelping. One of the squaws working at the fire stood up to kick among them. Big Starr burst into laughter. "They ain't all old folks, Joe. That squaw is big with a youngun. 'Bout ready to drop it, from the looks of her."

Fowler stared at the woman, puzzled. Pregnancy never kept an Indian woman from doing her work or going on a hunt or wherever else the village went. "She must of been left to mind the old ones," he said.

Another woman squatting by the fire got up then. She evidently heard the traps rattling for she turned in their direction and stood looking toward them, shading her eyes with her hand. "I be danged," Starr said, "that 'un is big, too. Them Bannocks has made good use of the winter, ain't they?"

"There's another one," Fowler said, "coming out of that lodge at the end."

Suddenly young Lashly let out a whoop. "They're *here!* Them are our women, Starr! That one's Annie just come outta the lodge! Yippeeee! Hi-yi-yi-yi! Annie! Hey, Annie! It's me! It's Ben!"

The squaws moved toward each other into a huddle and then stood still for a long moment, all of them shading their eyes and looking down the slope. The men couldn't hear them but they knew when they began jabbering to each other because they started pointing and then they began scurrying around. Then two of them broke away and came down the slope. They were awkward in their bigness and waddled more than they ran but they moved with extraordinary speed considering their handicap.

Young Lashly dug his horse into a lope. Just short of meeting the squaws he hauled him up short in a cloud of dust and flung himself off. When the dust cleared they could see him swinging his Annie off her feet, prancing with her round and round and round. Big Starr said, "That 'un with her is Mamselle."

Fowler said dryly, "What was it you said about the Bannocks using the winter to good advantage?"

Starr threw him a crooked grin. "Yore Betsy ain't as slim as you left her, I hope you've noticed." He pulled off his cap and scratched his head. "Size Mamselle is, this hoss is wonderin' jist *who* bigged her, me or Fouchette. How in cat hair . . ." He let it go. "What the hell. Don't make no difference." He tickled the ribs of his horse and went to meet his waddling woman.

Bonneville was in a fit of laughter, doubled over, slapping his knees, sputtering when he tried to talk, then seized with further spasms that choked him and made him cough. "Free trappers," he managed to get out finally, "three proud free Taos trappers! As hitched and hogtied as any other family man! *Sacré,* but this is unbelievable! How could all three of you—?" but he went off into sputters again.

Fowler felt his face get hot but he made the best he could of it. He shrugged and laughed, too. "Easy, Captain. Three men . . . three women . . . three kids. You gonna put it in your report?"

But Bonneville lay on the neck of his horse, shaking and choking, helpless with laughter. Impossible, Fowler heard. Unbelievable. Marvelous. Wonderful.

He didn't think it was so wonderful. He slowed the big roan to a walk. Betsy had not joined the other two women in their rush down the slope. She had continued to stand, watching, one hand over her eyes, until the others had reached the bottom of the slope. Then as if it didn't matter, as if men came back from the Columbia every day of the week, she had turned about and picked up a paddle and had begun to stir the inevitable pot of stew hanging over the fire. But no mistaking it, she was, like the others, as round as a barrel and her skirt front hiked up ludicrously over her big belly.

A slow rage began to seethe in Fowler. She had done this thing deliberately. Annie was young and perhaps had not learned wisdom in such things. Mamselle had probably been careless and lazy. But Betsy was wise and she was never careless or lazy. Purposely and deliberately she had chosen to have a child. And she had chosen purposely and deliberately this special time.

A dry cottony taste came in his mouth. That was the trouble with them. You give a squaw an inch and the best of them would stretch it into a mile. He had never before let Betsy travel with him. He had let her talk him into it this time. And so. Having got her way about traveling with him, she would now tie him with a family. She would hitch him closer and tighter. Many beaver men acquiring a brood of halfbreed younguns became squaw men altogether, quit ever going to the settlements, turned Indian and almost forgot they had ever been white men. Was that what she wanted of him?

He walked the big blue slowly and made his anger flatten out, waited for the surge and storm inside to die out until there was only a cold heaviness. In all the years, she yet didn't know him or she would not have dared do this thing. Joe Fowler had a squaw but he was not a squaw man nor would he ever be one. No squaw had ever put hame strings on him and no squaw ever would. She would learn that. Having a brat was no way to go about putting hitching lines on him. He had always left her when he got ready to go back to the settlements and he would leave her *and* her youngun when he got ready again.

He rode up to the fire. She left off stirring the stew and went toward him. He got off the horse and flung her the reins. Her eyes searched his face. He met them with a long, direct look, coldly blanking all feeling out of his own eyes and keeping it off his face. He presented her his accusation and his anger and his refusal with a studied stoniness. She dropped her eyes and waddled away. Ordinarily he would have helped her with the unloading and unsaddling and the picketing of the horse and they would have chattered and laughed together after this long absence. But he let her lead off the roan alone. He went to the fire and picked up a wooden bowl and although he wasn't hungry, didn't want food, he heaped the bowl full of stew and began to shovel it down.

Young Lashly and Big Starr were taking their time up the slope with their women. When Bonneville had seen to his horse he joined Fowler at the fire. Fowler jerked his head at the stew. "Meat," he said. "They've killed a cow."

"I'm not hungry," Bonneville said, "perhaps later." He stood a moment longer, then he said, awkwardly, "I take it you are not pleased with this turn of events." As soon as he had opened his mouth he knew he shouldn't have and wished he hadn't. One thing you did *not* do, under any circumstances, in the mountains was butt in on a man's private affairs.

Fowler made no reply, did not even look up. He just went on eating.

Bonneville looked at him squatted on his hunkers shoveling big hunks of meat in his mouth. He shrugged and let it go. It was none of his business. But he wondered at Fowler's displeasure. Why was he so angry about it? What did it matter? There were hundreds of little halfbreeds in the mountains. Hardly a trapper but had two or three, or a dozen, by as many different women. If you took a squaw surely it was to be expected. And nobody gave it a second thought. It was nothing. Look at young Lashly and Big Starr, yelping, laughing, joking with their women about it. It was a strange strain in this man to be displeased about it.

Young Lashly had veered Annie toward the lodge at the end of the street and they were walking along, leading his horse, arms locked, heads together, laughing and jabbering together like children. That was one young man to whom it certainly did not matter. And Starr. The big man had hoisted Mamselle onto his horse and he was walking along beside her. There wasn't a cloud on Big Starr's face. He was laughing, too, and probably teasing the woman about whether the papoose was his or Fouchette's. The squaw's face was merry and she was giggling in happy fits of laughter. "I suppose," Bonneville said, "you will want to stay over a night here."

Fowler finished the stew and threw the wooden bowl carelessly on the ground. It went skidding through the sand collecting a mess on its wet sides. Fowler shoved up and wiped his mouth with the back of his hand. "Why?"

"Well . . ." Bonneville began, uncertainly. It was obvious. The boys had just found their women again. They wouldn't want to move on right away, even with the women traveling with them. They would want a little time. He said, "We can wait till morning to leave."

"No need," Fowler said. "Soon as the boys have eat and the women get packed we can start. We can get to the mouth of the Blackfoot by night."

Bonneville shrugged. Fowler was angry in a way Bonneville had no experience of. When he was angry he sputtered and erupted and boiled over and everybody knew it. But Fowler had become like granite, a hard, implacable, unyielding rock that you could break yourself against. "If you say so," Bonneville said.

Betsy came back hauling Fowler's heavy saddle. He made no move to help her. He let her lug it into the lodge. Then she went back for his pack. When she had put it in the lodge, when she had taken care of his possessions, she came to the fire to feed and care for him. But she saw the dirty bowl on the ground. She picked it up and tried to brush the sand off. She gave up and rested the bowl on the shelf of her big, outrounding belly and she began to talk. In a quiet monotone she began to talk. There was something to be told, she said.

Fowler made a chopping, shutting-off movement with his hand. "Not now. It can wait."

The woman breathed heavily. And so. But it could not wait. It must be told now. It concerned the man called Mose and the man called Pete. They were dead. They had been killed. Not long ago. In the Blackfoot mountains. With no emphasis of any kind in her voice, keeping it low and flat and level, only the tongue clickings against the teeth, the occasional glottal stops changing the rhythm, she told him. That was why she and the other women were here. When the man called Mose and the man called Pete were killed she had led them to this place to wait for him. To tell him.

Bonneville could not understand the Utah language but he saw the look of unbelieving shock on Fowler's face. "What is it? What is she saying?"

Fowler shook his hand off his arm. "In a minute. Wait." To the woman he said, his voice grating with a dry harshness as if the spit in his mouth had all dried up, "Tell it."

She turned the wooden bowl in her hands but her eyes stayed on his face, though not meeting his eyes directly. They seemed fixed instead on his mouth. Her voice kept low and flat. It was the middle of April, she said, the Plant Moon of the Utahs. They were in the Blackfoot mountains—and she nudged south with her chin. The men were taking many beaver. Many. She and the other women were very busy with the skins every day. The beaver were fine and fat and heavy. The man called Mose and the man called Pete trapped together each day, and they came back each day with skins from all their traps. One day they did not come back. The bowl made a half turn on her stomach, and her eyes moved up Fowler's face to meet his eyes.

Two of the other men, *his* men—she nudged her chin toward Bonneville—went to look for them. And so. And yes. And they found them.

Fowler's mouth worked but he said only one thing. "Pete had worked too fast, up ahead of Mose."

And yes. They found the man called Mose first. He had been shot and he had been scalped. He was dead. As far as from here to there—nudging down to the flats below—up the stream they found the man called Pete. He had been shot and he had been scalped but he was not dead. His spirit had not gone away from him. His spirit remained in him until he could tell the other men it was five Indians . . . the ones called Poordevils . . . and with them was the man called Bastro.

Fowler's breath grunted out.

The Utah woman went on. And the man called Bastro took the beaver and he took the traps and he took the horses and he went away with the Poordevils. And then the breath of life left the man called Pete. The other men brought the two dead men to the camp. And they buried them there. And so. And thus. And then she and the other women came to this place to wait for him. The Shoshone woman who had lived in the lodge of the man called Pete went with one of the other men. She did not come to this place with them.

"They try to trail 'em?" Fowler said.

The woman's head went slowly from one side to the other. They did not follow. The men were afraid. They hid their furs and they pulled up their traps from the streams and they went away to the place called Beer Springs. It was so. And the Poordevils, she said, went north. When she and the other women started to this place they found their tracks. The tracks then turned northeast—her chin pointed—after half a day. She and the other women followed the river to this place.

When she had finished Fowler stood like a piece of stone for a long timeless moment. Then without moving, standing absolutely rigid, he began a slow, grinding, grating cursing. He did not raise his voice, he did not shout or yell, he did not become shrill or strident. There was no stress or emphasis in the flat ragged voice. It just went on and on and on, dull, strained, repeated, monotonous. His face had turned gray and his eyes were flat and opaque-looking, blank, hooded like a snake's. It made Bonneville's flesh creep, standing beside him, hearing, watching without knowing, but knowing it was something terrible and awful and unbearable to this man.

The oaths spewed out of the thin twisted mouth like vomit, vile, venomous, bitter, unrelenting, unremitting, unsparing, pitiless, outpouring. In their flatness and in their repetition and in their monotony they were like the beat of surf or the moan of wind or the drum of white water. Coldness iced down Bonneville's back and he felt the hairs rise on the back of his neck and down his arms. Fowler must stop this! He was out of his head! He was losing his mind! But Bonneville could not force himself to touch him.

Big Starr came catapulting out from between two lodges. He threw himself at Fowler and took hold of his shoulders and shook him. "Joe! Shut up! Joe! Stop it!"

Fowler's voice cut off in mid-oath, his mouth hanging open. He stared at Big Starr without seeing him. Then a long cry broke from the Utah woman, a long, shuddering, keening cry. Fowler turned his head to look at her, the cry penetrating some dim inner consciousness. Her head was thrown back stiffly, and she had torn her hair over her face, and her mouth was twisted with the cry. Her eyes were rolled back in her head and her hands were clawing at her face. She drew in a long sobbing breath and cried again. Suddenly Fowler's stone face crumpled and his mouth trembled. He reached blindly for the woman and she went into his arms and hid her face against his chest. And he led her into the lodge. They could hear his voice, quiet now and gentle, comforting the woman.

It was over. Wherever his soul had gone, wherever it had wandered out of his body, however far it had wandered, it was back inside him again. In great fear for its lonely journey the woman had cried for it. In great grief for its desolate loss she had mourned for it, and her fear and her grief had been strong enough, and his spirit had heard and come home.

A shudder ran all through Bonneville. Something so wild, so haunted, so savage, had just taken place before him that he felt as if a ghost had walked, a strange wind had blown, a tongue had uttered and he did not know the language. A man like Fowler knew it. And a woman like the Utah knew it. And it took years to learn it and he would never learn it . . only men as wild and haunted and savage as the people of this place, and the place itself, could ever learn it. Elemental as the gray rocks of the mountains, as the wild water of the canyons, as the animals that haunted the wild places, no man like him, crusted with civilization, veneered with learning, could hope to understand it. Witness it, record it, but not ever, not ever once know what it was.

Big Starr slid slowly down to the ground. He pulled his knees up under his chin and folded his arms across them and laid his head on his arms. His big shoulders shook. No sound came from him but he was racked with a terrible shaking. Bonneville dropped down beside him. "In God's name, what is it?" he cried. "What has happened? What terrible thing is going on here?"

Big Starr raised his head. Mamselle had just told him, he said, addle-pated as she was, not thinking to tell him for the longest time, and he had come straight to tell Joe and found him going crazy. Bonneville shook the man's arm. "Tell him what? Tell him *what?*"

Starr stared at him, then shook his big head as if to clear it. "You ain't heard yet? Didn't *he* tell you?"

"Nobody has told me anything. The woman told Joe but I couldn't understand her. What is it that has happened?"

Starr told him, his voice almost as flat and level as Fowler's had been. "We are to blame," he said when he finished. "That's what sent Joe off. Me and him are to blame for this thing. We ought to gone after that bastard 'stead of goin' with you. If we had, Mose and Pete would be alive now. We didn't tend to our business, way we ought to. We let it wait. Said we'd git him come spring. Now, it's too late. We oughtn't to waited. Mose was gittin' old and not as spry as he used to be. And Pete was crippled. They was both fair game for that sonuvabitch." He hit his hands together, then shoved up from the ground, pushing himself up in one long flowing movement, and he strode away.

Bonneville sat where he was. He felt stunned, and there was nothing he could do. Nothing he could say. He knew about the man, Bastro, of course. He knew how Fouchette had been killed and how the man had deliberately shot Pete in the knee, crippling him. But it was something he had had no part in, and this, now, was something he could have no part in, not even to advise or counsel. This was purely the affair of these men, to whom he owed so much, whom he liked so much, whom he would have helped much if he could. Nothing of his gratitude nor even his hopes and wishes could serve him, or them, now. He could only wait and see what they would do. He guessed every plan would alter considerably now. He doubted Fowler would do another thing until he had tracked this man down now.

He waited a long time. No one came. There was no stir of movement in the lodges. They did not even seek each other out yet. Whatever they were doing, whatever they were feeling and thinking, they were excluding him, but he accepted it. It had to be. He got out his journal and wrote it up, then he wandered over to talk with the old Bannock people at the other end of the street, not knowing what to expect or when, just taking up the slack of time.

When beaver men lived with Indians they took on many Indian ways. They quit, for instance, having any set time for eating. With all Indians, food was always cooking and ready to eat and each individual ate when he was hungry or when it suited him. There was no gathering around together except when there were visitors to be honored. But late in the afternoon, as if they had agreed upon it, Fowler and Big Starr and young Lashly and the women converged upon the fire in front of Fowler's lodge and the men ate together. Fowler sent young Lashly for Bonneville. Betsy filled a bowl for him.

"I reckon you know," Fowler said immediately, "me and Starr will go after this sonuvabitch now."

"Yes. I believed you would."

"Well. Well, then, we'll put out in the morning. But Ben, here, will go with you."

Young Lashly looked up puzzled, and Bonneville guessed he was hearing for the first time of this decision. "I would a heap ruther," the boy said, "go with you. I thought—"

"No." It was cruelly short.

"But I thought I was a Fowler man, too. You said—"

"There ain't no more Fowler men," Fowler said bluntly. He made the flat, downward, cutting-off motion with his hand. "There's just me and Starr. That's all that's left of Fowler men. And a job to do. You'd just be in the way. Go with Captain Bonneville."

He didn't say more, but it was this kind of thing Fowler wanted no more of. This kind of having to explain. He didn't want the kid along. He didn't want any more of a young man having to be taught and looked after and seen to and told and hauled out of his mistakes. He felt as old as the mountains. As timeless, as gray, as stony and hard. He didn't want any green sapling in this rocky grayness. Starr and him, neither ever having to talk, knowing without talk what it all meant, anything they saw, anything they did, never having to say. Seeing, doing, absorbing, distilling, using. The kid would be like a sore thumb, bothering, useless, in the way. "Go with Captain Bonneville," he said, and he repeated, "There ain't no Fowler men no more."

The youngster looked scared. He glanced obliquely at Bonneville as if he feared he, too, might reject him. Behind him his young squaw's dark eyes were round and frightened, too. She could not understand what was being said but she knew her man was troubled and if he was troubled she was frightened. Bonneville hurried into the breach. "Of course, Ben. You will be helpful to me. I'll be glad to have you. Good men are hard to find out here. Your wages will continue as one of my party."

Big Starr thumped the ground. "Thar, now. Good job for ye, Ben. Good wages. Ye couldn't ask no better."

Young Lashly nodded but he still looked bewildered and unhappy. Bonneville wondered if he even knew what this was all about. "You know, don't you, Ben, what has happened?"

"Oh, sure," the youngster said, "Annie told me. And I figured we'd be going after Bastro. I would—"

Big Starr butted in. "Shore ye would. Me and Joe knows it. It's jist, well, it ain't your put-in, Ben. We kin do it our-selves quicker and easier. Ye see—"

Fowler clipped in. "Quit. It's settled."

What was puzzling the kid was his behavior, Fowler knew. He should have taken time to talk to him and explain. He shouldn't be short and blunt with him. But he didn't feel like taking any more time. He didn't want to talk about any of it any more. The kid would have to grow up, was all. Learn men were one thing one time, another thing another time. Joe Fowler was willing to teach a greenhorn when the time was right, willing to take time when there was enough of it. But when time ran out, he wasn't, and that was it. He had a bigger obligation to the man who had taught him, in the time and the place that was right for it. Lashly would have to find his own place with his own men, and it wasn't with Joe Fowler and Big Starr right now. *And let it go!* His nerves were frayed to the raveling point and he didn't want any more talk about it.

Bonneville asked if they would be going down into the Blackfoot mountains to pick up the trail. Fowler shook his head. "It's too old down there. We'll ride with you to the mouth of the river is all." He didn't say where they would be going from there.

"Well," Bonneville said, accepting it, "maybe we'll see you at rendezvous."

"Maybe."

"And if you're free, I'd like to have you go back to the Columbia with me this fall."

"No."

Bonneville glanced at him, brooding over his coffee, then quickly looked away. He didn't know what Fowler meant. Didn't know whether he meant he thought it would take longer to find Bastro, or whether he wasn't interested in going back to Oregon. He didn't ask. He accepted that, too.

Fowler swallowed down the last of his coffee. "You got enough ammunition in your main cache on the Green to sell me some?"

"What's there you're welcome to," Bonneville said quickly. "We shan't need it. Michel Cerré will meet me at rendezvous with fresh supplies. I won't even be going to the Green until time for the rendezvous. I'll give you the sign marks and a map." He went for his notebook.

When he came back Fowler said, "Give me a piece of that paper and I'll make you out a draft."

Bonneville tore out a page and handed it over. Fowler wrote quickly, authorizing payment by the Johnny Osage stores. "I've left the amount blank," he said. "We'll leave a message in the cache saying how much we took and you can fill it in."

Bonneville nodded. He was copying blaze marks and signs on another piece of paper and sketching in a rough map. He handed it over. "You find anything else you need in the cache, Joe, take it." He owed this man all the help he could give him.

"I'm obliged," Fowler said, folding the sketch and tucking it away. "Might take some trade goods. But we got our own traps and it's calf time so powder and flints is mostly what we'll need."

A gust of wind blew sand across the fire and all of them stood and looked around. A slate cloud bank had formed to the north and a few turkey tracks of lightning were playing about. The women hurried to put pots and bowls and kettles away, to carry in skins and robes and bedding, to fasten the lodges down more securely. Betsy, as usual, was scolding and muttering and fussing as she hurried. The men went to see to their horses and then without more talk they dispersed to their lodges.

Fowler lay awake a long time that night listening to the hiss and spray of rain driven against the sides of the tepee. Beside him in the robes Betsy was asleep, her knees drawn up, curled, like the child within her. The wind drove the rain and the cone of the tepee was lit often with the flare of lightning and the thunder rumbled and cracked. Little by little, as if slowly turning pages in a picture book, Fowler did the thing he was most afraid of. Like reopening old wounds, as painful as picking dry scabs off old sores, he deliberately went back and opened up all his memories of Mose.

The first time he saw him on that cold, blowing snowy corner in Taos and he had been so green and scared and Mose had spoken to him in friendliness and had taken him in. The winter in Taos when they had lived in the old hovel in the edge of the town, but had lived well and even saved for their first hunt together by making and selling Taos lightning. The first hunt up in the Spanish Peaks country, and the Comanches, and the first time he ever stood back to back with a man and like to heaved his stomach up, and he and Mose had stood back to back and had stood down the Comanches. The times since. All the hunts since. All the territory covered. All the streams trapped. All the mountains crossed and recrossed, all the rivers and plains they had learned together. Time ran in a swift current backward for him, separated and distinguished not by years but by parks and rivers and passes and peaks. The del Norte. The Yampa. The Arkansas and the Cimarron and the North Platte. The Laramie Fork . . . Sweetwater . . . Popo Agie. The Siskadee and the Wind River and the Tetons and Pierre's Hole and Jackson's Hole and Brown's Hole. And the Bear and the Gila and the Uncompaghre. And all the other nameless holes and passes and peaks.

All the gray-rock peaks and the willow-brush canyons and the spruce-pine timber and the quaking asp groves, the cotton-wood islands and the quicksands on the slow rivers and the white water of the fast ones—they all came into his memory and rolled and flowed and were timeless, marked only by the infinite number of blood-light dawns setting traps, and the blood-light evenings running traps, and all the camps and fires in the purple shadows of high peaks, and the vein-blood warm and coursing, and the muscles elastic and stretchy, and the high, proud certainty they were men like no other men before them, or ever would be again. They had it all, inside them—he and Mose and a handful of others—a little few, not wanting others, not needing others. They had done it, they owned it, it was theirs, and they were the men, a special breed of men. They had had a time of glory, a very special kind of glory and it would die when the last of them had gone under—been rubbed out. It would go because they had been the first and they had made it for the others and when they were gone, all of them, men might remember, but no one would ever again know what the glory was like, for it would go with them. They had used it up, him and Mose and some few others.

He buried Mose in his own way, with memories. He would not do it again. He knew he would not ever do it again. Then he turned on his side. The rain was quitting. It was only a soft hiss against the skin of the lodge now and the thunder was a fading growl. He curled around the Utah woman and she stirred in her sleep, murmured drowsily. He nuzzled his face into her neck and put his arm around her, around her big, bulging belly. Suddenly he grinned. Mose had known about this. Mose had been the one to see the first growing signs. And Mose would have been fixing up to carry him high. He never would have heard the last of this from Mose.

He went to sleep, the last of the thunder rumbling distantly around the horizon, mixing and growling along with Mose's old cracked voice blackguarding him with bawdy and ribald remarks.

thirteen

Captain William Drummond Stewart, the Englishman traveling with the fur brigades that year, called the valley of the Green the most beautiful place in the west. The Crows called it Absaroka, their homeland, and said the Great Spirit had put it in exactly the right place. Mountain men, short on words any time, simply thought it was paradise. They looked forward all year to the rendezvous on some fork of the Green and came back to the valley like pigeons coming home. As near as any place in the mountains was home to them, the broad sage plain that stretched from the Wind Rivers to the Tetons was home to them.

Easterners, traveling for whatever reason in the west and un-initiated, looked in consternation at it and wondered what was so beautiful about it. To them, it was flat, almost treeless, desolate, dotted with some kind of tough grass and the everlasting sagebrush which smelled like turpentine, so sharp and pungent and acrid. They did not know it abounded in every kind of game, that the bunch grass was the best forage in the world, and that the cottonwood that marked the course of the Green and most of its forks was the most valuable tree in the West. It gave ample shade in the summer, fuel in the winter, made lodgepoles for the tepees, and was a succulent food for horses. Put to it, you could smoke the crumbled bark in your pipe and you could even make a stew of it that would keep you from starving.

The valley begins narrowly in the north where the Grosventre hills nudge over near the Wind Rivers, then it widens to thirty, forty, fifty miles as the Grosventres break off. Most of the forks come down from the Wind Rivers. Where the basin spreads out to about fifty miles in width, before it pinches in again with a scattering of hills in the south, Horse Creek flows in. Here was where Captain Bonneville had built his Fort Nonsense, and it was here Fowler and Big Starr came the middle of May and dug into the caches. They took ammunition and some trade goods and then moved on.

They went probing among the Crow villages along the base of the Wind Rivers and on the upper streams. They took their time and they visited. They did a little trading but not much because the Crows were getting ready to move down to the big rendezvous. They smoked and traded a little and they asked discreet questions. Had a small band of Poordevils, this many, been seen lately? Had they been troublesome? Had any horses been stolen lately?

The Crows were polite. They smoked and they listened and they said, no, they had not seen any Poordevils at all. And no, no horses had been stolen lately by Poordevils. Blackfeet, yes. Blackfeet had made a raid just a short time ago and they had stolen some horses. But not Poordevils. Poordevils, they said, were like spirits, like the ghosts of men. They lived in the mountains and they were wild. They could be seen sometimes, up a canyon, or on the high side of a mountain, and then if one looked again they were gone. They did not often come out of the mountains.

"There is a white man with this small band of Poordevils," Fowler told them. "He will come out. He will not live like a Poordevil very long. His name is Bastro. You know the man called Bastro? He has lived among you."

And yes. They knew the man called Bastro. But he was the friend of Beckwith. Was he not up north with Beckwith?

"No. He is not with Beckwith now. He is with the small band of Poordevils." He took pains to tell them why he wanted Bastro. He told the headmen of each village that the white man killed his friend, Mose. Did they not remember Mose? And yes, they remembered him. And the white man had killed his friend,

Pete Smith, the one who wore the wooden leg. Their hands covered their mouths, then they made the sign of death with them, one palm erasing the other, the rubbing out of life. They were sorry. They understood he must find this man, Bastro. A brother killed must be revenged or his spirit would wander forever without a home. They would watch, they said. If they saw this man they would send word to him.

But there was an uneasiness among them you couldn't put your finger on. They put on a good act but it was as if they were looking over their shoulders all the time. "They're lyin'," Big Starr said, "they know where he is and they're helpin' him."

"Yes," Fowler said slowly, "I think it. They're caught betwixt and between. They been friendly to us ever since we been coming up here. Commonly you could count on 'em now. But they're friendly with Beckwith and Bastro, too. And Beckwith can do more for 'em around Fort Union and with the Company than we can. I been puzzling why Bastro's hiding out. Thought maybe him and Beckwith had fell out. But the Crows wouldn't befriend anybody Beckwith was on the outs with. So it's some other trouble he's had."

Big Starr flexed the fingers of one big hand and looked over at the massed humps of the Wind Rivers. "This coon would hate to have to commence combin' all them canyons and hollers in that mess of mountains."

"It would be like looking for a needle in a haystack," Fowler admitted. "No use us trying that. But maybe we won't have to. Bastro is not gonna stick with that band of Poordevils very long. He'll come out some time, some place."

Big Starr grunted. "Wagh! Trouble is, how are *we* gonna be there?"

Fowler shook his head. "Have to bait him a trap."

"What kind of a trap?"

"One he'll fall into," Fowler said, laughing. "I'm thinking on it. What day is it? Are we in June yet?"

"I have not got the least idee," Starr said.

Betsy was working nearby. Fowler asked her and translating her accounting he made out it was the fifth day of June. "We'll mosey down to the rendezvous," Fowler said. "Most of the outfits will be there by the twentieth."

Big Starr moaned. "Now, you done it. Mamselle's been naggin' me to go. She'll cost me ever' dime of pay I got from the captain. They won't be enough baubles and geegaws to satisfy her. New clothes, beads, paint, foofooraw foolishment. She'll want it all and won't quit till she gits it."

"Can't you say no?"

Starr squirmed. "Well, a man wants his woman to look as good as anybody else's. He don't want nobody to outshine her. Makes him look miserly if he don't open his hand."

"Don't lay the blame on Mamselle then," Fowler said, laughing.

2.

The rendezvous was in full swing when Fowler's little party reached Ham's Fork. Bill Sublette, carrying supplies for the Rocky Mountain boys, had arrived and set up his trading booths. The carriers for the American Fur Company had reached the flats and were set up, too. Nathaniel Wyeth, who had hoped to do business with the Rocky Mountain boys through Milt Sublette this summer, was out in the cold. Milt had had to stay in the east to have his wounded foot amputated. Bill wouldn't honor the contract and shouldered Wyeth out. Wyeth set up his booth and made do with what trade he could hook onto, but it wasn't much. Some of the free trappers did business with him, but most of them were too used to Bill Sublette to forsake him for a new carrier.

All the brigades were in, all the winterers, the hivernants, the

Rocky Mountain boys, American Fur Company hunters, free trappers, even a few Hudson Bay boys deserting and wanting to line up with the Americans. There were French Canucks, Spanish, Kanakas, Irish, Kentuckians, Missourians, British—name it and he was there at Ham's Fork, several hundred of him. And he was having himself a whale of a time after fifty weeks of beaver hunting. It was five dollars a pint and straight raw alcohol, but it was worth it. It made a man forget the peaks and the passes and the icy streams. It lent strength to his legs in the running and jumping and wrestling contests. It made him feel invincible at the gambling game of "hand" with the Indians, or at euchre with his friends. It made his Hawken shoot straight in the shooting contests. And when a grizzly ambled absent-mindedly through the middle of the encampment it made him brave enough to walk out to meet him bare-handed. It made him forget he could get an eye gouged out in a brawl. It made him a half-horse, half-alligator who could out-drink, out-shout, out-shoot, out-brag, out-jump, out-run, and out-eat anything else on two legs. And at night, in some lodge on "whorehouse row" he could out-last any other man, too.

The Indians were there, fifteen hundred of them it was said, their lodges making a tepee city of the plains. There were Nez Perces with great droves of the spotted horse they bred, the Appaloosa. There were Bannocks and Shoshones, Flatheads down from the northwest. The Crows were there with their fine white-cured robes and feathered headdresses, their beautiful quilled moccasins. There were Utahs and a few Cheyennes. The warriors, like the trappers, were carousing and brawling and gambling and trying their skills with the white men at shooting, racing, wrestling, and jumping, and best of all, showing off their horsemanship, dashing around and through the encampment, making their horses wheel and turn and prance and flourish.

The squaws had set up their booths with their beautifully

cured, soft, beautifully sewn shirts and moccasins for sale, their
sleeping robes, their feathered headdresses, to lure the trapper
into trading. In return they took beads and feathers, bells, necklaces, rings, yard goods, bangles, mirrors, fringing, dyes, face
paints of all kinds, frippery of all kinds.

Up the creek, a little way from the main encampment, were
the lodges set apart for the women with themselves to trade.
They did a thriving business both day and night. Prostitution
was not taken amiss in any Indian tribe, save perhaps the Cheyennes, and the rendezvous was the time when Indian women and
their husbands and their fathers became rich. Drunken trappers
never haggled over prices. At the end of two weeks almost any
squaw could accumulate enough wealth in goods to furnish her
whole family and all her relations for the balance of the year.
If she didn't succumb to the temptations of alcohol, that is, and
trade it all away.

Fowler and Big Starr and the two squaws rode in. Starr
grinned at the noise and the wildness and the spread and the
color and the boiling erupting mass of humanity. "What was it
the captain called a rendezvous?"

Fowler grinned. "He called it a saturnalia."

Big Starr combed his fingers through his long black hair. It
was fresh washed and curled and he had capped it with a new
beaver cap. "Well, whatever," he said, "this child is good and
ready fer it. I am gonna saturnate like nobody else at this hyar
rendezvous!"

They had dressed carefully for their entrance. They wore
their fancy Taos shirts with the heavy long fringe and the porcupine quilled fronts and the beadwork on the cuffs. They tied the
shirts in with scarlet sashes. They had on new buskskin pants
the women had made, with extra long fringing down the seams.
They had discarded their moccasins and put on their boots and
they attached their long Spanish spurs for extra jingle.

Behind them Betsy and Mamselle were equally well dressed,

in new dresses made of skins so perfectly aged and cured they were a creamy white, elaborately worked with quills and beads. Mamselle was decked out in all her ornaments and jewels. She looked, Fowler thought, like a living bangle-tree, bracelets going up her arms to her elbows, earrings dangling, necklaces swinging, and her big belly riding way out in front.

Betsy let the richness of her dress speak for itself, and it needed nothing more. It was, Fowler thought, the prettiest squaw dress he had ever seen. Soft as a baby's skin it was almost white in its pureness. She had fringed it deeply around the bottom and the edge of the sleeves and she had worked a design of her own dreaming all around the skirt and above the fringe. Little bells were sewn here and there and a richness of blue beads, shells, and silver went around the neck and down the front. She wore the silver chain necklace, as always, and hanging center from it was now the red garnet Fowler had brought her.

Fowler was proud of her. She was clean. She smelled good. She was richly dressed. But there was a little nag of discomfort. He wished she had had her baby before the rendezvous. He wouldn't have had to take near as much joshing from the boys about a fact accomplished as one still impending.

They came to the edge of the encampment. They halted to make sure the horses looked all right. Scarlet cloth, found in Bonneville's cache, covered the worn old saddle blankets, and the big roan and Starr's big black pranced with their blood-red caparisons and bells on their bridles. Starr settled his new beaverskin on his head and said, "Let's go!"

Fowler nodded and both men let out a wild whoop, both shot off their guns, dug in their spurs, and leveled their horses into a flat run down the middle of the street. Gamblers, Indians, traders, drunks, children, dogs, scattered out of the way, and a great cloud of dust rose under the feet of their horses—rose and swirled and fanned and choked and hid the whole long street, then settled again slowly in the still hot air. They heard shouts as they passed, yells and whoops. "Hi-yi! It's Joe Fowler! It's Fowler and Big Starr! Hi-yi-yi, you Taos men! Hyar's yer own boys!"

They let their horses run far out on the flats. This was ritual. A dozen or two men, knowing them, with fast horses themselves, would fling onto their mounts and race after them. They spurred their horses and the others pounded after them, joined them, shouting, yelling, whooping, shooting, and they made a crazy, wild, racing melee, all wheeling and circling and jostling. It went on and on until suddenly Fowler whirled the big roan about, slowed him, and set the pace back to the encampment. He shouted at half a dozen men in the bunch. There was the Englishman, Captain Stewart. There was Kit Carson, up from Taos. There was Joe Meek, and old Gabe Bridger, and Tom Fitzpatrick, and many more.

They cantered back down the street together, jostling each other, slapping Fowler and Big Starr on the back, promising more debauch and more great doings and fixings now that the two of them were here . . . and Mose . . . where was old Mose? Surely he had come with them. Fowler told them about Mose and it sobered them, but only for a moment. They regretted his death. "What? That old boy rubbed out? I'd of thought he'd live forever, wise old coon like him. Too bad. Won't be the same without old Mose. But didja know old Barrett went under this season, too. Up on the Three Forks. Blackfeet got him." And the talk circled around, went on to others, where they had been, what they had been doing, what had been happening since the rendezvous began. One more man gone, and a good one, but they were alive and it was rendezvous time.

They swerved around a bunch of Indians playing "hand" in the middle of the street and laughed at a naked little Utah squaw looking on disconsolately. "She's lost her shirt," Captain Stewart said.

"I'll remedy that," Kit Carson said, pulling up his horse. He dug in his pockets and threw their contents onto the ground in

front of her, spilling coins and beads and whatnot helter-skelter
in the dust. She scrambled for them, flashed him a radiant smile,
and threw her bet in the ring.

"You'll be welcome in her lodge tonight," Captain Stewart
said.

"Why else you think he done it?" Big Starr jibed.

Carson was a little banty rooster of a man, but his size didn't
keep him from being a gamecock. He joined in the laughter as
the group moved on. "Come over to my tepee fer a drink," Old
Gabe said, "the bunch of ye. I got plenty."

"No, to mine," Fitzpatrick put in, not to be outdone in hospitality.

But Captain Stewart took charge with a high hand. "I will
drink no more of that mountain poison. I'll stand all of you to
a drink of real whiskey."

Then the boys spied Betsy and Mamselle and the whooping,
the joshing, the lickerish bawdiness began. Fowler and Big
Starr took it, trying to give back as good as they got, as the bunch
moved on down to the captain's big lodge. It was twice as large
as any other and it was fitted out with every kind of luxury, even
folding chairs and a camp bed and a bearskin rug on the floor.
The man had dollars to fling about, all right. He brought out
brandy and real keg whiskey and dispensed it with a free hand,
and it went down slow and warm and silky-soft, and it made a
man feel easy inside, and it took away some of the miss of old
Mose.

After a couple of drinks Big Starr and the others went whooping off and Fowler settled back to hear the news and the gossip
from the Englishman. The captain gave him a fine cigar and lit
it for him, lit one for himself, and began. Talk at rendezvous
always began with who was there and what was happening.
Nathaniel Wyeth was sore as a bear about his raw deal from the
Sublettes. Claimed he had lost better than five thousand dollars
by it. Called the whole bunch a great lot of scoundrels.

Fowler chuckled easily. "He should have known better. He

contracted with the wrong Sublette. It's Bill Sublette you do business with out here."

Stewart asked if he had heard that Bill was building a fort at the mouth of the Laramie Fork. "Left a bunch of his men there to build it as he came through."

Fowler thought about the location. "It's a good place for a post," he said noncommittally.

"And the Bent brothers have built a fine post on the Arkansas —near the Big Timbers. They have the Cheyenne trade all sewed up."

Fowler smiled. "Yes. I heard that before I left Taos. They have always been traders. Never did do much trapping."

The captain went on with his news. Wyeth, he said, was planning to build a post over on the Snake, at the mouth of the Portneuf. Said he was going to get even with the Rocky Mountain boys. Figured to get the Bannock and Nez Perce trade there. Fowler raised his eyebrows. Having just come from that place, he wondered. Nez Perces, maybe. But Bannocks? He didn't think so.

Posts, then, he thought. Posts on all sides—the Arkansas— the Laramie Fork—the Snake. It was going to be the fort and stockade system in the mountains now. Going to be the old, old trading system like the Company had always used on the Missouri. The rendezvous would go, then, and the carrying trade. No need of either with stockades handy.

Wyeth, the captain was saying, had a bunch of greenhorns traveling with him this year. There was a countryman of the captain's, a man named Thomas Nuttall, who was a botanist and naturalist. He was going to the Pacific studying the flora and the fauna of the country. With him was an assistant named Townsend. Both seemed good fellows.

"I have heard of Thomas Nuttall," Fowler said. He added dryly, "He studied the flora and fauna around Fort Smith on the Arkansas when I was a boy."

"Well, well. Fancy that." The captain poured Fowler another brandy. "The boys have got real respect for Nuttall and young Townsend, but," he laughed wickedly, "Wyeth has a much less popular man traveling with him this year, too."

"It don't take much to make a man unpopular with the boys," Fowler commented. The captain's brandy was pretty potent, and Fowler was beginning to feel nice and unwound.

"Yes," the captain said, "you'll never believe it but civilization has come to the mountains, my friend. Nathaniel Wyeth has brought a missionary out with him!"

"Do tell," Fowler said softly. "Why would he do that?"

"Oh, it isn't Wyeth's idea. The man is traveling with him for protection. But we have a man of God in our midst, to preach to the heathen and the godless—and he has damned well been preaching, too. When he could gather a few of the faithful together." The captain hunched forward in his chair. "But mostly the good man execrates upon the habits of mountain men. He has never, he says, seen their like for debauchery. All the worst of men's sins are to be found here, he says—drunkenness, gambling, fornication—all of them. He says he must go about with his eyes closed and his ears stopped to keep from being offended."

"My, my," Fowler murmured.

The captain nodded somberly. "Yes. He says he has never seen such wickedness, nor so much evil in men before. He lays about him with power and thundering fulminations—and nobody heeds him. He is grievously disturbed. Especially because the Sabbath is not observed."

Fowler lifted sleepy lids and fixed astonished eyes on the captain. "You mean the boys don't observe the Sabbath?"

The captain touched his fingertips together piously. "I fear they do not."

Fowler clicked and clucked unhappily. "Who is this saint of the Lord?" he asked.

"The Reverend Jason Lee, sir. He is answering a call to minister to the Flatheads in Oregon. He is to establish a mission on the Columbia."

"He don't have to wait till he gets to the Columbia to commence ministering to Flatheads," Fowler said lazily. "I saw Flatheads here in the camp."

The captain was delighted. "Of course. You are observant, sir. And the good preacher has taught them a few hymns. Two, I believe. They sing them around their fires at night, Brother Lee leading them, naturally."

"Naturally."

"He says he has made a little progress against the darkness of their heathen state."

"Do you think they will be singing their hymns tonight?"

"I am certain of it."

Gray eyes met black eyes, lit, twinkling, in perfect understanding. "They need encouragement, wouldn't you say?"

"Precisely what I was thinking, sir."

"We will encourage them tonight," Fowler promised.

They drank to it and the talk moved on. Fowler was getting pretty drunk but not too drunk to recognize the captain's gambit when it came. It looked like a fine big rendezvous, didn't it? Same men, just as many skins, prices for plews high, trade goods a little higher, plenty of everything for everybody. It looked fine, didn't it? But there was trouble. It was not known to everybody.

"What kind of trouble?" Fowler said, watching the brandy swirl with the slight movement of his hand.

Stewart looked down at his own drink. "The Rocky Mountain boys have come to an agreement with the Company. They have decided they can't shake off the Company brigades and they are all tired of fighting. They have decided they should join forces and fight the Hudson Bay people. They have divided the territory. The Company takes the region west of the divide. The boys take the region east of the divide. And between them," he cut his throat with his finger, "death to the Hudson Bay boys."

Though he felt as if he had been hit in the stomach, Fowler didn't show it, and all he said was, lifting his glass, "Success to 'em!" He grinned, giving the captain no satisfaction.

But his thoughts were seething. So the boys were knuckling under. Settling up. Selling out. The Company had won. And with all the money of John Jacob Astor, he thought bitterly, why not? It had to come, some time. You couldn't beat the Company when they decided to move in. And it was the way the Company had always worked. Let a handful of men take the risks and open the country, begin to make money, then move in, cut their throats, run them out, and take over. They had swallowed the Northwest Company around the lakes that way. They had taken over the Missouri trade the same way. Now it was their turn in the mountains. It always worked. Endless resources always moved in where and when they pleased.

The captain was continuing. "Of course you free trappers will still be cock-of-the-walk. But they're saying there aren't enough beaver to go around. They've been too heavily trapped the last few years. The cream has been skimmed, they say. And the new posts will trade in robes and tallow and anything else the boys want to trade—as on the Missouri."

Fowler stood, swaying a little but thinking clearly. Maybe the cream had been skimmed, but he still knew some streams —knew plenty of them, never been seen by anybody but him and Mose—never been disturbed or trapped and hunted over. He raised his drink and swallowed down the last of it. "That's very interesting, Captain," he said.

The captain also stood. "You went to the Columbia with our friend Bonneville, did you not? What did you think of it? Is it as rich as we hear?"

Fowler looked at him steadily. "Captain Bonneville is at the rendezvous," he said, "why don't you ask him?"

The British captain met his look. Then he shrugged and

smiled. "I will do that, my friend. Are you leaving? One more drink?"

"No."

"When shall we have that race you promised me? The race between your horse and mine?"

"Anytime you say," Fowler said.

"The day after tomorrow," the captain said. "That will give the boys time to make all their bets."

"Suits me fine," Fowler said. He bowed slightly. He was afraid to try much of a bow. He'd fall flat on his face. He'd better eat a big bait if he meant to last out the night with the boys. "I'm obliged for the brandy, sir."

"It was my pleasure, sir, my pleasure." The captain also bent slightly at the middle. "Don't forget we must encourage the Flatheads tonight."

Fowler assured him he would keep it in mind. He made what he thought was a very graceful exit, only knocking over a chair and tangling his feet a little with the bear's head on the rug, then he made a beeline for his lodge, some food, and some sleep. He would be as good as new in a couple of hours.

That night when the Flatheads were gathered around their fire and were singing their new hymns, the preacher happily leading them, Fowler and the captain, Big Starr, Jim Bridger, Kit Carson, Fitzpatrick, and a few others crowded around to listen. One by one they slowly infiltrated the group, as if they, too, had come to sing and to hear.

Encouraged by the enlarged congregation and delighted by the presence of the trappers, Brother Lee led another hymn with vigor. He had not, however, counted on the vigor of the boys. At the end of the hymn, they began all over again. The missionary hesitated, then joined in, full voice and smiling. Through all four stanzas they plowed their way. The reverend held up his hand for quiet, then. He had decided this was too good an opportunity to miss. He would preach a sermon, here and now. Never had he had this many of the trappers gathered together.

But Fowler lifted up his voice and started the hymn again. The missionary beat his palms together and begged for silence. He implored. The boys ignored him. The Flatheads happily followed their lead and the two first stanzas were rendered. Then Old Gabe suddenly reached out and picked up a frying pan and a spoon and began beating out an age-old, heavy, elemental rhythm. His cracked voice began chanting. "Hi-yi-yi! Hi-hi-yi-yi! Hi-yi-yi-yi!"

The boys started pounding their palms, the Flatheads forgot their hymn and joined in, and in two minutes flat a full-fledged war dance was going good and strong. The good reverend was horrified. He tried to stop it. He shouted, he stormed, he ranted. He ran about sawing at the air. But the Flatheads were hearing the beat of their blood, and their feet must tramp it into the earth, and they must shout it and chant it, and they must beat their breasts and whoop. Finally the Reverend Jason Lee crept to his tent, annihilated. It was said next day that he had stopped his ears with wax to keep from hearing the heathen desecration. The Flatheads were not quite ready for Methodism, it seemed. And the wicked, the Reverend Jason Lee said, were like the troubled sea, and salvation was far from them.

3.

"I *am* ashamed," Fowler assured Bill Sublette the next morning. "I was never so ashamed in my life. To disturb and upset that good man so! I don't know," he said blandly, "what got into me."

"The devil and too much of Captain Stewart's brandy," Sublette said. "My God, Joe, we're already having a time with the boys and that old fool. They just might run him out of camp. I'm doing my best with 'em but it goes against the grain with 'em to be told they're all going straight to hell because of their wickedness." He wagged his head dismally. "Then you come along, just when I'd promised the reverend there wouldn't be any more trouble and raise hell with his Flatheads."

Fowler raised his right hand. "I swear I won't do it no more."

Sublette's severity broke up. He grinned. "Wish I'd seen it. Must of been something to see!"

"It was," Fowler said, "it mortally was. You ought to seen Stewart with a blanket around him and two feathers stuck in his headband. Looked more like a Flathead than any chief there."

They broke into good, relieving laughter and then Fowler got down to his business with Bill Sublette. "You going straight back to St. Louis?"

"Not straight, but I'll get back before cold weather."

"I'd be obliged if you would present this bill for my services to old Mr. Driant, Bill. Me and Johnny bank with DeSalle and Company. He can credit me with the amount there, tell him." He handed over a slip of paper.

"That your pay for guiding his son's party?" Sublette asked, putting the slip in his strong box.

"It is. I didn't want to do business with that fool Noel." He paused. "Heard anything about him? I notice he's not here."

"Boys say he give up before the winter was over and went back to Taos."

Fowler nodded. "I've got a notion he took some skins of mine with him. I misdoubt he left 'em in the cache. But that can wait. I'm going to cover every bet made on the race tomorrow." He grinned. "I'll win, naturally, but in case I don't, I'd like you to pay off for me."

Sublette nodded. "Noticed you didn't bring in any skins. You short of dollars? I can cash a draft for you."

Fowler shook his head. "I'll let you know if I need any. I'm expecting to win enough from Stewart to cover my losses this season and outfit me for the next."

"You've got a lot of faith in that roan of yours," Sublette said.

"Got reason to have, unless that little *paseo* last winter broke his wind some."

Sublette tidied some papers on the table in front of him. "I hear Bonneville thinks Stewart is spying for the British."

"Bonneville tell you so?"

"Oh, news gets around. I know why Bonneville's out here, Joe."

"Well. So what do *you* think about Stewart?"

"I dunno. I've not been around him. Brought him out last summer. Not seen him since. Boys say he's moseyed around some, though."

Fowler pondered. "You know, I got my doubts anybody will ever know. He could be what he says he is. He could be what he don't say he is."

"That's about the way I see it. But it smells. It smells high." He added, rubbing his nose as if he had smelled a bad odor, "He's going out to the Columbia next, to Vancouver."

"He is?"

"Yes. Him and Wyeth have come to some kind of agreement. He'll be traveling with Wyeth."

"I heard Wyeth aimed to build a stockade on the Portneuf," Fowler said.

"He does. But he's going on to the Columbia. Soon as rendezvous's over."

"And Stewart goes with him."

Their eyes met. Both were thinking what a lot the Englishman had learned while traveling with the American fur brigades —what a lot he could now pass on to old Dr. McLoughlin at Vancouver, and what a lot McLoughlin could pass on to the Canadian government. "It does smell, don't it?" Fowler added.

"Reckon Bonneville knows Stewart's going," Sublette said.

"I would guess it. But I'll make it my business," Fowler said.

They went on into a long serious talk then about business, the state of the trade, the new fort on the Laramie Fork. It was all changing, Sublette said. Nothing was going to be the way it used to be. "Two, three more years, Joe. That's all I'm going to stay in. Us boys that got here first had better cut and run while we still got our topknots. Now, fellow like you, you got another ten years or so. But the carrying trade? It's gone, boy. And the brigade system, and the beaver, they're going. You and Johnny are fine, though. You got another wiping stick to your gun—freighting."

Fowler nodded slowly, thoughtfully, and said, "If you like freighting."

A great hullaballoo began outside, a lot of shouting and yelling, whooping, running and stampeding about. "What in hell—?"

Both men got up to see what was happening.

A buffalo bull was charging down the middle of the street. He was old and he was bleeding from a wound but he was still going strong. Nobody was running from him, nobody was getting out of the way. Instead lines had been formed on each side to make a path for him. Hanging onto its tail, driving it along, prodding it with his lance, was a young Nez Perce. He was called Kentuck because he was always singing "Hunters from Old Kentucky." "Hokahey!" he was shouting, prancing and dancing behind the prodded old bull. "Hokahey! Hokahey!" The crowd was yelling encouragement and advice, running alongside to keep up, taking up the Nez Perce's shouts of goodby, farewell, "Hokahey!"

Bill Sublette pulled a long face. "That's my boy. I have a guest. General Clark's nephew is traveling with me. I let the word get around I would like to have him entertained while I am busy. This is Kentuck's idea of entertaining a guest, I suppose." He raised his voice, "*Bueno,* Kentuck. Take him away!"

The old bull put on a surge of speed and fled toward the river. Every man with a gun, which was practically every man in the crowd, made a target of the animal and the guns flashed and roared and the bull was soon filled with rifle balls. Kentuck and his friends dragged the animal down the bank and rolled him into the stream. "I hope the current washes that carcass downstream pretty soon," Fowler said. "If it don't, there'll be a pretty rich smell around here before long."

"It couldn't add much to the stinks we already got," Sublette said, wrinkling his nose.

"Oh, it ain't too high yet. Your nose is finicky is all. You have got out of the way of smelling strong smells, back east."

Sublette admitted the possibility. He said, musingly, he was thinking about getting married, when he cached his traps for good.

Fowler looked off across the flats, ran his eyes clear around the long horizon. "Well," he said, "they usually go together. A man don't think of marrying till he begins to think of caching his traps. Don't need it or want it till then. Marrying means settling down. Long as you're a beaver man, there ain't no settling down. If that's where your stick floats, I wish you well, Bill."

Sublette nodded, a kind of sad, agreeing wisdom in his eyes, and they parted.

4.

A track, of sorts, was laid out on the flats and a cottonwood pole was driven to mark the turn of the race. Half a mile out, round the pole, and half a mile back. For two days excitement and tension over the race had grown and mounted and the bets were wild. Nobody cared whether he had a penny left or not, just so he had all he could scrape together on Captain Stewart's

Jezebel or on Joe Fowler's big blue horse. They all had credit for the necessaries of the next season and no man at the rendezvous cared if he owed his soul, but a good horse bet was something to beg, borrow, or steal every dollar you could lay hands on to cover. Finally, even traps, horses, and squaws were wagered.

Fowler and Big Starr covered every bet that came their way. "If that blue don't win," Starr said, finally, "we're gonna owe so much we can't ever pay off. We'll have to leave the country. Go down to Chihuahua."

Fowler and Stewart had a five hundred dollar wager between themselves. Stewart coveted the big roan so much he wanted to make the horse a winner's trophy, but Fowler wouldn't. "No. I'll bet you any amount of money you want to put up. Money don't amount to nothing. But I won't bet my horse."

Stewart understood. "I wouldn't risk him either." They settled for the five hundred dollar bet, then.

The starting line and the finish were just outside the encampment and most of the trappers stayed nearby, but the Indians, wildly worked up, scattered on their own horses all the way out to the turning pole. Some of them would run their horses every foot of the race, outside the track. Some status would accrue to the winner, and Indians too poor to bet on the big race were laying wagers on the side race.

It was a wildly excited, restless, surging, noisy, brilliant scene as the two men walked their horses to the starting line just at noon. Bill Sublette was to fire the starting gun. They lined up. Stewart's Jezebel was a nervous young mare, a pretty fine-blooded bay. She took a long time to settle down, the noise and the crowd bothering her. She broke away often and finicked around. Stewart kept talking to her, soothing her. The big roan jerked his head at the bit a few times, switched his tail at the flies, but he stood quietly. Years of having one man on his back, the reins in his firm hands, the same steady voice speaking to him, had made him a beautifully disciplined animal. It was as if the big horse knew that all he had to do was what the man asked of him when the time came. The man did the telling—the horse did the doing.

Stewart's Jezebel broke fast when the gun sounded, but she finicked a few moments to get into her stride. The roan had a plunging start which put him into his stride in seconds. He was running, long legs stretching, eating up the ground a full length ahead by the time the mare hit her stride. She could run, though, and she narrowed the distance, nosing up on the big roan's left flank before they were halfway to the pole. Three quarters of the way and she was only a head behind.

Nearing the pole Fowler was on the outside. The mare had run too close and Stewart had been too clever for him to maneuver. There was nothing for it but to make the turn on the outside, but both horses made as tight a turn as possible. Now, straightened out, was the time that told. In a mile race, Fowler never ran the roan flat out from the start. He ran him hard but left him something for the stretch. Now he had to ask it of him, whatever was left in him, and he wouldn't know till he asked it if there was anything left. The hard winter journey may have taken too much out of the horse. They broke for the stretch and Fowler dug his spurs in, leaned way forward, and yelled, and the big blue responded. He leveled flat out for the spurt home. He gave him everything he had, long legs reaching and reaching and reaching, deep chest and great lungs standing up to it, head rhythmical in its sway, hooves pounding. It was so beautiful to watch that even the men who had bet on the mare forgot they were losing and watched in awed admiration. "Lookit that sonuvabitch run! Jist lookit him run! God, there ain't ever been a horse could run like him. Jeeee-sus, lookit him run!"

Then the whole encampment went wild, boiled over, erupted, stampeded. The mare was left halfway back at the turning pole as the big blue pounded across the finish line. "There ain't nothin' on four legs kin beat that horse!"

Men paid off their bets, moaned and groaned and went to drown their sorrow, not too sorrowful, for they had seen a real horse run. It was worth every penny. "Cleaned out, by ding," Joe Meek told Big Starr as he paid him. "Plumb cleaned out. Whyn't ye tell me that horse could run like that?"

"What! And lose my bet?"

Stewart rode up to Fowler shaking his head. "I was told he could run. I was told he could beat any horse in the west. I believe it. I would give two thousand dollars for that horse, my friend. Just to own him. Just to know that fine piece of horse-flesh was mine." He put out his hand and ran it down the roan's sweating neck. "My God, what a horse!" He looked up. "But you'll never get another race for him, Fowler. Not after beating my Jezebel. Nobody will run against this horse."

Fowler wiped the sweat off his face. "I don't figure to race him but once more," he said. "I got one more race for him to win and then I'll not run him no more."

"How old is he?"

"Five. It ain't that he's getting too old. But we'll both put racing behind us after one more."

They were rich, Big Starr said. Rich. Filthy rich. "We done won enough," he chortled, when it had been counted up, "to make up for the season and git us through the next."

"*Bueno,*" Fowler said, "I got a use for some of mine right now."

The next few days he bought horses. He bought a lot of horses and they were all the spotted Appaloosas of the Nez Perces. He kept buying Appaloosas until he had a string of forty. "Now, what in cat hair we gonna do with all them horses," Big Starr asked finally. He had looked on and said nothing for a day or two. Fowler always had a good reason for what he did. But Starr's curiosity got the best of him at last. "You aimin' fer us to drive 'em to St. Louis?"

"Nope. We're going up the Popo Agie with 'em, mebbe up

the Big Horn, and if we have to we're going plumb to Fort Union with 'em."

"The Company post? You aim to sell them horses to Mc-Kenzie?" Starr's mind was working slow.

"I don't figure we'll get that far," Fowler said, slowly.

Starr's brow furrowed while he puzzled that out, then as understanding dawned he broke into a long, low whistle. "Bait, huh? Jeeee-sus, what a idee!" He beamed his admiration. "How come ye to think of it?"

"He's greedy. He won't be able to keep his hands off a string of good horses. Commence telling it around where we're heading, Starr. Circulate it amongst the boys."

"Well, I *will!*" Big Starr's head wagged up and down. Then he slapped his thigh. "I like to forgot. That halfbreed, Tixier, you recollect him? Works for the Company? With Fontenelle?" Fowler nodded. "Well, he told me something jist a while ago. Said Bastro and Beckwith hadn't had no falling out. Said it was that old trouble croppin' up again. McKenzie learnt Bastro was back up with Beckwith and told him if he didn't git out he'd cancel Beckwith's contract. So betwixt the Crows and the Poordevils, Bastro is makin' hisself skeerce again."

"I figured it was something like that," Fowler said. "The Crows would have got him by now if it was Beckwith wanting him. You go mingle with the boys, now. I'm gonna pay a visit to old Broken Arm's lodge and sort of let the Crows know what we're doing."

"Shore." Big Starr broke into laughter. "My God, what a trap!"

"It ain't shut yet," Fowler said. "But if I'm not mistaken, a runner will go out tonight from Broken Arm and in the next few days mirrors will flash up some canyon in the Wind Rivers and our man will begin to drift down towards the Popo Agie."

Fowler hired a couple of Mexicans to wrangle the herd. He wound up his affairs and told goodby to a few of his friends—

young Lashly, the Englishman, Bill Sublette, the trappers, and Captain Bonneville. That good man was bustling about making ready for the next season. He was surprised that Fowler was leaving before the rendezvous was over. "This business of mine won't wait," Fowler said, "I reckon you know that."

Bonneville's head nodded. "I hope you find him, Joe. He's a real renegade."

Bonneville's supplies had arrived in good order, although his friend, Michel Cerré, had not brought them. He had taken a position with the Chouteau people in St. Louis. "I will send my report back east with my furs," Bonneville told Fowler. He chuckled. "It is a very lengthy report, I'm afraid. But I have included in it everything I have learned about this country. I have even written its history. I have given an accurate accounting of the Indians, and all the fur companies, and all the men engaged in the trade. I have included my recommendations concerning the Oregon country."

"You know Stewart is going to Vancouver next, don't you?" Fowler said.

"I had guessed he would and, yes, I know it. It is his logical next move—to report to McLoughlin and through him to the government. It's about as much proof as we need that the Hudson's Bay Company is acting for the British Empire. Our government is acting much more slowly, but thank heaven it is beginning to act. It is waking up to the great potential on that coast, in that country. It isn't only the fur trade, Joe. We need those harbors. There is a vast industry in whaling and salmon fisheries. There is a great commerce with China which could be pursued from that coast. And we need naval stations along it. And its potential for agriculture and stock raising, for resettlement of our people, has only begun to be explored. It is a country we cannot allow the British to swallow up, as they will if our government does not move and move rapidly." He shrugged. "I have done what I could, and mostly what I was sent to do. When I have made this journey to the Columbia again, my great adventure will be over. I shall have to go back to the army, then."

Fowler smiled. "You sound as though you kind of regretted that."

"A little," Bonneville admitted. "A little. It is a fine life here in the mountains—the finest life I ever lived. I shall miss it. But," he raised his shoulders, "a man serves his country wherever he is needed. I wish you would change your mind and go with me to the Columbia this fall." He changed the subject, dismissing his regrets.

Fowler shook his head. "When I get my own business tended to I'll have to get on down to Santa Fe. Me and Johnny will have some things to think about when I tell him all I've learned. But I wish you well." He grinned. "If you are posted back to Gibson, give Savanna my love, will you? And if General Arbuckle is still the commandant, give him my regards."

"It will be a pleasure to give Savanna your love," Bonneville said, "and have no fear. General Arbuckle will still be the commandant at the fort. The old buzzard is going to live forever and he will remain the commanding officer at Fort Gibson as long as he lives. It is my fate."

They talked on briefly, then went their separate ways. It would be twenty-seven years before they saw each other again, many things would have happened to both, the Spanish possessions would have become American territory, and Captain Bonneville would be Colonel Bonneville and himself a commandant—the commandant of the Territory of New Mexico. But neither, that day, looked farther ahead than the next task and neither wondered, much, about what the future held in store for him.

5.

In the gray-lavender light of false dawn on the morning of the first day of July the Fowler outfit splashed across the Ham's

Fork and headed northeast. They were a sizable train now—
two men, two squaws, four saddle horses, four pack animals, a
dust-raising herd of Appaloosas, and two Mexican wranglers.

They didn't hurry but neither did they loiter. Fowler kept
them moving steadily along. The third day they crossed the
Green at the mouth of Sandy Creek and took up that creek
until they came to a branch called Pacific Creek. Here they
took the branch and kept up it. These were both west-flowing
creeks.

They headed for South Pass, the easy way across the divide.
You didn't even know you were crossing. It was a sagebrush
plain, a saddle between the Wind Rivers and the Antelope
Hills below. They struck the first east-flowing river with the
Sweetwater and followed down to the valley at the foot of
the Rattlesnake range. Here they cut due north and made for
the loop of the Popo Agie, which flowed down from the eastern
foot of the Wind Rivers. It was a river in its own name only
until it joined the larger stream, the Wind River. The Wind
River rose high in the north in the Wind River range, flowed
south through a long basin flanked by the Big Horn mountains
on the east and the Wind Rivers on the west. When the Wind
River turned the Big Horn mountains, it became the Big Horn
River. As the Big Horn it flowed northeast to its confluence
with the Yellowstone. Turkey tracks, and you had to know
your country and which river and which part of each river you
were on.

Eight days out from the encampment they passed by the tar
spring near the Popo Agie. This was a place where oil oozed
up through the shale and collected in a shallow basin. You
could smell it for miles around. It was said to be good for the
rheumatism which plagued most mountain men. Betsy wanted
to get some of the tar to use for liniment, and Fowler halted
the outfit for an hour. They dabbled around in the thick ooze,
Betsy filled her jars, and then they moved on to a little brush-
bordered creek to camp.

They picketed the horse herd near the creek inside a rope corral. The weather was so pleasant the women were not putting up lodges these nights, but they made the camp in their usual orderly and routine way. The men ate and the camp settled in for the night.

For several nights, ever since they had turned the base of the Wind Rivers, Fowler and Big Starr had taken turns standing guard with the Mexicans—two men on, two men off. It was Fowler's turn for the first watch. When he woke Big Starr at midnight he said, "It looks about right tonight, Starr. The moon's down but there ain't a cloud in the sky. There'll be starshine plumb to daylight."

Big Starr came awake all at once and hauled up, pulling his gun up with him. He moved into the darkness of some willows and Fowler rolled in a blanket near the ashes of the fire. Starr on guard was like himself on guard so he went to sleep immediately, but it seemed to him he hadn't much more than closed his eyes till something was prodding him, something sharp. He brushed it away and saw what it was. Starr hadn't come out of the shadows. With a long pole slid along the ground he had poked Fowler awake. Fowler rolled out of the blanket and, still rolling, inched into the shadow with Starr. "Watch them bushes over by that arroyo," Starr whispered.

Nothing, for a time. Then an almost imperceptible movement of a few bushes in a larger clump of bushes, a shaking, trembling as if a breeze stirred them, then a slight crawling forward, six inches, maybe a foot, then a pause, complete stillness, then another inching forward. Fowler counted the bushes that moved. Six. It was an old Indian trick and a good one. If you were good at this kind of camouflage you could get within a few feet of a buffalo without being seen or heard— or you could get within scalping distance of an unwary enemy and he would never know what hit him.

Bastro had crossed the river far upstream, Fowler guessed, then he had circled out onto the flats and was approaching the camp through a brush-covered spit of land that lay between it and a shallow arroyo. He grunted with satisfaction, thinking of the location of the camp. Bastro and the Indians either would have to lose time trying to drive the herd across the river, or they would have to head out the arroyo. Either way, they would have them.

"Roll down the bank," Fowler said, "and warn Tomás. Wake Miguel. But tell 'em not to make a move till one of us fires a gun. Tell 'em to get ready but to keep quiet."

"*Bueno.*"

You couldn't tell when the big man left, you couldn't hear so much as a rustle of movement where he'd gone, and you couldn't have told when he came back, except that he spoke. "They're ready."

"We'll break when they do," Fowler said. "You and the boys get the Indians. I'll get Bastro."

Big Starr didn't argue. He would have, several months before, for Fouchette and young Pete were his friends, too. But on account of Mose, Fowler's right came first now. "Reckon ye'll know him?" he said.

"I'll know him. The light's good enough I can see him plain."

It took nerve to lie there, like a rock, not making the slightest movement or sound, and let the bushes creep slowly, slowly closer to the herd. Barely breathing, Fowler felt as tight as a fiddle string. He hoped the women stayed asleep until the thing broke wide open. They were sleeping a little apart and if they stayed down they oughtn't to be in the range of fire. He hoped one of them wouldn't waken now and have to go to the bushes. He hoped Tomás and Miguel didn't panic—but one of them did. Just at that moment.

There was suddenly a flash of fire, an explosion, and then bedlam. The Indians cast aside their covering bushes and broke, screeching and shrieking, for the herd. Fowler swore and ran, yelling. He ran for the big roan. For three nights he had not hobbled the horse. He had left him with only a side line attached. As he ran for the horse, he saw Big Starr and the Mexicans running into the horse herd.

With one swift move Fowler jerked the hitch loose from the willow and sprang onto the roan's back. The roan threw his head up and whirled about. Fowler held him, waiting, in the shadows. Then he saw the short, barrel-chested, chunky man he was looking for head an Appaloosa out of the herd, run hard along beside the horse a few steps, then with a running leap spring onto him. Fowler drummed his heels into the roan's ribs and the big horse plunged as if a starting gun had fired.

Through the brush, down the draw, the Appaloosa's spotted rump was like a white target in the bright starshine ahead of him. Fowler didn't want Bastro across the creek in the thick brush. He pulled the roan up a bank, cut him across the brush, and headed the Appaloosa off. He was close enough, then, to see that Bastro hadn't got a rope on the horse. He was riding him by hand and knee. But he turned the little spotted horse and headed him back up the draw. This was what Fowler wanted. The big roan pounded behind up the draw.

The arroyo flattened out shortly into the long level land. In the starshine the Appaloosa bunched his legs and took off across the flats. Fowler laughed and leaned far forward over the big roan's neck. "Let's go, boy! Let's go!"

The big horse went flat out, hooves drumming. Fowler's feet swung easily with the rhythm of the horse's long legs. He had the man now. There was no place for him to go. There was no hiding place—no trees, no brush, no rocks. He couldn't get behind anything and cut a man down the way he liked to do. There was nothing here but the long endlessness of the flats, which went on and on forever, into the black sky and the wheeling bright stars. There was nothing here but an eternity of space.

The little Appaloosa did his best, but slowly the big roan closed up the distance. When there was only one length between them, Fowler swung him a little wide, to the left. He saw Bastro's head turn toward him, quickly, briefly, then he humped over the Appaloosa's neck and drummed his heels into the horse's ribs desperately. The big roan was running as smooth as river water now. Fowler raised his Hawken and brought it level. He knew exactly where he wanted to shoot the man. He waited a moment. He did not want to miss. He steadied the big heavy gun with his father's initials on the brass plate in the butt. Then he fired. Bastro screamed like a stuck hog and grabbed his left knee. The Appaloosa veered a little but kept on running and Bastro hung on.

Fowler pulled the big roan around, now to the right, and kneed him to close up. The big horse gathered his legs under him and put on a burst of speed. Fowler waited till he came up so close he could have jumped the other man off. Then he pulled his pistol from his belt and carefully shot Bastro in his other knee. Bastro's head jerked back in a long howl of anguish. Fowler watched him slump and topple and slide off the Appaloosa and go rolling in the sand. The Appaloosa kept running.

Fowler shoved the pistol back in his belt, turned the roan in a wide, wheeling curve, slowed him to an easy lope to get his wind back, and without looking back once where Bastro had fallen, rode back to the camp.

Big Starr rode out to meet him. There was no need to ask, but he did. "Git him?"

"Got him. Both knees. The buzzards, the wolves, or the Crows can have him."

Big Starr grunted. "Wagh! That shines, that does. That's makin' 'em come, plumb dead center."

They had got two of the Indians, Starr told him. "They was Crows, like you said. One of 'em is old Broken Arm's own boy. You baited the trap real good. I let Tomás and Miguel have their topknots. The others got away, but we never lost a horse except that 'un Bastro was ridin'." He straightened his big shoulders and eased the muscles in them. "Good night's work," he said. "Now what do we aim to do with all them horses?"

"Drive 'em on to the Laramie Fork. Bill Sublette bought 'em off me. He needs a herd at the new fort. I told him we'd drive 'em there for him."

Big Starr howled. "Yoweeeeee! What a son-of-a-gun you are! What a ding-danged horse-tradin' bastard you are! I ought to knowed!" He cut his horse in a tight circle, then straightened him out into a dead run toward the camp.

Fowler let the roan walk. A small breeze had sprung up and there was a bleaching of the sky in the east. He looked off there where the Big Horns lifted up from the land and he watched a pale star skid a little, then fall. The breeze blew on his face and was cool. He was conscious of being very tired. It was the end of a long road. But the spirits of Fouchette and young Pete and Mose Strong would have to wander no longer. They could go home.

fourteen

W HEN HE GOT BACK to the camp the first thing he saw was
the white outlines of a lodge off to one side, a good distance from
the fire which had been built up, and near the creek. He knew
what it meant. It was Betsy's time. He did not go near it.
She would not have liked it. It would not have been proper
for him to. This was a woman thing and she would manage
for herself.

He rubbed the big roan down and hobbled him, patted the
glossy, sweated flank. "You done good," he told him, "you done
real good. And you've run your last race. I promised it and
I'll keep my word. You needn't ever run your heart out for
me no more."

He went to look at the dead Indians, grunted, and told the
Mexican boys to put them at least a foot underground so the
buzzards wouldn't bother that day. They wouldn't be moving
on till tomorrow, he told them. Miguel admitted it was he who
fired the gun before the signal. Fowler raked him over the
coals a little, told him he had to learn to obey orders. His life
might depend on it some day. "Sí, Señor. Nex' tam I remember. But dose bushes, dey come vair close. I get the fits to
shoot."

Fowler laughed. "They might have got a fit to shoot first."
He praised them both for their help, then. Not one horse lost.
That was something to be proud of. And he admired the
scalps they already had stretched on small willow hoops. They
would take them back to whatever little village they came from,
on the Chama, the del Norte, and be heroes with the girls.

Day was breaking now and Big Starr had a pot of coffee on

the coals and hump meat roasting. He looked up as Fowler came up and grinned at him. He jerked his head toward the lodge. "Looks like you're gonna be a pappy this day."

Fowler glanced at the lodge. Not a sound came from it. "Where's Mamselle? In with her?"

"Nope. She's gittin' up some more wood. We ridin' today?"

Fowler rubbed his chin. Big Starr poured some coffee and handed it to him. "Don't reckon we will," Fowler said.

"Well, we got a extry day to put in we jist as well kill some meat, hadn't we?"

"Just as well."

They ate the half-done meat. Fowler wanted the big roan to take it easy so he saddled one of the Appaloosas and they rode across the creek into the brushy foothills. For half a day they rambled around before coming on a small herd of buffalo. They killed a cow and butchered out the hump. They ate what they wanted of the raw liver, then meandered unhurriedly about looking at the oil slicks and shale basins in the area. They were a curiosity to them, just one more strange thing in the country which had so many strange things in it, like the boiling springs, the petrified forest, the big salt lake, the lava rock and cracked earth near the Snake. You never knew what peculiar thing you would stumble on out in this western country.

The middle of the afternoon they got back to the camp. The lodge was down and Betsy was sitting cross-legged on a buffalo robe, a small rolled bundle beside her. She spoke crossly to Fowler. He need not, she told him, have lost a full day of travel. They could have been, she said, another sleep in the direction he wanted to go. Her man, she said vehemently, did not have to alter his plans for his woman. His woman was clever at managing things.

Fowler flung himself down on the robe beside her. "Yeah," he said, laughing, "it looked like it about daybreak this morning. You were being real clever along about then."

And so. She scowled at him. Did he not know these things were done quickly? Did he not know she would be ready to travel by the time the sun came up?

No, he didn't know. "And besides, we ain't in no hurry now. Got plenty of time. This the kid?" He poked at the bundle.

And yes. She drew back the coverings and he peered at the baby which lay naked in the fine, soft, creamy robe she had prepared for it. Big Starr crowded up and hunkered over his shoulder. "Dang, Joe," he said, "you got ye a boy! And ain't he a dandy, though? Jist look at him suckin' on his fist. And ain't he fat? Fat as a little possum."

The baby was *mestizo*, like his mother, copper-colored instead of dark. He was small but he was so fat he looked almost as broad as he was long. His wrists and ankles were lost in wrinkles of fat and his round small head sat on a short, fat-wrinkled neck. He was tiny but perfect, whole, not a mark or a blemish on him. Thick dark hair thatched his head. Like all new babies he was featureless. He had a nose and a mouth, which his fist filled right now, and he had two eyes, but they were squinched tight shut at the moment. He nuzzled on the fist and kicked his short fat legs.

Fowler caught one small foot. It was lost in his big hand. He had a queer feeling as he touched the baby, a funny, rippling feeling in his stomach like a pang of hunger, or the contraction, unbidden, of a muscle. He dropped the foot and ran his finger down the blown little belly, down to the tiny perfect male organ. Boy. Manchild. Son. Son of Joe Fowler. Grandson of Matthew Fowler. Great-grandson of Hannah Fowler. Son of a Utah woman, she who was the Mist Rising from the Valley. Grandson of Old Cholly. Great-grandson of some nameless Spanish trader from Taos. Kentucky . . . Arkansas . . . Taos . . . Saguache. About as much different blood as you could cram into a human being was crammed in this little new manchild. And if any one of the people in his background had gone astray for a minute, he wouldn't be here. It took each one of them, coming onto the stage at exactly the right time and in the right place, to make him. He was sure a mixed blood, all right—Indian, Spanish, American.

Kid, Fowler thought, I ain't sure you been done any favor, being made. He thought of Charbonneau—Baptiste Charbonneau, Sacajawea's boy, who was a common ordinary hand to anybody, any outfit, any company, that would pay him wages. General Clark had got so fond of him he had taken him to St. Louis to educate him. Baptiste went to school there. Then some prince from Germany had come to St. Louis and he had taken Baptiste back to Europe with him and the kid had lived with this prince for six years. He had got a real high-class education. But when he came back, he went right straight to the Shoshones. And now he was anybody's hand at whatever wages he could get. Half French, he was, for his father was Touissant Charbonneau, but he wound up as much Indian as he could find for himself.

Fowler touched the little copper-colored leg. Might have been better if you'd stayed just a notion of your mother's. But she wanted you and she got you and here you are, mixed as hell, and nothing you can do about it. You'll have to make out, one way or another, best you can. Like Baptiste.

He poked the little fat belly. The baby drew up his legs and kicked strongly, took the fist out of his mouth, screwed up his face and took a good breath, then began bellowing loudly.

"God," Big Starr said admiringly, "he's sure got a set of good lungs, ain't he?"

Fowler laughed. "And a temper, looks to me."

For a moment, Betsy watched proudly while the baby howled, then she gathered him up and cradled him and soothed him.

"What ye gonna name him?" Big Starr asked.

Fowler lay on his back and folded his arms under his head,

squinting at the bright sky. "I ain't," he said. *"She'll* call him something, when it's time."

"She'll call him something can't nobody say," Big Starr said. The baby's foot had worked free of the robe and was kicking rhythmically. Starr touched the sole of the tiny foot, then counted the toes. "All of 'em thar," he said, and squeezed the foot. "Little old Popo Agie baby. Ought to have a name. Ought to have a plain name folks can say."

So he had one. From then on he had one. They called him Popo Agie at first, for a few days, then they shortened it and he became Popo.

He was a noisy, squally baby, strong, lusty, and from the first knowing, it seemed, precisely what he wanted and how to go about getting it. He could howl loud enough and long enough when he was hungry or uncomfortable to drive a man clean out of camp. He never cried or whimpered or sobbed plaintively. He bawled like a bull calf, he kicked vigorously while he bawled, and he fought at anything with doubled fists until he could clutch them onto his mother's breast. When he was full of milk and comfortable, he was a bright-eyed, laughing baby. But he was never a placid, easy-going baby. Wiggly as an eel, strenuous to handle, strong from the beginning, he was either all sunshine or all storms. And you never knew which it was going to be. Fowler was glad the weather was pleasant. Betsy put up the lodge at night on account of the baby, fearful he would be cold or some slight moisture might fall on him. But Fowler slept near the fire. Him and the youngster were too many in one lodge.

Two weeks later they reached Fort Laramie. Bill Sublette had left fifteen men to build the fort and they had the stockade finished and were working on the blockhouses and the tower over the central gate. It was a good, strong fort they were building here where the Laramie Fork met the North Platte. The men had some carpentering skill and they had hewn the logs and put the slab sides out so that the stockade had a smooth, planed look on the outside. Inside, they had run quarters around the four sides, with roofs sloping down from the upper wall. There was a parapet, chest high to a man, all around the top of the wall and a walkway. Stairs would go up to the tower over the gate. It was going to be as comfortable a fort as had ever been built, and the location was good.

A long stretch of hard-going plains unwound eastward, and another long stretch of worse-going plains stretched west. But here at the Laramie Fork was grass, some timber on the North Platte, and as a backdrop the Laramie Mountains rose in the distance behind the fort. A good meeting place, where all trails crossed, a good stopping place for anybody with any business anywhere in the west.

They rode into the courtyard and, too astonished to say a word, they watched Mamselle slide off her horse, look frantically around, then scoot all hunched over into the nearest quarters. An hour later she had a little girl. "She was hard put to wait till we got hyar," Big Starr explained later. "If there'd been a bush she could of got behind she'd of had it on the trail and then caught us up. Way it was, she begun to think she was goin' to drop it off the horse."

Fowler and Big Starr tried to decide, by studying her, whether she was Fouchette's or Starr's and couldn't. "Jist have to wait till she's bigger," Starr said, "and commences to look like one of us. She ain't nothin' but another baby right now."

They stayed two days. They turned the herd of horses over to the men at the stockade. The Mexican boys thought they would wait here for *Señor* Sublette. He had promised they could go to St. Louis with him. *"Bueno,"* Fowler said and paid them off.

They were saddling their horses next morning when Big Starr said, a little sheepishly, "Mamselle's nose is out of joint."

"What for?"

"Well, we give Betsy's papoose a name and we ain't give her'n none."

"Hell!" Fowler laughed and finished tightening the cinch.

"Don't jist say hell," Starr said morosely, "help me think of somethin'. We don't, Mamselle is gonna have the sulks and she ain't no fit company when she's got the sulks."

Fowler glanced around to make sure nothing had been forgotten. He ran his eyes over the four corners of the stockade, the flat, sandy courtyard, then followed around the walls to the parapets. "Call her Laramie," he said. "I reckon she's the first kid born inside these walls."

Big Starr yelped gleefully. "By ding, you done come up with a real ringer. That name'll really shine with Mamselle. Both kids got the name of where they was borned. Popo and Laramie—now, that'll make 'em come!"

"Better than Snake and Powder, ain't they?" Fowler grinned.

"Or Stinkin' and Bitter," Starr said.

"Or Platte and Arkansas."

"Or Bear and Portneuf."

"Or Chama and del Norte," Fowler said, and that put an end to it.

Big Starr whooped. "Del Norte, hyar we come! Whichaway we goin'?"

Fowler thought on it. "I dunno as there's any use going by the cache in the North Park. Don't much think them furs are still there."

"Hell, man, you know they ain't. Noel took 'em. If he's honest he taken 'em and has got the dollars banked with Johnny. If he ain't, he taken 'em and pocketed the dollars hisself."

Fowler said, "Well, whyn't we mosey down to the South Platte and on in home that way."

"Suits me fine."

So they moved almost due south and their days were clocked

by the creeks and streams as they came to them and put them behind them. Bear Creek, Horse Creek, Lodgepole Creek, Crow Creek. August, now, and the country was the color of the light which plated it over—yellow and tan and tawny and gold, and the dusty gray of the sage, and the willow thickets on the creeks turning yellow already, and the cottonwoods and box elders losing glisten of green. Dry and hot at noons and beginning to be cold at night, and the days shorter, and a lavender dawn later and a quick dusk earlier, purple and a little melancholy.

The miles and the creeks fell behind them regularly, then there was the South Platte and they took up Boxelder Creek to avoid the big looping bend. Now the mountains loomed again, and they cut over to the South Platte and followed up it as far as the canyon. They went on south and found the Arapaho trail through the gorges and peaks. Three days of hard travel, climbing, descending, climbing, descending, climbing again, until they moved down the last slope into the Bayou Salade.

The first men ever to see this hole were undoubtedly French hivernants and there was no doubt at all about the time of year they had first looked down on it from some high pass. It had to be the summer of the year, when all the fretwork of little streams was full and splashing, the little ponds and the big ponds lapping full to the banks, sparkly as frost with the sunlight on them. And the meadow grass had to be thick and as lush and green as plush and as tall as a man's waist. The cottonwoods had to be sprangled with their great fanned leaves and the willows had to be fringed with green plumes and the alders had to be full-leafed. It had to be high summer, the whole wide park spread green and silver before them, the rimrocks gray around it, the sky like a sheet of blue silk, for the Canucks to call it the Bayou Salade. There were times of the year when it looked neither watery nor green, but the first men to see it had seen it when it was both, and they had given it the right name for the look and the season.

Fowler and his people found the grass still kneehigh and still green although it was brittling and beginning to turn. The alders and aspens were jaundiced a little, the streams were pure silver, and the air was crisp.

They camped in the same copse of trees in which they had camped last fall, and they found signs of their old camp undisturbed. Men had crossed and recrossed the basin in the year since they had been here, beaver men and Indians had used it, but this little copse of alders and willows and cottonwoods had been passed by. Necessity had caught no one near it. It was one of hundreds of such camping places, all as good as or better than it was.

A little litter was still strewn about, odds and ends which they had discarded, a frayed length of rope, a piece of rotted elkskin, the link of a trap chain. There were even sticks of half-burned wood just as they had left them, with the old ashes packed and turned black beneath them. Big Starr kindled a fire in a new place with the dried pieces of the old fires. "Don't hardly seem reasonable, does it," he ruminated, "that it's been nearly a year. And all that's happened since. When we was hyar, Mr. Driant was still livin' . . . and—"

He cut it off. No use saying Mose had been with them, and Pete and Fouchette. You couldn't brood over what happened to men in this country, for what happened to one man could happen to another, and it might be your turn next, but as long as it wasn't you kept going on. You got to brooding you went queer in the head, the way Old Bill Williams was said to be, became a real loner not able to stand your own kind around you. Hunted by yourself, lived by yourself, talked to yourself, and avoided all the rest of mankind. They had done what they could for Mose and Pete and Fouchette. They had paid Bastro out.

They only stayed over a day to kill meat, then they moved on. Across Poncha Pass, down the San Luis, then around the splayed hills toward Saguache and the cottonwoods and the camp by the sparkling creek. The last day the squaws were chattery with excitement, pointing out landmarks, giggling together, wanting the men to hurry. Neither man had ever said a word to his own woman about where they were going, but ever since the encampment on Hams Fork both women had seemed to know. White men, beaver men, after all stayed out only so long. Both women knew, too, that the men would go on to Taos and Santa Fe. If either of them thought it might mean the end of her marriage to this particular man, neither mentioned it. They did their work as well as they had always done, they took care of their babies, and they served the men and followed. But now, in their own homeland again, they were like happy children with their feet on the home path once more. Fowler and Big Starr humored them and pushed the horses a little.

They were seen by the vedettes, the news was flashed back, and the usual escort rode out to meet them. There was great excitement, noise, wheeling and circling of horses, firing of guns, and then there was the village and the long street and they were walking their horses down it and old Cholly was waiting by his fire to welcome them. His blanket was around his shoulders, his tomahawk across his folded arm, one tall eagle feather a little askew in his headband. It did not in the least impair his inherent dignity.

The women melted among the other women, showing their babies, jabbering, laughing. Their tasks would be light tonight. They would put up the lodges, unsaddle the horses, unload the packs, and turn the animals over to the young men to take to the corral. But they would not have fires to build and food to cook. The men would be fed at old Cholly's fire tonight. They, the women, could enjoy their homecoming. They could tell their own news with pride, could boast about their babies, could astound these women who had remained with the village with their travels and experiences. And show their finery, their new baubles, all the wealth which accrued to all women who belonged to white men.

Old Cholly had a big feast for Fowler and Big Starr. There was a lot of drinking and a lot of smoking and a lot of talking. Spanish traders had been by recently and there was Taos lightning in quantity. Fowler and Big Starr did justice to it. The Utes did most of the talking, which was usual at an Indian feast, and it suited the white men just as well. They didn't want to talk yet. They just wanted to eat and drink and smoke and lie back and enjoy themselves.

And where had the Utahs been? They had been west. They had visited their Cochetopa relatives. And they had been north. As far as the big river in the Uncompaghre country. And they had come home this many days ago—a month. And yes. They had taken much beaver. And yes. They were fine skins. And no. They had not sold them to the Spanish trader. Only a few. Enough for whiskey, and a few unimportant baubles for the women, some calico and vermilion and beads and such, and for some powder and lead, and some tobacco—

"And likely," Fowler growled to Big Starr, "he's traded all but a few mangy skins won't be worth two dollars apiece."

Old Cholly's grin split his face. Did he not know, he said, that his friend Fowler would be back and would want the best of the furs? And did he not know his friend Fowler always paid the best price? And did he not save them for him? Fowler would see. He would be astonished at how many there were and how fine they were. The grin broadened. And did he not know that his friend Fowler would have a "big dry" and want much whiskey? And did he not get much Taos whiskey for him? Did he not always consider the needs and the wishes of his friend, Fowler?

Fowler made a nice flowery speech in reply, using all the right words in all the right ways. It took him ten minutes to assure old Cholly he was indeed Fowler's good friend and that he was certain he would find the finest beaver skins ever seen and that among all his Indian friends the Utahs were certainly the most hospitable and the most honorable and the bravest.

The amenities observed he then slid easily into the question which the glittering eyes and the restlessness of the young men told him was being waited for. And had his friends, the Utahs, been at war this year?

And yes. There had been a war with the Arapahoes. Early in the summer. Up north. The young men had killed many Arapahoes. Old Cholly waved grandly at the scalp poles in front of the lodges. Then it must be told, in detail, each young man telling his part, at great length, with much boasting and vaunting. It took them almost till morning, until whiskey and war chants and all the boasting and bravado rendered them limp and ready to collapse. Fowler and Big Starr collapsed with them. Neither of them could have walked as far as their lodges.

They slept till noon next day and then did their trading. Fowler was fooled. The Utes had a full pack of beaver skins, nearly one hundred prime plews. Each plew would bring eight dollars in St. Louis. One way or another, they had come out well ahead on the season. With all the time they had lost, doing no hunting to amount to anything on their own, they had still come out ahead. They had wagered everything they owned and their future for half a dozen years on the long legs of the big roan, and that had paid off. They had made a good profit on the herd of Appaloosas. And now old Cholly had a pack of prime plews for them. Fowler flipped a pelt back onto the pile. There wasn't much doubt trading was the way to make money. If money was what you wanted.

They didn't linger long. There was an exchange of loads which didn't take much time. The lodges, the paraphernalia belonging to the women, most of the odds and ends were left behind. Instead of equipment the pack horses were loaded with furs.

There was no need to tell the women they were going on. Any time a trapper headed for the settlements he left his squaw behind some place. They had been lucky that these two men had brought them back to their own village. They had not been traded to some other trapper or left with some strange village of another tribe to make their way back as best they could. Their men were good men. They had brought them back to their own people. They had achieved status by belonging to these two men, by traveling with them. But they were at home again. Neither of them sulked or grieved. They had helped with the loads but they were standing apart now, laughing and talking together, their papooses slung on their hips. "I swear this coon believes they're glad to be shut of us," Big Starr said, as they saddled up.

Fowler glanced at the women. "Maybe," he said. "They get homesick same as white women, I reckon. Glad to be back. Not traipsing for a while."

He usually left Betsy without any to-do about it. Just rode off. But this time he turned over to her considerable wealth. He left her the otter skin robe, all the trading goods left over, which was a handsome amount of calico and mirrors and awls and beads and such; he gave her a handful of Spanish silver won at Ham's Fork; and he gave her her horse, replacing him with another from old Cholly's herd. By Utah standards she would be a rich woman.

Neither of them said anything about when he would be back, or if he would ever be back. There never had been, nor ever would be, any talk like that between them. If she thought the generosity of his gifts meant this parting was permanent, she didn't show it. Nor did she express any gratitude for the gifts. She saw he wasn't taking the things. He left them in the lodge and she knew he meant for her to have them. But neither by word nor sign did she acknowledge them. Later she might exhibit them with noisy pride. But not now. Not in front of him.

Not given to self-analysis, he didn't examine his reasons for leaving her well off, better off than ever before. He had no sense of guilt nor any feeling of easing his conscience. If he had had to think about it, he might have thought, well, she had the kid now and would need more. But consciously, he didn't need the things. She did. And that was it.

When he went to get on his horse he passed her and she was nursing the baby. He gave the youngster a light swat on his rounded little behind. The baby turned loose of the breast and broke into a bawling howl. Fowler grinned. The kid, even at two months, took nothing lying down. Even a little pat was something to get up on his hind legs and bellow about.

When the men mounted, Mamselle deliberately turned her back and went into her lodge. It was not good to watch someone leave. To watch someone leave, especially to watch until that person grew small in the distance, went all the way out of sight, was to let that person take some of you with him. You would never, until that person returned, be entirely whole. Some of your spirit would be gone away. It was very dangerous to watch someone leave. She peeked out her doorway once, when the horse's hooves had grown faint, but even then she kept her eyes well down so as to see only the hem of Betsy's skirt and her feet, so there was no chance she would see the smalling backs of the men, and she was appalled that Betsy was standing there, still watching. She shuddered, knowing she would never have dared to do such a thing, and firmly closed the flap over the door opening.

The men cut out across the flats at a mile-eating fast walk. Big Starr was feeling fine. It would be a spree to end all sprees when they got there, he said. He was going to get likkered up and stay that way for a week. And he was going to find himself a little Mexican *señorita* the first thing. He was dad-blamed tired of red blood. He wanted somebody that would laugh and talk something besides pig-grunts with him, and somebody that wore clothes that weren't made of skins, and somebody who would kick up her heels when the fiddles tuned up for a *fandango*. By dang, this coon was ready for a little civilization.

He turned around once and looked back. "But you know," he said, "I kind of wished I knowed if that papoose is mine or Fouchette's. A man jist plain likes to know."

fifteen

WALKING OVER to Johnny's new house for supper, Fowler thought that what took the most getting used to again was the lights in the windows. You were around people and Indian villages and forts and animals and tepees enough that the crowd and jam and pack of houses so close together you couldn't spit between them didn't seem strange. And the groan and creak and rattle of wagons and carts, and the crack of the whips and the shouts of the drivers around the plaza didn't seem strange. Not even the jostle and the jabber of a half dozen different languages and the mill and stir of people seemed strange. But it took a time, every time he came back, to get used to see lighted windows. It was strange every time to walk about Santa Fe after dark the way he was doing from La Fonda, where he had a room, over to the new house on the street of the Palace of the Governors, to see squares of lamplight and to see the yellow checkered patches they made on the packed dirt and to walk through them. It was even stranger to be able to see where you were going by the glow from the windows.

Away a long time in the mountains, you got used to black-dark nights when the only light was a little glimmer in a little circle around the fire, and the moon and stars. You got so used to it you got to where you could see in the dark about as well as in the daytime, with your feet and body almost as much as your eyes. You sort of forgot there were towns and houses, in some place you had left a long time ago, where there were candles and lamps and where when dark came they were lit and people ate and talked and danced and drank and life went on by their light. Civilization, he guessed, laughing and wading through another patch of gold, meant light to him.

He and Big Starr had got to Taos a week ago. They had had their big spree and he had settled up with Starr and left him there. Starr didn't much like Santa Fe. It was too big and too crowded for him, he said. Besides Taos was home to him and he wanted to stay home for a while. "Jist send word when you're ready to put out ag'in," he said, "I'll be ready when you are."

Fowler hesitated and then said, "Dunno when that'll be, Starr. Me and Johnny have got some talking to do. You want to put out with somebody else, go ahead."

Still boozey, Big Starr had wagged his head. "I understan'. This coon'll take keer of hisself."

Fowler laughed. Starr was rich for the time being. His pockets were full and he was banked for more at the Johnny Osage store. But give him a month or two, the end of the winter at the longest, and he would be flat broke. Nothing but his horse left. He would spend it like chicken feathers flung in the wind, on finery and bangles for the girls, on finery and bangles for himself, on whiskey and good food, and what he didn't spend he would lose at the monte tables. Then he'd have to find somebody ready to put out and he'd have to outfit himself on credit. Which he had as high as the sky and knew it and so he never worried. Living was now. You might not be here tomorrow. Riches were to spend and there was always more and more up in the mountains, little brown animals whose skins turned into dollars. Big Starr liked to cut a wide swath when he was in town; a big man, he always said, had to have a big time in a big way. But it was strictly Big Starr's business.

So Fowler left him in a *cantina* and rode down off the high Taos plateau, down through the rough gashed canyon, up and around high bald shoulders, past Truchas and Chimayo, down by the Nambé pueblo, the Tesuque pueblo, into the long

golden land which lay under a tranced golden light. In the
town the adobe houses were a warmer and darker brown than
the homes in Taos. Taos houses were creamy and honeyed
and tan. Santa Fe people liked richness and depth in their
color, or maybe it was some difference in the dirt of which the
adobes were made. Whatever, Santa Fe looked pinker and
warmer and earthier than Taos. The end of the season, the
inn he liked best had not been overly crowded with drovers
and freighters and a room was made ready for him.

Yesterday, then, Fowler and Johnny had talked most of the
day. It took a while to tell it all—where he had been, whom
he had seen, what he had seen, what he had heard, what was
happening—Johnny listening, asking shrewd questions, understanding, nodding, commenting. The conclusions reached were
inevitable. "Say another ten years," Fowler summed it up, "a
man can still take a little outfit and come back with enough
plews to make a little profit. I know some places yet. But
sooner than that the big money will be gone, Johnny. Bill
Sublette gives it just another two or three years. He'll be hanging up his traps then. General Ashley was able to make a fortune, Sublette and Campbell are well off, but Bridger and
Fitzpatrick and the other Rocky Mountain boys aren't more
than breaking even. And the Company is taking over. When
the Company makes its move, you just as well get out. They
can take a loss year after year and hang on and crack you wide
open and crush you flat.

"But the worst is that beaver is going. Them boys up there
have been takin 'em by the thousands, the hundred thousands,
for years and years now. They don't give time for a new crop to
come on before they're back working the same ponds and creeks.
And they can work out three or four mountain ranges in one
season. Whoever got there first always used to get the cream.
But the cream is about gone. The way it went down in these
mountains. Overhunted. Overtrapped."

"And the prices are falling," Johnny said. "St. Vrain got

back from St. Louis last week. Said he didn't get but five dollars for beaver." He spilled tobacco in a brown cigaret paper and rolled it. "Last season," he said, "we got nine."

Fowler shrugged. "That was the price war. Way the Company broke the boys. But they can pay as low as they want now that the boys are knuckling under—and they will."

Johnny leaned his elbows on the counter. "Freighting's the thing, Joe. You know how much trade there was over the Trail this season? Got any idea?"

"I wouldn't even try to guess."

"A million dollars. A cool million dollars." He straightened up. "You know what they're buying in Santa Fe now? And Taos? Not just hard goods and calicos and linseys and bangles and baubles. We're bringing nearly everything you could buy in St. Louis in now. Furniture—tables and chairs and chests and beds. They want American furniture, not the old-style things from Vera Cruz. And we're bringing in spices and medicines and tobacco and chinaware and silver and oil lamps and the oil to burn in 'em, and wines and iron and machinery and plows and tools. I brought a sawmill in the first train this season, and a lathe and planing tools. That's how Judith got wood floors for her new house. They're wanting the same things in El Paso and Chihuahua and they got the specie to buy, and the wool, and the hides and mules and horses to trade. Every beaver skin we can get our hands on will be that much to the good, but the money, the big money, the real money is gonna be made in freighting and trading, Joe."

Fowler knew it. He didn't have to be told. The handwriting was on the wall for any sensible man to see. But it made him a little sick at his stomach. "How much we make this year, Johnny?"

"A hundred thousand. Next year it could double that."

Fowler grimaced, then grinned. "Well, it beats beaver, don't it? Sublette didn't make that. Not even with a thousand percent mark-up on his goods. How many trips you make yourself?"

"Three, and they like to killed me. We got plenty of men can take a train through, but you got to go yourself once or twice a year to look over the stock and tend to business. You can't do it all by letter. Them St. Louis merchants get careless if you don't show up yourself pretty often. Charles Bent and St. Vrain and John Scolly, they keep the road hot going back and forth. And me. I think I've jolted my liver loose and I *know* I've unhinged my backbone."

He didn't say, he never had said, and never would say, that he wished Joe would hang up his traps and take over the wagon trains. It would have been the biggest help he could give to the firm. But when Joe put his money in, it had been understood it was just money. Joe didn't go with it. Johnny needed more backing, more investment badly. He needed extra money to spread out with and for a sort of cushion if he had a bad season, or lost a train. Joe had some money to invest. He had kept putting in more and more until he had more real dollars in the firm than Johnny. But it had always been Johnny who managed and administered the business, made the decisions, changed and shifted with the times, took the risks, made them pay off. Joe had always kept himself out of it. If, now, he was ready to hang up his traps, take an active part in the business, it would have to be him that said so. He knew it was waiting for him, all he had to do was say it was time.

Johnny had always believed the time would come. It had to come. Joe would get the mountains out of his system some day. He hoped it was now. But this nephew of his, only twelve years his junior, and as much like him as a twin brother, would take his own time making up his mind. He couldn't be talked into it, nor would Johnny have valued him if he could have been. Joe would mill it around in his head, ponder it, weigh it on every kind of scales he knew, and maybe before the winter was over say what he had decided.

They walked over to the *cantina* in the inn and talked until dark over their whiskey. Lighter things now, news and stories and chuckling laughter. Johnny knew about Bonneville. "There was talk about him in St. Louis. Kind of a whispering about. Most of the fur men know what he came out for. You can't keep that kind of thing quiet."

They talked about Bonneville a little. Johnny also remembered him from old Fort Smith. "The St. Louis men think the government'll settle the Oregon line without war, though. Benton's the one shoving and pushing to get it settled so quick. General Ashley's in Congress now and he's shoving and pushing along with Benton. They want it for settlement and they're all talking the fifty-fourth parallel as the line. Straight across, one ocean to the other."

Fowler shook his head. "England won't turn loose of that much of Canada."

"No. Likely they'll run the line west from the Great Lakes."

"Well," Fowler reflected, "that would give us the Columbia and enough room north of it to turn around in."

Johnny wanted to know about Pierre Driant's death. "That clerk of his, that Noel fellow, come back to Taos soon as he could get through the snow in the passes. Told that Driant had died up in the mountains."

Fowler told him about it.

Johnny nodded. "He said about the same. I reckon Santiago told you he brought some furs belonged to you back to the Taos store."

Fowler said yes, Santiago had told him. "Kind of surprised me. I didn't much think he'd be that honest."

"You didn't like him much, did you?"

"Not the least bit. He was a pushy sort of feller. I didn't know but he'd seize 'em for himself. Where is he now?"

"He went back to St. Louis this summer with St. Vrain. Seemed like he had got his craw full of the country."

Fowler grinned. "I would think he had." He raised his glass slowly, thinking back. "He was the sort that wouldn't ever learn. Not that first danged thing. He knew it all. If it didn't work out the way *he* knew it, he wouldn't ever have changed his way of thinking. He had better stay in St. Louis."

Fowler learned that there was a new house, which didn't astonish him, for Judith had been wanting one for a long time. What did astonish him was the news there was a baby now. "A youngun? After all this time?" He could hardly believe it. He didn't say, though he thought it, a young one that lived after all this time of trying. Three had either been born dead or died within a few hours. "Boy?"

"No. Little girl. Judith named her after Becky. Named her Rebecca Jane. She's a pretty little thing. And I dunno. The others were all boys and weak and died quick. But she's as husky as my mother, Hannah. You remember your grandma, don't you?"

"Sure. I remember her well. And the baby looks like her?"

"Not exactly. She's not so dark as Ma. But she's a big baby, big-boned and long, and she's stout. She'll do for this country, Joe." He laughed. "She'll do the same way Ma did for Kentucky."

"And the way Becky did in the Arkansas territory," Fowler said.

Johnny nodded. "Rebecca was like Ma, too. Enduring and strong, in her heart same as her body. It takes something in a woman to go into a new country and make out. I'd not thought of it much, but as little and drinlin' as Judith looks, she can stay with you. She come out from Connecticut with that mission bunch to the Arkansas territory. And then I brought her here. She's little. She's not big and raw-boned and stout like Mama and Rebecca. But I don't know but what she's got more heart for being so little."

"I'm glad for her," Fowler said. "Maybe she'll be more contented here now."

Johnny laughed. "Oh, you couldn't find anybody more contented. There ain't a thing wrong with this country now. She's got her a house and a baby. And the house has got wood floors and papered walls and real windows and a tin roof, pitched, with a regular roof-comb and eaves like she thinks a house ought to have. There's too much Connecticut in Judith for her ever to like a Santa Fe house. She wants a house to look like a Connecticut house."

"You built her a frame house?"

"No, it's 'dobe, but it's wood-framed inside and floored. And you know what color she painted the 'dobe on the outside? White! Said she wanted a white house and a green roof. And she got 'em. She'd have got 'em if it had harelipped Rachel, but about that time I was so scared she was gonna lose another baby I'd have give her the moon with a fence around it if I could. I didn't quarrel with a white 'dobe house one minute."

They laughed about a woman's whims, in particular a New England woman's whim, transplanted to this high, dry, red land. Nothing would do her but she must make a bit of New England for herself. Hungry for the tidiness and neatness of green and white in a mud-colored town, she would have it. More than one eastern woman coming after Judith Fowler would hunger and thirst for what she had left and would try to recapture it as best she could with an eastern house, eastern grass, eastern trees and flowers. Unlike the Spanish, whose home, either in Spain or Mexico, was so much like this land there was no strangeness in it, it was the only way the eastern Anglo woman could bear the harshness and the bareness and the strangeness. Judith was one of the first to try to graft the east onto Santa Fe, with her white house and its pitched roof on the street of the Palace of the Governors.

She cooked the Mexican way, though, more or less. A little less hot, but hot enough. And a little more lightly and a little better. "Most any cookery," she told Joe that night when he complimented her supper, "is better for a light hand, and a little mixing with other ways. What you eat in my home is some of New England, some of Arkansas, and some of Santa Fe."

He held and admired the baby. And just for a moment, when

he first took her, he thought of the little Popo Agie baby. He hadn't much held or handled the boy. Indian women took all the care of their babies and they carried them in cradleboards or slung in shawls constantly. There wasn't much need for holding or handling them. But all babies were soft and round and they all snuggled and felt alike in your arms.

"She's a nice baby," he said. It wasn't a very inspired comment, but he never knew what to say about babies. She had dark hair but her skin was fair like Judith's. Her eyes were blue, like Johnny's.

The Mexican girl came for her then. Judith had help in the new house, a girl for the baby and a quiet, middle-aged woman for the kitchen. She and Johnny were living in style nowadays.

They sat on around the table with more coffee, brandy for the men, and talked. Judith brought some sewing to keep her hands busy and listened, putting in a word or two now and then. When Bonneville's name was mentioned again, she exclaimed suddenly, "Have you told him yet, Johnny? About Savanna and David?"

"Not got around to it yet," Johnny said.

"What about 'em?" Joe asked. "Savanna got another set of twins already?"

"Oh, no. Nothing like that. But they're coming out here—to Santa Fe! With the first train next spring! Isn't it wonderful? I can't wait. I am dying to see Savanna. She was—why, it's been more than ten years. Poor Captain Brooks was still living."

"They gonna live out here?"

Johnny spoke up. "Gonna see if they like it. David's been here. He'd like to move out. Savanna . . ."

"Savanna has an open mind," Judith said. "And she'll like it here. I know she will. My goodness, Santa Fe is a vast improvement over Three Forks! She can't help but like it better." Her head was bent over her sewing, and she didn't see the amused looks exchanged by her husband and Joe. Not so long ago she had seen nothing, nothing at all, to like about Santa Fe. "And

I will have her as a neighbor," she went on. "One of the family right here in the same town. And I can help her get used to things—sort of smooth the rough edges off for her. Oh, it will be so nice. They'll stay. I know they will."

Fowler lit his pipe. "Reckon David could be talked into coming into the business?"

Johnny, rolling a cigaret, looked up. "I hope he can. We need him."

Judith looked up and said sharply, "Don't press him. Give him time. There will be plenty for him to do in this town as a doctor."

Both men denied quickly they meant to rush him. "But he always did love to get out on the prairie. Hunt. Ride," Joe said. "He is a good doctor, I reckon. But I sometimes used to wonder if maybe he wouldn't rather been something else. He'd of made a good beaver man."

"Leave him alone, you two," Judith said. "Let him make up his own mind. And as for you," she turned to Fowler, "what are you going to do now? Go back up in the mountains? It's time you quit all your wild and rough ways, jaunting off to the mountains every year. You ought to settle down. Get married. Help Johnny with the firm. You're a grown man now, Joe. You're past thirty years old. All that beaver hunting and trapping was fine, as long as you were a youngster. But you ought to settle down now. Raise a family. If you ever intend to." She shook her needle at him. "You'll keep on and on and the first thing you know you'll be too old. There won't be enough time left."

He put up his hands as if to ward off a blow. "Now, who would have a tough old mountain lion like me?"

"Almost any pretty Spanish girl around here. And there are plenty of them." She was emphatic. "Girls of good blood. Nice, well-raised girls. There is the Ortiz girl, and the Flores girl—oh, there are dozens. But if you'd rather, think of all the nice girls in St. Louis . . ."

Joe grinned. "I can just see one of them convent-raised girls marrying an old hivernant like me and coming to Santa Fe to live. They don't leave St. Louis, you know. You marry one of them, you make your home there. You leave 'em behind when you go out on your business."

"Very well. Don't go to St. Louis for a wife. There are plenty of girls here and in Taos."

"Or Chihuahua," Johnny put in, "or Vera Cruz or Mexico City."

"You too?" Joe said, raising his eyebrows.

Johnny grinned and shrugged. "It's a way of living you've not tried. You might like it."

He thought about it. He thought about it a lot. He thought about it enough during the winter to go up to Taos and out to Don Mateo's *hacienda* pretty often. He thought about it when he rode with the old man over all the spreading acres and looked at all the thousands of woolly backs when the great sheep herds grazed near. He thought about it when he looked at the comfort and the ease and the richness of the *hacienda* life, with all the peons to make it easy and comfortable.

Don Mateo was not *hidalgo*, but no *hidalgo* had accumulated more riches or lived more handsomely. If he had acquired his wealth of land and sheep by the shrewdness and cleverness of his forefathers, by theft and corruption on his own part, he had also acquired a veneer of gentility that went with wealth. Descended from a common soldier, a sergeant in the army of De-Vargas, he was not wholly peasant. And his soldier ancestors had married daughters of the colonists and worked slowly upward, acquiring a little more land, a few more sheep, each generation, until in Don Mateo the line had strengthened to the point he could wrest the final fifty thousand hectares of land out of the governor through his own political maneuverings. He was the first to add the Don to his name, but he was not disdained for it. Not openly. He had power in the palace and no one dared disdain it. The man who married his daughter would come into a very comfortable life. Fowler thought Don Mateo would not mind a Yankee son-in-law. Especially if the Yankee was a partner in a very profitable business.

He thought about marriage when the Uliballos came into Taos for a long stay to avoid the worst of the winter. He was welcomed in their Taos home and allowed to take the young Carmelita, and her duenna, to the *fandangos.* And he sometimes thought quite a lot about it when he was with Carmelita. She was as pretty as all young girls, slender, dark-eyed, dark-haired, quick to laugh, light-footed to dance with, gay, tempestuously exciting. There was enough of the peasant in her to make her lusty. He guessed she would have him. He wasn't a bad catch, not even for her, and he knew it.

They went to the *bailes,* he had many meals in their home, he gambled at monte with Don Mateo and rode about with him. And he would think he was going to speak to him, next time, next day. Some nights, after a ball, when Carmelita was especially pretty and gay and in a mood to dispense favors freely and was flirting with him outrageously, he would think the very next morning he would speak to Don Mateo. Then she would be in his arms and he would kiss her and, by ding, he never kissed the girl but that he didn't somehow think he smelled sheep wool. And it put him off. So all winter he didn't get around to saying anything.

And then it was spring and he ran into Big Starr and they took Johnny's first wagon train to St. Louis. And they brought David and Savanna back with them, and then for a month there was a lot of family visiting and talking. They had to find David and Savanna a house and help them get set up in it and then there were parties and balls and so much going on he didn't get back up to Taos. And then he and Big Starr took a train down to Chihuahua and by the time they got back it was September.

They had been drinking in the *cantina* in La Fonda. They came out of its dimness into the bright hot light of middle afternoon. It had been a drought year, not even the scanty rain to which the Santa Fe plateau was accustomed had fallen. The little river was dry, its bed as white as bleached bones. The grass had browned and turned brittle. The red dirt was red dust, like red sifted flour over the plaza and the sky was starved and empty. Fowler looked up at the Sangre de Cristos. The red earth was dull and bloody looking under the black of the piñons. High up, the aspens were not their bright yellow gold. They looked tarnished and haggard and drought-bitten. The whole land looked tarnished and starved and thirsty and haggard.

There came in his mind suddenly the look of a long grassy meadow, long and swelling and rolling, the grass like green plush on every swell and roll. And there was a creek, as clear as veinsilver splashing and boiling through the meadow. And there was a shelf on a rolling knoll behind the creek and a grove of trees. And the air was soft with moisture, mild and silky and easy to breathe, soft against the skin, soft to smell, soft on the hair and eyes and lips. Water soft, rain soft.

He drew in a lung full of the dry hot air that lay so thinly over this high dry plateau. He swiveled toward Big Starr suddenly. "You want to go to Oregon?"

"Oregon?" Big Starr fumbled it around in his mind a little. Then he grinned. "Shore, *amigo*. Why not?"

"*Bueno*. Let's go."

"When?"

"Right now."

It took a little longer, but in less than an hour they were riding out the road to Chimayo and Taos. Two days later they were in Taos, gathering together what they would need, buying ammunition and a few trade goods, filling their possible sacks, acquiring a couple of pack horses. And traps. They would as soon have gone without buckskins as without their traps.

And then they were riding out, fast and jangling, steel traps and Spanish spurs rattling. It was September again. The sky was a white glare of light squinting the eyes and making them run water. Their horses raised a fog of red dust which trailed behind them. There had been one last spree in Taos, one last fandango, and their heads were pounding, but they said goodby in fine style just the same, fancy beaded shirts on, new long-whanged buckskins covering their legs. They would pack them away tonight, but for leaving Taos they were the right kind of foofooraw.

Big Starr was in a high, wide, and handsome way, singing, whooping, skirmishing his horse around. It took him almost to the pueblo to begin to settle down and then he was still easy unsettled. "Ye know," he said, "this child didn't know but ye'd git married this time. Ye made up to that little Uliballos girl a right smart."

Fowler jerked the pack horse's lead rope. "I made up to her," he said, then he added, drawling, "but I never could abide the smell of sheep wool."

Starr whooped and made his horse prance and curvet around. The big roan shied at a tumbleweed and Fowler steadied him. They were passing the pueblo now and he looked over at the terraced adobe houses set back from the ancient cracked, flaking wall. Dust devils swirled about the bare court. A blanketed sentinel stood on the highest roof, motionless, wrapped, looking as Taos sentinels had looked for the first sign of any enemy for untold generations. A pack of dogs fled across the bare court, yelping. Indian women, high-booted, worked about the beehive ovens, around the little creek, among the piles of wood.

Big Starr skirmished his horse back and hauled him up. "Whar away, *amigo?* East side the del Norte? Under old Blanca?"

Fowler looked west into the blue-hazed distance. "How about if we head for Pagosa?"

Big Starr's eyes squinched with humor. "They won't be thar yet, man. They're still up at Saguache."

"Well, Saguache ain't out of our way."

Starr broke into a warwhoop. "Howgh-owgh-owgh-owgh! Howgh-owgh-owgh-owgh!" Then he howled old Pete's ditty:

Sugar-eye Betsy,
Cotton-eye Joe;
Oughtto been married,
Forty year ago!

Fowler grinned at the big man's caperings. His head was pounding but he never felt better in his life. Saguache, and the sparkling little creek . . . the San Luis, and the glittering basin country . . . and up over the Poncha Pass . . . the Bayou and frost and new ice . . . and that little creek after you made up over Rabbit Ear Pass . . . the Yampa . . . the Popo Agie . . . the Siskadee . . . the massed, humped rootbed of the Wind Rivers, and the sharp peaks of the Tetons. And the Sweetwater and the Bear . . . and sometime . . . some day . . . the grassy meadow.

Starr worked off his capering and settled alongside him. "I jist thought of somethin'," he said, screwing his eyes up against the light. "That papoose of Mamselle's. She ought to be big enough we could tell who she looked like now, oughtn't she?"

"She ought to be," Fowler said.

Epilogue

CAPTAIN Bonneville made his second journey to the Columbia in the summer and autumn of 1834 with a party of twenty-three men. He explored the Burnt River canyon and the Powder River route this time and found it a more practicable way through the mountains. Later it became the western end of the Oregon Trail.

Captain Bonneville, however, met with no better success at the hands of the Hudson's Bay Company than before. He moved down the Columbia River as far as the mouth of the Umatilla when, his provisions running short and unable to buy so much as a fish or root from the Indians, it was necessary for him to turn back. His journal reports that the Hudson's Bay Company had coerced the natives into refusing to trade with him.

He remained in the west through the winter of 1834–1835, then made his way back to civilization in the summer of 1835. He reported for duty at Fort Gibson, his old post, in 1836.

Subsequently Captain Bonneville served in the second Seminole War and in the Mexican War, where he was wounded at the Battle of Churubusco and advanced in rank to Brevet Lieutenant Colonel. Following the Mexican War he served at Fort Kearny and at other posts in Wisconsin, New York, and California. After the treaty of 1846 with Great Britain, when the Oregon boundary was fixed at the forty-ninth parallel, Fort Vancouver came under American command and it was Colonel Bonneville's happy privilege to serve as commandant of the post from 1853 to 1855. It must have given him great satisfaction to command the post which had denied him succor in 1833–1835.

In 1855, Colonel Bonneville was made commander of the Department of New Mexico stationed at Fort Marcy, in Santa Fe. He was variously stationed from 1855 to 1866 at Fort Fillmore, at Fort Clark, Texas, and Benton Barracks and Jefferson Barracks, Missouri. He retired in 1861 but during the Civil War came out of retirement and served in recruiting service for two years and as chief mustering and disbursing officer in Missouri for an additional two years. In 1865 he was made Brevet Brigadier General.

In his permanent retirement he returned to Fort Smith, Arkansas, to make his home. His first wife having died, he married late in life a young Miss Susan Neis, who survived him by many years. When he died on June 12, 1878, at the age of eighty-two, he was the oldest officer on the retired list.

Captain Stewart fared much better on the Columbia that winter of 1834–1835. He was an honored guest of Dr. John McLoughlin, the Hudson's Bay Company factor at Fort Vancouver, and when he returned to the mountains in the spring of 1835 it was with a Hudson's Bay fur brigade.

Captain Stewart continued to hunt and travel with various fur brigades, both American and British, until 1838. In September of that year he was informed that his brother, Sir John Archibald Stewart, had died. Captain Stewart had now become the seventh baronet of Grandtully, Murthly, Scotland, and it was necessary for him to go home.

Sir William returned to the United States in 1842 and in the summer of 1843 was again in the western mountains. So far as is known this was his last journey west. He died at Murthly in 1871 in his seventy-seventh year. His son and heir had preceded him in death in 1868, therefore Sir William's younger brother succeeded to the title and estates. A series of suits and countersuits involving the succession immediately followed. They concerned Sir William's adopted son, Francis Nichols Stewart. He was know to be an American, and it was said he was Sir William's illegitimate son. Twice Sir William had tried and failed to have the entail of Murthly and Grandtully broken on the young man's behalf. In the end the best Sir William could do for him was to leave him forty thousand pounds in his will. If Francis Nichols Stewart was Sir William's own son, it is tantalizing to wonder who his American mother might have been. Inevitably one thinks of the "dusky beauties" of the mountains, about whom Sir William wrote and for whom he always had such an eye.

It cannot be proved or disproved that Captain Bonneville was directly commissioned by the War Department to spy out British activities in Oregon in 1832–1835. In the National Archives there is, however, a letter from his commanding officer, General Macomb, authorizing Captain Bonneville's leave of absence and instructing him to "learn all he could about the quality of the soil, the productions, the minerals, the natural history, the climate, the geography and topography as well as geology of the various parts of the country within the limits of the territories belonging to the United States, between our frontier and the Pacific."

The letter, dated 29 July 1831, also instructs Bonneville to obtain the proper instruments for making the "best maps of the interior to be found." He is also told to learn all he can about the various tribes of Indians, and "in short any information which you may conceive would be useful to the Government."

At this particular time, when the government was restive under the joint-occupation treaty with Great Britain, information concerning the activities of the Hudson's Bay Company and its attitudes toward Americans certainly came under the heading of information useful to the government.

In the National Archives there is also a very lengthy report from Captain Bonneville to General Macomb dated Wind River, July 29, 1833. This report faithfully details what Captain Bonneville had learned to this date in obedience to the instructions given him in General Macomb's letter. A second report, made after his first expedition to the Columbia, was lost in being sent back to Washington by messenger. However, the daily journals Captain Bonneville kept the entire time he was in the west, all of his sketches and maps and detailed calculations and charts, were turned over to the War Department upon his return to Washington in 1835. He did survey, chart, and map the western country, and he provided the first really accurate map of the region.

Historically there is no proof that Captain William Drummond Stewart was spying on the Americans for the British. But he was a retired officer of the Fifteenth (The King's) Hussars, and in the years 1833–1838 he certainly had the best opportunity any Englishman in the country had to obtain information concerning the activities and attitudes of the Americans. That he did not pass such information on to Dr. John McLoughlin and other Hudson's Bay factors seems highly unlikely.

The northern boundary of the Oregon territory was settled with Great Britain in 1846, by negotiation and at its present parallel.

A complete list of all the men employed by Bonneville at various times during the three years he was in the west is not in existence. It is not known, either, who the three men were he took with him to the Columbia on his first expedition the winter of 1833–1834. It is known that one was a Kentuckian by birth. I have not therefore usurped the place in history of any known individual by placing Joe Fowler and two of his men with Bonneville on that historic journey.

JHG

Spout Springs
Knifley, Kentucky
February 14, 1966

Bibliography

Bancroft, Hubert Howe, *History of Oregon,* San Francisco, 1886

Blacker, Irwin R., *Taos,* New York, 1959

Bonner, T. D., editor, *The Life and Adventures of James P. Beckwourth,* New York, 1856; reprint edited by Bernard DeVoto, New York, 1931

Chittenden, Hiram M., *The American Fur Trade of the Far West,* vols. I and II, Stanford, California, 1954

Connor, Daniel Ellis, *Joseph Reddeford Walker and the Arizona Adventure,* edited by Donald J. Berthrong and Odessa Davenport, Norman, Oklahoma, 1956

Coues, Elliott, editor, *Forty Years a Fur Trader on the Upper Missouri,* New York, 1898

Dale, Harrison C., *The Ashley-Smith Explorations and the Discovery of the Central Route to the Pacific,* revised edition, Glendale, 1941

Devoto, Bernard, *Across the Wide Missouri,* Boston, 1947; *The Course of Empire,* Boston, 1952; editor, *The Journals of Lewis and Clark,* Boston, 1953

Fremont, John Charles, *Narratives of Explorations and Adventure,* edited by Allan Nevins, New York, 1956

Garrard, Lewis Hector, *Wah-to-yah and the Taos Trail,* Norman, 1955

Gregg, Josiah, *Commerce of the Prairies,* edited by Max L. Moorhead, Norman, 1954

Hafen, Leroy R., and W. M. Ghent, *Broken Hand,* Denver, 1931

Horgan, Paul, *The Centuries of Santa Fe,* New York, 1956; *Great River, the Rio Grande,* vols. I and II, New York, 1954

Hulbert, Archer Butler, editor, *Southwest on the Turquoise Trail,* Denver, 1933

Irving, Washington, *The Adventures of Captain Bonneville, U.S.A., in the Rocky Mountains and the Far West,* edited by Edgeley W. Todd, Norman, 1961

Keleher, William A., *Turmoil in New Mexico,* Santa Fe, 1952

Lavender, David, *Bent's Fort,* New York, 1954; *The Fist in the Wilderness,* New York, 1964

Parkman, Francis, Jr., *California and Oregon Trail,* Centenary Edition, Boston, 1937

Preuss, Charles, *Exploring with Fremont,* translated and edited by Erwin G. and Elisabeth K. Gudde, Norman, 1958

Russell, Osborne, *Journal of a Trapper,* Boise, 1921

Ruxton, George Frederick, *Adventures in Mexico and the Rocky Mountains,* London, 1847; *Life in the Far West,* edited by Leroy R. Hafen, Norman, 1951

Sabin, Edwin L., *Kit Carson Days,* revised edition, New York, 1935

Sandoz, Mari, *The Beaver Men,* New York, 1964

Stewart, Sir William Drummond, *Altowan,* New York, 1846; *Edward Warren,* London, 1854

Vestal, Stanley, *The Old Santa Fe Trail,* Boston, 1939

Wissler, *The American Indian,* second edition, 1931

DATE		

© THE BAKER & TAYLOR CO.